JERRY ABERSHAW;

OR,

THE MOTHER'S CURSE.

———

BY THE AUTHOR OF " DICK TURPIN," " CLAUDE DU VAL," &c.

———

LONDON:

W. CAFFYN, 31, OXFORD STREET, MILE-END;

AND SOLD BY ALL BOOKSELLERS.

JERRY ABERSHAW;

OR,

The Mother's Curse.

CHAPTER I.

THE BIRTHPLACE AND YOUTH OF JERRY—HIS EDUCATION—A QUARREL—JERRY
CAUSES HIS FATHER'S DEATH—THE WIDOW AND HER NEIGHBOURS.

In the year 1784, the plot of ground still known as St. George's Fields,
presented an aspect much more consonant with its name. Standing a little

beyond and to the right of the spot where the Surrey Theatre (originally the Circus) was afterwards built, the space, looking northward, presented an uninterrupted view to the river's bank, and all the extensive triangle, formed by the radiation of the Waterloo and Blackfriars roads from one common centre, was dotted with ruinous sheds, the hovel-like dwellings of labourers on the water, and those who sought precarious employment, or who cried perishable commodities about the streets of the great city for their daily bread. Another part of this district, now covered by streets of a questionable character, where dwell the daughters of infamy, who nightly crowd the saloons of our theatres, and flaunt in stained silks and tawdry finery beneath the gas-lights of this moral city, was occupied in a way less socially harmful ; namely, by a vast expanse of cabbages, cauliflowers, celery, lettuces, mint, onions, and other esculents, intended to nourish the bodies and gratify the palates of the denizens of the good city of London, which rested under its canopy of sea-coal smoke on the opposite side of the then smooth-flowing Thames. To the east of the spectator stretched the rows of squalid buildings forming the Clink Liberty, Southwark ; and amid these rose the square towers of St. Saviour's, adjoining that time-honoured obstruction Old London Bridge. The westward view rested on lines of building constructing in what is now called the Westminster road, or on the scattered suburban villas of independent gentry and wealthy citizens in the vicinity of Vauxhall, and the ancient tower and palace of Lambeth. Here, too, the line of the Thames defined the prospect, close to which were situate the dwellings of lightermen, watermen, and others who lived by the river-trade, interspersed with waterside tea and pleasure gardens, bowling alleys, taverns, and other resorts of idleness and dissipation.

At this period the occupation of a waterman was one of the most lucrative among those of the labouring classes, and their high rate of earnings, hard labour, and consequent bodily strength, made them a formidable, an insolent, and a reckless set of fellows. It was from these that our navy drew its best seamen, and many were the desperate conflicts between the Thames watermen and the men-of-war's boats sent up the river in time of war upon the impressment service.

To this class did old Lewis Abershaw belong ; and to this calling he brought up his only son Jeremiah, having in his fourteenth year duly indentured him to himself in the Hall of the Waterman's Company, thereby entitling him to the freedom of London, and the privileges of the City. We have already spoken of the breadth of market-gardens near where Waterloo-bridge now stands ; crossing thence towards the Cornwall-road and Broadwall, was a ditch (not many years since filled up), and a narrow footway through the gardens, with a swivel bridge, and a cottage known as the " Halfpenny Hatch." Here each passer through these enclosed grounds paid the fine of a copper for the privilege of free transit, and thence he emerged upon a path leading across a swampy ground to the " St. George's Bun-house," on the side of what is at present Great Surrey-street. In these marshy fields dwelt, in a humble cottage, old Lewis Abershaw, and here, in play and mischief, with ragged, uncared-for urchins like himself, young Jerry grew to his fourteenth year, as wild and uncultivated a young savage, mentally and morally, as ever dwelt in a Hottentot wigwam, yet with the cunning, the hypocrisy, and self-acquired knowledge of all the worst vices of that sort of civilization with which a boy so situated would be likely to come in contact.

At the age of seventeen, it was the fortune, or misfortune, of Jerry Abershaw to lose his paternal parent. Old Abershaw was a brutal, rough, swearing, hard-drinking, hard-working old fellow, tough as junk, and obstinate as a pig ; and he must needs, after a five hours' pull, wherein he and his son Jerry had rowed a person of distinction in their wherry as far as Twickenham, indulge in several extra libations of gin-royal, out of the gratuity presented him by his generous fare. The consequence was, that, in a state between drunkenness and exasperation, he forgot that his boy Jerry had grown into a man, and accordingly, a quarrel arising between them on the passage down, when opposite Millbank (such skirmishes had of late been frequent), the old fellow, after exhausting his vocabulary of hard words, resorted to harder blows, and catching up the stretcher from his feet, he dealt young Jerry, who was pulling aft, a blow on the side of the head, which at once sent that promising youth into the river.

" Take that, ye young devil's spawn !" exclaimed the affectionate parent, as his first-born rolled off the thwart, head-foremost, into the tide, which was just past the flood, and was running rapidly down. Then, gazing at the water with a drunken stare, the old man seemed somewhat sobered by an inkling as to the probable consequences of his rash act; with a grunt, therefore, and a hitch of his braceless inexpressibles, he stood up in the boat to look after his son and heir.

But Jerry was destined to a drier death; he arose in a few moments to the surface, and spluttering out an oath equal in coarseness to his father's, seized the side of the wherry with both hands.

"Say ye're sorry for it," said old Abershaw, "and I'll——"

The enraged youth cut his speech short, by giving the boat a sudden cant, and over fell the old man, in his turn, into the rippling tide.

"Tit for tat," exclaimed Jerry, as he gained the inside of the frail wherry, by dexterously throwing one leg over the gunwale, and raising his body from the water by the mere strength of his arms.

"Holloo, old 'un! how do you like that? What's sarce for the goose is sarce for the gander, eh?"

No voice replied; and Jerry, with a sudden misgiving, looked at the rippling face of the water. All was silent. He peered anxiously, more anxiously than he would own, even to himself, into the tide. All was silent. The deep water rolled on (there was a great depth opposite where the Penitentiary is now built), its surface just dimpled by the evening breeze, for twilight was fading in the west. No object was visible. Jerry looked along the counter, and under the overhanging side of the boat, astern and ahead, in momentary expectation that the old man was playing off one of his practical jokes, just to give him a fright; but no, nought was visible.

"Come, stow this larking, dad!" cried he, in a tone of incredulous remonstrance; "come, old buffer, were are yer?"

No voice replied, and Jerry began to feel nervously uncomfortable.

"I didn't mean it," muttered he to himself; "they can't hang me for it, nayther, I think—nobody seed it—I'll run away to sea——"

These were his first reflections, from which it is clear that his intensity of grief was by no means such as to extinguish his regard for self. Again he looked round, the sculls playing loosely in his hands, and the boat drifting rapidly down stream.

"I'll pull back to where he tumbled in—he was very drunk, sure-ly; but who'd ha' thought he'd ha' drownded like a blind pup at his time o' life. I didn't mean it, though; I'll swear I didn't; and nobody was by. Besides, what bis'ness had he to hit me first."

Having reached the spot where the catastrophe had taken place, Jerry hallooed again and again; echo alone answered his voice. At length he concluded that he would remain where he was till some boat came by, to the people in which he would relate his father's accident. He waited till dark came on, but none passed; he was above the great tide of traffic and amusement in those days; for such of the wherries as plied to Vauxhall, Cuper's, or the Apollo Gardens, hugged the Lambeth shore to avoid the set of the down tide, and the fast increasing darkness, with the breadth of water, placed him beyond their observation. He grew uneasy and alarmed, for the most ferocious natures are often most affected by superstitious fears; and, at length, unable to bear his solitary situation any longer, turned the head of his boat, and pulling vigorously, soon darted the wherry into the shed a little above "The Old Barge-house," where it ordinarily lay. As he removed the cushions, ornamental back-rail, sculls, &c., from the boat (a practice always observed by the watermen for the sake of security), the thought of home, of his mother, and his sister Susan, first distinctly presented itself.

"I'm sorry for Suke," thought he, "'cos she liked the old hunks much better nor he ever desarved. I couldn't help it, though," he added, in a tone of self-justification; "he'd never ha' felled over onless he'd been beastly tosticated; it was all along of hisself, that's what it was. Kious* though, s'pose they should pull† me for this here, will the beak‡ stand this here patter? I should say not. He did it hisself—to be sure he did. Why, the gatter-speeler,§ at Battersea, said as he wouldn't sarve him no gin, 'cos he warn't safe in a boat, by no means; and he'll take his davy‖ as he wouldn't ha' give it him at all, only the vi'lent old beggar swore he'd chiv¶ him. To be sure, he was very drunk; and how could I

* Softly; be quiet.   + Take me up; apprehend me.   ‡ Magistrate.   § Publican; beerseller.
  ‖ Take an affidavit; make an oath.   ¶ Strike him with his chive (knife); or stab.

be accountable for his standing up and rollin' overboard?   Didn't I do all I could
—except jump in in the dark—and there was no help nigh?   I'd better be wet
through, though." And here the ingenious youth, having deposited his burden on
the head of the crazy wooden stairs leading to the water, proceeded to duck himself thoroughly, head over ears, in the muddy river. "That'll do," thought he, as
he scrambled up the slippery steps. " I'll dirty my eyes and face, too, as if I'd
been cryin'. I'll not go to sea—why should I? Let me alone—I'll pitch it strong
enough, I'll make all the soft-uns pity me—I've only to hold my whist, and who'll
be the wiser?"

So saying, he shouldered his tackle and stock of moveables, and in ten minutes
stood before his mother's humble cottage door.

He peeped through the casement ; there sat his mother and his only sister
Susan. The former was engaged in preparing the supper for himself and the old
man : little did the unconscious widow suspect that her husband was at that
moment rolling, a soddened corpse, among the oozy mud of that river whereon he
had so many years toiled. The girl busied in thrumming a worsted cap for her
father's wear, when wintery weather should bring occasion for such a covering for
his bald head. Jerry's heart misgave him, as he looked upon the scene—for no
man is bad at once. Though the disposition may be originally prone to depravity,
yet it is only by a course of crime that the soul becomes seared, the conscience
callous, and the heart desperately wicked. Young Abershaw, for a moment, felt a
pang of remorse, and was inclined to rush in, fall at his mother's feet (for she
was an indulgent, though careless parent), and, confessing all, seek her advice and
consolation. He did not doubt she would screen him, as she had often done
before, in less serious, though more predetermined offences ; but the next instant
his worst spirit prevailed.

"She's a foolish, blabbing woman," thought he ; " and what such people don't
know they never tells. Besides, it was an accident, arter all ; though I wish, for
that matter, it hadn't have happened. So here goes—in for a penny, in for
a pound!"

Thus resolved, he walked a few paces softly away, then, giving a noisy run
towards the door, he bundled down his load at the very threshold with a crash,
at the same moment setting up a wail of lamentation, that brought mother and
daughter to their feet in a panic of surprise and alarm.

"Good heavens! what's that?" cried the terrified Mrs. Abershaw. "It's
Jerry's voice. What *can* have happened?"

"Open the door, mother! Oh, Lord! oh, dear! father's drownded, and I'm
nearly drownded too! open the door !"

Poor Susan sunk, half fainting, on her chair ; Jerry, dripping wet, and covered
with mud, presented himself to the view of the alarmed women.

"I can't tell you how it happened," said the lad ; " give me a glass of something hot, mother ; but father got so very drunk, that, as we were coming by
Millbank, he fell overboard. I jumped in, but after swimming half an hour or
more, I couldn't find him—oh, dear! oh, dear! what shall I do ?"

The acting of the boy, clumsy as it was, completely imposed on the simple
woman, who, seating herself, burst into a flood of tears. Jerry continued his
over-acted moanings, but the orphan Susan sat in silence, pale and colourless as
a statue. In a few minutes, the female inmates of the two or three neighbouring
hovels joined the mourning group ; and as Jerry still kept up the show of
the noisiest grief, he had soon a large share of the sympathy of those assembled,
independent of the monopoly of their curiosity, for from him alone could the particulars of the catastrophe be learned. Amid sobs and groans, he delivered his
broken but plausible tale ; and as there appeared nothing absolutely improbable
in such a death befalling a drunken waterman, he received full credit for veracity.
The gin-bottles of the neighbouring gossips were brought in as a consolation to
the desolate family ; and so liberally and pressingly was the bereaved son
supplied—sorrow, moreover, being dry—that he rolled to bed, at a late hour, so
drunk, that all remains of compunctious visitation was drowned in the excitement
of the ardent liquor, and young Jerry Abershaw never slept more soundly than
on the night that he had caused his father's death.

CHAPTER II.

JERRY AND HIS SISTER—THE BODY FOUND—TOM TRIMWELL—JERRY SUCCEEDS TO HIS FATHER'S CALLING—BLACK SAM, THE RESURRECTION MAN—JERRY THREATENS HIS MOTHER, AND ABANDONS HIS HOME.

WHEN he awoke the next morning, he found Susan at his bedside. Her eyes were red and swollen, and her whole appearance betokened that her rest had been broken by grief at their sad bereavement; for sad it was in more than one point of view, inasmuch as old Abershaw, drunken and dissolute as he had been, was the main support of the family.

"How can you sleep so soundly, Jerry," said she, mildly, "after the dreadful sight of our poor father's death? Mother and myself have been crying all night. Pray do tell me again how it all happened; I can bear to hear it now."

The brain of Jerry was still confused with the fumes of the liquor, and he bethought himself, with an almost instinctive cunning, that he might have said something the overnight which would clash with his tale, should he repeat it. He therefore fenced with her questions, and endeavoured to recall what had passed, even to the most minute circumstances. Meanwhile Susan pressed her enquiries with such simple-minded earnestness, that the young ruffian grew provoked and surly.

"I'll tell ye what it is, Sukey," grumbled he, "the less said about last night's work the better. Father's drownded all through his own drunkenness—and there's an end of him; and I s'pose I must get a partner in the boat for oars. Leastways, I can't well work her myself, 'cos she's too heavy. I've been thinking then, though, as I'll only have half, or say two-thirds its earnings, and there's mother and us two to keep——"

"Oh, Jerry, dear Jerry, do not talk so, I beg," exclaimed Susan; "I did not ask about the boat, but it would give me a sad pleasure to know how father came by his death. He was a good father, Jerry, to us both, though cross and cruel at times; I hope you didn't quarrel with him before the ac——"

"And what if I did," said the ruffian fiercely; "there was nobody by, and what's done can't be helped—but come, Sukey, you're too good a girl to——"

"Merciful heaven, it is then as I feared——"

"Hold your silly, blabbing tongue, can't yer," retorted Jerry; "I was a precious fool to talk to you at all. See where he struck me across the cheek with the stretcher," and he exhibited a livid bruise and cut on his ear; "now mind yer, Suke, I'll stick to it as I got that when I jumped out of the boat after him," and he laughed defyingly at the bewildered and terrified girl.

"In the name of God," said Susan, earnestly, "do not, dear Jerry, madden me by talking in this way. Do not drive me crazy. You did not——"

"Murder him! no, no, that I didn't; he hit me where you see, and then tumbled over the gunnel, he was so precious drunk."

"You did not strike him, Jerry?"

"No, that I didn't, I'll swear," replied Jerry. Susan buried her face in her hands, and sobbed loudly. "Why, what ails the girl; you take on as if I had killed the ould man—there'd been small blame to me if I had—but it so happens I didn't."

"I wish I had never asked you about it," rejoined Susan; "I shall be miserable for ever, now I know you quarrelled and fought just before——"

"Who said we fought? it's a lie," retorted Jerry; "he struck me, and——"

The last few sentences had had a second auditor, in the person of their widowed mother, who now threw herself on her knees beside the bed, in a paroxysm of grief.

"Oh, my son, my son," cried she, "that ever I should live to hear this. All night long I've been haunted by terrible fancies—I feared—I feared—something told me, what at first I did not suspect, that your father met his death by violence."

"It was his own violence, then," growled Jerry; "and if you think you can make it otherwise, why, go and 'peach — nose upon me, and get your son scragged,*—see then who'll work the boat for your living—Tom Trimwell, I dessay, as is so nutty on Sukey there—he'll splice her, and then p'rhaps you can do better by a stepson than your own flesh and blood."

* Inform against me, and get me hanged.

"Oh, my dear boy !" exclaimed his mother, while Susan's cheek reddened with a blush of mingled modesty and indignation ; "how can you talk so ! neither me nor Susan would hurt a hair of your head. But pray tell me the truth—the horrid truth—and I'll never——"

"You've had the whole truth, s'help me," retorted Jerry ; "I told you it before, but if you want to make me out a murderer between you, why, try and prove it. He tumbled overboard—and if you don't like that, make it some other way ; or ask him hisself, for I dessay they'll pick him up when he floats. I'll tell you no more, if you teaze me for a month of Sundays."

With this resolve, the obdurate Jerry turned himself in the 'bed, and drawing the clothes over his head, pretended to sleep ; he was, however, listening attentively to the whispered conversation of the two females, who with broken voices communicated to each other their conjectures on the sad event. From their discourse, Jerry gathered that they mutually entertained a dreadful suspicion of foul play ; and though his mother and sister declared their intention of securing the safety of the reprobate by a guarded silence, their very suspicions awakened a bitter feeling of hatred in his ill-regulated mind, and from that moment he felt a rankling hostility against them.

The body of old Abershaw was, as his son had surmised, soon found ; indeed, much sooner than he expected ; for by noon the next day he was brought home by some brother watermen, and, unluckily for Jerry's character, already none of the best, the corpse exhibited an extensive lacerated wound on the back of the scalp, owing to the following circumstance. It was just flood, and a spring tide, when the accident happened, and as the old man fell from the boat, his head struck with violence against the iron-bound top of one of the massive piles driven into the river-bank below the low-water-mark, for the purpose of preventing the floats of timber in process of seasoning, from being carried away by the tide. This ponderous log, usually above the surface, even at ordinary high water, was now about a foot beneath it, and the concussion depriving the unfortunate man of all sensibility, was the immediate cause of his sinking in the manner we have seen. On the following morning—for the affair was soon bruited about among the neighbours—Tom Trimwell's wherry, with a companion, was early on the spot, and at low water the body was found in the mud, lodged against another pile, which had prevented its being washed away.

It was fortunate for Jerry that Tom Trimwell was the only one who perceived the wound, or public indignation might have cut short the career of young Abershaw. The young waterman had a sincere affection for Susan, and he felt how dangerous it might be to excite suspicion. The corpse was, therefore, enveloped by him in an old sail, and thus conveyed to the cottage. The coroner's inquest soon sat ; but the story of Jerry, who was examined before it, appearing plausible, and the examination of the body by the careless and unsuspecting jurors never extending to lifting up the head, the suspicious wound was not even alluded to ; and the knowledge of its existence was confined to Trimwell, the mourning Susan, and her bereaved mother. Jerry was accordingly cleared by a verdict of "Accidental Death ;" and in a few weeks the matter ceased to be talked about, except by a few crones, who did not hesitate to hint their suspicions that, "in spite of the crowner's quest, *they* didn't think the matter was half looked into."

Jerry now took into partnership, as his fellow-oarsman, a companion in the person of Samuel Tummons, better known by the cognomen of " Black Sam"—not less from the swarthiness of his complexion, and the blackness of his hair, than from his habitual scowl and forbidding aspect.

Black Sam occupied a ruinous tenement, down a narrow alley by the waterside ; and, although he worked but little, was one of those mysterious sort of personages who contrive to live better, and waste twice the money in idleness that can be earned by more industrious fellows. The Dog and Duck gardens and skittle-grounds, in St. George's Fields, then the resort of the disorderly characters of the scattered neighbourhood, engrossed the afternoons of Sam ; there he was always to be found, in the midst of the idlers and gamblers, dressed in the vulgar, flash style of the time, and his pockets seemed always pretty well lined whenever a bet was offered, or a flat to be pigeoned by a display of cash. Indeed he seldom was much seen till afternoon, and common report belied him, if much of the means whereby he made an appearance, were not earned during the hours of darkness. In few words, Sam had the credit of supplying the hospitals in the

Borough with subjects for the experimental skill of those theatres of surgical instruction. Though none dared say it to his face, he was a reputed resurrection-man, and the position of his dwelling seemed well calculated for his trade. At that period the abhorrence of dissection, among the lower orders, was far deeper and stronger than at present, and hence Sam was despised and shunned by the more respectable and honest members of his ostensible calling, which was that of a Thames waterman.

Sam and Jerry had of late become inseparable companions; and his mother saw, with increasing anxiety, and dread of worse to come, that her son, since this connexion, seemed to be more plentifully supplied with money, though his industry and attention to his calling had considerably relaxed. He was from home too, occasionally, the whole night, returning from his nocturnal expeditions, weary and half-intoxicated, at unseasonable times in the morning, and then sleeping till far beyond the early hour at which he was wont, in his father's time, to leave his bed. Remonstrance, she found, only exasperated his savage temper, and she at length ceased to expect money at his hands; seeking a scanty subsistence by washing and bleaching clothes for a respectable family in the City, to whom she had obtained a recommendation, while her daughter plied her needle to eke out the pittance. But this would not have sufficed had not the same kind patron recommended her and canvassed the voters, and thus obtained her a small pension as the widow of a waterman, from the city company of which her deceased husband was a freeman. This too was still further augmented by the kind attentiveness and generosity of Susan's sweetheart, Tom Trimwell, who never allowed the day

which comes between
The Saturday and Monday,

to pass without bringing some present, or serving them in any and every way which lay in his power.

Jerry nevertheless had taken a rooted aversion to Tom. Vice abhors virtue— and he felt bitterly aggrieved at the simple praises which his singlehearted mother never failed to lavish on Tom's name, whenever it was mentioned in her son's presence. Poor woman, she thought, in the innocence of her heart, that her commendations might spur her son to amendment, and never failed to expatiate on Tom's excellencies, by way of example. Her words heaped coals of burning fire on his head, they dropped like molten lead on his reprobate heart, and he mortally, savagely hated Tom, because—everybody praised him. From sneering at his goodness, he progressed to slandering his character, and these calumnies being warmly combated by Susan, the family quarrels grew frequent, and at length young Abershaw almost entirely absented himself from home. Sam's uninviting dwelling was his usual resting-place, while the day was devoted by the pair to drinking, skittle-playing, and the like. Tom Trimwell, too, as may be supposed, disliked Jerry for his bad behaviour to his widowed mother and orphan sister; and at length a quarrel taking place between them, on the seeking of Jerry, the latter ordered him to quit the house. Trimwell refused, and a fight would have ensued, but for the interposition of Susan and her mother. The outrageous son now called on his sister and mother to choose between him and Tom Trimwell. He had better not provoked the choice. Mrs. Abershaw, with tears in her eyes, for once roused into reistance, boldly declared her preference; and the ruffian quitted the cottage, dealing out dark threats of vengeance against the whole unoffending family; who, though they felt his absence a relief, could not help, with the exception of the fearless Trimwell, dreading his desperate denunciations.

CHAPTER III.

A CHURCHYARD SCENE—AN ENCOUNTER—AN ESCAPE—THE CORPSE—AN ALARM—
THE BURIAL—A SISTER'S FEARS—SUSAN'S RESOLVE.

THE night was boisterous, dark, and rainy; the rattling showers descended heavily on the flooded fields, which the vivid lightning made visible for a moment, only to immerge the landscape the next moment in impenetrable gloom. Two men were abroad in this terrific storm, bearing between them a heavy load. They picked their way carefully and cautiously along the narrow lane which led from the water-side churchyard of Putney, and, reaching the causeway, deposited their burden in a boat which was there made fast.

"The stiff-'un's* none o' the lightest, Jerry," said Black Sam, as he drew a long breath after his labour; "I should like to sell him by weight—he'd be a good night's job. Hallo! what's that? hark!" continued the speaker, laying his hand on his comrade's arm.

Next moment a large and furious dog, of the bloodhound breed, came bounding down the causeway, and, guided by his unerring instinct, set up a deep howl.

"Damme, Sam, they're on us!" cried Jerry, aiming a blow with a long pointed iron bar, used in their nefarious occupation, in the direction of the baying dog.

He missed his stroke, and the infuriated animal repaid his intended compliment by fixing its teeth in the fleshy part of his assailant's arm.

"Knife him—knife him, Sam!" exclaimed Jerry, trying in vain to tear the beast from its hold.

Sam drew his knife, and plunged it in the brute's ribs, which turned furiously on its new assailant; but the two men got the animal down, and while Jerry stamped on it with his boots, Sam disabled it by plunging his knife repeatedly in its side. Footsteps were now heard on the gravel road, and voices in pursuit. The two resurrection-men threw themselves into their boat, but as Sam was busied in casting loose the headfast, the foremost of the pursuers aimed a blow at him with a knobbed stick, which alighted on his shoulder; the man was about to repeat his blow, when Jerry, having cocked his pistol—for they both carried fire-arms—discharged it at him, with as good aim as the darkness would permit. A cry of anguish followed, and the man, falling forward from the causeway, plunged into the water. Another man, armed with a gun, had now arrived; but Sam at that moment launching the boat, the tide quickly carried them off. He called to his companion, who cried—

"Shoot them, Bill! Fire!—I am wounded."

"I will," was the reply; "where are they?"

The boat was yet near enough for them to hear the click of his flint lock, as he brought it to full cock, and next moment they laid down, while the man discharged his piece in the direction of the skiff. The slugs whistled by harmlessly, and Sam, using the sculls with professional skill, they had placed the old wooden bridge between them and their pursuers, before the former had time to reload.

"That cursed hound," said Jerry, "has torn me savagely. I shall want this arm dressed; harkee, Sam, I can't row."

"Never mind, old fellow," replied the other; "I'll make you all right when we get to Bankside."

Few more words passed until London, with its glimmering lamps of oil and cotton, rose on their view. The storm, which had in some measure lulled, now broke out afresh, and, amid thunder, lightning, and rain, the drenched companions ran their boat in at the stairs nearest Sam's dwelling. Arrived with their load, in carrying which Jerry's assistance was but small, a light was procured, and having washed and bound up his wounded arm, a consultation was held as to the next step to be taken.

"Ve mustn't keep the stiff-'un here," said Sam, "for fear of the traps; nor, to my thinking, vill it be quite safe to take him to the Sawbones, 'cos, d'ye see, mayhap the cove we spifflicated may turn up his toes,† and then *they* mightn't like to know as ve vere out all to-night. These things require thought, d'ye see, else I should ha' been lagged‡ long ago. Yet I don't like to put the old bloak to soak,§ arter all the trouble ve've had to get him, so we must plant him somewheres for a day, till ve see vhat comes of our night's spree. But first let's see the old chap's box of dominoes."

So saying, Sam untied the sack in which the corpse had been thrust, and disclosed the head of a handsome and corpulent man of thirty.

"No such old bloak, neither," said the hardened ruffian, forcing open the lips of the dead man. "See here, Jerry, here's ivories—vorth a goldfinch‖ to any front-railing maker¶ in the long village."

Black Sam now sought an iron instrument from one of the pockets of his capa-

---

* Dead body.   † Die.   ‡ Transported.   § Throw the old fellow into the river.
‖ A guinea.   ¶ Dentist: manufacturer of artificial teeth.

cious quilted jacket, and, procuring a small hammer, proceeded deliberately to punch, or rather chisel, out the teeth of the corpse.

We need hardly here explain the cause of this proceeding, after Sam's speech; yet it may be as well to observe that, eighty years since, the thousand and one inventions of " incorrodible metallic," " mineral succedaneum," " enamel," and " marmoratum," for supplying the deficiency of nature's masticators, were not discovered, and hence good and undeniable grinders bore a high price—so high, indeed, that, after one of the battles in Germany, a London speculator made a considerable sum of money by employing persons to collect for him the teeth of the slain.

Jerry looked on, and held the light during the horrid operation, and when it was completed, Sam, giving the corpse a thrust aside with his foot, coolly observed that—

" The buffer 'ud vant a pair o' nutcrackers, if so be there vas any nuts in hell."
Then, having washed the teeth in some salt-and-water, he deposited them in the
pocket of his coat.

" I've just been thinking," observed Jerry, " that I've hit on a plan to get my
arm dressed, as 'll do nicely. It's only to step to mother's, and, though she may
grumble a little, she'll see to it for me. We'll plant the stiff-'un in her back
yard—no one 'll ever think of sarching there for it."

" It's a precious night, sure-ly," replied Sam ; " but it's no go for *him* to lodge
here ; so I'll carry the bos, if you'll pick the vay across the drains and bogs."

" Agreed," said Jerry ; and Sam, who was a powerful man, with the sack on
his shoulders, and his comrade as a guide, started, by the side of the ditch, along
the lane now known as the Cornwall-road.

Thus they proceeded, until they neared the dwelling of the widow Abershaw,
where, having knocked and gained admission by arousing Susan, Jerry and his
companion (who had deposited the corpse outside, against the garden fence) were
not slow in making themselves at home. Susan, at the request of Jerry, kindling
a fire to dry their soaked garments, and Sam producing a pocket-pistol of " rum-
royal" for their mutual comfort, whereof he in vain pressed Susan to take a
dram.

Poor Susan ! her mind misgave her sorely ; and if ever fellow was calculated to
confirm evil impressions, Black Sam was the man. Mrs. Abershaw, who had
not seen her son since the night of the quarrel with Trimwell, aroused, though
it was long past midnight, prepared some frugal food for their supper. Jerry
next exhibited his wounded arm, describing the hurt as having occurred through
a fierce dog in a timber-yard hard by ; and his sympathising and credulous mother
soon washed and bandaged the wound, applying to it a herbal styptic of high repute among the " old women" of " sixty years since." Thus liquored, fed, and
healed, the comrades grew talkative ; and the selfish Jerry, having supplied his
wants, was by no means slow in intimating to his sister and mother that he could
dispense with their services, and they, knowing his violent temper, gladly retired.

It was now resolved by the precious pair, that the body should be deposited in
the garden at the rear of the house, and this agreed on, they stepped out softly to
execute their intention. The clouds had cleared, and a grey light shone through
the whirling rack, while ever and anon the watery moonbeams struggled faintly
through the vaporous air. A slight hollow was quickly dug in the loose earth,
and within it they deposited their unconscious burden. The moon shone occasionally as some rifted cloud with fleecy edges passed from before its face, but
only in the next moment to be again obscured. It was in one of these " lucid
intervals" of the queen of night, that the nefarious pair conveyed their graveyard prize to its shallow bed. They were in the act of lowering it, when Jerry
thought he heard a suppressed scream of terror. " Listen !" said he, in a whisper ; a sob followed. " I'm danged if I didn't hear summat," observed Sam.
All was still. " It was only the wind soughing among the pollards and sallies ;*
I've often heard it make a noise like that, afore now," replied Jerry, depositing
his end of the burden.

" I'm danged if *that's* vind, nor pollard neither," retorted Sam, pointing towards the hedge, where Jerry saw, or thought he saw, a moving object. They
strained their eyes at the suspicious spot ; a rustling and crackling was heard, but
at this instant the moon became gradually more obscured.

" Hist, Jerry," said Tummons ; " maybe ve're piped ;† and if so be Oliver‡
have blabbed on us, vy, the gaff's blowed,§ and lagging's our share on it. Kim
on, and stick to me, and ve'll leave the nose∥ no bellows to pipe his story afore
the beak ; for I'll slit his veazand, and let out his vind. Kim on !"

Jerry needed no second invitation, and they both hastened towards the place
whence the sounds proceeded. Here they paused, for the darkness baffled their
search.

" It von't do to strike a light," hoarsely whispered Sam ; " but the upstairs
lantern there 'ill sarve us in a minute, I see," and he pointed to the moon.

Again an imperfect light was shed across the dreary scene, which momentarily
increased ; but what was the alarm and surprise of the pair, as the landscape grew
clearer, on beholding, at some hundred yards' distance, the moving figure of a

---

* Willow wands, or osiers, grown in swampy grounds.   + Discovered.   ‡ The moon.
§ We're discovered.   ∥ Informer.

man, who, darting suddenly from the shadow of the most distant tree of the straggling rows of stunted willows, started off at a famous pace along the high-road! To pursue him would be madness, as, long before they could possibly overtake him, he would easily reach the houses on the way-side, whose inhabitants might come to his rescue; besides, he *might not* have been watching them. But to this their bosoms both said nay, and each looked at the other in the pale moonlight, and saw his blanched cheek reflected in his companion's visage.

"This darkmans* sells us, Jerry, or my name aren't Sam," said that individual, slowly; "but there's nothing more than a forestalling o' the worms† agen us, arter all; provising alvays, as you ha'n't croaked the cove at Putney—vot do you think? Shall 've dig up the stiff-un, move him, and then cut and run? or shall ve cast anchor? I'll do jist vot you decides."

"Cut and run be hanged," retorted Jerry, contemptuously; for, young as he was, he was fast assuming a superiority over Tummons, such as eminent villains ever exercise over inferior ones; "cut and run! you're always for bolting. If the cove that's showed such a good pair of heels just now has seen us, it 'ill be worse to move the stiff-un, which is a 'natural visitation' for any crowner's 'quest in the kingdom: but if we *do* bolt, why it 'ill be made a 'wilful murder' business, and ↄe can say, when they do nab us, won't clear it nicely. You can go and dodge ↄou like, but I'll dorse‡ it at old mother's; and if they *do* nail me, I'll peach on somebody, I knows who; and if I don't wipe off a score, and save both on us for a future skrimmage, call me a muff, that's all! Take care o' yerself, old boy; keep dark a-bit; and if I don't play a trump card this time, I'll give up my hand to a better sharp. Good bye!" Thus saying, Jerry went round to the front, and entered the cottage; while Black Sam, who had several retreats, whenever circumstances might render it politic for him to make himself scarce, walked off at a stiff pace towards the Kent-road, and, by the time that morning shewed itself over the undulating outline of the Kentish hills, was sleeping snugly under the tilt of a gipsy encampment on Blackheath. Here he was cordially welcomed by the black-eyed mother and swarthy patriarch of the Egyptian tribe, with whom it needed but a casual observer to discover Black Sam might claim a somewhat closer affinity in blood than he ordinarily chose to acknowledge. Jerry, on his part, soon betook himself to his bed beneath his mother's roof-tree, for it was not occupied, and, exhausted by fatigue and suffering, soon after slept.

But there was another in that lowly cottage, who, although guiltless of crime, passed moments of misery till dawn "broke from the opening east." Susan Abershaw, her senses quickened by solitude and apprehension, had heard their muttered discourse; she, too, had overheard them leave the cottage, and while yet she watched them in the little garden, had beheld, by the same gleam of moonshine which assisted their labours, the corpse of what her fears told her was a murdered victim, deposited in his damp and narrow grave. It was from her that the involuntary cry of terror had proceeded, and with the heavy sob which followed she sank swooning on her bed. She knew not how long she lay there insensible, but when she recovered, her brutal brother was murmuring his half-intoxicated dreams, or snoring in heavy slumber. Sleep came not to her eyes: the harrowing sight of the victim, and the figures of his supposed murderers, seemed to sear her sight. In vain she closed her eyelids: they were still there, engaged in their horrid task. Anon, a dreadful idea presented itself. She recalled the terrific denunciations of Jerry against her lover; she had heard of the sanguinary brutality of Tummons; and, with the earliest day, she donned her bonnet, and wrapping herself in a warm woollen shawl, which had been presented her by her sweetheart Tom, she hurried off to his mother's dwelling, to confirm or dissipate the horrid imaginings which haunted her.

Arrived there, a new and heart-rending fear awaited her. Tom Trimwell was not at his mother's house. He had, she said, gone the preceding day to Gravesend with some goods, and would not return till the second up-tide that day. Alas, what an age of misery and suspense! Thrice did she repeat her questions to old Mrs. Trimwell, who, alarmed by her manner, sought in vain to draw from her the cause of her alarm, and, at last, began to think her distracted—and so she was! Her mind was torn by conflicting emotions. Should she betray her brother? Then the horrid sight of which she had been an involuntary spectator! Hope whispered that Trimwell *might* live, and she might causelessly betray her

* Night.　　　† Resurrection job.　　　‡ Go to sleep.

brother, whom she loved, despite his vices. She suppressed this feeling for a time ; and, having decided on her first step, hastened back to her mother's cottage, where a new trial awaited her.

———

CHAPTER IV.

A THIEF-TAKER—JERRY APPREHENDED ON A CHARGE OF MURDER—A CROWNER'S QUEST—PERJURY—TOM TRIMWELL APPREHENDED—THE FORCE OF APPEARANCES.

POOR Susan, her bosom throbbing with painful anxiety, was crossing the fields with hasty steps, her agitated feelings escaping in involuntary mutterings of half-formed prayers for the safety of her true-hearted lover, and the innocence of her brother of this damning crime, when she suddenly became aware of a man, who, with cautious stride, kept step and step with her, even at the rapid pace at which she was hurrying on.

The slowly-breaking fog of a chill November morning rendered objects, even at a moderate distance, very imperfectly discernible, and the intention of the stranger to keep her company was by no means equivocal. Apprehending she knew not what, she kept on in the road home till she arrived at a turn which led across a stout plank-bridge by a short cut to her mother's cottage ; here she paused, as though to allow the stranger to pass over first, should he intend so to do ; but the man stopped also, and Susan, her heart leaping to her mouth, now, for the first time, scanned his person. He was a stout, square-built man, between thirty and forty, of determined aspect, dressed in strong, black jack-boots, and a heavy great-coat. There was something in his bold, inquiring look, which sadly intimidated the innocent Susan, and he did not long leave her in suspense as to his character and intentions.

" Fine morning, Miss Susan," said he, with coarse familiarity ; " early abroad —but not so early as ve vas. I s'pose you thought to give the office* to your sweetheart, didn't yer ? He vas out, too, last night. The vatch is set, and it's no use votsomever for young Jerry to try to give *them* the slip as is vaiting to grab him. Howsever, I'll use my kind hoffices to get him through this ugly job, vich, at any rate, desarves a kiss, by vay o' binding the bargain. Vot ! so coy ? Ben Turner's not the cove to kiss and tell—come, vun smack, my pretty vun ; and I'll see if I carn't *halibi* this consarn for you knows who ; purviding alvays as you ——"

Susan had listened thus far, half-stupefied with terror and surprise at the sudden boldness of the thief-taker's address, who, it was clear, had watched all her movements since she left the cottage ; his coarse advances towards using what he thought his advantageous position as a cover for personal rudeness, however, recalled her maiden courage, and, indignantly thrusting him back, she declared she would shriek for assistance, unless he desisted. The fellow looked at her amazed, and slightly abashed.

" Oh, oh !" said he, " you're skittish, are yer ? Very vell ; then if yer von't make friends now, you may be soon glad to. Jerry's in for a lifer,† and Tom— *my dearest Tom*—(here the unfeeling villain mimicked the tone of Susan's first inquiry, which he had overheard, at the widow Trimwell's)—vot ha'n't been home last night, vill keep him company to Antigguee, or, maybe, Bottomy Bay,‡ if-so-be *I* only chooses to say the vord in the mounter,§ vich depends on how ve two drives our hosses, you see."

" Heaven grant me strength !" murmured Susan. " What horrid meaning can this man have ? Tom accused of being my brother's accomplice in —— He's innocent, my good sir ! he's innocent ; indeed he is ! He's gone to Gravesend, and ——"

" Oh, ay !" replied the fellow, with a grin ; " he's hinnocent, in course ; but other folks has to be convinced o' that. There's no von knows vere you've been this morning but myself and you ; moreover, there's no need of no von knowing,

———

* Give information ; forewarn.   † Transportation for life.   ‡ Antigua, or Botany Bay.
§ Give evidence in the witness-box. Giving testimony was called *mounting*, from the position of a witness in criminal courts, he being placed in a sort of elevated rostrum, ascended to by several steps, equidistant from the bench and the jury-box.

provising, as I said afore ——'' Here he again attempted to salute Susan, who shrunk from him with disgust.

"Very vell, very vell; then it's yer own fault," grumbled Turner. "Howsoever, step on, if you please; I likes to see mischief go afore me. I'm at your sarvice, now; perhaps you'll be glad to be more at mine, by-and-bye.''

The thief-taker gave a clumsy bow of derisive politeness, and pointed to the bridge, over which the terrified Susan hastened. On nearing the cottage, they perceived two men similarly attired, the one at an angle of the cottage, the other at the rear of the hedge which skirted the garden. To the first Turner addressed a few words.

"Come on," said he, "we've trapped the bird; but I'll tell you more presently. The twig's limed for t'other; and we'll cage him, too, afore the darkmans. My pretty darling here's been kind enough to favour me with his name and abode, for which she desarves my best respecks. Now, Miss Susan, ve only vaits your pleasure to knock, and ve'll make ourselves more at home than velcome, in no time.''

"Jerry's up and stirring," observed the other, as he unbuttoned his uppercoat, and disclosed the butts of a pair of brass-mounted pistols, and the hilt of a heavy cutlass in a black-leather scabbard.

Susan's companion did the same; and each drew out a pistol, of which he raised the pan and examined the priming. Poor Susan grew faint with terror.

"Now, miss, if *you* please to knock, vell and good; if not, ve'll hannounce ourselves. Ve understands politeness, you observe, unless ve're obligated to be rude.''

The sneering insolence of the fellow was unendurable.

"He can't get off, nohow, you see; so be so good as to knock, or I vill.''

Susan tapped, and, staggering into the room, threw herself on a chair; the panic-struck Mrs. Abershaw screamed aloud; and the thief-takers, rushing in, seized their prisoner, who was at the moment sitting in a careless attitude on a corner of the strong deal table, engaged in an abusive altercation with his mother, upon the threadbare topic of her very natural remonstrances against his evil courses and vile companions.

"I arrest you, Jeremiah Abershaw, in the king's name, for murder!" said Turner, as he seized him by the arm. "Come, come, it's no use slumming innocent; you'll have summat else to laugh at by-and-bye.''

Jerry had burst into a fit of laughter.

"Hold his elbers, vill yer," said Turner to his comrade, "vile I slips on these darbies.''

Jerry, during these proceedings, offered no resistance, merely laughing at his captors; while Susan, overwhelmed with grief, sobbed aloud, and Mrs. Abershaw gave free vent to her lamentations. At length Jerry found speech.

"Well, old Mare's-nest," said he, "whose pig's killed now, that you're squeaking like this? I've a notion you've got the wrong end o' the stick altogether. What am I to be shoved into these bracelets for? But I s'pose you'll have your own way for a turn or two. Who gives me in charge, and what for?''

"Come along here a little vays, and you'll see," replied Turner; and the two officers, leading the manacled Jerry by the back-door into the garden, where, by this time, several idlers and neighbours had assembled, approached the spot where the third man, whom Susan had seen watching, was busily engaged in disinterring the corpse which Sam and Jerry had buried over-night.

A group of inquisitive and eager faces were watching his movements, and to these, in another moment, was added poor Susan's. The light earth was soon shovelled off, and the mould cleared from the face of the dead man. Every eye was now abstracted from the prisoner, who looked on with a hardened grin, to the unaccountable behaviour of his sister: rushing towards the corpse, as its shoulders were upheld by two of the bystanders, she eagerly scanned its features for a few seconds with a gaze of frenzied earnestness; then, as if her heart was relieved of some load too mighty for further endurance, her countenance brightened, and falling on her knees, and fervently exclaiming: "Thank God, *he* is innocent of *that*; it is *not* ——'' she sunk fainting on the damp earth.

"Poor girl, she's crazed for sartin!" observed a sympathizing neighbour. "Lend a hand while we carries her in to bed.''

So said, so done; and with tender care Susan was borne from the scene.

It was clear, as the school-books say, to the meanest comprehension, that the body before them was a " natural" death, for it was yet clad in a handsome frilled shroud; and, although some old women who loved the marvellous would have it that a murdered body was found, the best-informed knew that the charge against Jerry was of no deeper dye than " body-snatching."

> " Men are the sport of circumstances, when
> Mere circumstances seem the sport of men,"

sung my Lord Byron, and the guiltless Tom Trimwell was destined to prove an illustration of the truth of his lordship's axiom. He did *not* return all that day, and, not to keep the reader in suspense, we will tell him the reasons why.

Trimwell had, as his mother had informed Susan, gone to Gravesend with a load of goods, much of the carriage of commodities and persons being in those days performed by these labourers on the " silent highway" of the Thames. Tom was not, like the heroes of your fashionable hot-pressed novels, either an unmitigated scoundrel, nor one of

> " Those faultless monsters which the world ne'er saw,"

but a straight-forward, cheerful, good fellow, who could take his pipe and his glass like a man, and had, moreover, no objection to a spree. Accordingly, happening to meet at Gravesend with an old acquaintance in a seaman of an India ship just paid off, at that as yet unimproved rendezvous for shrimps, smugglers, slang, sport, shell-fish, and emancipated sailors, he accepted an invite from his well-breeched friend for a day's stroll; further incited thereto by the temptation of procuring a bandanna or two for his Susan's neck, and a supply of " Queen's"* tobacco for himself and friends. Indeed, Tom, like most of his fraternity, was not very straight-laced in his notions upon the revenue-laws, which were and are pretty generally viewed by all his amphibious race as restrictions to be evaded if practicable—impositions to be submitted to only by those who cannot help it. While Tom was on this excursion, in which he went as far down as Yantlet Creek, important events were in progress, which seriously compromised his safety.

On the following morning, the coroner for Surrey summoned an inquest at the Compasses in St. George's-road, whereat assembled a worthy jury of small traders of the neighbourhood, " good men and true," who were duly sworn to inquire into the circumstances of the finding of a body in Mrs. Abershaw's garden. As the penny-a-liners would say, " the excitement in the neighbourhood was intense." Before this jury young Abershaw was brought—for coroners and paid police magistrates had not then squabbled about the limits of their respective jurisdictions—and the enquiry was duly proceeded with. The cauliflower-wigged functionary having heard the evidence of a surgeon, who declared that the body submitted to his examination had died from natural causes, Jerry, after being cautioned that what he said might hereafter be used against him, was asked whether he had any statement to make.

After some well-feigned reluctance, he cast his eyes at Susan, who was permitted to be present, and with much apparent ingenuousness spoke as follows :—

" I knows, yer honour, it ar'n't no good me denying of this here business; but I wishes to know whether, if so be I *do* tell the whole on it, I may be made a witness of—then, maybe, I *could* tell a summat as 'ud save a good deal o' trouble to all of you."

The coroner readily caught at the bait. He was a pompous, pragmatical lawyer, and like most of the public functionaries of the time, far too ready to give credence to what is called " evidence for the crown;" a failing which, coupled with the premium then given in the shape of blood-money,† in several cases led to dreadful perjuries, and the sacrifice of innocent persons on the scaffold, as our criminal annals bear melancholy proof. He therefore thus addressed the prisoner :—

" I cannot promise you, young man, a free pardon; but if you are, as you say,

* Contraband tobacco; once so called, in contradistinction from " King's," which had duly paid the customs' duty.

† Forty pounds was given by the state to any one prosecuting a capital felon to conviction; and " Tyburn Tickets," privileging their possessor from being summoned to serve on juries, and other unpleasant offices, were bestowed on those who did not choose to accept the money-reward.

willing to further the ends of public justice, by disclosing your accomplice or accomplices, and giving such evidence and information as shall lead to the apprehension and conviction of the said offenders, I may venture to say that it will go far to release yourself and vindicate the majesty of the law. Moreover, although a *particeps criminis*, you will be viewed leniently, as one who has, after committing a crime, made the best amends in his power, by delivering up others to merited punishment. Mr. Clerk, write down the culprit's evidence, if you please."

"Why, you see, gentlemen," began the artful villain, "last Tuesday as ever was, I meets Tom Trimwell, and says he to me——"

"Oh, Jerry, Jerry!" exclaimed Susan, "do not add false swearing to your other crimes. He never——"

"Who is that young woman that audaciously presumes to interrupt the proceedings of the court?" angrily demanded the coroner.

"'Tis I—his sister," eagerly replied Susan, thrusting herself forward and embracing the prisoner's knees, who looked down at her with a grim scowl of satisfaction. "Indeed, indeed, sir, Tom Trim——"

"Remove her from the court, instantly!—but stay; has she any evidence to give? You seem, young woman, to know something of this transaction; we will hear you first."

But poor Susan knew nought; and, in her agitation, instead of stating the circumstances of Sam's visit with Jerry to the cottage, and their burial of the body, she confined herself to some vehement assertions of her lover's innocence. The coroner waxed wroth at this trifling with the dignity of his court, and the weeping Susan was thereupon thrust from the inquest-room, leaving a clear stage to the inwardly-exulting Jerry Abershaw.

Jerry now went on to state the whole particulars of the adventure at Putney churchyard, with which the reader has been already made acquainted, carefully substituting Tom Trimwell's name in the place of that of his swarthy associate, and not forgetting to charge on him the actual firing of the pistol, whereby the watchman of the graveyard had been wounded. The clerk's pen moved nimbly, and when he had concluded, the coroner, after deliberately reading over what he had written, said—

"Young man, the mode in which you have given your evidence does you great credit, and will certainly have its effect in the proper quarter. It is most importantly corroborated, too, by other circumstances. Where is this Tom Trimwell to be found?"

"I've a little bit of evidence to give as to this pint too," said Ben Turner, who, with an inferior myrmidon, had the prisoner in custody, "as will corehobborate this young man, as your honour says. Yesterday morning, jist as I and Bill Sharpus posted ourselves on the dodge, in consekence of private hinformation ve had procured, close to his mother's cottidge, who should come out, qvite on the sneak like, but that ere young voman as yer vership has jist sent out of the room. 'You stop here avhile,' ses I to Bill and my t'other *plant*,* 'and I'll keep step vith this petticoat, and see vot she's arter, for there's seldom no good ven a voman's about a lay.'* Vell, off she mizzles like bricks, and I arter her, through a fog yer might ha' cut vith a knife; and off she ikes it to old Mother Trimvell's, and in she goes. I does a bit o' the door-nobbling,† and overhears her say, 'Vere's Tom —vere's my dear Tom?' ses she. 'He's gone to Gravesend,' ses the old 'oman. 'Are you sure o' that?' ses she. 'Quite sure,' ses the old 'oman; 'he ha'n't been home all night.' 'Isn't he home now?' ses she. 'No, I told you so afore,' ses the old voman; 'vot's amiss?' 'Thank God!' ses she, 'thank God!' two or three times over, 'then he has escaped!' That vos all I heerd, becos they then took to vispering; and the young-'un, so far as I could gather, seemed to be tellin' the old-'un as she thought the crabs‡ might ha' caught him, and she vos glad to find it vosn't so. Presently she comes out, and I dogs her agen home, vere she acted more like a crazy gal nor anythink else, ven she found I knowed her secret. That's all, yer vership, as I have to add at present," observed Ben Turner, "and I thinks as it's very likely I may grab him afore to-morrow, mayhap yer vorship 'ill give your warrant."

"Of course, I shall issue my warrant," observed the coroner. "Your vigilance does you great credit, Mr. Turner—your testimony is an important

---

* A plot; plan, or contrivance.   † Eaves-dropping; listening.   ‡ Officers.

addition to the case. Gentlemen, I think we have enough before us to conclude upon."

The tinkers, tailors, barbers, and hucksters, forming the enlightened jury, having no opinion but that of the coroner, acquiesced; a special verdict, at the coroner's dictation, was returned; and in an hour or two, the twelve honest men were "bemusing" themselves with beer, and had so mystified their noddles with arguing and re-arguing the points of the case, that you would have supposed to each individual of the dozen belonged the sole credit of having unravelled all the intricacies of the affair, and setting Jerry and his associate well on their road to the gallows. Nevertheless, not a mother's son of them had said a word during the inquiry, nor, indeed, with one or two exceptions, at all clearly understood what they were about, till the proceedings were over.

The distress of poor Susan, the affliction of old Mrs. Trimwell, and the grief of the widow Abershaw, may easily be conceived when, on the second morning of his absence, the unsuspecting Tom Trimwell was apprehended by Turner and his myrmidons, on landing at Blackfriars-bridge with the silks and tobacco he had purchased on his excursion. Whence, after depriving him of his suspicious freight, he was straightway conveyed to the dreary gaol in Horsemonger-lane, to await his trial for the felony with which he stood charged on the evidence of his supposed accomplice.

CHAPTER V.

THE COUNTY GAOL—A FELON'S LAWYER—THE PERJURER—THE ALIBI—THE ACQUITTAL —THE TABLES TURNED—A PITCH-PLAISTER AND ITS RESULTS.

Six dreary and tedious winter weeks in the wretched, filthy, sordid, and ill-ventilated gaol for Surrey, were passed by the innocent Trimwell, before the assizes came on; during which poor Susan was unremitting in her attendance on the unfortunate victim of her brother's fiendish malice. By the united efforts of Mrs. Trimwell, Susan, and her mother, means were raised to employ a legal scoundrel in the shape of an attorney; one of the debased hangers-on of the criminal courts, who drew guinea after guinea from the anxious and unsuspicious females, under pretence of procuring evidence of an *alibi*, which, according to his declarations, was of certain and easy proof.

Mr. Crocodile Fuddlebrain was one of those public-house attorneys, formerly so common, who laid in wait for the ignorant and unwary friends and relatives of people " in trouble," as criminals were termed, and by playing the eaves-dropper at the ale-houses in the vicinity of the principal gaols, contrived to introduce themselves to the notice, and thus acquaint themselves with the secrets, of such persons. This race, now happily nearly extinct, owing to the passing of the Prisoners' Counsel Bill, and the improved practice of the courts, was a social curse of no small magnitude in the " good old times." They were, indeed, a cruel tribe of dirty, " obscene birds," seldom seen in broad daylight, but hiding their filth and villany in the semi-darkness of beer-smelling tap-rooms, in the obscurity of which they lurked in silence, till they found the opportunity of fixing on some unhappy victim, from whom

" The blood, the blood, the very blood to suck,"

was their vocation and profit; until, having exhausted the means of the unhappy wretches who employed them, they usually deserted the miserable prisoner in his hour of trial, leaving him in a worse plight than ever.

On the second day of Tom Trimwell's confinement, Susan and Mrs. Trimwell had presented themselves at the gate of the gaol, and, by means of a present to the turnkeys, succeeded in gaining admittance to the prisoner. They found him in a long, dirty room, with grated, unglazed windows, having a large fire-place at one end, herded with a motley group of drinking and smoking gaol-birds; debtors, felons, and persons committed for misdemeanours, all being crowded together. The smell of the place, and the frightful looks of the prisoners, shocked and disgusted Susan; but her anxiety for her true-hearted lover overcame every other feeling. Tom strove to comfort her, assuring her of his innocence, and narrating to her every particular of his proceedings, from the time he quitted home till his unfortunate apprehension; he concluded by requesting her and his mother

to use their best exertions to obtain him legal assistance. They remained with him until nightfall, when the rules of the prison requiring them to retire, they left the place.

Tom had informed them that, by leaving the needful cash at the bar of the Granby Head, in the immediate neighbourhood, he might be supplied with such beer and refreshments, by favour of the gaolers, as he might require; a per-centage being taken by those individuals for the indulgence. The public-house was soon found, and, while the women were making their arrangements with the red-faced landlady, a seedy-looking personage, who stood sipping a glass of Geneva at the pewter counter, thus accosted them—

"Beg pardon, ladies, for intruding myself so abruptly—but I think you said you were interested for one Tom Trimwell, unfort'nately just now lumbered, as they vulgarly call it, in the stone-jug hard by—I mean his Majesty's gaol. My name's Crocodile Fuddlebrain, ma'am, at your service. Had more experience, ma'am, than any five practitioners at these 'sizes—dare say you've heard of me, though. I got off Sixteen-string Jack twice, by finding flaws in the 'dictments; likewise proved *alibis* in seven clear cases of horse-stealing in one sessions, whereby I received the thanks of the whole bench o' judges and the grand jury for my perfessional skill. Though I say it as should not, there never was a jury I couldn't puzzle. My terms, ma'am, is low, and I does business on the maxim of ' no cure no pay;' only taking my travelling expenses, and a mileage for my witnesses. May I be so bold as to ask the nature of the charge? It *must* be a strong case that Crocodile Fuddlebrain can't get over. Rapes, murders, and arson, burglary, hos-stealing, perjury, highway robbery, and the likes, is my favourite cases—but if so be as yours is only a sheriff's job—debt, or the like—why, I flatter myself Crocodile Fuddlebrain is *the* man to settle with the creditors. I draw all sorts of petitions, too, at the lowest charge, for commutations of sentence, mitigation o' punishment, and the like. Mrs. Barglass here will speak for me in that line. I'm hand and glove with the judges and officers of the court; and, though I say it myself, if there's anything to be done for the unfort'nate prisoner, there's no one can do it better than your humble servant at command."

While the legal harpy thus volubly delivered himself, he fixed his gooseberry eyes on the face of Susan, who looked inquiringly at Mrs. Trimwell; she, equally ignorant of the ways of the world, nodded her wish that she should reply to the speaker. The landlady now chimed in, recommending Mr. Fuddlebrain; for he was indeed a good customer, inasmuch as he spent all his fees at the Granby Head, besides drawing others to supply his own never-ceasing thirst.

Poor Susan, too much absorbed in the troubles of Tom to think or reason much upon the subject, eagerly caught at the proferred services of Fuddlebrain, and, in the simplicity of her heart, briefly acquainted him with the facts of the case. The pretended attorney winked at the landlady, and said—

" P'r'aps, ladies, this had better be talked over in a private room. Mrs. Barglass, can we be accommodated ?"

The landlady acquiesced, and the trio were admitted to a small parlour within the bar.

Mr. Fuddlebrain now procured pen and ink, and proceeded, with an air of professional accuracy, to write down what he called the " leading pints of the case;" he soon succeeded in impressing the two ignorant women with a high notion of his wondrous legal attainments and vast ingenuity, and their good fortune in thus, as it were, accidentally procuring his valuable assistance. His next step was to ascertain the amount of their united stock of cash, and was not long in obtaining ten shillings as an earnest of two guineas, which he declared would be his charge for defending the prisoner at the ensuing Guildford sessions, whereat he would be tried.

Susan and Mrs. Trimwell departed for their homes, lighter in heart and in purse for their interview with Mr. Crocodile Fuddlebrain, who immediately thereafter fell into a confidential conversation with Mrs. Barglass, which ended in the obliteration of a long string of O's, ✕'s, and other hieroglyphics, from the back of the bar-door, leaving the panel clear for another score on the strength of Mr. Fuddlebrain's renewed credit.

The day of trial came, and Tom Trimwell, handcuffed, and fastened with a chain to three other prisoners, was conveyed outside the stage-coach to the assize-town of Guildford, in custody of Turner and another officer; Abershaw having been committed thither on the coroner's warrant in the first instance. The jury were sworn, and Susan, with her mother and Mrs. Trimwell, having placed themselves in the body of the court, the case was proceeded with.

The unblushing Jerry, called from the dock to the witness-box on the suggestion of the counsel for the crown, gave his evidence with cool and collected effrontery. The prisoner was now asked whether he had any questions to put to this witness.

Tom, overwhelmed by his feelings at the dreadful perjury he had heard, could only reply that he had understood counsel was engaged to cross-examine the witnesses for the crown, and that he had expected persons present to prove an *alibi*. Turner and his brother officer now added their statements, and the judge inquired of the bar what gentleman was instructed for the prisoner—but no counsellor held a brief.

Mrs. Trimwell and Susan, who had hitherto sat on thorns, looked around in despair for their legal adviser, who had not only promised to attend, but had deluded them, even to the latest moment of the previous day, with stories of the witnesses he had engaged and paid; and that he had further necessity for two guineas, to fee Mr. Serjeant Blather, and half-a-guinea for his clerk, which sums the heartless scoundrel had also obtained from them.

"Do you wish to call witnesses to character?" inquired the judge.

Poor Tom now found that he stood alone, and, summoning his energies for the occasion, he proceeded to state his defence. He told his lordship of his departure for Gravesend; of his absence with a friend, one Benjamin Stacey, of the Surat Indiaman, paid off on the very day named in the indictment; of his purchase of the smuggled goods, which lay upon the table of the court, and which Turner, the thief-taker, had artfully insinuated were probably the produce of robbery; and concluded by throwing himself on the mercy of the jury.

At this point, the judge was evidently about to sum up severely on the improbabilities of his story, standing, as it did, unsupported, in the face of such positive testimony, when a bustle took place in the body of the court, which, for a few moments, interrupted the proceedings. It was occasioned by several men in the garb of sailors, one of whom, despite the remonstrance of the officers, who wished to exclude him, called out—

"Avast there, my honourable judge and gentlemen o' the court, I've got a something to say; give me the book—I'll not spare myself—no, nor friends neither, to save an innocent fellow!"

"Who is that man?" inquired the judge.

"It's I—the very Ben Stacey as the prisoner's bin talkin' about. I can prove every word that down-looking lubber there has been a swaring to is a pack o' ——"

"Crier! keep order in the court," said the judge.

"Please you, my lord," persisted the fellow, "there's half-a-dozen o' my messmates, hard by can prove ——"

"This is totally irregular," said the judge, calmly; "nevertheless, place this man in the witness-box, and swear him. What is your name?"

"Benjamin Stacey, my lord," replied the blunt sailor. "I'm here, my lord, to-day, relating to a robbery committed on one of my messmates, by a land-shark hereby, and I ——"

"We cannot waste the time of the court in irrelevancies," observed the judge, who was in reality a good and feeling man. "It is informal, gentlemen of the jury, to hear any witness whose name has not been furnished to the crown prosecutor, except upon the point of character; nevertheless ——" The crown counsel here waived this objection, whereupon the judge added: "Let the witness, then, be sworn."

The sailor kissed the book fervently, and proceeded to state, clearly and earnestly, the whole proceedings of himself and Trimwell, on the two eventful days of his trip to Gravesend and Yantlet Creek. While he delivered his "round, unvarnished tale," the features of Jerry underwent a strange alteration—his scowl grew demoniac, and he bit his lips with baffled rage and vexation.

"My lord," concluded the honest seaman, "if you don't believe me, there's Bill Cropley, as is persecutor in the robbery case, and Sam Thwart, at a house hard by, let them be called, and see if they won't prove as yonder villin there ——"

"Stand down, witness," said the judge; "you do not seem to understand the respect due to this court: let William Cropley be called."

The crier went outside, and Cropley, in two minutes, was in the witness-box.

"Let Stacey be put out of court, but held in custody," directed the judge.

Cropley was then examined. With what eager joy did Susan listen to each word that fell from his lips. He, too, proved that on the evening of the churchyard exploit—which was the day of paying off the Surat—he had never left the company of Tom Trimwell and his friend; and produced the warrant of his discharge, together with a signed character from his captain, bearing date on that very day. These documents were submitted to the counsel for the crown. That gentleman declared he must give the prisoner the benefit of such evidence as this; and the jury, without hesitation, returned a verdict of "Not Guilty," amid a cheer from the crowded court, which the officers in vain attempted to suppress.

"The prisoner is not yet done with," said the judge; and poor Susan felt her

heart crushed at these words. It was, however, but for a moment, as he added—
"Let Thomas Trimwell, Benjamin Stacey, and William Cropley, be severally brought before me, at my private room, there to enter into their own recognizances to appear against Jeremiah Abershaw, on an indictment for perjury, to be preferred against him at the next assizes; and let the witness Abershaw be taken to the gaol from whence he came, on that charge. Mr. Clerk, make out the warrant of his committal."

Another murmur of applause followed; and amid the heartfelt congratulations of his mother, his sweetheart, and his sailor friends, Tom Trimwell walked from the dock, overwhelmed with the providential deliverance he had so unexpectedly experienced.

But there were other adventures in store, ere Jerry should hold up his hand at a felon's bar. We have already alluded to the old practice of conveying prisoners by stage-coaches on their various removals. At noon next day, the necessary proceedings having been completed, Jerry Abershaw, chained with a convicted felon, set out in custody of Turner and his comrade, by the coach for Southwark. It was a chill and foggy day, and, short as was the distance, daylight was consumed by the time that sluggish conveyance had reached Kennington-cross. Here Turner proposed to the coachman a drop of cordial, an invitation which these worthies were never known to refuse; and two inside passengers joining in the proposition, they entered the Rose and Thistle to take a "fog-cutter," as Ben facetiously termed it, leaving his brother officer in charge of the chained culprits. That personage also descended from the roof, keeping an eye on his prisoners, while he performed sundry gymnastics, intended to restore the circulation to his benumbed extremities.

"Hist! Jerry, is that you?" asked a voice from the dark road, at the off-side of the vehicle.

"Ay, ay," was the low response.

"Who's there?" inquired the officer, stopping in his stamping round, which bore no remote resemblance to some of the steps of the fashionable polka.

He had no time to repeat the enquiry. A large plaister of Burgundy-pitch enveloped his whole face, a knee was thrust in the small of his back, and two pair of powerful arms laid him prostrate on the frozen ground with a rude shock.

"Steek the gate,* Bob!" said Sam, for he it was, "and come and put your hoof on this grabbing-cove."

The door of the public-house was wedged tightly with a piece of wood sloped for such purposes, and in a trice Sam ascended the roof; one wrench of his ready jemmy† tore away the side-irons of the front seat of the coach, through which the chain was passed, and with but little assistance the liberated prisoners were soon safely down on *terra firma*.

"Across the common—mizzle, you cripples, like Newgate!" said Sam, in a hoarse whisper, as he accompanied them to the other side of the narrow roadway. "The corner of the Mint—old Hobbs's—in a hour. I'll be there by another way."

Jerry and his comrade needed no second bidding; ducking under the rails at the farther side of the road, they scoured along, under shelter of the friendly darkness, rendered yet more impenetrable by the intense fog.

"Now, Bob—here, Bill—nammus like bricks!" cried Sam to his companions.

The three villains took short leave; and when Ben Turner, the coachman, and his passengers, returned to the coach, they found, to their no small consternation and dismay, how much mischief had been effected during their few minutes' absence. Loud were the imprecations of Ben, and humble the expostulations of his half-suffocated understrapper, from whose face the plaister could only be detached by taking him to the tap-room fire, and there liquefying the well-compounded mixture. When this was effected, however, they were but little the wiser, as the partially flayed wretch could only tell them half of what the reader is already acquainted with.

* Fasten the door of the public-house.   † Small housebreaker's instrument.

CHAPTER VII.

THE MINT, AND ITS DENIZENS—THE THREE BREWERS—A WEDDING PARTY—BOB WALPOLE—LOOSE LYRICS, AND A DEBAUCH.

About an hour after the escape narrated at the end of our last chapter, Jerry, his personal appearance somewhat altered by a yellow tow-wig and a smock-frock, was standing with his fellow convict near the place of rendezvous.—But first a few words on the locality.

The space of ground extending from Union-street, as far southward as the Queen's Bench Prison, on the western side of "Long Southwarke," was known, in days of yore, as Southwark-park. Here was situate Suffolk House, the residence of the celebrated John Brandon, Duke of Suffolk, who espoused the sister of Henry VIII. The wife-killing monarch becoming possessed of the mansion, converted it into a "royal mint," of which there were then several in various parts of the kingdom. On the coining apparatus being removed to the Tower, the ground was sold to Archbishop Heath, who again, in the reign of Mary, of Smithfield memory, disposed of it to a company of building speculators. These gentry pulled down the palace, and covered the ground with a labyrinth of small streets of wooden houses, which, soon becoming ruinous, were let out to tenants of the lowest description; and, as described by a contemporary writer, "the Mint" became a spot

> " Where cadgers, and buffers, and such sort of fellows,
> Were mixed with a vermin bred up for the gallows;
> There *puttocks* and *files*, housebreakers and padders,
> With cut-purses, *sweeteners*, and such sort of traders :
> Informers, *thief-takers*, sheep-stealers, and bullies—
> Old straw-hatted ——'s, and their vile spunging cullies:
> Some drinking, some smoking, some lying, some swearing—
> Some dancing, some fighting, some ranting, some tearing :
> While some with the tapsters do get up a fray,
> That their pals, without paying, may slink safe away !"

Of the delectable neighbourhood thus poetically delineated, in a poem entitled "The Humours of the Mint," published in 1775, we need add little to the rhymester's sketch. This colony of riff-raff retained their appellation of "Minters," till but a few years since, and one of its entrances may still be seen by the curious inquirer, in a miserable lane, nearly facing St. George's Church in the Borough, which retains the name of Mint-street.

In the time of our hero, the buildings of this rookery exhibited lamentable signs of having become ruinously dilapidated, not less from their antiquity than from neglect of necessary repairs. Originally insufficiently erected, the squalor, filth, poverty, and recklessness of their inhabitants had aggravated the injuries of time and the seasons. The loosened weather-boards of the gables clattered in the breeze, while the roofs of many of the dwellings were open to the rains and dews of heaven. Unhinged doors, incapable of shutting, leaned against the no longer upright door-posts, while heaps of dirt in the uneven passages forbad their being closed, even had the inmates desired it. The windows were shutterless, their wooden flaps having long since been converted into firing; while the windows themselves displayed many curious contrivances by which old hats, shoes, straw, rags, and petticoats, were made to perform every duty of glass but its transparency. In the principal street, which was narrow and muddy, the apologies for shops seemed perfect museums of antiquities. In one fluttered habiliments of every fashion but the one then in vogue; next door stood a crazy building, from the door-posts of which dangled kerchiefs of every and of no colour; and at every few paces you came to a den, to furnish which the gutters seemed to have been raked—rusty iron, toothless files, broken hoops, screwless vices, broken keys, hiltless swords, notched screw-drivers, edgeless chisels, nails, clamps, and padlocks. Hospitals for disabled furniture, too, consisting of armless chairs, legless tables, bottomless chests of drawers, and mutilated household utensils of every sort were amazingly numerous. Magazines of salted herrings and stockfish, bird-fanciers, translators of shoes, barbers, and ale-houses, completed the catalogue. The ground seemed an odoriferous compound of drainings from dung-heaps, mixed with the offal from slaughter-houses; while the kennels—for the place was without sewers

—sent up their steams to mingle with an atmosphere redolent of fried fish, tobacco, sausages, faggots, baked puddings, tripe-cleanings, and steaming ox-cheek soup —purveyors of which article were, in times of yore, common in this and other low nighbourhoods.

Seated on the steps of the doors, or lolling out of the windows of the tumble-down houses, here and there might be seen faded, dirty, and bloated females, or squalid girls, who stared rudely at the passer-by, or addressed him with coarse blandishments; and above, tier above tier, floating like tattered banners in the black-laden air, hung yellow cottons or onec-gaudy chintzes, intermixed with foot-less stockings and tailless shirts, borne aloft on superanuated brooms or cashiered mops, stayed and steadied by knotted cordage.

Nor was the place without its charms for the sense of hearing as well as those of sight and smell: the squalling of children, the scolding of women, the riotous shouts of profane swearing, ribald songs, drunken ravings, and boisterous laugh-ter, issued in Babel-like confusion from the dens of misery, and the numerous drinking-houses, with which the Old Mint abounded.

But these sights were lost on Sam and his companion, on account of the dark-ness; while the former was too well used to the olfactory salutations to heed them; Jerry, however, could not refrain from comment.

" What a confounded stinking road you're bringing us," said he; " isn't there some better way to ——"

" Hist! silence!" replied Sam; " it's a sweet road that leads to safety. Do you see yonder smoky red lamp at the court end?"

Jerry grunted an affirmative.

" Well, then, that's the ' Three Brewers;' and now I think on't, this is Vensday night, and they're keeping up the vedding of Conkey Bean."

What this speech might mean Jerry was not yet made acquainted with; but he was not long left ignorant. Passing along Wheeler's-rents, a dirty alley leading from Mint-street towards St. George's-fields, they entered the Three Brewers; and Sam, together with the newly-escaped convict who had been Jerry's com-panion on the coach, being recognised by the tapster, the party were ushered into the apartment of revellers assembled to celebrate the wedding of the gentleman designated, on account of his nasal projection, " Conkey Bean."

The company was composed, for the most part, of those " mercurial" spirits, who are afflicted with a morbid desire to pry into the mysteries of their neigh-bours' pockets; and to whom, consequently, vice was too familiar in all its aspects to present much novelty, in whatever form it might be exhibited. Upon the centre table, at the top of the room, was a large leathern black-jack, full of some smoking liquor, wherefrom the pewter-pots of the company were replen-ished: around were strewed fragments of pipes, bread, cheese, onions, and the ashes of tobacco, the fumes of which, added to the rank whale-oil smoke of the shadeless lamp, and the compound of villanous smells, might have well disgusted any unseasoned stomach.

At the upper end of the room sat, in bottle-nosed importance, the landlord; a pursy, slip-shod, braceless lump of bloated humanity. He had once been a thief-taker; but had now, by a transition common in those days, become a publican; a convenient calling for his kindred profession of a fence, or receiver of stolen goods. To this worthy was Jerry introduced by Sam; his companion needed no such ceremony.

" What! Leary Joe, as I live!" exclaimed the ' quondam fisher of men;' " why I heerd only yesterday, as you was—— But, never mind, now's not the time for telling us—luck's all, my brave boys—take your seats vere you can get 'em. Now, genelmen, order for Slumming Bob's chaunt."

The tables now received a vehement shower of blows, accompanied by a concerto of kicks and stamps on the saw-dusted floor, during which uproar we will take a short survey of the company henceforth to become Jerry's associates and comrades.

The majority of the assemblage rather deserved the name of youths than men; debauchery, disease, the gallows, and the colonies, consuming them in such large proportions, that the very existence of such a class required a constant supply of juvenile recruits. Yet, though young in years, vice had, in most instances, worked such defeature, mental and bodily, that the youngest were not a whit behind those whom the law had spared a longer term of villany. The females—for there were beings who wore the outward form of a woman, though every characteristic of the gentler sex had well nigh departed—we will not pollute our pages by describing. Each was accompanied by her "fancy man," as she termed him; and amid the confusion of voices, the roar of blasphemy, and the din of imprecation, the voices of those libels on womankind bore their more than due proportion.

"Leary Joe," as the escapado, who had an hour before been Jerry's yoke-fellow, was called, soon made himself and his companion at home; and in a breath performed the office of *cicerone* to our hero.

"Do yer see yonder downy-looking old card, as is vispering to the young-un?—that's Ikey Long, the 'angling cove;'* he's making a deal with Jem the Buzman,† for a yack and inguns,‡ and a vedgelobb.‖ Ikey von't get the best o' Jem by a long pull, thof he be but a young-un. There, that chap as is rising now to speak, is Slumming Bob, the cracksman,§—and a hout-and-houter he is! Hear him! Order for Slumming Bob!" continued Joe, adding his voice to the Babel of sounds.

The landlord now plied his mallet vigorously, and the tumult subsided.

"Genelmen—hem!—genelmen," said Bob, "you've called on me for a song, so here goes!" and, moistening his throttle, he droned forth, in "linked cadence long drawn out," the first stanza of the ancient flash ditty, commencing

"As ve sailed down the river clear,
    On the tven-ty-nin-eth of Ma-ay,
Ever-y ship as ve com-ed near,
    We heerd the peep-el say,
'There goes a lot of rum-mi kids,
    All bound for——' "

The recollection of numerous pals, "who had left their country for their country's good," combined with an over-moistened throttle, or a drop of liquor gone the wrong way, here cut short the pathos of Slumming Bob. He sneezed, drew the cuff of his jacket across his eyes, and apologised. His doxy, too, seemed affected, and begged him to try "summut livelier;" anon he dashed off something in the following fashion:—

The coves they calls me Slumming Bob,
    Vell known upon the *mall;*
I'm fly, I'm down, I'm vide avake—
    And nutty on each gal;
The beaks¶ has often seed my mug,
    And pigmen, too, a lot,**
But still I sports my lil-y tile,
    Like-r-vise my svellish mot!
        Ticlum, ri-fol-lol, rifum, tooral, hey!

My father vos a cracksman good,
    And svags o' rowdy bagged,
Until his pal did nose on him,
    So he, poor bloak, vos scragged;††
But the peaching cove he vos sarved out,
    As you shall quick-er-ly hear,
For he vos nailed on the frisking suit,‡‡
    And napt it for fourteen year!
        Ticklum, &c.

So I vos left a horphan,
    As you may plain-er-ly see;
But to foller in the ould cove's vays,
    I'd a pro-pen-si-tee.
So I knibbles all vot I could ketch,
    And vos seldom ketched myself;
And many a svag‖‖ I yet vill lay
    All on the fencing shelf.
        Ticklum, &c.

Then here's success to leary coves,
    Vot's habsent and vot's here,
And may ve all have pluck enough
    The sarcy pigs to scare.
Success to those vot's in the start,§§
    Likervise to them vot's out,
And may the cussed clinkers¶¶
    Sit light their shins about.
        Ticklum, &c.

* Angling cove—purchaser of stolen goods.   † Buzman—pickpocket, cut-purse.
‡ Yack and onions—watch and seals.   ‖ Silver snuff-box.   § Housebreaker.
¶ Magistrates.   ** Officers.   †† Hanged.   ‡‡ Stealing trifling exposed articles.
‖‖ Booty.   §§ Gaol.   ¶¶ Fetters.

> Good luck to every nimming cove,
>   Vot's tramping in the town,
> And may he never vant a hog,*
>   A gold-finch,† nor a crown.
> Here's health to those vot's gone to sail,
>   All on the brin-y sea—
> Success attend each right cross-cove,
>   Verever he may be !
>   Ticklum, &c.

"That's all, genelmen," snuffled Bob, in the same tone as he had chanted the last note of his peculiar ditty. The applause was tremendous. Joe's chant, to use a newspaper flower of rhetoric, "had come home to every man's business and bosom," in that vile and lawless knot. Pots, jugs, sticks, and feet, vibrated in approval; song after song followed, and the hour of midnight passed, before Jerry bethought himself of departing. In fact, the liquor had made considerable inroad upon his understanding. Nor was this wonderful; he had, for the last week, led a life of unwonted and compulsory abstemiousness, attended with much anxiety, and the sudden revulsion of feeling, consequent upon his recent transition from chains to unexpected liberty, aided the liquor in its effects.

He communicated with Sam, who, half-intoxicated, also seemed to have forgotten the perilous position of Jerry; but Leary Joe quieted his doubts, by declaring that he knew a crib where they might rest in safety; and thither, after more than one of "the wee short hours ayont the twal" had chimed from the tower of St. Saviour's, Jerry and his new-found comrade repaired.

Sam, who was least "gone," preferred to betake himself to the road, to rejoin his gipsy companions; not however without promising Jerry and his friend to meet them at the "Three Brewers," on the following evening.

CHAPTER VII.

A CONSULTATION—A ROBBERY—ROBERT WALPOLE CHAMBERLAIN INTRODUCED.

'Twas high noon of the next day when Jerry awoke, parched and feverish, from his long sleep; his first thoughts rambled confusedly over the leading points of his recent escape, the scene of the overnight, and the companions he had met with. He had not, however, been long "companioned with his sweet thoughts," when Joe entered his squalid bed-chamber, and, with friendly facetiousness, inquired after his bodily health. This was followed by a metaphorical declaration, by that worthy, that he would stand "a double nip o' juniper, and a dash o' brown,'‡ by way o' cooling the copper of his pal; a motion readily assented to by Jerry. The liquor, with pipes and tobacco, being procured by the Leary one's lady, the trio forthwith sat down; and in about an hour, more gin having been swallowed, and a modicum of bread and cheese, with some raw onions, despatched, Jerry's visitors retired, leaving him to take "a siesta" till the shades of evening should bring the hour for the proposed meeting with Black Sam, at the Three Brewers.

Jerry had donned his clothes, and Joe having rejoined him, the pair sat hanging over the embers of a fire in an unset grate, inspiring and exhaling the fumes of the Nicotian weed in listless indolence, when Nor'ich Poll, as Mister Joe's " wife for the nonce" was termed, came up the stairs to announce the arrival of a visitor, in the person of Samuel Tummons.

"He's yarly, and no mistake," observed Joe; " I vonder vot's in the vind now?"

Sam entered, and the trio were soon in solemn concalve :—

"Vy, you sees o' late I ain't bin a-doin' much," observed that personage; " so this morning I borrows a moke and drag,|| and takes a turn round the svell houses and mansions about the heath§ and thereavays, just on the touting-lay ;¶ I likes to keep an eye to business. Vell, I reckons up a crib,** the third vith an hiron gate from the top o' Maize-hill. There's a highish vall behind, but that's nuffin, and there's a savage mastiff, but I've a doctor†† mixing for him as he'll have delivered this evening for his early supper; so he's purwided for; and now comes the best on it. I goes up the lawn, and peeps in at the folding vinders, and there I

---

* A shilling. † A guinea. ‡ Two glasses of gin and some porter.
|| A donkey and cart. § Blackheath. ¶ Looking out. ** Inspected a house.
†† A piece of meat, prepared with a poisonous or a narcotic drug.

sees a heap o' lobb,* real wedge, and no mistake, spread all over a sideboard, and buffets with stands full o' cups and kivers, and the like. Sam, Sam, thinks I, them *must* go to sveat,† or somebody else must sveat for 'em: so I takes a plan of the premises in my eye, and if-so-be ve are righteous vuns to each other, the thing's as good as a gift to us."

"And the household—who lives there?" asked Leary Joe.

"That's reckoned up, too," observed Sam; "there's two maid-servants—they're only dangerous for squalling: and there's an old gardener; there's a butler, he's fat and old—I've the ticket as to vat part they all sleeps—leastvise, I shall have it, for Ebony Nance ha' been into the kitchen, to tell both the gals their fortins, and I ha' bin in the hall to sell my brooms—vot flats these svell slaveys are, sure-ly! The hold hadmiral, as they calls their governor, is gone to Vindsor, or St. James's,

* Plate.   † Be melted.

4

I don't know vich, and von't cum back, maybe, for three or four days, and he's taken the vhipster and the flunkey,* with his own valet-de-cham, so if we ar'n't in luck's way I don't know them as is."

"To-night must do it, I see," observed Leary Joe, meditatively, counting his finger tips ; " it 'ill take four on us, Sam, at the least. I'm one, and, Jerry, what say you ?"

" Of course," replied Jerry, who had hitherto said little ; " but mightn't *three* be enough of us ?—the fewer in the job, the more to share."

" No," replied the Leary one ; " onless you've a boy, Sam, as is close enow to mind the rumbler.†"

"That's easily purvided," said Sam; " but four 'ill make a safer job on't. There's Bob Valpole, I should like him for a pal—he's an out-and-outer in the line, which is more nor I can say of either Jerry or myself; though our hearts is in the right place, I'll pound it."

Leary Joe, accordingly, set out in search of that individual, whose proficiency, as we have heard, stood so high in the estimation of Black Sam, and in a few minutes that celebrated cracksman was added to the party.

The reader must not here suppose that we have wantonly, or of *malice prepense*, taken the name of a great minister of state, who robbed his countrymen on the grand scale, as the cognomen of a mere retail thief; Robert Walpole Chamberlain was one of the most noted burglars and footpads of his day, a companion of Jerry Abershaw, and suffered the extreme penalty of the law in the year 1791, for highway robbery, as may be fully seen in the pages of the Newgate Calendar, and the Sessions' Paper for that year.

Walpole was dressed in a flash style, that completely astonished Jerry ; he wore a feather-edged hat, with a broad buckle and band, knee breeches of a bright ochreous yellow, a blue coat, trimmed with narrow white galloon on the edges and seams, a white neckcloth like a pudding, powder in his hair and curls ; his dexter hand carried a grotesquely carved stick, crooked as a ram's horn, and of most awful dimensions.

" Good evening, Sam—same to you, Master Joe. Well, my pinks, how goes it ? Pretty smartish booze at the wedding, last darkmans. Low toby‡ suit queer, Sam, ch ? I've been trying to do business lately at the buz and cover‖, but the family-people§ are getting so infernal hard-mouthed since old Izzy Abrams, the fence, got his travelling ticket, that, demme, if all trade isn't gone clean dead. But what's the go now ? The Abram suit's¶ flat ; and as for buzzing, dragging,** and hoisting,†† they're stagnated, because there's no market. So, now, out with what you've got to say new, Sam."

Having delivered this mercantile speech with the air of a speculator on 'Change discoursing on the state of commercial depression, Mister Bob Walpole seated himself on the side of Jerry's turn-up bed. His next act was to send for a shilling's-worth of ale, and then he declared himself ready to hear Sam's proposition. This was soon dispatched, and Bob Walpole, having satisfied himself, by sundry questions, of the feasibility of the robbery, thus gave them the benefit of his experience and judgment—

" The thing's a gift to us—we'll settle the rest as we drive down. You, Joe, with Sam, must start directly for Blackheath, get a cast on the road, if you can, and see the dog you speak of has got his feed. I, and our young friend here, will come down in the rattler, with needful traps for *unlocking* the strong-boxes and window-shutters. At eleven o'clock, under the trees, on the right hand of the Green Man, at the top of Blackheath-hill : driving later up that road won't do. And now, Jerry, my lad, we must be up and stirring, for it is already not far from nine."

Bob Walpole was evidently not one to let the grass grow under his feet, for, by half-past nine, he had procured a light cart, with a false bottom, belonging to a denizen of the Mint, that had many a time and oft been used on such expeditions, together with a smart, powerful, and fast little cob. In the false bottom of the vehicle were stowed the house-breaking implements necessary to the achievement

---

* Coachman and footman.   † Cart to convey the booty.   ‡ Footpad.
‖ Picking pockets, with a confederate or stalking-horse to " cover " or screen the depredator in his operations.   § Cant term for receivers.
¶ Begging-letter imposture of shipwrecked sailors, burnt-out tradesmen, and the like.
** Robbing carts or carriages during the absence of their drivers.   †† Shoplifting.

of their intended burglary; and having armed himself and Jerry with a brace of pistols, the twain jumped into the cart at the corner of the Kent-road, near the old Stones'-end, whither it had been sent under charge of a boy, for the purpose of avoiding suspicion.

Nothing worthy of note occurred during their drive, until they reached the appointed spot on Blackheath-hill. But as this burglary, the first in which Jerry was engaged, involved important consequences to some of the actors therein, we must postpone its details to our next chapter.

CHAPTER VIII.

A GIPSEY ENCAMPMENT—INGENIOUS COOKERY—A BROWN BEAUTY—JERRY SMITTEN—
JEALOUSY—THE BURGLARY—THE MURDER.

" PAST ten o'clock, and a cloudy night!" had been drowsily bawled by some hundreds of those hoarse, drab-coated, woollen-nightcapped guardians of the night, in days of yore yclept "Charleys," but now departed like a dream from the memory of the present generation—a pleasant, soothing dream, whose semi-somnolency is ill-exchanged for the wide-awake reality of the spruce modern policeman. The tidings that it was " past ten o'clock," had thus been published to the numerous dwellers in mighty Babylon, when Bob Walpole, Jerry, the fast cob, and the " light chay-cart," turned to the right, and quitting the highway which leads athwart Blackheath, in the direction of Shooter's-hill, commenced a slow walk across the undulating surface of the heathy turf.

The inequalities of the ground, which caused the vehicle to roll very much after the fashion of a surf-tossed boat, rendered riding so exceedingly uncomfortable, that after Jerry and his comrade had pitched against each other twice or thrice, dealing mutually involuntary bumps, Abershaw exclaimed—

" Gently, Bob; let me get out, and I'll lead the horse; ah! yonder's the signal—that's Sam's lantern—see!"

At this moment a dim light exhibited itself for a few seconds among the broom-tufts at a few yards distant, and they were speedily joined by its bearer and Leary Joe.

" All right, my trumps," said Sam; " come on: I'll call the kid to mind the rattler:" and that individual proceeded to do so in a characteristic fashion.

Stooping down and plucking a blade of spear-grass, he doubled it and applied it to his lips, then, blowing it with sudden jerks of the breath, he produced a noise so strongly resembling the chirruping of a grasshopper, that at such an unseasonable period for those merry minstrels, the note might have puzzled the acutest fellow of the Entomological Society, had such an one been within earshot of those low but piercing chirps. In a few seconds this singular call was responded to, and a ragged young shoeless urchin, whose brown, oval countenance, and bright black eyes "bespoke his oriental origin," came jumping through the gorse.

" Ben, my kinchin, watch these here gentlemen's hos, and see it don't stray, and they'll gie yer a tanner. And mind, if any of the Philistines comes nigh hand, chirrup and lead 'em off tow'rd yonder wall as skirts the park thereaways. D'ye twig?"

" Rightus, master, as a trivit; I'se awake," replied the small urchin; and the quartette of thieves, leaving the boy in charge of the vehicle, made off towards a gipsey camp in the hollow of one of the numerous sand-pits on the heath.

Here they found a family of that roving race, who welcomed them as friends of Sam, and very shortly were seated at a savoury supper composed of the gatherings from the hen-roosts and duck-ponds of the neighbourhood, together with a fine hare, the spoil of a wire laid down that evening in the ancient park of Eltham.

The mode of cookery among this wandering community astonished and enlightened our hero and his comrade, Bob Walpole. The fowls were not picked—such a process would endanger detection—but the birds having been drawn, were rubbed the reverse way of the feathers with damp clay, in which they thus became embedded to the quills; they were then covered completely with a crust of the same material, till they assumed the appearance of lumps of earth. A hole being next made, several heated flints, as nearly round as procurable, were placed therein; on these the enveloped fowls were pressed, and some more hot stones being laid above them, a fire was kindled on this compound hearthstone. Long practice told the "ladies" of this migratory establishment the time at which the birds were what the cooks call "enough," when lo! the ashes were raked away, and the steaming poultry, freed from the hardened clay, presented themselves, their feathery appendages coming clean away with the intermingled mass of baked earth!

Nor was their meal a dry one; the beverage being a strong infusion of the Chinese leaf, obtained from their smuggling friends. Tobacco, too, was there galore; and some "small-still spirit," with a powerful twang of essential oil, was proffered by way of "digester." Song followed the repast, until Jerry had almost forgotten the purport of their visit. But it was neither drink nor song that produced Jerry's obliviousness; there was one in that wild group, a coarser Cleopatra, a dusky Egyptian maiden, whose cheek needed no staining with "juice of berry," and whose dark bright eye and rounded but slender form, rivalling that of a Mahomedan houri, might well have attracted and fixed the admiration of a higher judge of female beauty than the "jolly young waterman," whose vices had transformed him into a lawless desperado. Nor did the damsel, who claimed some nineteenth cousinship or other mysterious genealogical affinity with Sam Tummons, appear in anywise to discourage Jerry's attentions; though there was one slouching vagabond of the party who looked with evil eye on Jerry's familiarity. Perhaps it was mere coquetry—smile not, reader—woman loves to display the empire of her charms; and whether clad in the sweeping gorgeousness of the velvet robe—laced in the gay boddice of the country maiden—or bare-foot and with kerchief-bound head, as was Jerry's gazelle-eyed inamorata—woman's nature knows no change. But we are not going to write a chapter on the "loves of the gipsies," so we will hasten on.

Rebekah Morse (for so the maiden was called) and our hero were getting fast upon that footing by "favours secret, sweet, and precious," which would soon have made the latter utterly forgetful of the business in hand, when Sam broke the charm and dissipated the "fool's paradise" of young Abershaw into thin air, by exclaiming—

"Now, then, friend Jerry, ven you've quite done with Bekka, I'll say a summat. How these young fellers is given to petticoats," added he, winking significantly at Leary Joe; then turning to Mister Valpole, as he styled him, who was also doing the amiable to an elder and dingier damsel—"howsever, it's arter twelve, I take it, and as black a darkmans as ever crow roosted in; Mister Valpole, might I ax the time?"

Bob Walpole rose from his seat on a bundle of hay covered with a blanket, and with the air of a swell from Hockley-hole, produced a massive Tompion, about the shape, size, and colour of a garden turnip, whence depended a triple chain of cut steel, ornamented with rows of cut plates, each the size of a shilling. As these glittered in the light, a small exclamation of admiration and covetousness broke from one or two of the infantine gipsies at the dazzling display.

"It's half-past twelve by Somerset House," observed Walpole, smiling; "but really, time has flown so pleasantly, ladies, that I have not noticed it."

He then politely apologised for the "pressure o' business," and declaring himself ready, the four set out on their midnight foray; Rebekah Morse accompanying Jerry to the outside, and wishing him "luck" with a cordiality which completed his infatuation—and his rival's hate.

The cart was brought silently across the sward to the top of the steep declivity called Maize-hill. In ten minutes, Jerry having furnished himself with a dark lantern, and a short iron bar with a "sheep's-foot" end, Leary Joe with a bunch of skeleton keys and a similar weapon, and Walpole with a "jemmy," a picklock, and a dark-lantern, the plan of procedure was arranged.

Sam was first to scale the back wall, with a tackle and hook he had provided, while Leary Joe watched the front and road; and when Sam had made good his entry, Abershaw and Walpole were to follow him. All went on favourably. The night was dark as the worst criminal could desire, and the wind soughing and moaning among the lofty trees which lined the wall of Greenwich Park, rendered slight noises inaudible.

" 'Tis a lovely darkmans," observed Walpole;·" I should say that Oliver has been served with a subpœna to give evidence in some other 'case' instead of ours. What a delightful rattle those bare branches make! One might dance among these dry, whirling leaves for a month in wooden shoes, and the next neighbours be none the wiser. Come on, it's chilly going at this pace."

The back garden was reached by a circuit through a paddock—Leary Joe, as before said, remaining in the front—and Sam Tummons was soon on the inner side of the wall; the dog was silent, the house was dark; and, in a few seconds, stealing gently along a closely-shaven lawn, the trio reached the parlour window.

"Blinkers * by ——" whispered Walpole. "There's no light within, though. This way."

Jerry followed him stealthily, as they crept round the house. All was dark and silent. They returned, and again surveyed it.

"'Tis a queer-built crib," said Walpole; "that staircase outside there leads us up to the pannum shed,† without troubling ourselves to force these lower ports."

There was, as is common in many old-fashioned suburban erections, an outer staircase covered with a verandah, whereby the guests could descend to the pleasure-grounds, without passing through the lower part of the house, and issuing at the grand entrance. Up this Walpole gently crept; but on arriving at the top, he deemed it inexpedient to force the door, which was of massive wainscot, and, doubtless, well secured. Casting one cautious gleam of his "housebreaker's best companion" from its bull's-eye aperture, he perceived that a railing of some four feet high separated him from a long balcony, which ran in front of the drawing-room windows, and round two sides of the house, commanding a delightful view of the river, and the opposite county of Essex; over this he noiselessly climbed, and with cat-like tread traversed its whole length.

"Beautiful!" he muttered. "This crib's been built for me to crack, that's certain. They do say when an unwelcome guest comes in at the door, maybe he goes out at the window; now here, if luck holds good, we'll just reverse that saying. So here goes in at the window, and if I *do* go out at the door, it shall be because it suits me better."

Thus saying, the facetious felon applied his little instrument to the slight fastening of one of the door-like windows, and it yielded to the gentle, but firm, persuasion, with the most accommodating alacrity. Walpole stepped in, threw another glance of his sliding light round, and retreated as gently as he had entered.

"Now, Jerry, sharp's the word and quick's the motion. Have you the sack?"

"I have."

The burglars ascended.

"Shall we secure what's here first, or go and nail the slaveys?" interrogated Jerry.

"Hush! the cleanest done things are those that are never suspected till they're over," responded the experienced cracksman; "there's *your* job!" pointing to a well-loaded sideboard.

Jerry needed no second bidding. With as little noise as was possible, he proceeded to transfer one article after another to the wide-mouthed sack. Walpole, meanwhile, completing his examination of the apartment.

"I'm for finishing with this room," observed he. "There are four servants at home; we could quiet the two old men, but mayhap a screech from the woman-kind might spoil us. All's not safe that's in danger, and though I don't mind a scrimmage when it does come, it's best avoided."

Jerry agreed: and Walpole and he were fast filling the sack, when they were joined by Leary Joe.

Walpole was about to remonstrate, but Joe assured him that all was right, "there wasn't a mouse stirring within a mile; besides," said Joe, "I wants a bottle or two of wine," and he suited the action to the word by uncorking one. Pouring out a tumbler full, he quaffed it to his own health, and his example was followed by Walpole and Jerry.

It is amazing how soon boldness as well as fear will steal on men; Joe took a second goblet, pronouncing its flavour excellent, and his two comrades followed suit.

"Sam's out o'this," observed Jerry; and Joe, taking the hint, snatched another bottle, and made his exit by the window, to treat their sentinel on the lawn below.

* Shutters.   † Dining-room.

Some delicious sweatmeats were next abstracted from a cellaret, and the party (for Sam had sacked his bottle to himself) were chuckling in confident security, when a slight noise, as of an opening door, struck their practised ears.

"Hist! hark!" whispered Jerry; "there's footsteps on the ladder!"* then applying his ear to the keyhole (from which dangerous and incautious position he was gently withdrawn by Walpole), he listened for a few seconds. All, however, was still.

"This will guard ag'in surprise, I reckon," observed Leary Joe, as he gently lifted a large heavy wine-cooler, bound with hoops, and lined with a compound metal, which he placed against the door.

They now resumed their occupation: drawers, cupboards and cellarets were busily ransacked. Walpole had just possessed himself of a splendid pair of duelling pistols, and Jerry of a magnificent small-sword, when a slight noise in the balcony again arrested their attention, and next moment a loud warning whistle from Sam sounded through the night air. The guilty scoundrels turned their eyes towards the door, and thence towards the window by which they had entered. A dark shadow was visible against the dun sky.

"The Philistines,† by G——!" shouted Sam from without; "down vith 'em, lads, down vith 'em!"

A bright flash, and a loud report followed his speech; the momentary light revealed a stout man, who had discharged a bell-muzzled, brazen blunderbuss at the marauders.

"Down with him, Jerry," said Walpole, faintly; "I've got my gruel—I'm peppered, by goles!"

The wounded burglar staggered towards the sideboard, but Jerry at the same instant rushing towards the open window, struck desperately at the assailant with his crow-bar; the blow alighted on the barrel of the blunderbuss, and struck it from the man's hand. Jerry followed up his vigorous assault, and at the next thrust hurled the unfortunate butler over the balcony railing with fierce violence on the gravelled walk below! One groan—and ere he could heave another, the ferocious Sam Tummons had shattered his skull with a heavy bludgeon, nor did he cease his blows till the unhappy man was a mere disfigured mass of lifeless flesh. Jerry, perceiving the coast was clear, and that this single servant had alone come forth, proceeded to assist Walpole from the apartment, while Joe, dragging down the sack of booty with Sam's assistance, hoisted it over the wall. This, however, was not effected quietly. The house was thoroughly aroused: female screams issued from the front windows, and the old gardener, who had more discreetly than valorously ran off on perceiving the awful catastrophe of the butler's fall, had got hold of the great dinner-bell; its ding-dong, so often heard with pleasure by expectant guests, mingled with the shrieks of the women, raised a pretty clamour among what novel-writers call the "sleeping echoes of the neighbourhood." This clamour, however useful it might be in accelerating the flight of the burglars, brought no assistance; for it was a good half-hour before the gardeners and flunkeys of the vicinity, having joined forces with two private watchmen, thought it prudent to attempt the relief of the shrieking garrison of old Admiral Boscawen's house from the perils of their midnight assailants.

At length, however, when the noise had subsided, they approached: and the murdered body of the poor old butler having been laid in the hall, lights were procured, a good fire was kindled, and several of these valorous plush-breeched champions, seeing all danger was clean past, volunteered to stay and guard the terrified womankind of the plundered house till "daylight should appear." Their offer was gratefully accepted; strong ale was brought; and, with the serious drawback of the presence of the awfully mangled corpse, which lay in ghastly goriness in the hall, any visitor who had looked in at Admiral Boscawen's two hours after the robbery, might easily have supposed *that* night had been devoted to merry-making, and not to murder.

* Staircase.   † Philistines, a cant term in gipsey and smugglers' slang, for enemies of any kind.

CHAPTER. IX.

REFLECTION — THE GIPSEY TRIBES — THEIR ORIGIN — THE WOUNDED MAN — A DILEMMA — A PAIR OF SMUGGLERS — THE SPRIGHTLY NANCY — MR. SOLOMONS OUTWITTED — A TRIP TO SEA.

" 'TIS a strange world we live in," has been iterated until its very strangeness has become familiar, and we begin to doubt whether anything strange ought to surprise us. The robbery at the old admiral's house, and the atrocious murder with which it was accompanied, formed a nine days' wonder for the newspapers, sluggish as they then were in their intelligence, and gave a profitable month's engagement to the thieftakers, who, well paid by the plundered owner of the mansion, found that they had a good job, and, accordingly, protracted their pretended services, while *detection* was farthest from their views. Indeed, in the "good old days," it was a mere question of "profit and loss" with the *thieftakers*—as they were conventionally termed—whether it was worth while to apprehend the felon; hence, although those "vigilant and active officers, Turner and Davis," as we read in the papers of the day, "had instituted the most searching inquiries, the villains remain undiscovered." But we will not pursue this, so return to the adventures of Jerry Abershaw.

In our last chapter we said a few words on the gipsies; and as our hero's preservation to adorn the "bad eminence" of the gallows-tree was materially promoted by their agency, it is fit we should say a few words of the strange community which sheltered him, and which so eventfully contributed to colour and mingle the varied web of his future life.

This extraordinary vagrant race first made their recorded appearance in Europe in the year 1427, then coming among the people of the "western world" as penitents or pilgrims. They declared themselves to be Christians driven from Egypt by the persecution of the Musselmauns, and obtained from various princes and rulers in Germany, France, and England, permission to reside in their several dominions, on account of their proficiency in certain arts, and more especially from their pretended knowledge in the "occult sciences," then liberally patronised by the ignorance of the ruling few. Other Oriental erratics followed, and wandered in all directions ; the men committing, as the few scattered notices lead us to believe, petty depredations and wholesale impositions, while the women invariably assumed the calling of prophetesses or fortune-tellers. In France they were called "Bohemians," being supposed to have passed over from Bohemia. In Germany they received a name equivalent to Egyptians ; in Italy and in Spain they were "Zingari ;" in England, "Gyptes, Gipsies, or Egyptians." A word may be excused as to the French term "Bohemians," so nearly resembling their German name. The old French, or rather Netherlandish word "Boehm," signifies neither more nor less than "a sorcerer," and hence some historians may have been led to attribute an erroneous etymology to their modern Gallic appellation. Be this as it may, the race became dispersed, and was known over all Europe. Everywhere they preserved the same roving character, a repugnance to the fixed habitations of the people amongst which they dwelt, and an aversion to the arts of husbandry or of manufacture. A profound ignorance, an inexplicable cunning, and uncleanness in person and in diet, a disposition to pilfer, and a desire to impose on the credulity of others, sufficiently marked their Asiatic origin. Yet it is remarkable, though evidently the denizens of a warmer clime, these sturdy vagrants prided themselves on enduring the rigours of a northern atmosphere, and while other indigenous beggars sheltered themselves in stables, barns, outhouses, or ricks, the gipsy preferred the independence of his tattered blanket stretched on a few hazel rods stuck into the earth. Thus much of the people with whom Abershaw was now, to use an erroneous term, "domesticated."

It must be remembered that our hero was a young man—so young that though he had by constitution, inclination, and choice, chosen the evil way, he was still strong in the passions which, if rightly directed, prove man's blessing and salvation—if wrongly, his ruin and his curse. Rebekah Morse had all the attractions which could mould "man's vagrant fancies," but—and here we draw the veil; she had not—how could she have ?—one single principle of truth, honesty, or sincerity. From her first year to the seventeenth, at which she had now arrived, her life had been one continuous acted lie. Deception with her was triumph, dishonesty, a mark of spirit. To a form slight and elegant, but with the active strength inseparable from symmetry, dark Andalusian eyes, white teeth, raven hair, and the winning graces of beauty, which

"needs not the foreign aid of ornament,
But is, when unadorned, adorned the most,"

she added that warm benevolence which, despite every defilement of vice and its associations, still dwells in the temple of a true woman's heart.

The bell of the temple sacred to the worship of God man hourly and daily profanes, had sounded two, when Abershaw, with his blood-guilty comrades, reached the heath with their ill-gotten booty. They halted and listened, but none pursued. The state of the wounded Walpole was urgent, and might discover them. A short consultation was held.

" 'Tis as easily done as telling a lie," whispered Leary Joe, rendered unusually serious by the event ; " I'll drive Bob to town in the rumbler, and you coves can make it all right by toddling off down the road."

" But how about the swag ?" suggested Black Sam ; " we won't trust *you* with our regulars."*

" Never mind about that, now," observed Jerry ; " let him take a part till we can meet again."

But to this Sam stoutly objected, and, in pursuance of his objection, Joe received a massive cup, five guineas, and the sword, with an understanding that Jerry should meet him that same evening to learn what had befallen Walpole, whose condition, as he lay fainting in the cart, into which they lifted him, was extremely doubtful.

Leary Joe and his maimed charge set out for town, while Jerry and Sam made their way towards the gipsy tent. Arrived there, Sam, with an air of authority, gave the signal for departure.

" Now, Mother Fly-by-night," exclaimed he, addressing the ancient crone, who issued from the tent at his first summons, " we want you to show us how soon you can move your bones. Me and my friend here have got some luggage, which must go with the rubbish and boys, while the two on us starts for Cobham-park. Come, no grumbling—send Ben out, and I'll talk to him ; for there's eighteen miles afore us, and we two mean to tramp it."

An elderly gipsy soon appeared, and Sam having, in very few words, made him acquainted with the state of affairs—at least, so far as he thought it prudent to disclose them—he and his companion started off, at a smart walk, over Shooter's-hill, leaving the easily-struck encampment to follow them, according to order.

" 'Tis easier said than done," though a common-place remark, is not less true than it is hackneyed. Leary Joe, trusting in his own sagacity, had declared that nothing was more easy than to get the wounded Walpole to town, and lodge him in a place of safety. He had reckoned without his host. Patent boxes, countersunk linch-pins, and the score of inventions which have been discovered by the ingenuity of man, to prevent the obvious dangers of a " spill," had not then been applied to wheels, and the light chay-cart, which conveyed Leary Joe and his comrade, had only just reached the New Cross, on the other side of Deptford, when, lo ! a faithless linch-pin treacherously forsook its duty to the common *wheel*, and, after wobbling a few yards, to parody the nursery rhyme, " down came chay-cart, fast trotter, and all."

Leary Joe swore ; the sorely hurt Walpole groaned ; and the horse said nothing.

" Here's a putty perdicament," exclaimed Joe ; " this is a tarnation onlucky night's job, Robert, and I'll do whatsever you think for the best."

"Take me to some place where I can get my wound dressed," replied Walpole ; " a fellow may as well be scragged as die for want of a doctor."

Joe looked about : the spot was solitary ; and at that hour there was no vehicle, nor even a foot passenger of whom he might ask assistance.

While thus consulting, two men, wearing the garb of sailors, came along the road, in the direction from Greenwich. Joe resolved on addressing them, and requesting their help—for a con-si-der-ation, of course. The strangers came up ; but what was Joe's joy when he recognised in them two old acquaintances and frequenters of the Three Brewers and the Justice's Head. They had been on a smug-

* Share on division of booty.

gling expedition, and freighted with a cargo of silk handkerchiefs, India shawls, and the like, which they intended mixing with a large proportion of inferior goods. With these they were wending their way to London,

The needy villain's general home,

where they intended selling their contraband wares, as a blind to their other duffing and pilfering exploits. To these fellows Joe briefly explained the pitiable state of affairs, when one of them, by name Bill Naylor, at once suggested an arrangement, which materially altered the destination of Walpole. But we will leave him to explain the matter in his own words.

" 'Twont never do, d'ye see," observed the amphibious Bill Naylor, " to ventur Mister Walpole, in his wounded state, in the Boro', amongst all they traps, landsharks, nobblers, hinformers, and long-shore coves. Shiver my timbers, but there's no safety whatsumdever on shore—that's my motto. Besides, a jolting in a cart ain't no go for a man as has got peppered: there's nothink like water-carriage for that, too. But, here, let's right ship fust, and jaw over the matter arterwards. Wot's carried away here?—a bolt—oh, ay—well, and the wheel's unshipped. Werry well. Lend a hand, Ben, my hearty, here's a wessel in distress."

Thus saying, Joe, Billy Naylor, and the fellow the latter addressed as Ben, soon raised the cart, and the wheel being replaced on its axle, a temporary linch-pin was inserted in place of the absent one, which was nowhere to be found.

This effected (for the reader must bear in mind there were then no "night coaches," and that travelling after dark was by no means safe, either for foot-passengers or horsemen), Billy Naylor again urged his proposition in a more definite form, and as there was more than one of the party who had a desire to see it carried out, it was pretty quickly agreed too.

Firstly, Ben, the companion of Billy Naylor—and who now carried the weighty pack containing the merchandise, had no objection to be rid of his load; secondly, Billy Naylor thought, and rightly too, that the chaise cart was just the thing to distance the old "Charleys," if any of them should be inquisitive as to its contents; he had, moreover, a mind to earn a guinea or two, especially as he could at the same time serve a friend; and thirdly, Bob Walpole himself had suffered so cruelly from the jolting of the vehicle, that he was glad to hear the proposition which Billy thus promulged.

"D'ye know Deptford Creek, at the mouth o' the Ra'nsbourne?* well, there, snug enough, lies till next tide, which flood at four, the Sprightly Nancy; as tight a little craft as ever run a keg o' Nantz or a kildy o' Cognac; now I'll tell'ee my plan: Ben here shall shove my freight aboard your wehicle, and you shall steer me up to town, Joe, 'cos, d'ye see, I don't know much o' navigating these here carts and hosses: meanwhile, Ben, as I said afore, having discharged his cargo, shall take Bob, as is so cruelly crippled, under convoy, and make all sail to jine the Sprightly Nancy. Whereby all mistakes will be saved, as Ben knows 'xactly the spot she lies. Once aboard, he'll find as how her skipper, when he knows he's a friend o' mine, is the right sort, and there he may lay and get his hull-damage repaired at leysure. What d'ye think o' my signal and manœuvre, eh?" inquired Billy Naylor, rolling his quid, hitching his trowsers, and squirting half-a-pint of saliva on the hard roadway.

"I should prefer it vastly," said Walpole, whose wounds were now becoming intolerably painful and stiff; "I could walk, with anything like help, to this Deptford Creek; where is it, and how far?"

"Short of a mile, across the fields," replied Ben; "and if-so-be we makes sail, it's my notion we may reach her by a *long leg*, east by north, in a quarter of an hour."

Walpole seemed relieved of half his agony; so much did he dread the jolting of the cart.

Billy Naylor accordingly mounted beside Leary Joe, who handed Ben a guinea as his fee, and Walpole two guineas, to pay for any services he might need. The fast trotter started towards London, and Walpole, by the assistance of the sturdy Ben Boltrope, after a short walk, found himself safe in the cabin of the Sprightly Nancy, a littled lug-rigged smuggling vessel, of Dutch build, engaged ostensibly in the turbot and flat-fish trade, between Flushing and the port of London, but in reality as arrant a smuggling craft as ever queered a Custom-house galley, or gave the slip to a coast-guard cruizer.

Here we will leave Walpole for a time, and return to look after our hero and his pal Sam Tummons, who were last heard of on their way to Cobham.

It is generally some strifling oversight which first furnishes a clue to the detection of malefactors. Sam and Jerry had safely reached Cobham, and the gipsy encampment followed them without note or suspicion, but, on the following day, Sam having occasion to visit the town of Gravesend, there entered the shop of a Jew, and offered for sale a small and beautifully mounted pistol, with a gold medal, which he had carefully defaced. The Jew bought them, but perceiving that the stock of the pistol was engraven with some letters, which Sam, from his deficiency of education, not being able to read, had mistaken for mere ornaments, he carried the same to the mayor of Gravesend for inspection.

* The river Ravensbourne, which, traversing Lee and Lewisham, falls into the Thames at Deptford Creek.

This proceeding would never have entered the mind of the Israelite, but for an unpleasant cloud which just then hung over his fair fame, in the shape of a charge of purchasing government stores of a seaman on board one of his majesty's ships. Mr. Solomons suspecting his customer, thought the present a beautiful opportunity for gaining favor; he therefore despatched his son Moses to watch the steps of Sam Tummons, while he, Mr. Solomons, hurried off to a magistrate to show the articles he had purchased, and the seller of which he expected to be able easily to find.

The news of the robbery and murder had not yet reached his worship; but his clerk, perceiving that the weapon bore the inscription—"B. Boscawen, Captain R.N., 1759." naturally concluded that it had been the produce of a robbery; a suspicion which was confirmed by further discovering that the gold medal was a testimonial of honour for a great naval victory achieved by the same distinguished officer.

This was enough. Mr. Solomons was praised for his vigilance, and a constable was despatched to apprehend the vendor, whom his son was then engaged in tracking.

But there was one who heard the whole of this important plot. It was Rebekah Morse, who chancing, in the pursuit of her profession of fortune-telling, to be in his worship's kitchen, had a question put to her by a domestic, concerning the robbery, by way of testing her powers in the discovery of theft.

From this fellow's narrative, as he detailed what had occurred up-stairs between Mr. Solomons and their master, to the maid in the kitchen, Rebekah became acquainted with the impending danger. She accordingly hastened from the house, and taking a circuitous path to avoid suspicion, hurried to the encampment. On her road thither, she overtook Jerry and Sam, to whom she communicated her fears and her discovery.

Their resolution was soon taken.

"We must bolt, Sam," said Abershaw, "or the traps will be on to us hot-foot. The river offers best chance; don't you think so?"

"There's no two words to that," replied Sam, "I should say: but, hist! I've a bright thought. This very morning I met Ben Boltrope o' the Sprightly Nancy; she dropt down this early tide, and Barney Bradwell's my old pal and her skipper; once aboard her, they don't take us easily,; but how's the chink?"

They "took stock," and half-a-dozen of guineas was found in store.

"We must kid old Benjamin and Bekka to plant the swag aboard for us, at some spot on the river's bank, and the thing's done. The Dutchmen 'ill give us value for all the wedge we can take 'em, and save the fences the trouble of taking our prize-money."

To this arrangement Jerry gave assent, and by the time his worship's constable, accompanied by Mr. Solomons, had arrived at the gipsy encampment, Jerry and Sam were on board the Sprightly Nancy in mid-stream; where, to their equal surprise and satisfaction, they found the wounded Bob Walpole.

The waterman's experience of both Jerry and Sam made them acquisitions to the crew of the little smuggling vessel, which, certainly, looked unlike anything but what she pretended to be, namely, a turbot and plaice boat. A communication having been made to the gipsies, that the Sprightly Nancy would lie, the night following, off Lower Hope Point, eleven miles lower down the river, to receive the booty on board, prior to its transportation to Holland, the smack tript her anchor, and stretched away down the Reach, as though off to sea on one of her usual fishing voyages.

CHAPTER X.

A FOUL WIND—A SURPRISE—THE TAKERS TAKEN—THE BILBOES—AN UNPLEASANT PREDICAMENT.

At the close of the last chapter we left Jerry Abershaw, Bob Walpole, and their swarthy companion, on board the Sprightly Nancy, bowling along the Lower Hope before a spanking breeze, which by nightfall had carried them below Yantlet Creek. Scarcely, however, had the welcome shades of darkness fallen on land and river, when a consultation was held, at which Ben Bradwell, the commander, Sam Tummons, and our hero, assisted; the result of which was, they put helm about and returned up the river as far as Gallions. After three hours of tedious tacking with the up-tide, the lively craft was moored off Battery Point, and Sam with Jerry went ashore in the boat, making their way across dyke and meadow towards the little village of Clift, three miles distant, where, at a small alehouse, the meeting with old Ben, the gipsy patriarch, and Rebekah Morse, had been appointed.

Here they found the pair they were in search of, with the portable valuables, which, it must be observed, were of such a description that Ben well knew must be unsaleable, except in a proper market. Leaving Rebekah at the public-house, the two started back by the road they came, in search of the Sprightly Nancy's boat, which awaited them under the lee of the river wall. The re-embarkation was safely effected; but the wind had now changed, and it was found at daylight that they had made but a few miles on their seaward voyage by the down tide: she accordingly lay-to.

The elements proved unkind; for the wind, which had hitherto been merely unfavourable, freshened into a breeze, and from that to a gale, and ere the tide they so anxiously expected had again turned, it blew "great guns." Night came, and still found the little barque straining at her anchor, and it was the afternoon of the third day, when, after several fruitless attempts to put to sea, Ben Bradwell declared the necessity of putting in for shelter in a creek off Southend.

All was now made snug, and as the Sprightly Nancy lay under bare poles rolling in the little sheltered haven, the crew proceeded to make themselves as happy as their weather-bound position would allow. But Walpole, whose flesh-wound had now only left a stiff soreness, had become wearied with the confinement of his hammock, and had sat down with Black Sam in the after-cabin, to while away the tedious hours of suspense in the mysteries of a game at put, when Sam, turning his eyes towards the cabin door, suddenly beheld an unwelcome sight.

Behind Walpole stood an officer with a pistol in each hand, while another thief-taker placed himself between Sam and the murderous weapons wherewith the side of the cabin was thickly hung.

The housebreakers were paralysed. No alarm from the deck had told of their approach: and they were forced to surrender at the first challenge of the officers, in the king's name.

Walpole endeavoured to put a good face on the matter, by inquiring their business; but the fellows laughed, and he who seemed the leader, replied—

"Vy, you don't think, Mister Valpole, as I don't know *you*, anyways; and as for our friend here, for sartin he's in very bad company, so I shall be obliged to borrow him likewise for a short time. Now, if so be you'll be so good as to split vere the svag is—the teapots and the vatches, and the vedge—may be it 'ill be none the vorse for yer; as there's a revard for the recovery of the property according to the amount, and if so be ve *can* settle it, you'll find us by no means onreasonable, considering the trouble we've been at."

"My good fellow!" said Bob, with barefaced assurance, "you are certainly mistaken. I've been on no cracking suit; but if you've anything particular, as you no doubt think you have, against myself or my friend here, let's have the particulars, and we'll consider whether it's worth trying."

"Hem!" observed the thieftaker: "mayhap you *might* know a crib near Blackheath; and, moreover, you might know a little summut about some wedgelobb* as the right owner is inquiring after. Mind, I only say *might*, at present; but if you names anythink well worth while, I mayn't take the trouble of inquiring farther. Howsever, what we must do must be done at once, 'cos vy, it's known by the dock-guard here hard by, as four on us are come to overhaul yer; and if so be ve don't think fit to find nothing, ve must be quick in getting back agen, in order that you may cut and run. So name what ready stephen† you can post, and ve'll tell yer vether——"

A loud splash interrupted the speaker, and at the same instant the Sprightly Nancy rose forward in a style that fully convinced the experienced Sam that her hawser had been cut; the next instant she heeled, and rolled in the trough of the sea.

The officer, who though of great personal courage, was a regular landsman, looked aghast for a moment. Then presenting his pistols, declared, that if either of his prisoners stirred, death should be their instant fate; which, from his determined looks, and that of his well-armed companion, seemed likely to be the case.

* Silver plate.   + The amount of cash.

"Dick," observed he, and there was certainly a tremour in his voice, "I thought you made all safe on the fore-hatchway. Call to Ned Bates, and see——"

A bubbling cry for help was heard above the rattling of cordage, and the creaking of the ship's timbers.

"It's Ned's voice! he's overboard!" said the fellow.

The cabin door, which had been left open, now slammed violently, and some weighty substance was thrown violently against it.

"Leave me here," said the officer, endeavouring to assume a composure he did not feel; "and go on deck and call our comrades."

"We are made fast," replied his follower, trying the cabin door.

A heavy fall was heard directly over their heads, and presently they clearly distinguished the tones of a man's voice earnestly supplicating for mercy.

"It's all right above-board, my hearties," cried Ben Bradwell, from the deck; "how many customers have you got there below?"

The officers stared at each other in blank dismay. Walpole smiled at the two armed men, but moved not from his place, while Sam Tummons laughed hoarsely, although two pistols were yet presented level with his head.

"I'm beginning to think," observed Walpole, sneeringly, "that we shall find the boot on the other leg, here, and that you will have, Mr. What's-your-name, to bargain for your own ransom. How much might you have of the ready stephen?" retorted the burglar, mockingly; "because, you see, your friends are waiting for you, and if you find nothing aboard here, it won't look well to delay."

"All right within there?" enquired Jerry, from the outside of the cabin door.

"All right," replied Walpole, "except our card-party is made up for whist by the addition of two gentlemen, who won't lay down their pistols and take up the cards."

"Ha! ha!" laughed Boltrope.

The Sprightly Nancy was now evidently careering through the waves under the propelling power of a small portion of her canvass: the officer seeing how matters stood, resolved upon a bold stroke.

"Both your lives are in our hands," said he, with a braggadocio air, "and it depends upon a chance whether we cannot fight our way to our boat. If we fire, the alarm will bring help. Choose at once, then, for we'll sell our lives dearly, whether you will let us retire quietly, or——"

"Pooh! pooh! my good fellow," replied Walpole, drily; "is it we who are to dictate terms!"

"Shall we raise a plank on deck, and pepper those two troublesome customers you have there?" inquired the skipper, "or will they surrender quietly?"

The officer, though a bold man, saw it must be useless to struggle against numbers, he therefore changed his tone, and merely stipulated that they should be permitted to leave the ship unmolested.

"Before we hear a word of that kind," said Walpole, coolly, "you must lay down your weapons. That done, we will parley."

The officers flatly refused.

"Then," said Walpole, "your blood must rest on your own head. I promise you shall receive no personal violence if you use none; persist in your refusal to surrender, and I will call to my friends here to force the door, and, as you told us just now, your lives will pay the forfeit."

"I surrender," said the officer, doggedly, and he laid his pistols on the table; Sam appropriated them, and Walpole did the same by those of his assistant. The door was now opened at their signal, and Bradwell, Boltrope, and Jerry entered. From them they learnt the particulars of their deliverance: it appeared that the four officers had boarded the Sprightly Nancy so suddenly, that before Boltrope, Jerry, or Bradwell, who were unsuspecting of danger, had time to stir from the fore-cabin, wherein they were solacing themselves with some stiff grog, the assailants had fastened down the fore-hatch, where they placed one of their party, on guard, while their chief and his follower made their way to the chief cabin, they had then placed a second officer at the companion ladder, and by these precautions surprised Walpole and Sam as already described. A minute's deliberation decided the three imprisoned men; having armed themselves with stout handspikes, they made a simultaneous thrust at the hatchway cover, and capsized the lubber who stood on it, who fell violently on the deck. The trio immediately emerged, and before the fellow had recovered from his surprise he was flung overboard. He, however, held on by the gunwale of the boat. The other man, seeing three desperadoes about to assail him at once, and conceiving "discretion the better part of valour," cried "peccavi," and beseeched quarter, as we have already heard. Thus quickly were the tables turned, and the intended captors caught in their own trap. Mr. Grabum now began to think he had made a foolish job of it; and bitterly to repent that he had ventured off *terra firma* in his professional capacity; but as there was no help for it, he put the best face on it he could.

"You can't say, gentlemen," said he, turning to Walpole and Sam, "but I was doing my duty with as little disagreeableness as was possible, when this unlucky affair turned up. In course you'll set us ashore agen, and I'll promise yer whenever——"

"Nay, Mr. Grabum," observed Walpole, "we won't think of sparing you till we have transacted a little business we have in hand on the other side of the herring pond, so you must make up your mind for a cruise with us; after we have settled that, perhaps we may leave you somewhere on the coast of France. What say you, my worthy skipper, to my proposition?"

"Not the least objection in life," was Bradwell's reply.

The officers saw it was useless to remonstrate with the lawless crew into whose hands they had fallen; and they were conveyed on deck, where Boltrope, having procured four stout iron staples of a horse-shoe form, and passed a chain through them, they were driven firmly into the deck, at distances of about nine inches apart; between this chain and the deck the feet of the unfortunate men were placed, the chain crossing their ancles as they sat on their nether ends. One end of the chain was now drawn till it was moderately tight, and being fastened by a stout-headed spike, driven into the planking, an extemporaneous set of bilboes, or marine "stocks," was quickly contrived. By the civility of Walpole, each prisoner was now accommodated with an old sail, whereon he could rest his body and head, their confinement by no means precluding a recumbent position. Boltrope was placed near them as sentinel, and they were left to repose as best they might, in their sad and comfortless situation. They had, however, some consolation in learning from their brother prisoner, that the last time he had seen their missing comrade, he was sculling away as hard as he could, with a single paddle, having gained the boat; and as he would, doubtless, soon reach the shore, or be picked up, they felt but little pity for his disaster, when they compared it with their own more unfortunate situation.

CHAPTER XI.

THE VOYAGE—A DISMAL NIGHT—A PRIVATEER—THE CHASE—RUNNING THE GAUNTLET—A LONG SHOT—DEATHS OF BRADWELL AND BOLTROPE—JERRY AND HIS COMPANIONS MADE PRISONERS OF WAR.

IT would neither edify the reader, nor in any way assist the progress of our narrative, to set down all the sage and philosophical reflections made by Mister Grabum, the thieftaker, and his two companions, during the long and tedious night passed by them in their straitened limbo, which marvellously resembled, in more points than one, "the enchanted castle," so admirably described by Butler, as the place of durance of Sir Hudibras and his puritanical squire hight Ralpho :—

> In all the fabric
> You shall not see a stone nor a brick,
> But all of wood, by powerful spell
> Of magic made impregnable:
> There's neither iron bar nor gate,
> Nor door, portcullis, bolt, nor grate;
> Yet men in durance there abide
> In dungeons scarce three inches wide:
> In circlet magical confined,
> With subtle walls of air and wind,
> Which none are able to break thoro'
> Until they're freed by head of boro'.

In such a "little ease" did Mr. Grabum and his two fellow-sufferers pass a rainy, dark, and uncomfortable night. The wind howled, the thunder rolled, the lightning gleamed, the canvass rattled, the shrouds strained, and the timbers creaked, until to their land-bred imaginations the little vessel seemed within an ace of strewing the raging deep with her scattered timbers ; and the unlucky Mr. Grabum, without having read the works of the great Dr. Johnson, felt the full truth of his dictum, that "a ship is a floating prison, with the additional horror to a thinking mind, that there is but one frail plank between yourself and eternity."

Morn, welcome morn, at length broke—

> When, like a curtain torn
> Suddenly, from the east, the parted glooms
> Withdrew, south, west, and to the howling north.
> Thus demons driven from some holy shrine
> By incantations, or a *god's bright frown*,
> Forsake the temple, and with desp'rate shrieks,
> Cast them upon the wide and viewless winds.
> The storm grew silent, and the thunder spake
> No more.

With the return of daylight and the cessation of the storm, the prisoners grew a little more cheerful, and their gratification was yet enhanced by one of them espying a lofty church spire at some miles distance, although the flat waste whereon it was situate was as yet invisible. Nevertheless, they argued, and with some reason, that as churches were seldom seen afloat, that they were, at any rate, near land ; a circumstance which, to their unseamanlike notions, was a great consolation. Indeed, they felt very like the Irishman in Sam Lover's tale of " the Gridiron," and at that moment "would have give up their title to any number of square miles of the most beautiful salt water ever met with, for an acre, or even less, of dry land, supposing it to be even nothing better than brown fern and whinstones."

Thus they ran along shore, till nearly noon. Their wet clothes, for they had been drenched all night with the breaking sea, gradually drying in the sunshine.

Bradwell, who stood at the helm, scarcely condescended to bestow a word on them, and with the exception of a glass of rum and a biscuit (for which they had no appetite), they had tasted nothing since the previous day. They had laid themselves back on their roll of canvass, and each had shaded his closed eyes with his arm, when a sudden bustle among the crew of the Sprightly Nancy attracted their attention.

There was evidently something unusual in progress. Bradwell, resigning for a few moments the helm to a lad, walked forward and joined Ben Boltrope, Jerry, Walpole, and Sam, who, with a seaman and a stout boy, were all assembled on her larboard bow ; Ben being busily engaged reconnoitring some distant object through a telescope.

"I tell you 'tis no such thing," exclaimed Ben, doggedly ; "I know the cut of they *chasse marées* too well to take one on 'em for aught else as swims. Mister Sam here, may opinion as he knows, but it ain't nothink Dutch—and that's what *I* don't like."

"Get up the French colours, and be ready to run 'em up to the peak at my first signal," said Bradwell to the boy, who departed to do his bidding.

"We can oustail her, at any rate," observed Sam ; "we've the weather-gage, too ; and she's no clipper. Has she seen us?" added he to Ben, who still kept the glass to his eye.

Bradwell had by this time provided himself with a better telescope.

"She not only sees us," observed the skipper, "but is making a long leg and stretching off, to intercept us in our present course, before we round Point Grosnez," (for it was the lowlands of Normandy that the adventurers were now coasting), "but we'll double 'em, my lads. Hold hard on as we are, for the present, and unless she changes her course, we'll not tack till we've opened yonder hummock and the church tower. We can run nearer to the wind than her, and with the aid of our sweeps we'll tip Mounseer the go-by, in a way he don't reckon on."

During this conversation, of which but a portion reached the understandings of the manacled Mr. Grabum and his fellow-prisoners, the Sprightly Nancy had been cleaving the waters like a sea-fowl. Suddenly her helm was brought up hard a-port, her topsail shivered, and the flapping canvass for a moment fluttered as though the vessel's course was undecided on.

"Does she show colours?" asked Bradwell.

"The Mounseer's tricolor, by all that's unlucky," cried Boltrope,

"Run up the tricolor," exclaimed Bradwell.

The command was obeyed. But the small, long vessel, which they had been so long eyeing with suspicion, seemed by no means inclined to take their word as to their nationality; for she fired a shot athwart the bows of the Sprightly Nancy, as a signal to lay-to, and then trimmed her sails to run her aboard.

"Helm a-weather," shouted Bradwell. "Let go the mainsheet: closer, closer, there, with the jib and fore! Now she feels it! And,

> "Merrily, merrily flies the barque,
> Before the gale she bounds;
> So darts the dolphin from the shark,
> Or the deer before the hounds."

The *chasse marée*, for such she was, appeared unprepared for this sudden manœuvre, and lost distance sadly before she recovered from her surprise; indeed, the superiority in sailing capabilities of the Sprightly Nancy was very manifest. The Frenchman, however, got out a pair of long sweeps to help his progress, whereon the smugglers did the same, and with an equal improvement in their sailing; and, in about two hours, the Sprightly Nancy had hulled down her pursuer, who, "though lost to sight," was by no means "to memory dear."

There is an adage current to the effect that a jump is sometimes made out of the frying-pan into the fire; and hence, while the little crew were congratulating themselves on their lucky escape, a more formidable opponent arose in the shape of a splendid schooner-rigged vessel, which rose in the offing at a short three miles distant, just as the *chasse marée* had been distanced. There could be little doubt, as the schooner now in chase of them had been sailing almost on a parallel line, that the exertions of the French coast-boat had been relaxed only upon seeing the better pursuer taking up the chase.

"A privateer, and with as pretty a row of teeth as ever chattered over a basin of salt-water," said Bradwell, bitterly, as he viewed this new-comer, who, unlike his previous foe, had the weather-gage on her side of the question.

"A French prison, or ——!" said Boltrope, turning his quid with a perplexed air.

"It's not lost yet," said Bradwell; "if we can but run the gauntlet of her fire without injury to our rigging—but no, it would be madness. We can beach the Nancy, 'tis true—but that's from bad to worse, for we're no friends on this coast. We must run for it, boys, and when we can't, we'll strike."

Again was the course of the Sprightly Nancy altered, this time to a line converging to the course of the French privateer—the French tricolor still flying at her masthead.

"These *letters of marque*," observed Boltrope, "have generally pretty knowing commanders; but if we can double this one, 'twill be worth the risk of a life or two."

The privateer considering the vessel now sufficiently near, backed her topsails, and lowered a boat, which was soon filled by active fellows, who hastened with alacrity over her side. We have said there was a fresh breeze, and the current which sets along this part of the coast, swung the privateer into an unfavourable position. As yet, the Sprightly Nancy had not taken in an inch of canvass, and it was not till she had passed the stern of the privateer at some distance, that the lubberly Frenchmen had the slightest idea of the audacious trick which the little craft was trying to put upon them. The truth flashed on them at once: the French boat's crew rushed to their oars—the tough ash bent to their strokes, and off they went, at a wager pace, after the escaping smugglers. The schooner, too, got up her head before the wind, and the bustle and row on board her, as her sails one after another bellied to the breeze, would have amused our adventurers, had not their lives been involved in the result. The captain of "*La Belle Marquise*," *sacre'd* and *jean foutred* his crew, with all the gesticulation of a monkey, or a French dancing-master; and at length, at the peril of losing way, seeing the rowers in the jolly-boat were already spent, and had no chance in the chace, he resolved to try the effect of a long shot or two on the Sprightly Nancy, ere she should get out of distance, or into Dutch waters, wherein a two hours' sail might bring her. Accordingly, *La Belle Marquise* payed off, and the next instant a pretty little brass nine-pounder spoke eloquently from her deck. The shot hopped harmlessly by.

"Rather too close yet to be pleasant," said Sam, observing Jerry attentively watching the shot which hopped along from wave to wave; Jerry feeling not in a

slight degree astonished at the distinctness with which he could perceive its course till it buried itself in the sea.

"Now," exclaimed Bradwell, "luck's all! if they miss us twice more, a fico for their pursuit."

Another bright flash was seen to issue from the well-armed deck of "*La Belle Marquise*," and with the booming report which followed came a heavier and better-directed shot. An awful crash was heard aft, splinters of wood flew from the quarter, and a joint-stock shriek from the lungs of the chained captives, drew Jerry, Boltrope, and Sam, towards that part of the vessel. Bradwell had taken the helm from the lad. They, of course, traversed the deck in a stooping posture to avoid being marked by the enemy.

"Confound their yelping," said Bradwell, looking contemptuously at the officers, whose pale countenances evinced the most ghastly terror; "are any of you hurt?"

None replied to this question, but each looked piteously at the other. Jerry and Sam, despite their perilous condition, could scarcely repress a laugh, when they saw that this partnership scream had been occasioned by the hulling shot.

The Sprightly Nancy yet flew on unharmed.

"We shall do 'em, by —— " swore Jerry; "see, see ——"

He was wrong: the privateer had wore, and had now brought her whole broadside to bear. A dense volume of blue-white smoke obscured her brightly-painted gun-strake, traversed by crimson tongues of forked fire; a whistling sound followed, and ere a breath could be drawn, or the loud boom reach their ears, the little barque of the desperadoes met the reward of its temerity. The mainmast went crashing over the side, cut by a chain-shot some three feet from the step, and amid the rattle of the falling shrouds, the cursings of some, and the groans of others, poor Grabum, assured of nought but his own existence, offered up the only prayer he was ever known to utter. A loud cheer from fifty pair of French lungs formed its "amen!" and next moment the Sprightly Nancy lay a dismantled wreck on the rolling waters.

"Sam, are _you_ safe—Sam! Bob Walpole, where are you?" were the first sounds heard on board the smuggler's vessel. It was the voice of Jerry, who, himself unscathed, called after his companions.

"All right, Jerry—except a bruise: and Bob, where's he?"

"Here," replied that personage from behind a water-cask, "are those d—d fellows going to play that trick again? If so, hadn't we better strike, before we're unable to do that or anything else?"

"Right!" replied Jerry; "but, by the Lord Harry, they've struck our colours for us," looking aloft to where the gaff a few moments before had borne the Gallic emblem of revolution.

"They'll not fire again," said he, looking towards the Frenchman, whose side was now crowded with men, watching the progress of the boat that was fast nearing their prize.

They were interrupted by a groan from the stern, where a heap of canvass, once the snow-white mainsail of their pretty little craft, lay, completely hiding from view what might be under it.

"Where's Bradwell?" asked Jerry.

"And Boltrope?" said Walpole.

"Who's groaning there?" enquired Sam, removing part of the sail.

The three prisoners, despite their manacled situation, had escaped almost miraculously; but it had fared otherwise with the skipper and poor Boltrope. The remains of Bradwell, cut in halves by the same shot which had lowered the mast of his little vessel, lay a scarce recognisable mass of mangled flesh, near the wheel whereat he stood at the moment of his death; while, a few yards from him, his mate lay mortally wounded: one arm, his right, had been carried away near its socket, and the "wind" of the shot which had thus injured him, had burst the bloodvessels of his lungs: a falling spar had completed his disfigurement by crushing his head till all feature of the "human face divine" was utterly obliterated.

The burglars turned from the sickening sight, and hardly noticed the French officer, who at this moment boarded and took possession of the vessel.

As for poor Grabum and his fellow-sufferers, so acute had been their feelings, that they positively hailed their captors as deliverers; and almost felt happy at the thoughts of exchanging the horrors of a French prison, for

"All the delights, and fun, and joys,
Of a cruise in the Sprightly Nancy."

CHAPTER XII.

A PRIVATEER CAPTAIN'S WRATH, AND HIS NOTIONS OF FAIR PRIZE—TREATMENT OF PRISONERS OF WAR IN FRANCE—JERRY AND HIS COMRADES VOLUNTEER INTO A FRENCH SHIP OF WAR—A SHIP ON FIRE—EXPLOSION OF L'INDOMITABLE—ESCAPE OF JERRY ABERSHAW, SAM, AND WALPOLE.

THE survivors of the crew of the Sprightly Nancy were quickly transferred to the deck of their French captors, where they underwent a short but severe cross-examination, from the captain of "_La Belle Marquise._" Grabum and his companions told their story with unvarnished simplicity, and clearly explained their own innocence, and the powers with which they were invested ; dwelling largely on the audacious criminality of Jerry Abershaw, Walpole, and Sam Tummons ; to say nothing of the fearful delinquencies of the slain Boltrope, Bradwell, and the smugglers, who had thus kidnapped his majesty's officers of justice. The Frenchmen listened, such of them at least as could comprehend the outline of his narrative, with puzzled attention, and Mr. Grabum began to think his oratory had had the hoped-for effect, when his hopes were annihilated by the French commander observing, in broken English—

"Ah! ah! I do see, ver' vell : you are de catch-a-teef—de officer of de justeece—de gendarme—de vat you call de poleece vagabone, vot go share vid de riche teef and hang-a de poor von. I comprend, *tres bien*—ver' vell—for I vas *restez* in your dam countree dis von, two, tree, five year agone. Ah! ah! by *gar*, you vorse teef dan de house-a-break demselves? *Sacre non de* ——! and all dis *orfévrerie*—de gold and de silvare pot and de dish, be got by von *grande*, vot you call a de bourg laree? Ver' vell! I haf de bonne fortune to pick you up, ah! ah! De *pierrerie* and de *epée*—de sword, I vas mean," (here monsieur scrutinisingly examined the rich articles found on board the Sprightly Nancy), "vos belong to him you call de Capitaine Bosca'en, ha!"

Mr. Grabum here made a low bow of assent, and added—" Yes, your honour, these scoundrels here had robbed the house, as I told you, of the brave old Admiral Boscawen, and I and my ——"

" *Ventre bleu!*" roared the Frenchman, " de brave, vat you call him dat to my teeth? Poltroon—vagabone—*au diable* vid your brave !—you ras-cal rosbif, you ox, you ass, you stupid *Jean foutre*, John Bool—*au dia*—— ;" and rushing at the bewildered Grabum, the irate Frenchman with one kick sent him down the companion of the mizen hatchway. There he lay with a sorely bruised back, while the commander, foaming with rage, strode back to his standing-place on the quarter, in vain endeavouring to resume his equanimity. " De brave," muttered he, " *sacre tel brave dis-je! Morbleu!* de impudent jackanape! *Parbleu*, but I'm ver' glad dese teefs have rob him—I ver' mosh vish dey had cut his vindpipe at de same time !—I sall be glad," said he, turning to Jerry, Sam, and Walpole, who stood surprised but not displeased spectators of this singular scene; "I sall haf mosh plaisir to treat-a you vell, bycause you haf don de spite-a on de brave ammiral—ah! ah! Ver' good! Give dese fellows *une verrèe d'eau de vie*—ah! ah!— I am please vot dat old scoun'rel, Bosca'an, vos serve out, for he teach-a me to speak your dam English tongue like a natif, bycause he take-a me and lock-a me up in dat diable stinking Ports-de-Mout for tree year! ah! ah! And dis be his fine cup, and de medailles, and de sword!—ah! ah! Dat is better joke dan all de rest! Gif dese fine fellows some brandee, steward, and keep-a dese von, two, tree, vagabones (here he pointed to the two other thieftakers) *au du pain noir*, and de bilge-a vater, and see how deir Anglish stomach sall like-a dat—ah! ah!"

The three criminals were straightway marched forward, and there given some of the ordinary ship's provision, with a glass of Cognac each—a refreshment they much needed — while Grabum and his unlucky companions did penance in the dark cable-tier, for the mortification which the thieftaker had inflicted on the vanity of the privateer's commander, by his eulogy on the English admiral. Unfortunately for Grabum and his comrades, Admiral Boscawen had, some years before, taken this very Frenchman prisoner in a naval action, and thus condemned him to three years of misery in an English prison, ere he had been enabled to get exchanged upon cartel.

The prize, with her captor, soon after cast anchor in the Bay of Hodierne, and the prisoners were disembarked about a couple of miles distant from the town of that name. And here their sufferings began. They were marched that day to Douline, under escort of three reliefs of soldiers, about twenty-five miles, and at night put into a cold church, with a supply of not over-clean straw, which, as Walpole remarked, was their "meat, drink, washing, and lodging." At early morn the unhappy wretches were called, by roll of drum, to prepare for another day's march, and started, almost barefooted, with about sixty others in the like unfortunate condition. The object of these cruel fatigues, doubtless, was intended by their captors, with the denial of sufficient sustenance, to reduce the number of these chargeable prisoners by death or exhaustion.

The subjects of our history, however, encouraged each other as well as they could, and being rather better treated than the tipstaffs, held out till they reached Chatolin. As for Grabum and his two brother officers, ill-treatment on board ship, and their subsequent fatigue and privations, so disabled them, that they were left in hospital at Quimper, a small town, on their third day's journey. At Chatolin they received, for the first time, a good substantial meal of bread and beef, after which they were visited by a government inspector, who questioned them all, taking down their answers in writing.

They had not been in this wretched place above four hours when an officer appeared, and, entering the prison, called aloud the names of all those who were able seamen. He then made a short address, in which he stated that all those who chose to volunteer on board the fleet of his most Christian Majesty the King of France, would receive ordinary seaman's pay, and, although still prisoners of war, could materially better their condition. This proposition, which in war-time has been usually proffered by the French, from their great desire to enlist able seamen, was received by the majority of the blunt Jack tars to whom it was proposed, with surly scorn, or honest indignation. A hoarse murmur, occasionally forming itself into articulate d—ns, or blunt expressions of rough loyalty, showed the French officers the offensiveness of this offer to the rude but brave and honest fellows to whom it was addressed.

While this scene was going forward, Jerry nudged Sam, and spoke as follows—

"I don't see no pull whatsever, in this here humbugging nonsense. If these pig-headed Jack tars here are going to wait till they gets out o' limbo by their country's gratitude, as they calls it, it strikes me, Sam, as they'll find it cold coffee afore they gets home to breakfast. I've no hidea o' this here loyalty, and that sort o' stuff, keeping us rotting in gaol, and dying o' fever. What say you, Bob, shall we volunteer, and take our chance o' the fortune o' war? We *may* cut and run then, but I'm blowed if I see the likelihood of it here."

"Sartinly," replied Sam; and Walpole, leaving it entirely to their decision, Jerry stepped from the crowd, and amid the execrations of the bold blue-jackets, who had refused the proffered temptation, offered himself and two companions as volunteers in the service of France.

They were at once separated from the rest of the prisoners. Indeed, it was doubtful whether their personal safety could have been secured, if they had been left among their indignant fellow-countrymen. The following morning the three renegadoes were *en route*, by easy marches, for Brest, where a formidable fleet was preparing; the destination of which was as yet secret, but surmised to be intended for an attack on the English West India Islands.

We will not detain the reader by a tedious narration of all the sufferings, privations, hardships, and contumely, which Jerry and his two companions were doomed to experience—and not undeservedly: their lot being cast on board a French frigate, bearing the swelling title of l'Indomitable, and which formed a portion of the French fleet under the Comte d'Estaing. Whether the Gallic man-of-war, on board of which our three fellows were, was proof against British steel and British courage, was a problem which the fates had decreed should never be solved in this individual instance; for, having been detached from the fleet for the purpose of reconnoitring the coast of North America, to see if any British force there cruising appeared powerful enough to interfere with the projected exploits of M. le Comte d'Estaing, a disaster befel l'Indomitable, which may well be classed as the most awful in all the catalogue of dreadful calamities which await those " who go down to the sea in ships."

The noon-day meal of coarse lean junk and execrable brandy (for rum grog was unknown in French ships of war), was despatched, and the frigate's crew were lounging about her decks, and leaning over her sides—watching with lazy, uninterested eye the sporting boneta, or the flash of the white shark's belly, as that tiger of the deep turned to grasp his prey—when the alarm of "fire" was given. The "word of fear" ran from mouth to mouth, and, all aghast, officers, men, and boys, crowded towards the spot, where a disorderly crowd ran to and fro in confusion and dismay. Flames were now seen bursting through the lining of the forecastle, and at the same instant the heading of a puncheon of rum started with an explosion resembling the report of the cannon. All that could make their way below, now rushed there; but were soon driven back by sheets of liquid fire. The spirit room was in a blaze. " The powder ! the powder !" cried fifty tongues, and all rushed to the boats. Of these, the pinnace was under repair, and to the long-boat and launch immediate attention was directed. The flames by this time burst in fearful volumes from the fore-hatchway, curling their forked tongues around the bows of the long-boat, as it hung suspended in the slings, and a cry of horror and despair rose on the startled ear, as the planking of this, their main hope and reliance, crackled and burnt (for she was fresh painted), as though in love with the consuming flames which licked its inflammable timbers, all reeking with turpentine and varnish. This retreat cut off, many hastened to endeavour to stifle the furious element with swabs, rugs, blankets and hammocks, saturated with sea-water. Vain efforts! The raging flames advanced! and now the deck was scuttled, and all the crew, animated by the common instinct of self-preservation, engaged themselves with alacrity in the task of handing buckets, the boldest pouring their contents on the crackling timbers below. Every struggle proved fruitless. The scalding water, hissing defiance, rolled back in volumes of blinding vapour, mingled with ashes, compelled them to retire—destruction stared full in the faces of the unhappy crew.

But while the gallant company of seamen were thus unavailingly engaged, it behoves us to look after Jerry and his duet of forced men, Sam and Walpole, as those in whom the reader is more immediately interested. The sailors of l'Indomitable, urged by many motives—patriotism, obedience to superiors, fear, or self-preservation—worked with pump, bucket, and damper, to subdue the fire; but the three house-breakers, on whom the last-mentioned impulse alone acted, demeaned themselves far otherwise. The yawl of the vessel, the most serviceable of the smaller boats, hung by the davits, and they seized the admirable opportunity afforded by the dire confusion to steal this boat, in conjunction with five cowardly French seamen. Hence, while their comrades were battling with flame and death in its most fearful form, the yawl and its crew made good a retreat, leaving all hands to extricate themselves as they best might, and thus depriving their worthier fellow-seamen of another of their resources in extremity. Nor was this awful extremity long in arriving; the crew were yet in the height of their exertions, when the small party of renegadoes were startled by a strange sensation—you might have thought the universal air had made one deep, strong, and powerful inhalation—as though Nature had drawn in her breath to heave it forth again in one mighty groan:—the ambient fluid in which "we live, and move, and have our being," seemed as though it were the exhausted cylinder of some vast receiver, and that the atmosphere, itself anihilated, had left a vacuum. The boat's crew opened their mouths instinctively—another instant, and the deep and awful pause was broken by a crash loud as the volleying thunder! One sheeted pall of livid flame enveloped sea and sky, and from its riven centre flew vast and massive fragments, the wreck of the gallant ship, and the mutilated remains of what, but two seconds previous, were two hundred living men. Athwart main and sky were driven the shapeless forms; nor could the eye recognise the hurled block of flaming timber from that which had but now been the clayey tenement of a thinking soul. The fire had reached the magazine—and man was the poor helpless sport of the murderous nitre he had invented and prepared for the slaughter of his fellow-creature.

"There they go!" exclaimed the callous Jerry, as the pieces of burning wood strewed the waves around them, each hissing as it was quenched in the rolling sea: "There they go!—But where the devil are we? What an almighty crash the old 'Domit-able did go with, sure-ly! Well, messmates, whereabouts do you call this?"

None of them knew. Frenchmen are rarely remarkable for geographical knowledge, even at the present day; but upwards of half a century ago (we speak from good naval authority), nineteen Frenchmen out of twenty knew as much of geography (or any exact science, as to that matter), as the subjects of his "celestial majesty," or the slaves of the "golden-footed" monarch of Ava.

Thus tossed on the wide Atlantic, without chart, compass, or provisions, they passed two days; the morning of the third dawned—but still no sail nor friendly shore presented itself, and it seemed as though they had been spared the sharp short pang of a fiery death, only to experience one more dreadful in its painful protraction and suffering.

CHAPTER XIII.

A PERILOUS SITUATION—HUNGER—CANNIBALISM—A DESERT ISLAND—JERRY AND HIS
COMPANIONS RESCUED.

AFLOAT in a frail boat on the trackless ocean, the third weary day went down
ere either of the little crew yielded to the pressing call of nature for sleep; so
deep had been their anxiety, and so intensely painful their watchings for some
friendly sail, or still more welcome shore to heave in sight. The weather, too,
was hazy, and the frequent fog-banks deluded their eyes with mocking phantasma
of ships or land, with buildings, sails, or trees, as unreal and torturing as the
mirage to the desert traveller.

A dull gleam, which marked the sun's position, however, enabled them (as
they were still sure of *their* northern position as regarded that great luminary) to
decide on the relative points of east and west, and, after some consultation, it was
decided that a north-westerly course must bring them rapidly to some part of the
northern coast of America. An oar had been already elevated as a substitute for
a mast, and to this such linen as they could muster was attached, as much for the
purpose of a signal to any vessel which might near them, as a sail to assist their
progress.

With the third nightfall came the foul weather, so prevalent in those regions—
for the unfortunate crew were in the latitude of the banks of Newfoundland; and
they were enveloped in clouds of misty vapour, alternated by drenching showers.

> " Still fell the flooding rains !
> Day, eve, night, morning, came and passed away,
> No sun was known to rise, nor none to set !
> 'Stead of its glorious beams, a sickly light
> Paled the broad east what time the day is born :
> At others, a thick mass, vaporous and black,
> And firm like solid marble, roofed the sky,
> Yet gave no shelter from the piercing sleet !"

And now the terror of death seemed to seize on each despairing soul of that
devoted few. They sat moody and apart, none spake, and they gazed across the
gloomy waste of shoreless waters with vacant stare for hours, save that now and
again one eyed the other with a savage glare; anon, as if startled at reading the
reflection of his own thoughts in the gleaming eyes of his comrade, each shuddered and shrunk within himself, then relapsed into his former apathy and
despair.

The sixth day came—the small portion of tobacco possessed by the mariners had
been equitably divided, some leather had been chewed, and cold, hunger, and
want of shelter had made sad work amid that gaunt and despairing crew. Thirst
they had as yet staved off by wringing out the superabundant moisture from their
various woollen and linen articles of clothing :—

> " Six days had hunger, misery, and fear
> Been their companions, and now death was here !"

The difference of language had grouped the wretched sufferers apart. The
three housebreakers occupied the after part of the boat (for they had all long
ceased to use any exertion in rowing, or otherwise assisting its progress), while
the not less miserable seamen huddled together in its bows, each cluster endeavouring to keep warmth in their bodies by mutual contact.

Two of the French seamen were now what is termed " down ;" privation had
done its work on their less robust frames, and delirium was evident in their rapid
speech—they raved of home and their "*belle patrie,*" of their friends and relatives,
and held affecting converse with imaginary parents, sweethearts, or wives. Hoarse
murmurings, too, passed among their stronger companions; but they were not
whisperings of sympathy or compassion—no ! the whisperings grew louder—

> " And you might mark
> The longings of the cannibal arise,
> With gaunt despair, within those wolfish eyes."

At length one spake out, and found that he but gave utterance to his fellow's
thought. The weakest of the delirious sailors, a slender youth, was suddenly

strangled—yet by whom, none hardly knew. His remains were speedily divided —and three more days passed. The boat drove—no one seemed to care whither ; the sun went down on the tenth day—and then a blacker darkness fell. In the midst of that dread night, blows were heard, and stifled groans, on board that solitary floating bark—struggle, there was little or none—and when the next morning dawned, the yawl of the devoted Indomitable displayed but *three* living forms—they were those of Jerry Abershaw, Sam Tummons, and their companion ! Three lifeless bodies (their horrid store of sustenance) lay in the boat, the fourth had fallen overboard in the murderous fray.

That day the breeze freshened to a gale, and the gale to a storm, yet the boat lived gallantly on the rolling waves, where many a taller vessel had foundered :—

> " Still the tempest raged —
> No pity, no release, ho hope. Lightning and storm,
> Thunder and deluging rain, now vext the air
> To raging madness ; and the riotous winds laughed out
> Like bacchanals, whose cups some fiends had charmed !
> Thus the loud and hurrying winds
> Forced them along, till through the whitening waves
> The horrid rocks peered up as black as death,
> And the hoarse shingles rattled on the strand
> Destructive welcome ; then the gale sung loud,
> As the wild sea rose swirling round their barque,
> Roaring with hungry noise, till one huge wave,
> Curling tempestuous, dashed them on the shore !"

The boat which had so well served them strewed the rocky beach in a hundred fragments—and wounded, bruised, and well-nigh exhausted, Abershaw and his two companions staggered out of reach of the recoiling wave, lest it should engulf them in its return. They crawled to the shelter of the rocks, but after a short rest, hunger drove them from their retreat ; and Sam and Jerry, who were far stronger than Walpole, left him, after giving assurance of their return. They were not long before they collected a sufficiency of drift-wood for kindling a fire ; a necessary as indispensable to their existence as food itself : and they further brought the welcome tidings that an abundance of clams, muscles, limpets, and other shell-fish might be had for the gathering. The fire was kindled, the fish ejected from their shelly tenements by the action of the heat—and as they did not stand much upon culinary punctilio, in a very short time, the trio of villains had gorged themselves to satiety, with what seemed to them a richer repast than Sybarite ever tasted, or the skill of gastronomy ever devised.

But we will hasten over the tedious sojourn of our adventurers on this dreary shore. They had been cast by the winds and waves on a small rocky island, off the eastern coast of Newfoundland, well known to mariners for its dangerous breakers and the sunken rocks in its vicinity ; and here they abode thirty weary days. Drift-wood was plentiful on the rocky beach, though there was no tree near their dreary habitation ; and hence they found little difficulty in keeping up a signal-fire on the face of the lofty rocks, in hopes that its smoke might attract the notice of some passing vessel. For the first few days the watching of this forlorn hope devolved on Walpole, but his weakness gradually increasing, he became unequal even to this task ; and when at length a vessel appeared in the offing, and his companions had made themselves visible to it by signal, he was lying helpless in a precarious state in a rocky cave, some hundred yards inland, wherein they had sought nightly shelter from the cutting winds. The stranger sail proved to be a Canada timber-ship, driven from her course in consequence of the shortness of her complement of seamen, a deficiency common to the vessels engaged in that traffic. She was bound for Liverpool ; and with what feelings of joy did the shipwrecked mariners behold her boat as it approached the iron-bound beach to their rescue ! They were soon on board, and having communicated to their countrymen the state of their absent comrade, Walpole was shortly brought on board also.

A plausible tale was easily fabricated by our adventurers, to the effect that they had been serving on board an English vessel which had been captured by the French ; that from their prison they had been drafted on board l'Indomitable (the tragic catastrophe of which, and the detail of their sufferings, enlisted for them the sympathy of the English skipper and his crew), and escaping therefrom had been cast on the desert place whence they had been so mercifully rescued. The story was probable, and it was believed. About four weeks after, our three shipwrecked mariners were landed at Liverpool, where they received every attention and succour their destitute condition demanded; and by the liberality of several merchants, were enabled, when they left the hospital, into which they were received on landing, to quit that town for London, re-established in health, well-clothed, and in vigorous condition to pursue the career of hardened villany, which it will be the office of the future chapters of this history to develop.

CHAPTER XIV.

LIVERPOOL—THE ABRAHAM SUIT—A QUAKER—A METAMORPHOSIS—A ROBBERY.

THE Liverpool of our fathers, though then fast rising into great commercial importance, was indeed a different town from that which the present generation beholds. In those days of negro slavery, the Queen of the Mersey was rapidly challenging, by the industry of her traders, and the advantages of her natural position, a rivalry with the ancient port of Bristol, although her proud pre-eminence had not yet been achieved. She had not at that time become the rival, and in some branches the superior of the port of London; far from it. The New World, but yesterday raised from the crippled state of colonial dependency, had not stood forth great and mighty among the nations of the globe, and the reflected glories of her "onward" commerce had not yet made the most convenient of our cis-atlantic ports a monument of the wealth, the luxury, the splendour, and the architectural beauty, which modern civilisation, and the cultivation of the true interests of mankind—the arts of peace—invariably bring in their train. The town that Jerry Abershaw and his companions quitted bore little resemblance to the "city whose merchants are princes," which we of the nineteenth century know as Liverpool. The humanizing refinements, the glories of science, the triumphs of architecture, had not as yet made her streets their dwelling-places; and, although the quays were busy with the noise of traffic, the acquisition of "dirty pelf" was there pursued on a scale that makes trade contemptible.

> "In little trades more cheats and lying
> Are used in selling than in buying;
> But, in the great, unjuster dealing
> Is used in buying than in selling,"

says the author of Hudibras, and the merchants of Liverpool were as yet in the first stage. Whether society has benefited in the aggregate by the change, is a question that little concerns the life of Jerry Abershaw. We shall, therefore, return from this little digression, which we have rather penned to show that we can write *from* as well as *to* the purpose, by looking after our hero and his companions.

Leaving the town where they had been sheltered, and received kind treatment they so little deserved, the trio betook themselves, in high spirits, to an alehouse some three miles distant on the London road, and here their future plan of operations was determined on.

"I'll tell you what it is," observed Jerry, who had assumed, more by tacit assent than by any formal agreement, the leadership of the party, "we've seen quite enough to know which side our bread's buttered on. The land-service, I'm sartin, suits us all better nor the salt sea hocean. Howsomdever, the pigmen and traps* isn't so likely, to my thinking, to nail us with their 'dentifying, if so be we sticks to a huniform dress, like as we now sports. Now, here's my perposition: we'll separate so as not to be seen together, but take care to keep in sight of each other, all the same. I'll do the Abr'am suit† as a cast-away sailor; and in that-a-ways twig the cribs along the road, and nail the soft-uns as may be charitable inclined; and it 'ill go hard with us, but I'll pick up a few things that 'ill turn out a trifle better nor cadging: you, Sam, must pull foot and keep me in sight, while you, Bob, must keep up the charackter of a generous seaman, flush o' cash, as is jist come ashore, and don't mind how he melts the few shiners he has left in his locker—eh, my buskers,‡ what d'ye think o' *my* move—eh!"

Sam and Walpole owned the superior genius of Abershaw for villany, by having nothing better to offer as a suggestion, and the preparations were soon completed.

---

* Magistrates' officers, and constables.   † Shamming; imposture.   ‡ Strolling cheats.

With a wooden leg, in the socket of which he made a soft pad for his knee, and a patch over his right eye, our hero might have made a tolerably deplorable figure as the mendicant of the party, but Jerry had a talent above these easily-simulated disfigurements and calamities. Having chalked his visage, he rubbed it with dirt, and then withdrawing his left arm from the sleeve of his jacket, he doubled that member in such a way that by placing the palm of his hand upon his breast (inside his shirt), and re-inserting the elbow of the bent arm in his sleeve, he made a most pitiable spectacle of the moving stump.

Sam and Walpole laughed heartily at the metamorphosis of their active companion into a wretched cripple, and thus disfigured he betook himself to the high-road, Jerry making good headway, and his companions following in his wake, to act as circumstances might dictate.

They had not travelled thus above a mile, when they espied a gentleman's house near the road-side, and Jerry was just holding an interesting colloquy with

himself, when he saw a quaker-looking personage walking with staid and deliberate step along the gravelled walk which led from the mansion to the highway.
His first prompting was to address the stranger to ask an alms, for Jerry knew but
little of the close charity of " the friends," and supposed that it was probable he
might succeed in his appeal to his frigid sympathies. Assuming a painful hobble,
he limped painfully towards Aminadab, as soon as he had cleared the gateway
leading from his garden, and thus opened his masked battery of misery.

" Long life t'yer honner, and may yer niver feel the loss o'yer blessed limbs!
Spare a trifle for poor Jack, as has lost his larboard fin in the sarvice of his
majesty (God bless him), and has bin shipwrecked on a savage henemy's coast,
vere he lived forty days vith nothink to eat but salt-water and sea-veeds. Lord
presarve yer honner—spare a copper or two for a distress-ed seaman as has fought
and bled for his country, and han't a place to *lie* in, 'xcept this hard road.
Heaven presarve yer honner's goodness from the sufferings I've seed amongst the
cannibals, Frenchmen, and wild Injins, vere ve vos cru-el-ly——"

" Friend, I have nought to give thee," tersely responded Aminadab : " moreover, thou hast been punished by the sword, as they who live by the sword shall
be. If thou hast served thy king, let thy king reward thee. Dost thou not know
thou art a vagrant, liable to be committed to the stocks, for thy audacity, in thus
begging on the highway, against the law in that case made and provided ?"

Jerry had some difficulty in swallowing the rising curse with which he was
about to retort on the cold-blooded formalist; as it was, his hearty d—n, like
Macbeth's " amen," stuck in his throat.

" Won't your honour relieve a poor seaman, then ?" asked he.

" Go to, thou art a sturdy beggar, and there are places provided for such as
thee. Nevertheless, if thy wants are great, go to the village hard by, and inquire for the overseer, and he will relieve thee, and set thee on thy road. They
do enforce their taxes and payments on such as I, and I give not but to those of
my people."

" To h— with your cant, you snuffling old son of a —— !" retorted Jerry.

" I will procure a constable for thee, and place thee in the durance appointed
for wrong-doers," replied the quaker ; and, hastening his pace, he hurried onward
by the road on which Walpole and Sam were advancing.

Jerry was quick in deciding on revenge, and the change which took place in his
appearance, after a few seconds' retirement to the hedge, was like the transformation of a pantomime. Unbuckling his supplementary leg, he laid it in the dry
ditch ; the patch was quickly removed from his eye, and deposited in his pocket ;
his cramped-up arm withdrawn from his breast, and, in less than half a minute,
he was on the trail of the uncharitable quaker. He hailed Walpole, and Aminadab was much more surprised than delighted when he beheld a suspicious-looking
fellow, in the garb of a seaman, descend from a bank, and place himself in the road
he was going. Not liking the appearance of the new comer, Aminadab turned about
to retrace his steps towards his home, but he was soon made aware that this part
of his intentions would not be allowed to be carried out without question—for
here another sturdy fellow appeared, though little did he suspect that it was no
other than the mendicant he had so lately spurned. He affected, however, no
haste or emotion, and, deliberately placing his hands behind his back, began his
walk with cool nonchalance. Jerry walked rapidly to meet him, while Walpole,
with Sam, who had now joined him, soon came up to his shoulder. Aminadab
glanced suspiciously at the pair, and from them to Jerry, who, however, did not
keep him long in suspense as to their intentions.

" Now, old Broadbrim," exclaimed Abershaw, producing a short thick stick ;
" if-so-be as you're quiet, and forks over the stephen handsomely, why you sharn't
be mislested, but if-so-be as you don't, we shall be hobligated to help ourselves,
do you see. Down on your marrowbones—down, I say !"

Aminadab gave a heavy grown, but spoke not, for the spirit was sore grieved
within him.

" Alas, my friends," he began (dropping on his knees to avoid the contact of
the stout ash-plant which Jerry flourished in such a way over him, that it was
only by lowering his head that he escaped a sidelong blow), " alas, my friends,
what is it that ye would of me ? Silver and gold have I none ; but if such coin as
I have will content ye, behold it is here !"

Thus saying, the close-fisted quaker drew forth from the square skirt of his drab upper garment, a few coppers. The footpads set up a simultaneous laugh; while the quaker, who was merely procrastinating in the hope that assistance would arrive, knelt amid the trio with the upturned eyes of a martyr at the stake.

"What, thrums!"* roared Walpole; "ha, ha! well done, old Yea-and-nay! Must we take our dues as the rate-collectors do from your brethren—dive our hands in your cly, and draw the rhino out?"

Aminadab groaned again, while the footpads soon tested the amount of credit due to his assertion. First, from his breeches pocket, Sam extracted a brown net-purse containing a few silver coins and a guinea; a pair of silver-rimmed spectacles, a pencil-case, and a fine cambric handkerchief, were the next fruits of his search, but his other pockets presented nothing but a few loose memoranda and letters. Sam had been so busy in his search, that he had not watched the motions of Aminadab, and he exclaimed, when every pocket of his dress had been examined—

"Thirty hog, a tanner, and a whin!† S'help me, if the old curmudgeon oughtn't to be made taste the flavour of the nighest ditch for not coming out better blunted:‡ vy, it arn't worth sparing his canting carcase for. Ten bob a head—vy yer old ——" and he finished his expression by an emphatic kick on the posteriors of Aminadab.

"Don't be so fast, my good fellow," observed Walpole, who had been standing, stick in hand, during the search. "I've a notion as the old gentleman arn't quite easy in his breeches; get up, if you please, worthy friend."

But the quaker seemed to have an aversion to rising, and kept fumbling awkwardly at the waistband of his small-clothes.

"Ah! I see," continued his persecutor, "you've a pain in your back, poor man—stand up," (the unlucky quaker rose slowly on his feet). "Come, don't be fractious, a little rubbing gives great ease to that complaint."

The robber suited the action to the word, and passing his hand into the unmentionables of Aminadab, plainly felt some hard, thick, square substance, in form and size like a well-filled pocket-book. It was, however, too far thrust down towards his seat of honour to admit of ready withdrawal by the clenched hand.

"Here's a reader,‖ and it's a thumper too," said Walpole.

"Bring him here, behind the hedge," said Jerry: and no sooner said than done.

The quaker was grasped in three pair of lusty arms and carried from the roadway.

"I exhort thee, son of Belial, that thou shed not my blood," ejaculated Aminadab in terror; as he beheld Jerry, who had drawn a large knife, bring the murderous weapon near to his abdomen.

"Hold your canting prate, or I'll rip you up," said the savage.

The quaker only replied by a deep groan. The waistband (for in those braceless days that part of the garment, by fitting tight above the hips, was the sole support of the don't-whisper-em's), was quickly severed, and the pocket-book appropriated by Jerry, and their plunder completed.

"Shall we leave him here?" asked Sam.

"No, no, I'll show you," replied Abershaw.

The quaker's small-clothes were drawn off, and his hands and ankles tied, the one with his neckcloth, the other with his garters, and having laid him on his face with bitter threats, that if he stirred for one clear hour, they would return and murder him, the trio set off across the fields, as hard as they could run, returning by a circuitous route to the main road, and reserving for a future opportunity the inspection of their ill-gotten booty.

We will now, by virtue of the historian's prerogative, shift the scene once more to the great metropolis.

———

CHAPTER XV.

A GIPSY TENT—INFORMATION—JEALOUSY—A PAIR OF THIEFTAKERS—A CONFESSION—A THREAT.

"HURRAH! hurrah! hurrah!" Here's luck! A long life and a merry one to every cross-cove of the present worthy company!" cried the chairman of as ruffianly a gathering as ever assembled in a flash ken in the back slums.

* Threepence. + Thirty shillings, a sixpence, and a groat. ‡ With more money. ‖ Pocket-book.

"Hurrah! hurrah! hurrah!" repeated the guests.

The scene of the revel was a room in the White Hart, situate in the Coal-yard, near the Holborn end of Drury-lane, and in the immediate vicinity of the then un-purged Lewkner's-lane, and its surrounding ramifications of misery and profligacy. The house was well known as the resort of most of the tobymen and padders* of the day; and not a few of the company exhibited an odious compound of flash finery and dirty slovenliness, in their incongruous costume. Yet among these more lucky desperadoes (for crime, like misery, acquaints us with strange bedfellows), were mixed many dirty, unkempt, unshorn, unwashed ruffians, the sweepings of the gaols and hospitals of London. Some of them were duffers and begging impostors, who to their mendicant calling added no scruples of honesty; while others were hardened criminals; and not a few *touters* (a name which has survived, though its original meaning has become extinct), appeared among the motley group.

These touters, some sixty years since, and upwards, were indispensable to the system of robbery then in vogue. They *lurched* (like poachers' dogs about preserves) in the vicinity of the houses of the nobility and the wealthy gentry, and, by scraping acquaintance with the underlings of the stable-yard, at the neighbouring public-house, furnished themselves with information of the movements of the wealthy, which was of no small value to the highwayman and the footpad.

In like manner the inn-yards and hostelries of London and the great roads were haunted by these eaves-dropping scoundrels, who gathered intelligence without suspicion, while the appearance of the robbers themselves would have been dangerous, and have led to detection. Numerous *apparent* callings were assumed by these fellows—that of a cadger, or a dealer in cabbage-nets, turned bowls, wooden spoons, clothes lines, or turf, being most in favour. What was thus learnt was sold to the professed thief; and the *touter* was to him as indispensable as his dog to a sportsman—for without one of these to start or point his game, but little success could be hoped from his exertions.

But to return. In the midst of this riff-raff assemblage, "high in a chair of state," sate Bob Walpole, having as his right-hand supporter our hero, Jerry Abershaw: and while the tables are rattling, we will turn for a few moments to look what has become of their faithful companion in so many dangers and difficulties—Black Sam.

That individual had betaken himself to Hampstead-heath, which, at the period of our story, was much *farther* from town than at present; and there, in the bosom of his vagrant tribe, was carrying on petty larcenies, just to "keep his hand in" until a more distinguished felony presented itself; this, to a person of his active turn of mind, was not long wanting. Jerry and Walpole had been, on the day of the night we are now speaking of, doing a little on the "frisking-lay†" at Westminster, in the squeeze which took place on the occasion of his Majesty George III. (as yet untainted with lunacy) proceeding in state to open the sittings of his loyal lords and faithful commons; and they were now enjoying themselves in a rattling booze out of the proceeds of their ill-gotten booty. The mirth and fun were waxing fast and furious when a message was delivered to the president, by mine host of the White Hart, in a confidential tone, and the former having (equally *sotto voce*) communicated its nature to Jerry, our hero left his seat and withdrew with the messenger into the passage outside the door of the room wherein this thieves' saturnalia was held.

The bringer of the message was a swarthy tinker of gipsy caste, who briefly delivered himself of his information in a tongue which certainly would require translation into English for ordinary use, yet not one word of which seemed foreign to his auditor. He gave Jerry to understand that Black Sam had acquired intelligence of a good booty which was obtainable by stopping a north-road coach, which would take its way over the brow of Highgate-hill; that road, before the formation of the new highway from Kentish-town to Finchley by the Archway, being the main route of the York and Liverpool coaches. Jerry quickly returned, and Bob quitting the room at a signal, the pair left London by Tottenham-court-road for the rendezvous at Hampstead, where they arrived some hours before daylight.

Here they lay perdu the following day; and here, to Jerry's unqualified satis-

---

* Mounted highwaymen and footpads.   † Picking pockets.

faction, he met and renewed his acquaintance with the fascinating Rebekah Morse, his quondam flame of Blackheath memory. The vagrant family of Egyptians consisted of old Ben the Patrico,* Sam, and two other vagabonds of the race.

The arrival of Jerry, however, awakened a sleeping serpent in the bosom of one of the party—it was that of the rejected suitor for the favour of Rebekah, whom we have noticed in a former chapter. This fellow, who boasted some cousinship or affinity to Jerry's flame, had, since our hero's absence, endeavoured in many ways to supersede him, but in vain. And now that he saw him once more in the field, the old feud broke out anew. He did not dare, however, to exhibit it openly: not only because he was personally pusillanimous, and mistrusted his prowess against the strength of Jerry, but because the latter had firm friends (as he had experienced on more than one occasion) in the persons of old Ben, his queen (or *quean*)—the crone who acted as *mater familias*—and in the bosom of the handsome Rebekah herself. Thus situate, this gloomy breeder of revenge, on the morning on which Jerry and Walpole reached the encampment in the hollow formed by the declivity near Jack Straw's Castle, strolled forth to indulge his spleen, and " chew," in solitary wandering, " the cud of bitter fancy," while his rival slept.

He had strayed without noting even the passing wayfarer, down the slopes of Child's Vale, and had reached the end of Pond-street, when, in front of a humble ale-house, he spied two men taking an early lunch of bread and cheese. Drawing near them, and standing in the shade of some alder bushes, which lined the garden of the house, he overheard the following converse, which opened up to him a " medicine for his melancholy," in the tempting shape of revenge.

" I tell you what it is, Master Turner," said one of the men, a short, squat, thick-built fellow, with a neck like a bull, and apparently about of equal strength with that formidable animal : " I'll tell you what it is, there's no more chance o' nailing a fellow among these gipsies, than catching a flea in a truss of hay. They're here to-day and gone to-morrow ; besides, the warrant's only good for Middlesex, and it's more than likely as the coves we wants is in Surrey."

" Not a bit of it," replied his brother thieftaker ; " they'll not trust 'emselves in ayther Surrey or Kent, arter the ugly name they've got up for smuggling in those parts. I've a notion as old Ben the Patrico and that lot, was deeper in the murder and robbery at Blackheath, and the making away with poor Grabum and his man, than what people suspects—but that's neither here nor there. The cove as we wants is him they call Black Sam ; for sartin, he was thought to be gone abroad with his pals, but *I* knows better—he have been seen in London, and young Abershaw, too, within these three days ; and it shall go hard but I swing the lot of 'em."

The gipsy listened eagerly. The conversation continued, and he soon gathered enough to find that the speakers were a brace of Bow-street runners, who held a warrant against Sam Tummons, for a petty offence, and whose enquiries had thrown them on a scent, which had issued in their discovering that Jerry and Walpole, whose absence from the country was generally believed, were still lurking about London. The opportunity seemed to him an inviting one, and he resolved, even at the cost of treachery to his tribe, to embrace it. Stepping forward, he accosted the runners, and proffered his services to render them the information they required, in order to ensure the capture of Jerry and Walpole ; inwardly determining, nevertheless, to save the Patrico, and Sam, from a feeling for the blood of Egypt in their common veins.

A brief parley sufficed to show Turner and his follower that the intelligence of the gipsy was valuable, and having pumped him as far as they thought necessary, a conference took place apart between the two thieftakers ; Turner meantime ordering some ale and cold meat to regale the renegade gipsy.

" These bush-coves† arn't to be trusted no further than you can swing a bull by the tail," said the runner, in a whisper ; " besides, he's a great deal readier with his informing than I like. This luck's too good to be all true ; it's too rich a dollop for any but a gudgeon to swallow. Here's a chap, and all for love of us, so far as I can see, going to blow the gaff‡ on all his pals—without being in the slightest clinch o' danger—no, no, depend on't, this here's a trap for us. How-

---

* Father, or elder of a gipsy camp.   † Gipsies.   ‡ Turn impeacher.

somdever, Bill, we'll not let him see as we suspects him—only do you look sharp as he doesn't mizzle and raise the birds." The officers rejoined the gipsy.

"And so, young man," said Turner, " these owdacious villains is just now a contriving more robbery, eh? And they're in a place close hereabouts—to which you'll undertake to guide us, eh? Well and good, so far: but you say as how you will go and see, and then return to us. Now all you say seems very fair, but how are we to trust you? No, no; you must allow us to be best judges how these things ought to be done, and therefore you'll be so good as to walk with us as far as Sir Thomas Wilson's house, here on the Heath, whereby you will be able to give the necessary affidavys afore his worship the beak."

This was a most unpleasant hearing for the gipsy, and he was about to remonstrate—for his vagabond race have an instinctive horror of officers, magistrates, and all ministers of the law—when he was quickly made aware of the false position in which his own cunning had placed him, by Turner calling abruptly to his companion—

"Here, Bill, lend a hand—this bush-cove thinks as how he can play fast and loose with us, but that won't fit, old chap, at no price;" and the astonished gipsy found "the action suited to the word," by feeling his arms pinioned with a short cord with a slip-knot at its end, kept by the runners for the purpose; and being thus far disabled from offering effectual resistance, they made assurance doubly sure by slipping on a pair of darbies, despite his remonstrances and declarations that he would willingly accompany them, if left unbound. To these Mr. Turner and his associate paid not the slightest respect, and in ten minutes from the time of his unexpected capture, the gipsy found himself in the justice parlour of Sir Thomas Maryon Wilson, lord of the cockney manor of Hampstead, and a worshipful J. P. of the county of Middlesex.

Here the gipsy strongly protested against the manner in which he had been treated, but his protest was unavailing; inasmuch as, by the showing of Turner and his bull-dog,* he was not only intimately cognizant of all the circumstances of more than one capital felony, but had been the associate, probably the accomplice, of the criminals.

We shall not weary the reader by recapitulating the testimony; but it was deemed sufficient by the magistrate's clerk to warrant the detention of the gipsy. That cunning scoundrel easily saw that he was yet safe, provided he revealed nothing farther; he therefore wished his worship and the officers much joy of their information—seeing they did not yet know the whereabouts of their wished-for prey—and declared his intention of persisting in a dogged silence, adding that all he had hitherto disclosed was mere invention and lies.

This tack succeeded; and in order to induce him to follow up his revelations, he received the formal promise of his worship that he should be admitted evidence for the crown, provided he aided the capture of Jerry Abershaw, Walpole, and their confederates in the Blackheath robbery and murder.

"Time and tide wait for no man;" and the single hour wasted in these conferences, and the capture of George Cooper, probably added years to the life of the villanous Jerry. A slinking scout among the donkey-keepers on the heath, had seen the gipsy carried in custody up the road, and into the justice's house. The news flew like lightning to the tents; and when Turner, the gipsy, and two stout constables from the manor-house arrived at the encampment, Jerry, Walpole, Sam, and the Patrico, had made themselves scarce; so that the women, baggage, and children, alone remained the spoil of the captors.

But the revengeful gipsy had now committed himself too far to recede, and to his former jealous spite now added the motive of self-preservation; nevertheless, he could not restrain his feelings of exultation when he saw the scornful Rebekah Morse brought into the justice-room among the captives. Drawing near her, he whispered, in a husky voice—

"Look, when the smock-faced youngster, for whom you have rejected your own blood, shall dangle on the gallows tree, then, perhaps, Rebekah will be glad to accept the hand of the man she has scorned; then will be *his* turn to refuse.".

Rebekah darted a furious glance at the traitor.

"Take care," retorted she, " that you do not yet crave *his* mercy first."

The gipsy little imagined how few hours were to elapse, ere her words should prove prophetic.

* Officer's follower.

CHAPTER XVI.

AN EXAMINATION—FLIBBERTIGIBBET AGAIN—A PLOT—JERRY STABS HIS RIVAL.

THE examination of the captured gipsies was confined to that of the old woman, of Rebekah, and another female of the tribe. It was long and severe, but elicited nothing. At first, his worship was inclined to commit them to hard labour as vagrants for a short period; but discretion, as well as mercy, prompted him to forego this resolve. Firstly, because as a great landholder he had much exposed property, and the enmity of the gipsy race was a thing not to be despised in those days; and secondly, if he committed the females (who were certainly the most criminal), what was he to do with the infants, of whom there were five, as unreclaimed, ragged, bare-legged young urchins, as ever rode a donkey bare-backed, cadged half-pence, or turned " catherine-wheels" and summersets before a stage-coach on the highway. His worship consequently resolved to discharge the captives, as the most convenient way of settling a knotty point. Most assuredly he would not have done so, had he for a moment surmised the consequences of his step.

Among these lawless ramblers there are always appointed rendezvous and a code of signals, which, though not so elaborate as the naval countersigns, are quite as useful to these dwellers in an enemy's country—for such they deem the civilised, settled society which surrounds them. The old woman, the boys, Rebekah, and her sister, quitted the court-yard gates of Sir Thomas Wilson, and taking the main coach track across the heath, came out on the brow of Haverstock-hill; crossing the high road, they pursued their march to Hendon; but no sooner had they arrived at the curve of a hedge which concealed them from the view of the public-houses and the main road, than the party halted.

" Bekka," said the crone; " Bekka, dear, I'm very tired. Here, Benjee, boy, bring the sticks, and we'll warm a little something. Whistle, Benjee, whistle !"

The eldest urchin, who was no other than the flibbertigibbet of Blackheath memory, put a small piece of the hollow stem of the cow-parsley, wherein a slit was made with a sharp knife, to his lips; and after a few seconds this extemporaneous wind-instrument discoursed loud and sweet music, not unlike the tones produced by an accordian. A skylark's whistle replied.

" That 'ill do. Bless the boy, what a noise he makes," muttered the old woman, as if she thought it necessary to conceal her own trickery even from herself. "*He's* there, at any rate :" and she withdrew her hand from her ear, where she had placed it, as if listening for the bird. "I wonder if they're all safe. Well, well, Rebekah, my dear, you must take a small brown pitcher, and go towards the pond, and down by the pollards on the right, and cough three times : but I needn't tell you, you know the rest."

Rebekah caught up the pitcher, and had left the party before the old woman had ceased speaking, taking her way as directed; she drew near the pollards, which grew on a small embankment by a deep ditch skirted by a hedge. She coughed thrice ; and immediately after old Ben, Sam, Jerry, and Walpole, were seen sneaking through from the farther side of the bank. Rebekah greeted Jerry with her eyes rather than her tongue; but to Ben and the rest she was more communicative.

" Well, girl," inquired the Patrico, "which quarter's the wind in now—fair or foul? Do you know, my prime lads, I've more nor a ideey, as George has been striking his colours afore his worship, the beak there, and turning informer to save his own dirty carcase, else vy should Sir Thomas Vilson hissue varrants for our apprehension, as never did him any harm? Depend on't, there's a screw loose with George; it's jealousy, or summut of that kind, to my thinking; and if so, the sooner ve're rid on him the better."

" Indeed, father, you're right in your suspicions," replied Rebekah; " he hates Jerry, and has vowed his death. This day, at the justice's house, he swore revenge, and threatened me with the fate of a hempen widow; but I've more to tell you. George knew of your plot to rob some coach from the north; while I was in the justice's-room I kept my ears open to some purpose. I there heard it settled that two officers should accompany him to a certain spot, where he told them you would lie in wait, and take Jerry and Walpole. He further told them that this might easily be done, as Patrico and Sam would be stationed at a distant point at the top of the hill, and would not join till the coach came down to the spot where it was intended to rob it."

"Bravo! bravo! my dark-eyed 'un!" said Jerry, snatching an unresisted kiss; "you're a hangel."

"Come, come," said old Ben, laughing; "no billing and cooing now, when business is in hand. Jerry, we'll take your advice, as most concerned in the scoundrel's proceedings."

Jerry readily gave his opinion.

"Well, what I say is this: let's surprise the ambuscade of these precious traps, and turn the tables on 'em. Here are four of us: Patrico is stout; though, old 'un, excuse me, but you're a little past fighting."

"Past what?" said the Patrico, good-humouredly, and flourishing a formidable staff which he used to assist his pedestrian performances.

He had been a man of giant strength, and was still, for a short effort, a most formidable opponent at cudgel or single-stick play.

Jerry laughed at the old man's briskness.

"Bravo, Patrico; then we may reckon on you. Well, there's Sam and Bob steel to the back-bone; and, for myself, I'll do my best. And now, lads, what say you for the rendezvous at Milford-lane, where we will take a survey of the enemy, and act as chance may direct. Rebekah will return to camp."

"Nay, I will not," replied the damsel; "I will go with you and act as your scout: I may be useful, and more than that, can show myself where you must not. Look, therefore, to see me at the stile near the old cottage, below the park-gates of Caenwood."

She left them a few minutes, then returned with hot meat and bread from the fireplace; having eaten, and deposited the remainder in the Patrico's wallet, the party set out for Highgate-hill. Carefully creeping along the hedgerows and fences, keeping always on the farther side of the few houses it was necessary to pass, and occasionally crawling along the beds of dry ditches which skirted the fields, the men, under the guidance of the Patrico, again came to the highroad; this they crossed unnoticed, and struck into the plantation of young trees, near Caen-wood, the residence of the Earl of Mansfield: emerging thence, and taking their way by the embankments of the three pond-like reservoirs, they came to the hedge skirting Milford-lane, which opens, after an elbow-like turn, on what was, at the period of which we are writing, the great mail-coach road, over the heartbreaking ascent of Highgate-hill.

This was the appointed spot to meet Rebekah, and here they halted to lie awhile in hiding, to rest themselves, and await her appearance.

In about half an hour she was seen resting on the stile, and soon after she cautiously communicated to them, as they drew near enough to hear her voice, the following information, which she rather sung than spoke, without moving from her resting-place; so that no casual wayfarer, or even watcher of her actions, would have supposed her engaged in any more serious matter than singing a song upon a gate:

> Down by the hill there went three men,
>   Sing lira, lira, lay—
> With pistol and sword they armed them then,
>   Their enemies to slay.
>
> The first he was a runner stout,
>   Sing lira, lira, lay—
> The second his cad, who prowls about,
>   To seek on whom to prey.
>
> There's, too, a 'peaching, treacherous wretch,
>   Sing lira, lira lay—
> All three now lie in wait to catch,
>   On the right of the next highway, &c.

And thus Rebekah continued crooning out her monotonous rhymings until she had artfully informed the gipsy gang of the exact position, number, and force of arms of the officer's ambuscade.

"Now, my trumps," said Jerry, "let's drop down on these here cunning warmint, and beat up their quarters. It's now nigh hand on eight o'clock, and getting

duskish, and the long-drag* is timed for someways atween half-arter eight and
ten.† You three can take the traps, and leave me to deal with the sneaking cur,
what's been twisting hemp for me. I'll make him taste the soft end of an ash
plant, and find there are other uses for good rope than stopping the breath of a
right 'un—the 'peaching sneak !"

"Do as you likes vith him—ve disowns him—he's none of our'n," said the
Patrico, indignantly; "do as you please, you've our license, and the vorse you
sarves him the more you does him justice. The tribe I rules, and I says it vith
pride, never numbered hinformers among it, nor never shall, so long as ould Ben
is its Patrico."

* Four-horse coach.
† A striking difference between modern fast coaches, where ten minutes on a long journey was
" time," and our still more modern locomotives, where ten minutes late is equivalent to the probability of some calamitous accident.

"Bravo, dad!" said Sam, "spoken like a brick: and now, rum'uns, are we ready for the skrimmage?"

"Not a doubt on't," replied Walpole; "but I can't say I exactly approve of my weapon; it's cursed clumsy, and too thick for a gentleman's hand. I don't object to fighting, observe, but should like to have something civilised, though it's but a stick."

Jerry laughed, and so did the Patrico, and the latter soon procured Walpole a stiff blackthorn of moderate diameter, in lieu of the hedgestake he carried, and thus equipped they stole cautiously down the lane.

At this moment they heard the voice of a female passenger along the highway which they were skirting.

> "Then says Jenny, says she, unto her good man,
> More haste the worse speed—so better your plan:
> The friends that you wot of, they're now on the road,
> And in a few minutes they'll reach your abode."

"There's that cursed Rebekah, sneaking about the road," said George Cooper, the gipsy, to the two officers. "See, that's her before us; that bodes no good."

"Is that the pretty black-eyed maiden," said Turner, "what we grabbed and had at his worship's?—poo! poo! you're a coward. She's on no lay—not she. I'll tell you what, young feller, I suspects you're a rank cur, and if so be this turns out a sell, arter the trouble we've took, why look to get the worst of the round, for we won't be played with—these coves—leastways this here Abershaw and Walpole——"

"Oh, lord!" exclaimed the gipsy, as he fell prostrate, from the dull heavy thwack of a ponderous cudgel, brandished by the sinewy arm of Jerry Abershaw; while at the same moment the Patrico, Walpole, and Black Sam, leaped from the hedge and assailed the two runners. Panic-stricken by the suddenness of the assault, the officers fled before superior strength and numbers; nor did they stop until they were clear of the pursuit of the determined trio who had charged them. Meanwhile, Jerry, his breast burning with jealousy, challenged his treacherous rival to rise—he did not dare. At length, after some angry recrimination, in a style which it would be impossible to transfer to paper, George Cooper proposed to fight, provided Jerry would allow him the privilege of rising without molestation. Jerry assented, and the cowardly scoundrel rose; but at the moment that Jerry, brandishing his stick, advanced to the combat, he observed the left hand of his antagonist groping in his breast. A pistol, thought Jerry, and quick as the thought, he struck the left arm of his rival with such smashing violence, that a "life-preserver" dropped from his grasp; his next blow was at his head, and Cooper was again down.

"I'll live to hang you and your woman too," snarled the gipsy, in agony of mind and body.

The phrase brought back Abershaw's danger to his comprehension. This villain will betray me, thought he—dead men tell no lies. He grasped his long, sharp, Spanish knife, and without compunction or remorse, bared it to the view of the horror-struck gipsy.

"Murder! murder! mercy! mercy!" shrieked the despairing wretch: the last effort of his shriek was a gurgling groan. The knife had penetrated his lungs; the stab was repeated in his throat, and despite his struggles, Jerry, a third time, sheathed his murderous knife in the wretch's body—this time reaching his heart. The gipsy rolled in the dust a ghastly disfigured corpse. There was no time for reflection, and Jerry dragged the body through the hedge.

It was dark when the Patrico and his companions rejoined him. To them he glozed the combat as a fair fight, declaring his stabbing to have been in self-defence. The Patrico's sympathies were with the survivor, and that night, by mutual assistance, the four robbers buried their victim in a new plantation of firs, on the north-western face of the hill, in a spot which they supposed that was little likely to be disturbed or discovered.

———

CHAPTER XVII.

SUSAN ABERSHAW'S LOVER—HER MARRIAGE—DOMESTIC FELICITY—THE FIRST OF AUGUST—THE WATERMAN'S ARMS—A SNAKE IN THE GRASS—FOREBODINGS.

WE will now make a resting-place in our narrative, while we return and cast a retrospective glance at other personages in this history, of whom we have so long lost sight; and this no less because it is refreshing to breath awhile a purer atmosphere than that tainted with the foul misdeeds of robbers, murderers, and outcasts, than from the necessity of preserving unentangled and perfect the thread of our varied story.

The widow Abershaw and her excellent daughter, for some months after the absconding of Jerry, continued to occupy their humble cottage near St. George's Fields, where the honest Tom Trimwell was a constant visitor as the accepted suitor of Susan. Tom, it is true, often urged, with a lover's ardour, the celebration of their marriage, but prudential motives prevailed, and he deferred the wished-for event until his worldly circumstances should be such as to enable him to offer a comfortable home to the wife of his choice. Fortune smiled upon his industry and perseverance, and, inspired by hope, in a twelvemonth he had saved upwards of forty pounds. His aged mother, however, demanded his care; but her death, about this period, though sincerely mourned for by him, had an influence in accelerating the happy period. Old Mrs. Trimwell, as we have already said, was the widow of an honest, hardworking man, and, at her decease, besides the little cottage they had occupied together, Tom Trimwell found himself the possessor of upwards of a hundred pounds, the produce of her thrift and that of his father.

The decent funeral over, and the ordinary period of mourning expired, Tom proposed to his intended that he should purchase a waterside public-house, and that forthwith herself and her mother should be installed therein.

Had Susan's affection been less insincere than it was, there might have been sufficient reasons to subdue her coyness, but, loving him as she did, the prospect of the future appeared so fair, that smiles and tears welcomed his proposal, which was made in the presence of both the widow and her daughter. Matters were soon arranged, and many months before the period at which our story has now arrived, a neat and thriving public-house, on the Bankside, bore the inscription on its creaking sign-board of "The Waterman's Arms, by Thomas Trimwell." The cleanliness, civility, and good looks of Susan, the alacrity and industry of Trimwell, and the care and frugality of the widow Abershaw, soon raised the character of the house; and, by its good liquor, civil and prompt attendance, and the cheerful courtesy of its buxom landlady, the Waterman's Arms became a favourite resort. At night, its clean sanded parlour and blazing fire attracted not a few of the small tradesmen of the neighbourhood, who met there to blow a cloud and discuss politics; while, during the day, the benches before its door exhibited a full muster of the hardy, bronzed faces of the Thames watermen, and the wooden verandah above was enlivened by a succession of pleasure-seeking citizens, with their wives and little ones.

Trade flourished, customers increased, and it would have been difficult to point out a happier, a more thriving, or more deservedly prosperous family than the Trimwells.

It was the evening of the first of August, 1787, and the rippling wavelets of Father Thames were alive with gaily-painted craft. The gilded barges of nobility and gentry (for the "silent highway" of London was then the continual scene of brilliant pageantry, ere improved and widened streets, and above all, steam, had annihilated the old water-glories of the river), the gay sailing boats, the rude skiffs of the bargemen, the heavy wherries of the fire-watermen, and here and there a man-of-war's boat, with its trim blue jackets, and small union jack astern, lent animation to the scene, for it was the day whereon the oldest of our river contests, the coat and badge given by the comedian Doggett, was rowed for by the newly-emancipated apprentices. This venerable prize, now in its 134th summer, still survives, and though shorn of its glories by modern regattas, in the last century its recurrence was a sworn holiday-making affair to all the working denizens of London, Westminster, and Southwark. The public-houses along-shore were crowded, and among them it may easily be supposed not the least patronised was the Waterman's Arms, on the Bankside.

A constant throng of visitors had kept Mrs. Trimwell, her spouse, and a pair of tapsters, hard at it the livelong day, and a money-making season it had been with them. The lingering reflection of the crimson clouds was still glowing on the waters, and as the heavens and its reflecting mirror gradually softened into dull grey, the river became still, the doors of the houses were one by one closed, lights were brought, and the groups dispersed, or formed in the drinking-rooms of the various places of public entertainment more select and diminishing parties, who still discussed the merits of the competitors, and the various mirthful occurrences of the day. At this time, two swarthy men of by no means prepossessing aspect, entered the taproom of the Waterman's Arms. The one, an old man with grizzled hair, and huge false whiskers of the like mingled tints, was none other than old Ben, the Patrico of the gipsy tribe ; and his younger companion, who wore a black patch on his left eye, was black Sam, known to the reader as Sam Tummons, the reckless associate of the desperate and infamous Jerry.

The scoundrelly pair seated themselves opposite the open door of the thronged apartment, in a position that commanded a full view of the well-lighted bar, wherein, amid bright measures, china bowls, nets of limes, and polished glasses, Susan Trimwell, the smiling hostess, dispensed the good things of this life to the ready waiters, assisted by her husband.

"Dost see yonder smirking Jezabel ?" asked Sam of his fellow gipsy, in an under tone.

"What, the comely landlady, do you mean ?" replied the Patrico : "she's a likely piece o' goods—but what of her ?"

"That's my wife that ought to have been," said the ruffian, sulkily ; "but how the devil she came here, I can't guess ; and that smooth-faced suck-egg there's her husband, Tom Trimwell. See how they're counting off the pewter,* and there's a sprinkle of canaries† among that he's stowing away in the tankard with the lid. Do they leave that in the bar o' nights, think ye ?"

"I should say not," muttered the Patrico, abstractedly, for his eyes were steadfastly fixed on the landlord's motions ; "I should say not—in such a neighbourhood as this here."

"Kious‡ a moment," whispered Sam, as he rose from his seat and walked into the passage, affecting to look towards the door, while he narrowly watched Tom Trimwell, who little dreamt of such a spy upon his movements. "It's all right," said Sam, returning ; "he's bagged the ochre,‖ and the whites§ are left in the topped mug. Hark'e, Ben, Jerry must be one in this ; but don't let a word drop of whose crib it is, till I let him into the secret. There's a haul here that's a mere gift to three or four of us. You must come to-morrow and tout a little, so that we may find out who lives in the house, and where they snooze."

"Mum !" replied the old man, " a wink's enow for me ; and as there's no more to settle, let's drink to the success of our spec."

They called for liquor, and about half an hour before the hour of closing, Sam departed, leaving the Patrico to watch for any further insight he might be able to gain into the domestic economy of the devoted Trimwells. It was nearly eleven o'clock when the cunning old villain advanced to the bar and inquired whether he could be accommodated with a bed for the night.

"Thomas," inquired Susan of her husband, "can we give a bed to a stranger ?"

Trimwell looked at his customer, for the aspect of old Ben was by no means a promising one.

"Why, I don't know that we have one to spare," replied he.

"Lor' lov'ee, don't say that," urged the gipsy ; "I'm an old 'un, and I ha' walked thirty mile to-day out o' Kent, to seek a daughter o' mine as is married somewheres in town, about the Borough here, and I ha' lost the right direction ; but I shall be sure to find she on the morrow. Doun't'ee deny an ould man a lie down ; I'll pay ye readily, and thank'ee too,"

"Let the poor man have a bed, Thomas," said the compassionate Susan.

"He must make shift, then," replied Trimwell, "and sleep in the up-stairs front on a shake-down."

The Patrico thankfully embraced the offer, and retired to the tap-room.

---

* Silver money.   † Guineas.   ‡ Be quiet.   ‖ Gold.   § Silver coin.

So soon as the company had gone, Susan proceeded to make preparations for the stranger, and the Patrico, whose eyes were always about him, had the satisfaction of observing, himself unobserved, the spot where, in a strong safe, beneath double lock and key, honest Tom deposited his cash. Shortly after he was shown up to his dormitory, and it may be easily supposed that nothing escaped his scrutinising eyes, as to the position of the sleeping-rooms, and their various tenants, so far as he could either conjecture or ascertain them. In the morning, after an early breakfast, he made many seemingly innocent enquiries of Susan and her helpmate, as to the most probable means of discovering his daughter, and left the house to carry the tidings of his success to his villanous confederates.

At evening he returned, and with great apparent cheerfulness informed Mrs. Trimwell that his search had been crowned with success. That his daughter was with her husband in the service of a gentleman at Newington Causeway, whose name he mentioned—a name well known by repute to both Susan and her husband. He further stated that, in her dependent position, she could not accommodate him with a sleeping-room, and therefore he must once more trespass on their kindness for a night's accommodation. This was readily acceded to; but the direful consequences of this seemingly commonplace kindness must form the subject of the next chapter.

CHAPTER XVIII.

THE MURDER—THE CONFLAGRATION.

WE have already in an early chapter given the reader a sketch of the locality of the Mint, in Southwark, and shall therefore make no preface to introduce him to the parlour of the Three Brewers, where, on the morning of the third of August, 1787, four men were assembled, whose conversation sufficiently developed their character and intentions.

"I've my own eyes to answer for one part of it," said the oldest of the party: "there's not less that one hundred in white and yellow* in one plant; ay, ay, you cockney-bred cracksters† thinks yourselves downey a bit, but lor' love ye, get an old 'un as has bin on the tramp for years, if yer wants the touting and piping lay‡ done clean and safe. The one of the tapsters is spliced,|| and he don't dorse§ i' the crib at all; and t'other's no more nor a kinchin,¶ so to speak. Then there's the upstairs room where they snoozes—the bos-cove and his mot;** it's clean out o' hearing of anything short of crashing a dubber or blinker,†† or bending a glaze, as 'ud wake 'em, and there's no call whatsumdever for nothing o' that sort."

"Would you like the concern, Jerry?" asked Walpole; "because if *you* say ay, I'm one in it; if not, I'd as lief try our luck at Sir Jeffery Neville's, which I told you of—a much more gentlemanly crack—but I'll leave it to you."

"Why, as to that part of the affair," replied Jerry, "why we can't do both, I don't 'xactly see; and besides, I know Sam has a bit of a grudge, and I'm not far behind him. It's my thinking that Sukey wouldn't ha' much minded, if the pair on us had been scragged, when the last awk'ard job came off at Kingston; so I'm for just calling in—rayther late, of course—and giving the Waterman's Arms a turn of our custom—eh, Sam?"

Sam gave a chuckle, an unusual thing with him, at what he considered to be a stroke of facetiousness, and the rest of the preliminaries were speedily arranged.

It was agreed that the Patrico should, as upon the two nights previous, apply for a bed, which, doubtless, would not be refused him; and when the household should be buried in sleep, he should show a signal, by placing a piece of white cloth out of the casement of his dormitory; and that when all was in readiness and the time fitting for the purpose, he should descend, and the villains should be admitted to the lower part of the premises, where they doubted not to find a good booty.

Proceedings being thus agreed on, the party called for liquor, and drank "Success to their undertaking," with a spirit worthy of a better cause.

The full round orb of a summer moon rode clearly in the blue expanse, and tipped with silver the ripples of the silent river. The busy hum of labour was

---

* Silver and gold.   † London thieves.   ‡ Looking out and observing. || Married.   § Sleep.
¶ Child, lad.   ** Master, or landlord and his wife.   †† Breaking in a door or shutter.

still ; and the activity of the vast hive of industry, which stood upon the banks of the
Thames, was hushed in the refreshment of balmy sleep, renovating its strength for
the toil and labour of the coming day. At this hour, while innocence and honesty
slept, did the three criminals move towards the scene of their nefarious project
with stealthy strides. Pausing before the little abode of integrity and industry,
they scanned its upper windows, and quickly espied the welcome signal. Jerry
gave a low whistle, and, in reply, they were quickly made aware of the success of their enterprise thus far, by the gradual withdrawal of the bolts, and the
appearance of the Patrico. Admission gained, they paused awhile to assure themselves that all was still. No sound met the ear ; and the Patrico, having pointed
out the spot where the cash was kept, Walpole quickly set about forcing the
fastenings of the depository. This, however, proved a very different task from what
they had calculated on. It was a strong box, made of stout walnut, clamped with
iron at the corners, and possessing a lock of peculiar construction. It had once
been a plate-chest of some nobleman or gentleman, and had been set deeply in the
brickwork beside the chimney, by the skill of a neighbouring blacksmith.

Strong bolts held it in its embedded position, and being fixed so as to close flush
with the wall, it presented obstacles of no ordinary kind to its being either broken
open or removed. At this stout obstruction to their designs, Walpole had been
working with extreme assiduity for several minutes ; during which interval of
anxious suspense, his comrades had been sedulously watching his proceedings.
The stout wood, and stouter iron clampings, resisted every effort of his practised
hand and the little jemmy he carried, to force them to render up their trust.
The burglar paused, and a whispering conference took place.

"There's two ways," said Walpole ; "one is a long job, to bore a hole through
the door, so as to get in a spring saw, and cut away the lockbolt and fastenings ;
the other, a noisy one, to force the safe out of the brickwork with a crowbar.
We've disfigured the door too much to leave our work unfinished till to-morrow, as
the marks would show somebody had been here that hadn't the key—eh? What
say you?"

"There's none but him and the boy in the house as *can* show fight, and here are
four of us," observed Jerry ; "though I and Sam are known, which is unlucky,
in case we should be twigged."

The safe in the wall now underwent another strong scrutiny with a lantern,
wherein an additional pair of eyes were engaged, that were little calculated upon.
The widow Abershaw, who had rested but little that night, from some slight temporary indisposition, had lain awake for several minutes, listening to what she
supposed to be a suppressed whispering outside the house. Her bed-room was
immediately over the bar, and as the men stood near its fireplace, the chimney of
which had an opening into that of her apartment, their undertones very distinctly
reached the ear of the widow. Alarmed at the unusual sounds, Mrs. Abershaw,
well knowing the effect which a sudden terror might have upon the delicate situation of her daughter, rose cautiously, and slipping on a few clothes, crept silently to
the stair-head, whence, through a side window, a few steps down, a view of the apartment beneath might be obtained. What was her consternation at the sight before her.
She counted four men, and, while with bated breath and beating heart she strained
her eyes to perceive what they were engaged in, she saw them inspecting the safe,
where she knew all the wordly wealth of the Trimwells was secured. She was
hesitating how or in what way to give the alarm, on account of the interesting
state of her child, at which we have already hinted, when a new horror made her
blood run cold. It was the voice of her outcast son which met her ear; she could
not mistake its tones, and these were the words he spoke—

"I don't see any pull in goin' back now we've got so far—in for a lamb in for a
sheep. Let me and Sam plant ourselves outside the bos's snoozing room, and
keep the door—I'll pound it, there's nobody gets out without our leave; mean-
whiles you and Ben can prise out this here strong-box, and if you must make a
noise, why you must, that's all. Five minits 'ill do it, and we'll make the up-
stairs folks safe."

"That will never do, Jerry," said Walpole, looking dubiously at the securely-
fixed strong-box.

Mrs. Abershaw heard no more: she gently stepped into the bed-room of her
son-in-law, and, whispering in his ear, awoke him with a light touch. She did
not, however, unfasten the door so lightly, but what the housebreakers heard a

slight click as of a door lock, and paused in their conference to listen. Meantime, Mrs. Abershaw, having awakened her son-in-law, made him aware that robbers were below. Fortunately, Susan slept soundly, and although she gave an uneasy turn as her husband left the bed, did not awake.

Mrs. Abershaw related in a whisper what she had seen, and counselled Tom to descend from the window, and seek assistance in the neighbourhood : this Tom resolutely opposed. How could he think of leaving his wife, with four ruffians in the house, and no protection.

"No, no, mother," said honest Tom, as he slipped on some of his wearing apparel; "better they should take a few guineas, than any harm befall Sue. Give me the poker here; every cock, they say, can fight on his own dunghill, and I'll scurry 'em, if there were half-a-dozen!"

"Pray, pray, Tom, don't! Think—by yourself——"

"Hush! silence, mother," interposed the fearless Tom, as he walked quietly towards the door of the chamber; "don't wake Susan, if you can help it."

The next moment he was on the stairhead.

But an important change in the position of the burglars had taken place in the few moments which had thus passed. Jerry and Sam, convinced that they heard some movement up-stairs, had crept up to the bed-room door, beside which Jerry stood, at the instant of Tom Trimwell's sudden egress. Sam was in the act of descending the stairs to warn Walpole and Patrico to keep silent for a few minutes; his movement was unpleasantly accelerated by a downright smashing blow on the head from the poker of Tom Trimwell, which sent him rolling senseless, and covered with blood, into the passage below. Walpole and the Patrico had scarce time to recover from their surprise at this sudden onslaught, when poor Trimwell, in his turn, followed Sam, and fell a disfigured corse on the body of the burglar he had despatched. Jerry, we have said, was listening beside the bed-room door, at the moment Trimwell came out. The ill-starred man passed his most desperate and dangerous enemy, and struck down Sam. Jerry, unscrupulous and sanguinary, enraged at the fall of his friend, and impelled by hatred of Trimwell, hesitated not. In his hand he bore a cooper's dubbing-adze, a formidable tool, much used by boatbuilders; of this Jerry had possessed himself as a convenient and powerful wrench to dislodge the money chest, and now it ministered to his sudden vengeance and thirst of blood.

Springing from the place of his concealment, he uttered one low blasphemous exclamation, and as Trimwell turned to call his mother-in-law, that she might alarm the neighbours from the window, Jerry smote him with the murderous weapon full between the brows, and the unfortunate husband of the ruffian's sister lay next instant a mangled bleeding corse, on the body of Samuel Tummons."

Shriek following shriek burst upon the night air from that abode of blood and death, so late the home of cheerful industry and humble contentment. The first shrill scream of horror was drawn from the doubly-widowed mother of Jerry at recognising the wielder of the gory adze—her abandoned offspring; the second burst from the bereaved Susan, who saw no other object, as she rushed from her room in half-awakened terror, than the body of her husband, as he lay in a lifeless heap at the foot of the stairs, the full horror of the spectacle being momentarily developed by Walpole, who had just turned his lantern full on the ghastly object, to ascertain who was the second victim.

"Oh, my son, my son!" shrieked the miserable mother, wringing her hands in despair.

Jerry shuffled rapidly down stairs, leaped over the bleeding mass of what were lately living beings, and gained the street

"Come on," cried he to Walpole and the Patrico, in a husky voice; "we've done enow; there'll be a mob o' fools here presently. Come on!"

The instinct of self-preservation prompted them to follow his advice, and the three housebreakers turned along Bankside, threaded the labyrinths of the Clink, and were soon after in hiding, in that densely-peopled wilderness of misery and crime, the Old Mint.

We will not dwell further upon the scene which met the eyes of the neighbours, who were first on the spot, alarmed by the cries of the distracted women. Suffice it to say, that horror and indignation soon gave way to a determination to pursue the villains. Susan was happily not aware, when she slowly recovered from her swoon, of the part which her brother had taken in the dreadful catastrophe;

although the widow at once had denounced Jerry to the bystanders as the perpetrator of the atrocious deed, to their increased horror and disgust. The next day was spent in fruitless search after the murderers; but towards evening a singular accident put the officers of justice in possession of the person of Jerry Abershaw.

Among the casualties to which the wooden tenements of our ancestors were liable, the most appalling and irresistible was that of fire: and on the night of August 4, 1787, occurred a conflagration in the squalid region of the Mint, which wonderfully accelerated the march of improvement, by levelling with the ground upwards of fifty vile, ruinous wooden erections, and expelling their inhabitants from their dens of filth and misery. The fire broke out in a ruinous barn-like building, devoted to the unsavoury occupation of bone-boiling, and fed by the inflammable material of a neighbouring soap factory, the "devouring element," as the penny-a-liners phrase it, "raged with destructive fury." Jerry and the Patrico were wrapped in Morpheus' arms; the elder villain, worn out with their night of wakefulness and excitement, while Jerry was prostrated by copious draughts of spirits, which he had swallowed to quench the gnawings of an accusing conscience; for, wretch as he was, he felt miserably haunted by thoughts which he in vain strove to defy or shake off. The flames roared and crackled among the blazing timbers of the adjoining house to that in which the villains were harboured in an underground floor, communicating by a trap-door with the back-room of a low lodging-house; for in these places traps, concealed doors, and passages, were commonly found, as assistants to the security or escape of their law-breaking population. The Patrico was the first to awake; he heard the noise, the cry of many voices, the trampling of feet, and the fierce crackling of flames: the sounds grew nearer and increased in loudness; and at length he resolved to reconnoitre. Raising the trap gently, he found the apartment overhead filled with dense and suffocating smoke; self-preservation induced him to ascend, and he perceived the atmosphere in the rear of the premises one roaring glow of flame.

"Jerry! Jerry!" exclaimed he, shaking his drowsy and drunken companion; "all South'ark's in a blaze! Jerry, Jerry, save yourself, or you'll be suffocated vere you lie. Jerry! Jerry!" But to his urgent entreaty and yet more urgent thwacks and pinches, the old fellow could get no other reply than a grunt of lethargy and ill temper. "Vell, then, if so be yer von't save yourself, yer must be burnt," grumbled he; but he did not act exactly as he spoke, for as he said this, he seized Jerry by the heels, and dragged him by main strength to the foot of the step-ladder, then, raising him in his arms, he pushed up the trap, and ascending with his burthen, placed Jerry on his feet, in the apartment above. The smoke which he unconsciously inhaled, soon revived him; he coughed as if on the point of suffocation.

"Ay, ay, that's cotched yer breath, you'll do now; come, Jerry, man, save yourself! save yourself!" roared the Patrico.

Jerry opened his smarting eyes; the Patrico rushed from the burning house, and made his way unmolested through the crowd. Not so Jerry; his faculties but half awakened, were stunned and bewildered by the awful scene. He staggered out into the yard, and in the terror of the moment, imagined himself already an inmate of the infernal regions: he gazed with the stupefied stare of intoxication on the sheeted flame, then placed his hands before his eyes.

"Mercy! mercy!" howled the murderer.

"Why, what the devil have we here?" exclaimed half-a-dozen voices, surrounding the criminal.

"'Twas his own fault, if I did *murder* him! mercy! mercy!"

"It's Jerry Abershaw, the murderer!" exclaimed one of the party, recognising the culprit.

"Bind the wretch, and bring him along," cried another; and with imploring cries, which excited the mirth of the mob, the drunken wretch, who considered his captors as the tormentors of damned souls, was hauled to the prison at Horsemonger lane, followed by the hootings, peltings, and execrations of the multitude, whose furious gestures, vehement exclamations, and savage looks, added to the blood-red reflection of the flames, might have made a soberer man than the brutal Jerry doubt whether they were not more allied to fiends than men. His captors, however, succeeded in protecting their prize from personal violence, and having safely lodged him in gaol, we will there leave him, until returning consciousness shall awake him to the horrors of his situation.

CHAPTER XIX.

THE INCARCERATION—THE CORONER'S INQUEST—THE TRIAL BY TOUCH—THE
MOTHER'S CURSE!

To borrow the phraseology of Dr. Pangloss, " the thread of Jerry's web of life
appeared now well nigh reeled off the distaff of the fatal Lachesis, and the shears
of Atropos extended to sever its diminishing yarn ; for slumbering Justice seemed
at length awakened, and Retribution whetted her too-long-sheathed sword :" in
plain yeoman's English, his game seemed nearly U-P, and the term of his existence
henceforth to be reckoned not by years, but by days and minutes. Such in all
human probability might be presumed, but there are many things possible, and of
daily recurrence, which do not come within the scope of ordinary probability, and

confound the wisest practitioners in the dangerous trade of prophesying. But we will not anticipate our story.

The atrocity of the murder, and the general esteem in which the deceased and his lorn widow were held, so much augmented the indignant horror of the populace of the neighbourhood, that it was found necessary in the morning to procure the attendance of an escort of constables, ere the murderer could be safely conveyed to the Waterman's Arms, in compliance with the coroner's warrant. At an early hour the gate of the gaol had been surrounded by a group of people, eager to catch a glimpse of the ferocious ruffian, and as the hours wore on the the groups coalesced and increased into a dense crowd, which betook itself to the usual recreations of large assemblages of people with nothing to do, namely, elbowing, thrusting, shouting, fighting, occasionally "nobbing" a stray dog, or playing off a rough practical joke on some unoffending or remarkable individual. It was past noon, when a *posse* of constables, headed by the under-bailiff of Southwark, appeared at the prison-gate, to convey Jerry to the inquest, and bring him back in safe custody.

The spiked and studded door of the gaol now became the "cynosure of every eye;" at length the clanking chains and ponderous bolts were withdrawn, and the massive lock thrown back, and, heavily ironed, the malefactor appeared between two stalwart turnkeys. One mighty yell of execration, like the combined shriek of a thousand exulting fiends, greeted his appearance. Jerry, who had hitherto kept a morose silence and a savage look of dogged determination, trembled for an instant, then shaking back his somewhat long hair from his forehead (for his manacles forbade him to raise his hands), he gazed on the rolling sea of upturned faces, assumed a smile, and then burst into a hearty laugh of scorn and defiance.

"Well, dash me if he ain't a hout-and-houter!" exclaimed a costermonger, who had mounted a lamp-iron, in a tone of unfeigned admiration.

"Vhot a reg'lar trump!" echoed a dustman; and, although the more distant crowd kept up their yell, some of those nearest either sneered or held their peace in astonishment.

Such is the power of audacity over vulgar and undiscriminating minds, who forget the crime in contemplation of the first virtues of manhood—firmness under suffering, and contempt of danger. In those days the "county omnibuses" had not started, for the secure and private transfer of sensitive criminals from place to place, without exposing them to the vulgar stare of the rabble; Jerry, therefore, pedestrianised the whole length of Southwark, strongly guarded by the tipstaffs, who had much ado to prevent the crowd from squeezing them and their prisoner into a mass, so tremendous was the pressure from all points of the compass.

Arrived at the inquest-room, Jerry was ushered in, and placed before the table whereat sate the coroner and his clerk. The burglary was proved by the general evidence of the officers, and at length the question being asked if any other person had any evidence to offer, two or three proffered their oaths as to the declaration of the widow Abershaw, when she accused her son Jeremiah of the murder of her son-in-law. This evidence the coroner declined receiving, and he proposed that they should now adjourn to view the body, which lay in an adjoining apartment; after which they would consider the propriety of examining the mother of the accused, whose testimony they would willingly forego, if practicable.

A buzzing whisper now arose among the jurors, which, although the coroner and his clerk affected not to hear, they perfectly well understood the import. At length it assumed an articulate form.

"It's bin done many a time—I've heer'd it from those as wouldn't lie, as 'tis well known to ha' discovered murder, and why shouldn't it do it now?"

"We're growing wiser nor our fathers was," observed another, with a face of solemnity.

"Right, naybor Sandsugar; these here French hinfidels is hinfecting all our religious hinstitutions, and overturning the throne and haltar. Why shouldn't heaven do the same as it's done afore? I remembers when my gran'father a-tellin' us all how, when there warn't no proof at all agen a man as had murdered his wife, they brought him into the room where she was, and then her wounds busted out a-bleeding, whereby he confessed to all on it."*

_____

* This singular relic of gross superstition survived, even in great cities and towns, fifty years since. Even in the present century, a murderer, by direction of a Suffolk magistrate, was sent

"Ay, ay, neighbour Greaves, that's true as gospel writ: let's have him in to see the body. We'll have Abershaw in, if so be you've no objection, Mr. Coroner?"

The coroner assumed a smile of superior wisdom, but did not object.

The depraved and desperate are often superstitious, and this proposed ordeal struck more horror to the heart of the hardened Jerry, than could the presence of any real danger. His cheek grew deadly pale, he knitted his brows, and bit his lip till the blood started. His head whirled, and he felt so sick and faint, that for the first time he spoke, requesting a glass of water.

All eyes were fixed on him as he gulped down the draught, which seemed to hiss in his very throat; and handing the mug, hoarsely uttered—

"More! more water!"

It was brought, and again re-filled.

"He'll confess, depend on't," whispered a juror.

They were never more mistaken; such a thought had never entered his mind: he was but recruiting his determination for the awful crisis.

"Lead him in!" whispered the coroner's clerk.

Jerry assumed an air of dogged defiance, and the next minute was at the foot of the tressel on which the ghastly corpse was laid, in the exact state that it was found after the murder.

At its head stood an officer, with the blood-stained instrument, and beside the body, her face bathed in tears, and her eyes swollen with weeping, stood his doubly-bereaved mother, while his widowed sister sunk upon a seat, burst afresh into heart-breaking sobs at the dreadful scene of her brother, whom she had once loved with true sisterly affection.

Jerry screwed up his nerves, and succeeded in looking calmly and sternly at the blood-disfigured remnant of mortality.

The grief of his mother, and the bitter sobs of his sister, affected him but little; crusted in selfishness and brutality, he felt only for himself; and his sole awe was the suffocating grasp with which superstition compressed his heart; and his guilty conscience, though it feared not man, bowed in trembling, lest some supernatural phenomenon should force him to confession. This feeling, however, soon wore off; and at each sidelong glance at the corpse, he became more re-assured. The congealed blood flowed not; the features were inanimate and rigid, fixed only in the expression of acute suffering, under which the soul had fled its tenement. All seemed struck with silent awe, and not a sound was heard, save the occasional burst of an irrepressible sob of poor Susan Trimwell.

The jury even, who waited without the door the result of the solemn experiment, spoke not, or held their converse in such bated breath as to be inaudible within the chamber of blood.

Jerry looked again at the crusted and clotted gore; no liquefaction appeared.

"'Tis an old woman's bugbear! I'll speak; 'twill give me a better chance with the jury," thought he: "mother's a soft-hearted fool, and won't hang me at last; no, no!" He turned his look from the victim to his mother; but her face was buried in her apron, and he could not catch her eye. "Well, I'll not appear uneasy," thought he. He turned to the officer.

"If I'd done the deed," said Jerry, looking at the corpse, "it would have bled when I come near it, wouldn't it?" said he. "It's not that it's a pleasant sight for any one to see; but I've no objection to wait your pleasure. How long am I to stop here?"

"You've stood near, it's true, but you have not touched the corpse," observed the other man, who stood near the head.

Jerry made no reply, but walked coolly and indifferently to the side of the body,

to test the efficacy of this mute appeal to the interposition of heaven! Shakspere alludes to this impressive superstition in the speech of the Lady Anne to the Duke of Glo'ster:—

If thou delight to view thy heinous deeds,
Behold this pattern of thy butcheries:
O gentlemen! see! see! dead Henry's wounds
Open their congealed mouths and bleed afresh!
Blush, blush, thou lump of foul deformity;
For 'tis thy presence which exhales this blood
From cold and empty veins where no blood dwells:
Thy deed inhuman and unnatural
Provokes this deluge most unnatural.
O God, which this blood mad'st, revenge his death!
O earth, which this blood drink'st, revenge his death!

and was about to place his finger on the very wound, when his arm was arrested by a piercing shriek.

The widowed mother had just raised her eyes at the sound of his footfall, and beheld the audacious coolness of his manner.

" Hold ! hold ! horrid murderer ! Touch him not ! Oh, my son—my son ! that ever I should see this day ! Alas ! ——"

" Hold yer peace, you screeching madwoman ; if I'm your son, yer mad words, if yer warn't cracked, 'ud go nigh to hang me. Curse yer throat ; ain't it bad enow for others to try an' make me guilty o' what I know nothing of, without your tightening ——"

" Oh ! wretched woman that I am ! Alas ! Susan, I owe it to him that lies there, stark, cold, and bloody—to him that was the best of sons, and to you, Susan, my dearest girl—though my heart-strings break, and I die in the bitterness of my misery. Mine, wretch ! mine shall not be the hand to ——"

Jerry feared for himself, and he tried to interrupt her.

" Nay, I will be heard ! I will be heard ! Look upon thy butchery—thine ! for, though frantic, I know thee for his murderer ! May the bitter curse thou hast many a time and oft uttered against me and thy blood-stained brother be visited with ten-fold bitterness on thy unrepentant soul ! Thou shalt die by violence—thou shalt perish on the scaffold—thy mother curses thee ! she who watched thy infancy, and loved thee, curses thee, and denies her offspring, and heaven will hear her !"

The frantic woman, overcome by watching, faintness, and excitement, sunk on the ground in a senseless stupor. Susan, raising her voice in lamentations, threw herself on her neck.

The jurors, who had been spell-bound listeners of the awful denunciation of the murderer, entered the apartment, and Mrs. Abershaw and the widow were removed into another room. To take her evidence was now out of the question, as stupor succeeded the delirious ravings of frenzy. Jerry resumed his dogged silence ; he neither admitted nor denied anything, and after hearing some further witnesses, the jury, by direction of the coroner, fully committed Jeremiah Abershaw to stand his trial at the ensuing assizes, for the " wilful murder" of Thomas Trimwell.

CHAPTER XX.

A WOMAN'S LOVE—A DISGUISED FRIEND—AN ADVENTURE—PRISON REGULATIONS SIXTY YEARS SINCE.

JERRY, again an inmate of Horsemonger-lane gaol, became an object of morbid curiosity to that depraved class of sight-seers of the middle and upper ranks of society, who take delight in viewing the most notorious criminals ; and numerous were the fees received by old Briggs, the turnkey, for the favor and privilege of being allowed to have a peep at a ruffian who had made himself so abhorrent to every right-thinking mind, by the number, the audacity, and the blood-thirsty character of his crimes. His aged mother, her reason entirely overthrown by her domestic calamities and the dreadful sights she had witnessed, received the kind attentions of her unfortunate daughter with thankless apathy; more awful and heart-breaking from the quiet despair written in every line of her haggard countenance. As for poor Susan, her health was entirely broken, and her cheerful spirit fled; and, though removed from absolute want by the savings she and her husband had accumulated, and the proceeds of the sale of the goodwill of " The Waterman's Arms," augmented by the kindness of many friends, and the pension of her insane parent, was evidently slowly wasting away, consuming with the canker of her silent sorrow. All this, however, little moved, if he even thought upon such things at all, the desperate author of all this woe.

We will turn from these sad contemplations, to pursue the narrative of the fortunes of the chief actor in this tragic drama.

" When Nero, punished by the justest doom
   Which ever the destroyer yet destroyed,
Amidst the roar of liberated Rome,
   Of nations freed, and a world overjoyed,
Some hands unseen strewed flowers upon his tomb—
   Perhaps the weakness of a *heart* not void
Of feeling for some kindness done, when power
Had left the wretch an uncorrupted hour,"

says Byron; and, if this feeling for the worst of mankind dwelt in the bosom of *man* 2000 years since, it is yet alive in the eternal lifespring, the heart of woman. She *reasons* not, but *feels;* and, whether in lofty or in lowly station, to the man of her choice and of her heart, though black with crime and steeped to the very lips in vice, she is still faithful to the death. How many instances of this might we multiply for the darkest and most disgusting pages of our criminal annals; how commonly do we see its recurrence in the cases of the worst of felons. When the world, from casuistic selfishness or from interest, deterred by a thousand fears of identification with the branded ruffian, shrinks from him and abandons him; when, of all living creatures, none of his own sex remained faithful, there is still oft to be found some heart which is proof against all the world can say: deaf to its truths as to its slanders, blind to the defects, nay, the abhorrent villany of its object, still adheres to its truth, and would risk its all or its little to serve him on whom its faithful affection is fixed, with self-denying and single-hearted zeal. Such an one then yet existed, to whom the God-and-man-abandoned Abershaw was still dear; and that one was Rebekah Morse, the pretty gipsy.

Absorbed, concentrated in self, with no feeling higher than that of the caged hyena, which prowls its den with savage glare, instinctively seeking its escape from the bars of its den, to rend and tear the thoughtless gazers who look upon it with subdued awe, did Jeremiah Abershaw scowl on the many idle visitors who crowded the yard of the prison, where, heavily ironed, he was permitted daily to take exercise.

As yet there was no classification in crime in gaols, and this anointed ruffian, of necessity, took his daily walk among men who were confined in that loathsome, ill-ventilated lazar-house, for misdemeanours, petty assaults, or even for lacking the wherewith to satisfy their creditors; a *crime* yet punished with incarceration, in this enlightened land.

It was on the sixth day of his confinement, that, as he walked the yard, loaded with his heavy manacles, in dogged silence, that his keeper announced to him an indeed unexpected visitor.

"There's a smart, nice young feller in the waiting-room," said a turnkey, with a smirk, to Jerry (the scoundrel had been palmed with a golden fee, in the shape of a seven-shilling piece). "Your brother John is just returned from sea: he looks a likely sort o' chap, Jerry" (Abershaw was treated with distinction, on account of the pecuniary harvest which his detention brought to the lower functionaries); "and he wants a few minutes' prattle wi' ye: but it's agen the rules, Jerry; so cut it short—d'ye mind? *Lag* me if he isn't a nice young chap, and about as like you, no offence, as a goulden rennet's like a tater."

Having delivered this short and figurative speech, the turnkey, without observing Jerry's surprise, left him to introduce the unknown brother.

"*My* brother," inwardly soliloquised Jerry; "I have no brother; I have a sister, and she would hang me—and so would my mother, for that matter—it's none o' them. It's some fellow that wants to make himself great with me, that he may have to say he has talked with Jerry Abershaw, the murderer—ha! ha! I'll see him, though, and astonish him a little. I'm fated to hang for this last job; but I'll die game."

Such were the hardened felon's thoughts, and he was still pacing with measured step his peculiar and proper walk—for the less atrocious prisoners avoided him—when the turnkey drew his attention to an individual who stood at some yards' distance, attentively watching him. Abershaw had grown haggard, and his personal appearance, though a young man, was that, from neglect of dress, which added years to his age. Jerry raised his eyes, and there stood, in the sailor's attire of that day, the plaited jacket (similar to the old waterman's), with apron, encircling leather belt, and broad brass buckle, the slender and Apollo, or, rather, Psyche-like, form of Rebekah Morse.

Her dark hazel eyes were suffused with tears, but this the cunning turnkey attributed to fraternal affection.   At that moment the hardened ruffian felt unmanned—he trembled.

"He's not sich a hout-an'-hout cove as ve thought," remarked the turnkey to a by-stander; " ve vas led to expec' as he'd no more feelin' for man, voman, nor child, nor a crocodile or a millstun!   D'y yer see how shaky he is at the sight of his own brother?   Ay, ay, depend on't, these here slashing crimmunuls—and I've seed a few on 'em—ain't no more nor flesh and blood, arter all."

Having delivered himself of this piece of sound philosophy, though erroneous observation, the turnkey continued to watch his charge.

Rebekah saw, by the language of the eyes—the only language unintelligible to all save those who thus interchange electric thought—that she was recognised. Woman's courage—when was it known to fail?—inspired her.   She approached him, and the murderer was less firm than she was.

"What, Jerry," said she, in a voice that could be well heard by those that listened, " is it in this state I see you, after five years' absence? Oh! tell me, tell me ! is it true? for I'll not believe it but from your own lips! Are you here on a charge ——" she dropped her voice, and cast him a meaning look, " on a charge of murder?"

Jerry looked eagerly at her; he could have clutched her in his arms, but she saw his meaning, and retreated.

"Why, Jerry, you don't speak ! (how could he?)   Here have I been in London all day, and only just now heard from Frank, the waterman, that you were here. Is it—(she cast a glance at the listening turnkeys)—but I don't believe it."

She proffered Jerry her hand, which he eagerly grasped.

"Excuse me," observed the turnkey, approaching; " it's all very vell a shaking of hands, but it's my duty to see as nothing passes."

And he carefully watched that nothing had been given.

Jerry now reassured himself, and they paced the confined court-yard together. At first, by mutual language of the eyes, they conversed on indifferent subjects, and upon each successive turn in the immediate proximity of the watchful turnkeys, their dialogue was raised, and marked in its signification. They spoke of bygone times, of mutual friends and family connexions; which, of course, to use the phrase of one of the listeners, " was all as good as heathen Greek to them."   But when the favourable distance of a few yards intervened, they passed, in short snatches, such dialogue as the following :—

"Dearest Jerry, *how* can it be done?"

"Next turn, I'll tell you.—There was Bob Ruttock and the rest of us, but I know nothing about that, though they charge me with it—*a pair of shoes, you see I'm badly off, and between the soles a file*—we were all there, but though he and the rest of them——"

"*Shall I bring the shoes to-morrow?*—But Jerry, do they charge you with this dreadful murder, when you were not in London at the time that—*who will make them?*"

"*Sam will see to that—'tis all right, they don't suspect you.*—But to think that a mad woman should be believed, 'tis beyond my power of thought.   Yet here I am caged as a felon."

"Alas ! alas !—*to-morrow, at twelve.*   Oh, Jerry.—But here, these good men must have something to drink; I've gold galore, and I'll spend it !"

The few sentences caught by the listeners to this colloquy, were indeed sufficiently unmeaning, save the last; yet from it they gathered that which was to them most important, viz., that their already good profit must be materially enhanced by any indulgence shown to the young sailor.

Rebekah, having effected the object of her mission, departed; but not before she had left a substantial mark of her supposed liberality, in the shape of a money present for drink to the prisoners, an indulgence, anomalous as it may appear to the reader of the present day, so liberally granted to the culprit of the past century, that drunkenness was the exception, not the rule, with all those who could command the means, within the walls of our metropolitan prisons.

Accordingly, the turnkeys, having intercepted the gift professedly intended for the prisoners, besotted themselves that night; and once or twice, in remembrance of the first cause of the visit of the "founder of the feast" drank—

"Success to Jerry Abershaw, and may we never want such an out-and-outer in *our* stone-pitcher !"

Whether their drunken wish for the felon met its appropriate fulfilment, must, however, be reserved for the next chapter.

CHAPTER XXI.

A PLOT—REBEKAH'S INGENUITY—MR. BRIGGS AND THE RUM-BOTTLE—A PITCH
PLAISTER, AND ITS EFFECTS.

THE next afternoon the *soi-disant* brother of Jerry again visited the prison, bear⁻
ing this time a pair of half-boots with extra-stout soles; and Jerry, during the
night, had artfully made such articles appear of prime necessity, by tearing and
wearing those he had on, in such a way as to partially separate the soles from the
upper-leathers. The shoes underwent a careless inspection in the chamber of the
principal turnkey, an examination merely extending to putting the hand inside
them, and thereby ascertaining that no foreign substance was there concealed.
These apparently common-place necessaries, however, held that within their
fabric which was little suspected.

"Jerry's brother must have a tidyish hidear of his chance," observed one of the
gaolers, "if so be he thinks as he's likely to live to wear out such a pair o' stumpers
as these. He's on'y got twelve days to the sessions, and they won't be much worn
by then. Slap-up crabshells,* these," continued the fellow, striking the stout
sole with his knuckle. "We shall have old Abey, the topsman,† a stumping
about like a helephant in pattens, for a twel'month arter this scragging; for
I reckons as Jerry 'ull want no boots to keep his toes warm when he goes to Tum-
mus's hospital. Why the sawbones‡ there reckons on cutting him up, as safe as
if they'd bought his meat,§ and took the stiff-'un as a receipt for the gilt.|| But I
s'pose the pris'ner must have the loan o' these, and sartinly his brother's a trump
as well as hisself."

Thus saying, the official conveyed the much-desired articles to Jerry's place of
confinement, which was in a room, the window of which was strongly grated,
looking out (so far as accumulated dirt would permit) on the back-yard of the gaol
and the blank walls of the houses at the rear of the prison. The front of the
building, at the time we are writing of, commanded an extended view of the locality
of St. George's-fields, described in the opening chapter of this history. Jerry received the boots with assumed indifference, merely enquiring whether his
brother might be permitted to see him for a short time: accompanying the
request with the proffer of a coin, which was accepted without either question
or scruple.

The gaoler retired, and Jerry's look of indifference changed to one of eager
anticipation. He clutched the boots with a satisfied grin, then minutely scanned
round their seemingly well-stretched welts. Steps were heard approaching, and he
quickly and noiselessly placed them on the ground. The head turnkey entered,
accompanied by the disguised Rebekah.

"I'm blarmed, my young svell, if yer arn't in high favour to get all these here
'dulgences, clean contrary like to the regerlations o' the prison. But yer must cut
it very short, d'ye see, 'cos it's arter hours already."

This speech, in enhancement of the favour granted, was readily understood in
its intended sense; for the pretended sailor, drawing out a tolerably furnished
purse, placed a seven-shilling piece in the "itching palm" of Mr. Briggs, the
gaoler. Gold, eloquent gold, spoke to the purpose; and Mr. Briggs, after another
remark at the immense privilege conceded, positively retired to the door, *almost*
out of earshot of their whispered discourse.

Signals, half-uttered sentences, and the language of the eyes, soon made Jerry
and Rebekah fully comprehensive to each other, and their plan was readily devised. An escape by the window of his cell was hopeless. The massiveness of
the bars, imbedded in solid masonry, together with a formidable chevaux-de-frise
which fringed the sloping roof of a narrow pent-house, which ran along beneath
the windows, all chance of egress was here certainly cut off, to say nothing of the
lofty blank walls beyond. The front of the prison, too, was not likely to be

---

* Cant for shoes.
† Abraham, the hangman; the " finisher of the law," had the clothes of executed criminals for
his perquisites. ‡ Surgeons. § Bodies were then purchased at all the hospitals, and
" resurrection" a thriving calling. || Money.

cleared, as there was a sort of detached guard-lodge at the gate, built in the encircling walls.

Jerry, whose observant powers were quickened by the peril of his situation, had devised another plan. If the door of his cell could only be forced, and he could thus gain the passage leading to the back outlet of the prison, in the narrow lane leading into the Borough-road, he did not fear to escape into the labyrinths of the Mint, and once there, to baffle pursuit. But how the stout and well-secured door, opening upon the aforesaid passage, was to be passed, was as yet a problem; knotty, however, as that problem was, it was solvable, as many other puzzles have been, by the wit of woman.

When woman is once engaged heart and soul in a cause, what can she—what will she not achieve? Rebekah's first idea had been the self-sacrificing one of endeavouring to exchange clothes with Abershaw; but this, upon consideration, was rejected.

" Who locks you in ?" asked Rebekah, in a parenthetical whisper.

" The under gaoler; and old Briggs, there, comes round about half an hour after, to see all right. Sanders seems to keep the keys of these wards; but none but old Briggs himself ever turns the large door-lock of the back wicket. They calls him always to do that, and see everybody as goes out or comes in."

" I guessed as much," replied Rebekah. " Now for *my* plan: can you force *this* door ?" She rather looked than said this, as she glanced her full black eyes at the entrance to the lobby, where Mr. Briggs occasionally treated them to an impatient clank of his keys, by way of reminding them he was in waiting.

Jerry cast his eyes on his boots with a smile, and then replied with an affirmative nod—

" Good! then *I* will give you the key of the outer door."

Jerry gazed in gratified wonderment.

" Nay, don't be astonished: I've said it, and I'll *do* it. Good-bye, Jerry; keep up your spirits—you sha'n't want for a clever lawyer," added she, in a louder tone.

" Now, Mr. Briggs, I'm ready; and thank'ee for your patience," added Rebekah, as that functionary reappeared.

Briggs called his underling, who quickly secured Jerry in his narrow cell, by bolt and lock, then retired to the front lodge before spoken of.

" I should like to take a glass o' wine with you, friend Briggs, for your civility," observed the supposed brother, in an indifferent tone; " but I suppose you can't leave the prison without risk. I should like much to have a social half-hour with you, friend Briggs, but I suppose it can't be managed."

" This is a lib'ral young cove, ven he's sober," said Briggs, mentally; " no doubt as he's more so ven drunk."

" It's a nasty rawish sort of night, to be sure," observed the gaoler aloud; " but duty is duty, Mister Habershaw, and yer see as I carn't quit my post. Howsever, it isn't often as ve gets a genelman as pleasant as yerself, as ve confined pris'ners (for ve airc pris'ners, Mister Habershaw, as much as they ve vatches and vards), can make convarsible like; and it 'ud indeed be a pity to baulk so good a hintention of a pleasant hevening. There's my private room, Mister Habershaw, vere everything it commands, though I says it, but mum's the vord, and if so be as you *aire* inclined for that ere bottle of vine as you spoke of, vy, I'll step out myself, and see as the right sort's got from the King's Bench Coffee-house, and it's scarce a stone's throw off this very place."

" I certainly never make offers out of compliment, friend Briggs," replied Rebekah; " and my only reason for not asking you before was because, knowing your character as an officer, I thought you might think it a liberty."

The head turnkey now entered a little cellar-like room, wherein, although it was yet August, a small fire was burning, on account of the damp coldness of the stone floor, and the thickness of its arched brick ceiling. The night, too, was windy, rainy, and unusually chilly for the time of the year.

" Onseasonable veather, Mister Habershaw," observed Briggs, as he placed a worsted nightcap on his bald head, and surmounted that with a hat.

Rebekah handed him a guinea, and then seating herself near the fire, and beside the little square table, with the intention of concealing the feminine formation of her legs as much as possible, she gave the fire a hearty poke.

" Brayvo, Mister Habershaw; that's right, make yourself at home—shall it be

port or sherry?—for myself, I should like a rummer o' stiff Jamaikey—it's them as pays as is to choose!"

Rebekah declared for port, saying she had been in Spain and Portugal—an assertion which her nut-brown hue fully countenanced. Little did Mr. Briggs suspect the character of his visitor, or the eager gaze with which she watched his every motion as he moved about his little room.

"You see," said he, "as this here's the little master key, as puts the stun on 'em all."

And he removed from its nail, in a little cupboard, a curiously-constructed key, consisting of one stout pin, cross-cut on its upper end, and upon its sides numerous small projections, like abortive, or broken wards. A Chubb or a Bramah would laugh at such an affair, yet our ancestors considered their locks impossible to be picked.

Having contemplated the bright piece of metal with satisfaction, **Mr. Briggs** slipped out, and, passing noiselessly along the lobby, opened the postern gate, closed it carefully, and then hurried down a narrow lane into the Borough-road. Hastening to the tavern, he supplied himself with a bottle of port wine, balancing within himself whether (as he, of course, intended to keep all change, *virtute officii*), he should procure a pint or a half-pint bottle for his liberal young friend.

With the rum, however, he had no such scruples ; for, depositing a sixpence for the loan of a stone vessel, he purchased a quart of the best pineapple, and thus laden, he returned rejoicingly to the gaol.

Short as his absence had been, it had sufficed the nimble Rebekah to trip along the gallery and whisper Jerry of her presence and partial success. Briggs returned ; the door of the little room was closed, stiff grog was brewed, and Rebekah proved so good a listener, that old Briggs inflicted on the supposed youth a terrific yarn about his early experiences, from the time when he was " an unhowned orphant boy," till he grew up into a runner, and thence to the dignified post of gaoler.

Thus he ran o'er the story of his life, even from his earliest youth, like another Othello, much to the delight of Jerry's dingy Desdemona ; who rightly anticipated that the old fellow's chatter would prevent his hearing Abershaw at his operations. At length, in one of the pauses of his rambling discourse, Rebekah heard the low mewing of a cat ! It was the signal that Jerry was thus far at liberty.

"Drat it," observed old Briggs, who was by this time a long way down his fourth tumbler of grog ; " you don't drink, young seaman ; come, tie up yer stockings——"

Rebekah drained her glass, and refilled it.

"Vell, as I was a-saying, I got more ochre, and vhat vas better, permotion, through this here consarn ; let me see, vot vos I a-talking about—oh, about that 'ere feller, Nick Dowzer, as they called him, as escaped from old Nailer—dozy old chap he vos, for a hofficer, to be sure ; don't appint sich cripples now a-days to himportant charges ; vell, as I vos a-saying——Vy, vot the devil's that ? a cat a-miauwing in the gallery, I declares. Oh, von't I be about your house and garden in no time, marm, that I vill." And Mister Briggs was about to take down a heavy blunderbuss from its two hooks over the fireplace.

" You won't fire that piece in the gallery, will you ?" asked Rebekah, with ready wit.

" Vy, true, young man," said old Briggs, withdrawing his unsteady hand, " it vould speak rayther loud, and might vake the children," and the old fellow chuckled at his facetiousness. " But on'y to think, Mr. Habershaw, of the owdaciousness of a cat, to come a mollrowing just by von's door at the moment hof sich a hinteresting conversation—vell, here's luck !" and Mister Briggs took another "nightcap," as he called it.

"I'm afraid it's rather late," observed Rebekah ; " you'll excuse me, but some other evening ——"

"Ay, ay," replied **Mr. Briggs**, drawing from his waistband an old turnip-shaped watch ; " vy, bless my eyes, if it arn't half arter ten ; vell, how time does fly vith pleasant convarsible company ! As you says, some other hevening, I shall be happy —come, take another rosin—here's to our next merry meeting. That's a good toast, though it's an old 'un."

And the thirsty old gaoler, not troubling himself to see that Rebekah merely went through the motion of drinking, suited the action to the word, by pouring down his capacious throat the remaining contents of the rummer.

"Ve must be quiet though, Mister Habershaw, as, d'ye see, this are agen the rules ; not that *I* are subjec' (hic) to the regerlations (hic) of the under-turnkeys, and sich (hic) like : cos, d'ye see, I'm (hic) confidential (hic), as the sheriff said to me last veek but von, 'Briggs,' says he, (hic) ' you've been (hic) a faithful and wigilent (hic) servant (hic) ; there ain't been no (hic) irregulari, (hic) and the likes o' that, since—(hic) it's vonderful how this here vindiness does attack von's stomach arter eating o' much (hic) green meat (hic) ; excuse me (hic), but I'd pork (hic) and greens (hic) for dinner (hic)—but ve're a-vasting o' time (hic), I'll let ye hout—so says the sheriff (hic), say he (hic), ' No (hic) escapes, no prison-breaking (hic) since (hic) you've bin the (hic) gaoler,'—'No, yer (hic) vorship's honner says (hic) I ——"

Rebekah made a gesture of impatience, as though desirous to be gone.

' Ay, ay, but you're a (hic) prisoner," said the old fellow, chuckling, " till *I* shows yer the vay—now valk (hic) as if yer trod on heggs."

Rebekah opened the door, and prudently slipped first into the passage, while the old man with unsteady hand, after several bungling attempts, succeeded n placing a small piece of candle upright in the socket of a horn lantern.

At this moment Jerry sneaked by, and concealed himself in the deep recess of a doorway, near the end of the gallery, whereat the outer door of the prison was situated.

" Cautious ever, you sees," muttered old Briggs; " I never takes a naked (hic) candle (hic) into that 'ere gallery, bycause of the vind, (hic); now then, I'm vith yer—vere's my key?—oh, here it be. Vell, ven shall I see yer agen, my young friend? cos ve can't vell stand talking at the gate."

Rebekah, assured of Jerry's position, again stepped in. " To-morrow night."

" That's yer sort," replied old Briggs, groping for her hand; " vy, vot a very small daddle you has for a sailor," observed he; for, half-drunk as he was, the hand of Rebekah felt like velvet in his horny palm. " Come on then, to-morrow night! This vay, if you please."

The fuddled gaoler crept slowly along the arched passage; steadying his steps by leaning his right hand, which grasped the master key, against the wall.

They had now arrived at the gate, where Mr. Briggs made several abortive attempts at fitting the bright implement in the small round hole in the projecting socket of brass. He little thought who stood behind him, eagerly watching his uncertain motions. It was Jerry Abershaw, who, grasping a short iron bar, glowered with fiend-like exultation on his unconscious victim.

Rebekah, however, by a look and motion, prevented his intended blow; and, recognising her meaning, he nodded assent. Rebekah passed her hand behind her, and Jerry took from it a large piece of rolled white leather. It was smeared with Burgundy pitch, and Rebekah had kept it in a semi-fluid state by close contact of the leather with her person.

Jerry grinned, as he quietly unrolled it to its full extent, and placed it on his dexter palm.

Briggs made another and another fumble; he was evidently of the opinion of that facetious diner-out, who complained bitterly of the knave who had stolen the keyhole of his street-door.

" Allow me," said Rebekah.

" No, no," replied old Briggs, testily; " if I can't get the better on it, how should you?"

Jerry grew impatient: and there was indeed cause for alarm, as some person might come that way.

" I'll manage it, if you'll let me," said Rebekah, taking hold of the key with gentle force. It was inserted, and turned smoothly and slowly.

The well-oiled bolts of stout iron slid back into their box, and the heavy door opened softly.

Rebekah stood in the opening. " Good-night," said she, grasping the right hand of the gaoler.

What his reply might have been, must remain unrecorded; for the next moment sight, smell, and speech were gone: one vigorous application of the pitch-plaister effectually preventing either eyes, nose, or mouth, performing their natural functions. To add to the bewilderment of poor Briggs, Jerry further hit him such a tremendous drive in the poll of the neck, that the somewhat corpulent old gentleman fell stunned at the bottom of the flight of stone steps, which led up to the gateway; where leaving him in piteous plight, we will follow the flight of Jerry and his devoted deliverer.

We have said that the night was dark, miserable, and rainy, and this materially facilitated their flight; for, though it was not yet eleven o'clock, the dismal, dirty neighbourhood of St. George's-fields, which looked, with its unfinished houses, brickfields, and tumble-down cottages in progress of removal, a very chaos of odds and ends—a sort of warehouse for the surplus materials of a projected town or city, was literally deserted. They did not stay long to consider their route, but pushing across the Walworth-road, took their way towards Norwood, then, as for many years afterwards, the favourite resort of the gipsy tribe.

At this celebrated spot Rebekah conjectured that she was sure to meet with friends and shelter, until further steps could be determined on.

They arrived at the encampment about one o'clock, and Rebekah having explained, in the peculiar gibberish of the race (a pretended dialect of the ancient

Phœnician), the position of Jerry, he was readily made as comfortable as circumstances would permit. Not more from the kindred which Rebekah claimed, than from the inbred feelings of these sons of Ishmael, who, having, as they choose to pretend, the hand of every man against them, extend their hand against every man upon the principle of retaliation: indeed, it is a part of the gipsy creed, that as the *law* of the land in which they sojourn extends no protection to them, it is a part of their duty to protect and shelter those who may break or defy that law. At least, such *was* their principle when they were strong enough, and sufficiently numerous and exclusive to deserve the name of a distinct people. Enclosure acts, the increase of population, and the improvements of our rural police, have, however, exterminated the gipsies in their advance, even as the red man has perished and died out before the march of the civilised settler, until the crafty and peculiar knave, the darkness of whose speaking eye bespoke his oriental origin, "has degenerated into the drunken, travelling shoemaker or tinker," whose sprawling progeny beg by the roadside, or turn somersaults before the carriages of the travelling gentry, dividing their time between their out-of-door recreations and the insides of the various houses of correction, to which their vagabond propensities continually introduce them. But we are digressing, and will resume, in the next chapter, the thread of our story.

CHAPTER XXII.

JERRY SCORNS INGLORIOUS EASE—DUFFING—A LAND-GULL, AND A LAND-SHARK—
DANGER OF CHANCE-ACQUAINTANCE—A BARRICADE—FOOTPADS—A DILEMMA, AND
A HOT SUPPER

A FEW weeks were spent by Jerry and his *chere amie*, Rebekah, in wandering from place to place with the encampment of her tribe; but Jerry, whose active temperament " scorned inglorious days of ease," soon became weary of their pastoral life: the mere robbery of hen-roosts, or the stripping of washing linen from hawthorn-bushes or alders, was too petty a spoil for one like him, corrupted with debauchery and desperation, and used to the richer prizes of the footpad or the burglar. Such petty knaveries had no relish with them; they were like " thin potations " to the seasoned bacchanalian, or plain food to the pampered palate of the gourmand. Alexander the Great (homicide) killing flies (though Jerry had never heard of that wholesale murderer, whose history is specially preserved for the reading of our aristocratic youth), could not have been more weary of his trifling slaughter than Jerry, who had swallowed the strongest draughts of crime, and sounded its lowest depths, did at this milk-and-water sinning; these shallow pilferings of stray ducks and hens, and well-worn shirts, shifts, and towels. He therefore determined no longer to rust in inaction; and communicating his ideas to Rebekah, he found in her thoughts a ready response to his own.

" Bekha," said he, " I'm sick of this sort o' life; let's move out a bit into the world. I knows a thing or two as my seafaring life and the waterside business have taught me, and why shouldn't I turn it to account. These 'ere gipsy coves, it is true, are down to a thing or two, but they an't fit to hold a candle to such as have been put awake in the right school. We've a few shiners by us, and what say you to a trip through the country, on the duffing suit? There's them as I knows as does it up tidyish in that line, by never letting a chance go by."

Rebekah assented, and their future proceedings were thus arranged. Jerry was to go down to the coast of Sussex, whereon at that period dwelt many of the most notorious smugglers, engaged in running silks, shawls, and brandies, from France; tobacco, Schiedam, and cigars, from Holland; tea and bandannas, from inward-bound ships; and all the numerous commodities on which enormous duties offered a large per centage of premium to the contraband trader.

Jerry's plan was this: that after furnishing themselves with a stock of commodities, India shawls, bandannas, and tobacco for himself, and Brussels lace, trinkets, &c., for Rebekah, that they should travel through the country, ostensibly in search of customers, though in reality using their wares as a cover for ulterior designs; what they were he buried in his own bosom, though the reader may easily suppose they had little relation to trading. Even that pursuit which some satirists have described as systematic cheating, in Jerry's hands became something more; for he had no sooner possessed himself of a handsome India shawl of high price and value, than he immediately purchased a trumpery Manchester affair, of somewhat similar colour and pattern, which he folded to look as much like the real one as possible; thus being prepared, like a skilful duffer, "to ring the changes" on the unwary purchaser. Rebekah, too, was similarly supplied with a few good articles for exhibiting and attracting customers, and a stock of inferior ones to foist off upon those who might cheapen and purchase the really good. Jerry now equipped himself fully in seaman's attire, and having stained his visage to a reddish brown, and furnished himself with a jet black wig, with corkscrew ringlets, the hopeful pair set out on their adventures.

The first few days, keeping along the line of coast, they found few persons willing to inspect, much less to purchase their wares, so numerous were the vendors of contraband commodities in that district, and Jerry became somewhat tired of his new occupation, seeing that the farmers of Sussex and their dames kept the apparent smuggling trader at a whole yard's length from their front doors; and more than once some gruff householder talked of setting the big dog at them, if they tried to come nearer the house than the wicket at the end of the front garden.

"We wants no longsided dealers here, wi' them sham shawls an' laces, a gammonin' the womankind into all sorts o' extravagances, not we. Buy! ay, if the womankind had their way, they'd buy theirselves and their husbands and childers all out o' doors in no time, wi' your beyond-sea nicknackeries—come, trudge! pack! we want none on 'em here! Be off, or I'll set Towzer at ye, ye king-cheating vagabones!"

Jerry marked the abusive old fellow in his mind for revenge, and passed on.

They now resolved to try more inland counties, and accordingly quitting Lewes, they pushed off towards Croydon, in Surrey, where they met with better success. Arriving late in the little town, they rested there; Jerry, as was his custom, mixing with the guests in the parlour of the public-house, in order to pick out proper objects to practise on, and learn the news that might be afloat. He represented himself as a sailor just returned from the Indies, and had not long been among the agricultural party assembled in the parlour of the Jolliffe Arms, before he turned their conversation, which had before been of fat bullocks, weighty pigs, and "southdown" and "Leicesters," harrowing, horse-shoeing, dibbling, and broadcast; Farmer This's plough, and Farmer That's beans, peas, turnips, "whoats" or vetches, to the always-interesting subject to a landsman—of the wonders of the deep.

Jerry, safe of his audience, spared them not, and indeed he pitched them some salt-water yarns, which might have well passed muster among the best galley-stories that ever excited the wonderment of a mess on a sailor's Saturday night. Travellers see strange things, and Jerry took care to cram his gaping auditory with the strangest. He told them stories of shipwreck, privation, and suffering; of wars, battles, and merry-makings; of monstrous fish, phantom ships, albatrosses, and Mother Carey's chickens, and finally introduced his wares.

One wealthy old farmer was there, who resided some three or four miles from Croydon (for it was market-day), and who had prolonged his stay at the Jolliffe Arms, was much struck with Jerry's romances, and being in a state of strong ale and generosity, he invited the apparent seaman to accompany him home.

"'Twill be time enow in the morning," observed he, "for my dame to take a look at yer fineries; meanwhile, as you're 'one as has guarded our land,' as the old song says, order your grog, and I'll pay the reckoning. My horse and chay is down the yard, and I'll drive you home wi' me, if you likes the offer."

"Avast there, neighbour," replied Jerry; "I never allow any one to square the books for me, while I've a shot in the locker; no, no, it's time to dip in your neighbour's kit when your own's empty. Blow high, blow low, a friend's a friend, and Jack Sheavehole never imposes on good natur. I've rhino enow for myself, and I'll settle my own score; nevertheless, as I ain't 'xactly up to the navigation of these parts, I'll put myself under your convoy, for fear o' th' land-sharks."

The pipes were resumed, and about ten o'clock, Jerry, taking the opportunity of slipping out of the Jolliffe Arms, informed Rebekah of his success in obtaining an introduction to the house of a wealthy farmer; an introduction he doubted not to be able to turn to profitable account.   A rendezvous was, accordingly, appointed for Rebekah, at noon the following day, about two miles on the London side of the farm-house.   These matters arranged, Jerry returned to the drinking party.

More grog was drunk, and more stories told, each exceeding the other in improbability and extravagance; and it was near twelve when the well-fuddled farmer, with the seeming sailor, took his departure from the Jolliffe Arms, well strapped in by the apron of the leathern convenience, lest a stumble of his steed might roll his well-filled carcase into the road.

Farmer Thrasher having applied his heavy whip with a hearty thwack to the sides of his stout cob, the lumbering chaise jolted out of the paved yard of the Jolliffe Arms, sluing round into the roadway with a tremendous lee-lurch," as Jerry called it, and no small danger of a "spill." But fortune favours drunken men, and Farmer Thrasher's vehicle righted as they came to a bearing in the centre of the highway.

" Cussed awk'ard place that," exclaimed the farmer; " enow to break down anything but a well-timbered chay.   Made the old lancewood spring agen. So-ho, Ball! gently!" and they proceeded along the dark road at a swinging trot.

Once clear of the village, they were in darkness, and as the farmer appeared to be fast dropping off into a half-drunken lethargy, leaving the road to the choice of " Ball," who was certainly the more sensible and careful animal of the two, there seemed every probability of their reaching home without further mishap. Indeed, the horse evidently knew every step of the road, being well used to carry his master home, on such occasions as this, with little or no guidance.

As Farmer Thrasher was taciturn, and Jerry full of thought and scheming, they jogged on silently, until Ball, coming to a lane which led through the fields to Farmer Thrasher's homestead, slackened his trot to a walk, and turned into the narrow roadway with great care and judgment.   They had, however, scarcely gone a dozen yards, when the sagacious steed came to a dead stand-still.

" Cus the beast !" exclaimed the farmer; " what does he stop for? Kim up !" and he applied his thong heavily; an indignity which the horse resented by backing from some object just before him in the dark road, and by a diagonal retrogression planting the wheels of the chaise against the mudbank beside it. This woke Farmer Thrasher, who accompanied a hearty oath or two with another smart application of the whip; but Ball would have his own way, and that way was to attempt (in vain) a still further retreat.

" There seems to be something in the road," said Jerry; " shall I jump out and see what it is ?"

" No! blarm his carcase !" said the farmer; " there's nothing there—it's one of his old jibbing tricks, but I'll cure him.   Kim up! kim up !"

Another shower of blows put Ball so much upon his mettle, that he fairly reared up on his hind legs, and in another moment, had not Jerry sprung out and caught him by the bridle, they would have been all three rolling in the ditch.

Having brought the animal's fore-feet to *terra firma*, Jerry requested the farmer to sit still, a request which he, with an ill-grace, complied with; revenging himself for the self-restraint by devoting the horse's eyes and members to a place never " mentioned to ears polite." The cause of their obstruction was now manifest to Jerry.   Athwart the narrow lane lay a large log of wood and an overturned wheelbarrow; and just as he stooped to find out the readiest way of moving this evidently planned barricade, three fellows sprung from the hedge. The taller and stouter grasped Jerry by the collar, and brandished a formidable bludgeon over his head.   Jerry knew in an instant it was—the Patrico.

" What, don't you know Jerry—your pal ?" half whispered Abershaw.

The man's grasp relaxed instantly.

" Hist! don't you seem to know me," added Jerry: then changing his tone, he exclaimed: " Ah, you scoundrel!   Robbers, thieves, murder ! and performing a pretended struggle with the Patrico, who thwacked his bludgeon heavily twice or thrice on the log of wood, Jerry fell on the ground with a well-dissembled groan.

Meantime, the other two villains dragged the bulky farmer from the chaise; and, despite his remonstrances, rifled his pockets.   They then bound the farmer; and Jerry, having crept slily through the hedge with the Patrico, the following whispered converse passed between them :

" Why, how the devil came you in the drag with that old porpoise?" hastily inquired the Patrico.

" How the devil came you to stop us?" asked Jerry, in turn.

" It'll take too long to tell," replied the Patrico; " but Sam and Leary Joe are with us. We've bin a-watching for this old bloak two hours. How's the swag, Jerry; for you seem to have got the length of his foot?"

" All right," replied Jerry; " but I must lay down in the road—he mustn't suspect me, for I ain't half done with him."

" Brayvo, Jerry," muttered the Patrico; " you are a trump anyways. First I thought you was burnt, the night I lost you in the Mint, in that blazing fire—then you was booked to be scragged; but we heard from Leary Joe how you'd doubled the dubsman, and now we find you as thick as three in a bed, riding wi' an old bloak wi' lots o' gilt—what's to be the next turned wonders—but we mustn't prate here, as you rightly says."

Jerry again laid himself down beside the log in the dark lane, and interlarded the Patrico's calls to his comrades with piteous groans.

" Come, look alive, lads, and clean out the old 'un, for we must be off. I've plucked my bird, I can tell ye."

" Hurry no man's cattle," replied Leary Joe. " Now, old buffer, if you stir for half a hour from this here spot, we'll come and slit your puddin'-bag for you; d'ye hear?"

" Oh, Lord!" groaned Farmer Thrasher, whose dress they had completely rummaged, as he leaned, with his hands tied, in a half-reaching posture, against the bank. The robbers retreated through the hedge by the way they came, and hastened across the fields. No sooner did Jerry hear their receding footsteps than he called out to his fellow-traveller.

" Where are you, old friend?" inquired he.

" Ugh! ugh! ugh! the darn'd villains!" coughed the farmer: " which way did they go? I'll raise the county on 'em. I'll sue the hundred for my loss. They ha' robbed me o' eighty pun' in goold—oh, Lord, oh dear! And they ha' tied my wristes wi' a hard cord as cuts 'em like a knife. Lend us a hand to untie 'em, my good friend, and I'll take it as a kindness the rest o' my life."

" They ha' robbed me of ten guineas and all my shawls—have they took the bundle from the chay?"

" Nay, a' knows nought on't," replied Farmer Thrasher, sulkily: " but a'll hang 'un every one, or there's no law i' the land. Oh, my wristes! whereabouts are you—eh?"

" I'm tied both legs together," replied Jerry; " but I'll soon be loosed—there! Oh, the wretch, he's broken my back, I do think. If they hadn't taken me at a nonplush," added he, coming near the farmer, " I'd have shown 'em sport—the landsharks. There's no such thieves at sea, as ketches a feller up a dark lane, and hits him behind his back afore he's aware on 'em. Come, show us your hands: have you got a knife? They've taken mine."

Jerry now fumbled with his teeth at loosing the cord, which, having purposely taken a long time to untie, he helped the groaning farmer into the chaise. He next took some five or ten minutes to remove the log and the wheelbarrow, which obstructed their progress, and, having received the thanks of the farmer for his exertion, he got into the chaise, and they resumed their journey.

A few minutes brought them to the front gate of Farmer Thrasher; who, having roared lustily, and with unusual ill-temper in his voice, a shock-headed rustic appeared, bearing a horn stable-lantern, and led the horse up the yard, and by the farmhouse, towards the stable at the rear.

" I've turned over to-night's disaster in my mind, and second thoughts is best," muttered the farmer to Jerry in an undertone; " mum's the word to the woman-kind, mind ye, my young feller. There's my dame al'ays a foreboding as I'd be robbed some night a coming whoam late, and now it's happened, she'll discourse so, as I shan't never hear the last on't—so mark me, not a word about what's happened, and to-morrow we'll go to Justice Craven's, and tell 'un all about it. D'ye catch the idea, eh? Mum's the word."

The farmer's loss had thoroughly sobered him, and as this resolve precisely jumped with Jerry's wishes, he readily promised secresy. They were soon within doors, where, though the womankind of the house were gone to bed, they found a good fire kept in against the farmer's return, and abundance of substantial cheer, in the shape of bacon, eggs, cold salt beef, and humming ale, spread on a clean white table, in the large, oak-beamed kitchen ; for Farmer Thrasher was a surly, morose, domestic tyrant, and none of his household dared to neglect his creature comforts.

Jerry soon made himself at home. A hearty supper was eaten by both, and the misfortune of the night brooding in the mind of the old fellow, he revenged himself by swallowing horn after horn of the strong beer, pressing Jerry to do the same, that, in about an hour, he was fast asleep in his arm-chair. As for Jerry, after taking a survey of all around him, which bore the mark of comfort and competency, he was ushered by the rustic chamberlain before-mentioned (who had been kept employed for the whole time bringing tobacco, drawing beer, dragging off the boots of the old farmer, and administering to his many wants, which his ill-temper multiplied innumerably), to a sleeping apartment on the upper-floor, where, leaving him to revolve in his working brain the best mode of turning his present position to account, we will close this chapter, intending in the next to look after his further proceedings at the hospitable farmhouse, wherein the unsuspected scoundrel is now domiciled.

CHAPTER XXIII.

A DANGEROUS INMATE—A SCHEME—A BURGLARY—BORROWING A HORSE—EXECU-
TION-DOCK.

WE left Jerry at the house of Farmer Thrasher. On the morning after the robbery he arose early, and spent the hour or two previous to the farmer's getting up in a careful survey of the premises, under pretence of gratifying his sailor-like curiosity by wondering at everything he saw, from thrashing and chaff-cutting to the milking of the cows, and the churning of butter by the dairy-maids. At length the farmer made his appearance, and having taken Jerry into his confidence, informed him that it was his intention to let the matter rest where it was ; for the farmer was an obstinate, wrong-headed, and positive man, and he cared more for the mortification of letting it be known that he had been robbed, than the mere loss of the cash taken from him. Jerry, it may be easily supposed, did not very strenuously oppose this resolution : and the bundle of shawls, &c., which he had with him, being found safe and untouched under the seat of the chaise, so soon as breakfast was over he made a present of one of them to the farmer's wife, and another to his daughter, a proceeding which resulted exactly as he desired ; for it put him on such a good footing with the womankind, as well as the farmer, that he was pressed to stay a day or two at the house. This, however, he declined, upon the ground that he wished to go to Kingston, where he said that he had some friends residing, but he promised to call again in three or four days, when on his return to his ship, which he told them was lying below Gravesend ; on which occasion he would again trespass on their hospitality. He then took his departure, the farmer driving him a few miles on his road, when they separated to pursue their several routes ; the farmer to proceed to town to draw some cash from a cornfactor in the City, to cover the loss he had experienced, and Jerry to rejoin his scoundrelly associates, with the welcome information.

Jerry soon found the gipsy encampment, and having communicated to Sam, Leary Joe, and the Patrico, his good success, their plan for robbing the farm-house was soon devised.

The third day saw Jerry, true to his promise, again approaching the homestead of Farmer Thrasher, who welcomed the supposed sailor with as much cordiality as was consistent with his rough and uncouth nature. He further informed him, that he was about to ride over a distance of some ten miles to a dinner of agriculturists at a market town, and to this jollification he invited Jerry. The latter, however, declined the proffer, on the plausible pretext of the necessity of his departure early in the morning for his destination ; and the farmer was by no means loath to accept his excuses, and thus acquire what he thought a cheap reputation for civility and generosity in having made such an offer. Jerry was therefore left to the entertainment of the females. Feigning an indisposition, he retired early, and soon after dark, letting himself gently down from his bedroom window, he alighted

on a heap at straw covered with a rick-cloth, and stole cautiously out of the back of the premises, and making his way down a lane, soon joined his confederates.

"'Tis all right, my lads," said he, "and even better than I bargained for. Old Grumble is gone to a booze, and there's none to stop us. I've more than a guess, too, where the blunt is stowed, so give us my crape and the long coat, and I'll pilot you to the plunder in less than no time."

All was silent as they rapidly strode on towards their point of destination, which a few minutes' walking brought them in sight of. Cautiously they surveyed the outhouses and homestead: all seemed still; but in the apartment which served as a sitting-room for Dame Thrasher, and which was considered the best apartment, or parlour, of the substantial yeoman, her husband, a faint light glimmered. The room was on the ground-floor, at the side of the irregularly-built farm. Cautiously opening a gate which led into the rick-yard, Jerry and his comrades stole round the wall, until they gained a position by which they could obtain a peep at the interior. Jerry motioned with his hand for his companions to keep back. Through the curtains of red worsted, he perceived the dame, weary with watching, dozing in a high-backed chair; while, on the opposite side of the fire-place, in a like sleepy state, sat Moggy her maid.

Apprehension at their lonely situation, all their male protectors being absent, had induced old Thrasher's dame to determine upon not going to bed. He had scarcely time to take a synopsis of the apartment, when the dame awoke from her uneasy sleep.

"Moggy Moggy!" cried she, in a querulous tone; "drat the hussey, she sleeps like a top. Can't you keep your eyes open, as I do? Get up, and walk about, you lazy slut; your master might knock and bawl the house down afore you'd hear him."

And here, quitting her seat, she seconded her remonstrance by a tweak of the ear, and a slap of the back.

"Bless me, what's that?" exclaimed she, as Jerry made a slight noise, in treading over some loose sticks near the wall.

Moggy rubbed her eyes, and declared she heard nothing.

"It's a cat, I dare say," added she, in a deprecatory tone.

"A cat, indeed!" rejoined her mistress; "so you'd say, if there were a dozen of villains just going to break in and ravish us! Get up, you sleepy wretch! There it is again. It's your master come home!"

The last observation gave Jerry a hint; therefore, without further hesitation, they made their way to the front entrance, and there, with two or three lusty raps of a cudgel, demanded admittance. Moggy made her way, half-sleeping, to the door, and lifted the heavy oaken bar, which was its only fastening, and in one instant found herself seized round the waist, and her vocal powers completely extinguished by the tight application of a cloth to her mouth; while, before Mistress Thrasher had time for more than an abortion of a scream, the *persuader** of Leary Joe was so close to her head as to deprive her usually active clack of all its powers.

"Silence, or you're no better than a dead woman!" said Joe, in a deep growl of intimidation, so unlike his natural voice, that Jerry almost laughed outright at its mock-tragic tone.

"Seat yourself in that chair, madam, if you please," added he, in a tone of ludicrous politeness.

The lady, escorted by the horrid weapon, which ever and anon touched her ear, did so. Here Sam secured her with her own scarf and sundry handkerchiefs, and motioning Jerry, he also made fast the hands of Moggy by tying them behind her back; and, laying her quietly down on the floor, he fastened her thick ancles similarly together. These preparations made, and the back window having been unfastened, in order to secure a retreat in case of being disturbed, they barricadoed the front door. Jerry now, with the most horrid imprecations, threatened death to both the females, should they give the least alarm; and warning Dame Thrasher that obstinacy would be worse for her, demanded a disclosure of whatever valuables she might have upon the premises. She had, however, recovered from the first shock of alarm; fear of her violent husband rose on her mind, and she most doggedly resisted all attempts to force a disclosure; accordingly, the twain set about the search. A lofty oaken cabinet with panels first attracted their attention, and with many a fervent aspiration for the arrival of her spouse and his men, did the Mistress Kitty witness their endeavours to force it. At length it yielded, and displayed on its shelves divers pieces of ancient china, and smaller receptacles, in the shape of an escrutoire, with numerous nests of drawers, &c. These were consecutively overhauled, and as each delivered up its store of "apostle spoons," silver pap-boats, and other heir-looms of the wealthy family, a deep groan burst from the owner's bosom as they rapidly found their way into the capacious pockets of the housebreakers. At length they paused in their search, and the old woman's heart leaped with joy, despite the plunder she had witnessed; but her anxiety overshot the mark. Numerous things, too bulky or of too little value to carry off, were turned over and rejected.

"There is nothing more, good gentlemen, nothing more, I do assure ye," said she, finding her tongue. "Pray, good gentlemen, don't do us any bodily harm; you've got all we possess—I ——"

---

* Loaded pistols were called, in thieves' slang, *persuaders*.

"Silence, you old hag!" exclaimed Sam, "or I'll brain ye!"

He paused a moment, in the attitude of listening.

"The Lord send us deliver——"

Jerry cut the speech short by suddenly presenting his pistol.

"Have you no money?" demanded he.

"Lord bless you, no! My husband, good gentlemen, al'ays carries it with him —and—oh, Lord! oh, Lord!" burst from her, despite the fear of the presented fire-arms, for at that very juncture, Jerry, who had been scanning the shelves of the cabinet, raised a large inverted punch-bowl on the topmost ledge; beneath it was a small turned wooden bowl, above the rim of which a red canvass bag of plethoric bulk raised its tightened neck, encircled by a cravat of drawn yellow tape. To seize and lift its heavy body from its resting-place was the work of a moment: the ligature was severed, and into the bowl rolled the "good Queen Annes," and bright yellow "spades" guineas of "the three Georges," with that dull melodious chink, so peculiarly the property of the most precious of metals. Jerry's eyes glistened as he beheld the Pactolian stream, and tossing a strong silk handkerchief to Sam, he bade him secure them in it. This was soon done, to a running accompaniment of groans and exclamations from Dame Thrasher. Their task completed, the dame was contriving in her active mind how, upon their departure, which she now immediately calculated upon, an alarm might be most effectually given; but she reckoned without her host; they were in no such a hurry, and having supplied themselves with a cut of bacon from a gammon standing in a dish on the table, and a bottle of wine from her own private corner-cupboard, the unwelcome visitors demolished the good cheer with the utmost cheerfulness and sang-froid; then, after repeating their threats, and declaring that they would return and destroy them if any alarm were given for two hours, during which time they would stay upon the premises, they departed.

"By the bye, Jerry," observed Leary Joe, "now we are out, I've a little bit of a matter on my mind. D'ye know of any tidy stock hereabout, where we could borrow a horse?"

"The best I know in that line, is the very man whose farm we have just left; he takes the prettiest 'strings' to Kingston, in the saddle-horse line, of any man in these parts."

"He's one of the righteous sort," replied Joe, "and 'twould only be doing the thing complete to borrow horseflesh to carry off our rather weighty swag; shall we return?"

So said, so done. Guided by Jerry, whose accurate knowledge of the premises saved all loss of time, they were soon in Farmer Thrasher's stable; but, to their disappointment, found but four heavy cart geldings and one smart roadster.

"Take that and saddle him," said Joe; "I'll do with one of these 'punches.'"

"Stay a moment," replied Jerry; "he has a chaise-house, with a double-stall stable, in the other yard;" and before Sam had drawn the girths of a saddle which he found hanging up on the wall, and made ready the roadster, Jerry returned, leading an excellent stout galloway.

Sam surveyed the prize with delighted eyes.

Leading them from the yard, not without looking in at the window and terrifying the two manacled females by a farewell volley of threats, they were soon in saddle, and cantered merrily off towards London with their booty, first handing the Patrico twenty guineas for his share, and Jerry promising to let Rebekah know of his whereabout as soon as possible.

"I'm thinking," said Jerry, "that my name's too much up in the Mint to make Southwark a hiding-place for any of us; so what say you, my lads, to Wapping?"

The idea was approved of, and they made their way along Kent-street to old London-bridge, crossing which and turning to the right, they were among the vile dens near Execution-dock, as the day broke. Having tied their horses to the palings of a wharf, in a narrow lane, they there deserted them, thinking that longer retaining them might lead to discovery, and proceeded to look for shelter and refreshment.

CHAPTER XXIV.

WAPPING, IN THE EIGHTEENTH CENTURY—CRIMPS, KIDNAPPERS AND JEWS—A
RIOT—A CONFLAGRATION.

NUMEROUS are the incidental notices of this precious rookery, in books of the
early part of the last century, when it was notorious for containing a number of
infamous " crimping-houses," as they were called. Each of these bore the sign of
a liquor-shop ; and certainly the decencies of society have much improved, if half
we read be true of these dens of iniquity and debauchery. These crimps were a
race of human spiders, wretches who gained their livelihood by entrapping intoxicated and unwary young men, and having seduced them into one of these dens,
drugged them and robbed them ; these villains having thus done with their dupe,
he was in this state of insensibility carried on board a receiving ship for the navy ;
or, by a preconcerted understanding with some recruiting-sergeant, the luckless
victim, on recovering his senses, found himself kidnapped.

The uninformed reader may suppose this romance ; it is far from it. " Ward's
London Spy," and twenty other books of a later period, not only detail these matters, but such was the state of legislative morality at that period, that a reward
was given to these wretches for " procuring " an able seaman or soldier for the
king. In front of one of these dens, Jerry and Leary Joe stopped. Early as was the
hour, this neighbourhood was populous. Fellows who had been drunk in the
streets all night, houseless vagabonds, thieves, and prostitutes of a low order, resorted to it because of the " early houses " it contained. Indeed, owing to the
market there held for fish and vegetables, it was " all alive, oh !" hours before day-
break. They entered cautiously by a descending step into this cave of darkness,
peering forward to accustom their eyes to the imperfect light. Mingled sounds of
cursing, swearing, and merriment rose from within.

" We are safest in a crowd, Joe," observed Jerry ; and acting on this opinion,
they entered a low-roofed room, from the ceiling of which swung a train-oil lamp,
such as may now be seen at sheeps' head and tripe vendors' open windows in the
lowest neighbourhoods. This dirt-begrimed den was styled the parlour, and
therein sat five or six men, who, by their long coarse duffel coats of dirty white,
huge brown gaiters of undressed hair, and blue aprons coiled in a twist round the
middle, evidently belonged to the fish-market. They were apparently engaged in
business matters, had a tankard or two of ale before them, and were smoking their
pipes, though the sun had scarcely risen, while one of their party was cutting
away at some cold salt beef. They paused in their conversation and bargaining on
our hero's entrance, and looked at him suspiciously ; and as the mud-spattered
panes of the window of this apartment commanded a view of the street, he
thought he had better dive into some less exposed part of this hostelry. They retreated from the room, which the men, by their countenances, showed was considered by them as a good riddance. Pushing their way past a counter, at which
several wretched objects were swallowing liquid fire in the shape of execrable half-
rectified spirits, they found another apartment of much larger dimensions, and, if
possible, more filthy than the first. It was crammed with company of a still
rougher description than the occupiers of the room they had left. Several recruits,
in a beastly state of drunkenness, lay about on the benches ; in one corner a Jew
crimp was bargaining with a swarthy-looking sea-captain for the price of the unconscious piece of humanity which lay hard by, snoring under the influence of a
sleep induced by a drugged potation, from the effects of which he would wake
only to find himself a slave, in what Johnson describes in his day as " a floating
prison, with the additional horror of but one plank between yourself and destruction."

The reader must bear in mind we are writing of nearly a century since. Smol-
lett's novel of " Roderick Random " may give him some idea of the filth, misery,
and incoveniences of even a king's ship of eighty years ago ; but all these discom-
forts, multiplied up to misery by the total absence of all medical assistance ; the
prevalence of scurvy in the most loathsome forms, and the imperfect art of preserving the most ordinary provisions, rendered a mariner's life one of privations

and hardships, of which the seamen of our modern merchantmen can scarcely form a bare idea.

One of these scoundrels was putting the finishing ✕ mark to a dirty document, professing to be the "articles" for seven years' service of one of the stupefied fellows who lay near.

"S'help me, mister, but you're too hard! dere's five hog shpent on lush afore ve clapt the kybosh on the kiddy; half-a-bull arter ve'd nail'd him, to ma friend Lipey Aprims, who vill shvear to the 'articlesh' afore de shustish; pesides, de toime of maself and de rest. Shay tree ginnys, or, s'elp me, but I musht ike him on board the king's mashesty's ship for the forty bob;* pesides ——"

"Why, you extortionate Jew thief!" exclaimed the fellow; "you infernal dealer in flesh and blood ——"

"Nay, nay, ma coot Captain Tench, don't pe rash; ve'll shplit de differensh; two ginnys and a half, and you shall have tree strong fellows to-morrow for five more. Am I to haf de refusal?"

"Yes, and be d—d to you!" returned the rough seaman: "it's d—d hard that this hot press should force honest men to deal with such varmin;" and he turned a contemptuous glance from the Jew towards Jerry and Joe.

"Hast a mind for a trip in the good ship Fortune?" asked he; "bound for Virginia, and then on a trip down the Spanish Main. I like the look on ye, young fellows; and to show ye 'tisn't the vally of a canary† or two as makes me chaffer with these land-sharks, I'll give you ten as bounty money! Wilt sail with Captain Tench, my lads, eh?"

Jerry was spared all necessity for answering, for the Jew crimp, who was evidently much annoyed by the blunt seaman's remarks, and mortified at the offer, by which money seemed to be taken from his avaricious grasp, was cut short by a tremendous uproar in the street. Blows, shouts, and imprecations, resounded; the outer doors were slammed to with violence—cries of "Down with them! down with them!" were succeeded by the smashing of glass. It was clear that the populace outside were making an attack on the house. The two Jews grew pale with affright; they looked at each other with chattering teeth—the sailor laughed outright at their fear-stricken faces. The cries grew more tumultuous. Another more violent crash followed, and the two Israelites rushed along the passage in the back yard. A crowd of fellows, armed with bludgeons, burst into the house, and, despite the efforts of the landlord and his satellites, demolished bottles, glasses, and crockery, without stint or remorse. Some rushing up-stairs, commenced smashing the furniture and throwing it out of the window; while others piled it in a heap in the narrow street. Several of the men looked scrutinisingly at Jerry and Leary Joe, but it was clear it was not them they sought.

"By the heaviest holy-stone on the devil's quarter-deck," exclaimed the fellow to Jerry, "but I'm thinking this is no berth for us; so let us make headway and get an offing, or maybe we shall be hailed, and our papers overhauled rather unpleasantly, by some o' these queer craft; keep in my wake, comrade, I'll pilot ye!"

Saying thus, the seaman, slipping his tarpauling hat on his curly sconce, and grasping his stout oaken cudgel, made a way through the entering tide of rioters; but our hero did not follow him. Crash, crash, resounded above and below; the infuriate mob were bursting out the window-frames, tearing down the wainscotings, and even dragging up the floorings; huge pieces of the smoky ceiling of the tap-room in which he stood, fell on the floor—disclosing what a casual observer, five minutes before, would scarcely have conjectured—that a white material had originally been employed in its composition. The din was deafening; at its very height, a yell of triumph rose on the ear, and the next moment, all wan and wobegone, dripping with water and begrimed with soot and cobweb, the miserable pair of scoundrels, whom our hero had lately beheld make off, were dragged along the passage into the room where he stood.

"Smash the —— bloodmongers! slog 'em! murder 'em! down with the crimps!" were the confused cries which met his ears, as a gang of ruffianly fellows surrounded their victims, kept the rest off with their bludgeons, from executing instant justice.

* The then premium for procuring a man for the service.
† Guineas were so called.

"Hanging's too good for 'em!" exclaimed one fellow, who appeared to be a leader. "We'll keel-haul the —— killing Judases, till their dirty souls are washed out of their carcases with salt water!"

"We'll smear 'em wi' pitch, and set light to 'em!" exclaimed another.

"Tar and feather 'em," suggested a third, less sanguinary.

"Mercy! mercy!" shrieked the trembling Israelites. Their voices were drowned in the vociferous clamour.

All this time, Jerry had scarcely observed a slightly-made man, with a patch over his eye, and a flaxen wig, who had been sitting amidst the hurly-burly without attempting to leave the room. Jerry was proposing to Joe to quit the place, when he was checked by a pressure on his arm. He turned, and the stranger, making a significant gesture, remarked—

"Friend, meddle not with what is not your own business. These scoundrels' fate is richly deserved." Then thrusting his patch and wig on one side, he for a moment displayed a well-known face.

Jerry was delighted at recognising the features of Bob Walpole.

"Silence!" said Bob; "the bloodhounds are after me, and as this shindy will be sure to bring some to the spot that I do not wish to see, we'll be off, friend Jerry." So saying, the two left the house, and sallied forth into the street.

A strange scene here met their eyes: hundreds of people blocked up the narrow roadway; a huge pile of broken furniture was raised for a bonfire; and many and loud were the cries for the objects of popular vengeance, that, by a species of Lynch-law, justice might be done on those whom it pleased the sovereign majesty of the people to hang or burn. The fellows they had left inside now issued: they had, it appeared, decided on their plan of operations; for, "tailed" by a tremendous crowd, they made their uproarious way towards the river bank. Whilst they were gone, smoke was seen to escape from the sashless windows of the crimping house: flames followed. The pile in the street was kindled, and, in a few minutes, a conflagration was raised which threatened the destruction, not only of the immediately adjoining wooden tenements, but of the whole neighbourhood. A cry of "The soldiers are coming!" was now heard.

It was well for the safety of the inhabitants of the adjoining houses, and perhaps the neighbouring streets, that the military from the Tower did arrive at this juncture, or there is no knowing how far the work of mischief might have spread. That which was begun in the spirit of "revenge," which Bacon says is "wild justice," by a strong party of seamen, infuriated against those abominations the crimps, and whose design extended no further than the destruction of their den, and the infliction of summary justice upon their persons, was carried on by that numerous class in all great city mobs, consisting of the wantonly mischievous and the designedly wicked; the latter including the thieves and other scoundrels to whom any confusion or calamity is a harvest. Scores of these had already assembled, and, under cover of the riot, indiscriminate plunder and destruction were going on, when the detachment arrived and checked their saturnalia. They also succeeded in rescuing one of the Jews, half alive, from his persecutors; the other (for they had both been cast into the river with cords round their waists, to be dragged therefrom and again immersed at pleasure of their persecutors) had met his death from the blow of a stone, brick, or other missile, during one of his plunges. The arrival of the soldiery not only cleared the street, but they formed a nucleus round which the peaceable citizens gathered. Assisted by them the fire was subdued, but not before seven or eight houses had fallen a prey to its ravages.*

Life is made up of improbable contingencies. Yet how apt are we to say this or that is improbable, when scores of stranger and less likely things happen every hour.

Jerry, his companion, and the old pal they had thus unexpectedly met, took their way down a narrow lane leading to Irongate-stairs, then, wheeling about, the trio were shortly urged by a pair of stout oars, journeying down the river, and

---

* Two men were executed for this riot, in which a notorious crimping house was destroyed; and three or four others subsequently, for robberies thereat. Something similar occurred about 1750, in the Strand, when two brothels were destroyed near the Maypole (the New Church); and Henry Fielding, the celebrated novelist, wrote an account of the execution of a young man concerned in the riot, together with other tracts, he being then a justice of peace for Westminster.—See his collected works.

looking back occasionally at the fire and smoke which curled up from the blazing den of infamy they had just left.

The boat held on its way past Limehouse and Execution-dock, where swung the bodies of several men recently executed for the then every-day offences of murder and piracy on the high seas. Still they held on, passing Cuckold's Point and the noble hospital of Greenwich, until they gained Galleon's Reach; and here, on a swampy point of the Essex shore, the party landed.

CHAPTER. XXV.

A BANK OF DEPOSIT—BOB WALPOLE AGAIN—A MAN-OF-WAR'S BOAT—A PURSUIT—THE ESSEX MARSHES—BLACK SAM'S DEATH, AND CAPTURE OF WALPOLE AND LEARY JOE.

THE four scoundrels with whom our story is now occupied held their way along the path leading from the landing-place, but soon turned aside on to a track less frequented — indeed, only used by those who occasionally came to that desolate-looking swamp to cut osiers for the use of basket-makers.

"I dare say," observed Walpole, "that you wonder why I have brought you to this Noman's-land sort of a spot; but the fact is, that I've lately been doing a little crib-cracking hereabouts, and this is my bank of deposit. It's a pretty safe one, I'm thinking, and has no other customer but myself. However, I was obliged to cut and run about a fortnight since, and having waited till I think all search and alarm is over, I was this day coming down here, when I so opportunely fell in with you at Wapping. Here's a swag worth uncovering, I can tell you; and as I'm not the fellow to keep a share from regular trumps, why this is common stock until more luck shall turn up."

Jerry, Sam, and Leary Joe, briefly explained that they too were in prosperous circumstances, for the gold of Farmer Thrasher was yet about their persons. Nevertheless, the precious quartette went on until Walpole, who had been carefully noting certain marks on the bank of the raised causeway they were traversing, declared that he had found the spot. Advancing cautiously a few steps into the osier-bed, he seized the remains of an old sack, and bringing it out with him, disclosed to them a number of articles of silver plate.

"These go, as soon as possible, to my old friend Israel Crimble, of Bevis Marks," said he; "so now, my lads, who's for town again?"

Jerry, Sam, and Joe, however, agreed that a return to London would be anything but advisable under present circumstances: they were yet consulting, when Jerry observed a rustling among the osiers at some fifty yards distant from the spot they stood on.

"Look there!" cried he; "why, what the devil's that?"

They looked in the direction indicated by his finger, and plainly perceived a bending of the tall sallows near a pathway, full half the distance between themselves and the shore.

"There can't be any animal among these osiers large enough to cause that," said Walpole, doubtfully.

"See! see! there's a man's hat!" said Joe.

"There are one, two, three, if not more of them," added Jerry.

"Pooh! pooh! they've not seen us," said Walpole; "we've only to stand close."

This seemed probable, and they accordingly stood still and stooped.

"Peep over, Jerry, cautiously," whispered Walpole. Jerry did so.

"By G——, they're a party lying in wait for us, or I'm a shotten herring," was Jerry's reply: "there's four or five fellows running like good 'uns along the causeway: and more, there's two scampering along the path below. There, there! they're signalling to something on the river. Stand but a minute, and I'll hurry to the skirt of the bed, and look along the path leading to the river."

Jerry stooped, and ran rapidly along the way they had come; but the prospect was anything but encouraging. Pulling straight for the causeway and landing-place, was a large, bluff-bowed boat, which, by its neat trim, and the regular stroke of its oars, might have been recognised by a less practised eye than Jerry's, as one belonging to a king's ship, and manned by regular seamen. But he could further see in its stern-sheets the cocked-hat of an officer, whose bright epaulets glittered in the sun. He lost no time in speeding back to his comrades.

" Close run, and no mistake," exclaimed he; " let's stick together though, and we may yet tip them the double. There are five fellows on the marshes here; two of them have been watching us since we landed, and they have signalled a boat's-crew, which is now rowing into their aid : let's dash into the osier-beds, and chance it—one may help the other—unless some one has something better to advise."

" Why," replied Leary Joe, " it strikes me that it's nayther more nor less nor su-i-cide, to plump into all this here quagmire, unless we're obligated, and carn't run nowheres else. I'll stick to this here dry path so long as we can run, 'cos I arn't web-footed, and had jist as soon be hanged as smothered."

Jerry darted at him a look of scorn, and leaving the path, followed by Sam and Walpole, had gone some dozen yards before the treacherous soil refused support.

At this moment two of the pursuers, who had come to the end of the cross-path, seeing Leary Joe upon the hard footway, gave a sort of view-halloo, whereon Joe, his fear stimulating his speed, set off at a racing pace along the narrow strip of raised ground in an opposite direction. The halloo of the two fellows, who were of the Thames police, brought assistance, and they took up the pursuit. No sooner had they arrived at the spot where Jerry, with Sam and Walpole, had made their desperate plunge, than the foremost fellow stopped.

" Hereabouts, lads," said he, " hereabouts they've taken ground; and if they ain't bogged, it's queer to me. See, see! there they moves the reeds. Surrender, you varmint, or I fires."

The fellow suited the action to the word by levelling a carbine, or short gun, in the direction of Jerry and Walpole.

The latter, prompted by curiosity to learn how the pursuers stood, popped up his head, and cleared away a few reeds. The fellow thus caught a glimpse of him.

" Bravo!" exclaimed he, with stentorian lungs; " here they are, boys! here they are!" and he accompanied this exulting announcement by discharging his piece in the direction of Walpole's head.

Luckily for that individual, so far as his present escape was concerned, he had caught a sight of the enemy, and while the fellow was shouting to his comrades he shifted his position, so that the charge of large slugs spent itself idly.

The other men now came up, and it was clear to the burglars that the affair would be a close and sharp one. Jerry was now struggling knee-deep in slough, while Leary Joe and Walpole, warned by his position, were scrambling about to find a firmer piece of ground on which to retreat. Every step, however, the soil became softer; and now a new dilemma presented itself. The piece of marsh whereto they had committed themselves was skirted by another path running parallel with the one they had left, and making the plat of boggy ground a sort of parallelogram—at least, three sides of it were flanked by practicable foot-paths. The one—the main-road—ran along its eastern side, the other two on its northern and southern; but at its western end, where it was evidently most saturated with moisture, and therefore most insecure, it sloped into a perfect stagnant morass, terminating in a shallow lake, one of the " breeches" in the river wall, wherein, from its northern and highest end, anglers were wont to take their finny prey.

" This bog will be the death of us, Jerry," said Walpole; " I see no way but from bad to worse."

" If it's queer for us," replied Jerry, who held the presentiment that he was doomed to die a drier death, " it's as bad for them. They daren't follow us—but if they dare, why we can but die here, as well as in another place."

With this scrap of philosophy he nerved himself, and, making a few more plunges, discovered a dim speck, on which, after a few steps, he sate himself down, determined to abide there the worst that fate could bring. Sam, Walpole, and Joe, now took hands, but they were not so fortunate. Pushing straight, one knee deep in mire, and painfully working their way among the long reeds, they found that " union was not strength," in such an adventure, and they parted by mutual consent. Walpole still struggled slowly and with difficulty, his two comrades diverging laterally to the right and left. A small mound, terminating a ridge, presented itself; he hailed the discovery with joy, but it was destined to prove his destruction. He had scarcely gone ten yards, when he perceived that

it opened on to the footpath, and at the same instant this inexperienced bog-trotter came in view of two of the enemy. They rushed towards him, and he was immediately and helplessly captured.

Dragged to *terra firma*, he was confronted with a man in gentlemanly attire.

"The very man we want," exclaimed the official, who was no other than the deputy sheriff of Essex. "So far so good, lads: now for his comrades."

"They're crouched in the reeds here, not many yards from this," replied one of the men. "But how the devil to unharbour them, I don't see, unless we'd some mud-shoes: they're among the clumps to the right of us, and can't get off, for the men who are on the other side will drop 'em if they try it there, and down towards the beach the swamp is deeper and deeper."

Half-a-dozen stout sailors now joined the party.

"Here," said the deputy, "two of you lads take this prisoner down to the

Ferry-house, and see if you can get mud-shoes, and we'll follow these scoundrels into their lair."

His orders were obeyed, and Walpole was conveyed to his destination. Meantime Jerry had lain still, but Sam and Joe, uneasy in their positions, and finding the treacherous soil failing beneath them the longer they remained in one place, had desperately plunged and strove until they had partially retraced their way to the point they had quitted. Sam first became visible to the watchers on the northern bank, and no sooner did they catch a glimpse of his whereabouts, than three carbines simultaneously exploded a shower of slugs.

The burglar was pierced from head to loins ; he shrieked aloud with agony, and the gore, trickling from his many wounds, saturated his clothing. The foremost of the men, finding they had hit their mark, scrambled in among the reeds, and putting them aside, dragged (for he was a powerful fellow) the sorely-injured Sam from his position ; another followed, and in a few seconds he lay dying on the causeway.

" He's got his gruel, anyways, poor devil," remarked one of the fellows. "Ben, do you and I carry him down to the house ; perhaps hanging him would be more proper, arter all."

There was no need of this superfluous care. Sam's yarn was spun out : with a deep groan, and an inarticulate curse, his crime-burthened soul escaped amid a gush of black blood from his clogged lungs.

There yet remained Leary Joe and Jerry.

That there was still, at least, one other skulker among the reeds, the pursuing party had little doubt. Leary Joe, in reply to their frequent summonses of surrender, and having the death of Sam before his eyes, which he could in part observe from his lurking-place, determined to give himself up. To this resolve he was, moreover, unpleasantly urged, by finding that, every minute or so, his enemies fired from one side or other of the swamp, and, as his fears told him, often unpleasantly near to his carcase. He, therefore, raised his hands, and called aloud. His signal was acknowledged, and he was soon assured that all they sought was his surrender. He gave himself up ; and, in reply to their interrogatories, declared that they were mistaken as to the number of his comrades ; one having gone along the road to Barking.

It is curious how

> " Hope leads us on, nor quits us till we die ;"

for Joe, even in this perilous moment, felt somehow that the liberty of Jerry was the last hope for his own life, and that while he was free all was not lost. As for Jerry, he skulked (like the great Roman in the marshes of Minturnæ), until pursuit was past ; and the enemy was clear off when he betook himself to the road : but of his and the survivor's adventures we must speak in a future chapter.

CHAPTER XXVI.

THE POLICE OF SIXTY YEARS SINCE—COMMITTAL OF WALPOLE—A FLASH CRACKSMAN'S DEFENCE—ST. GILES'S GREEK, AND JUDICIAL IGNORANCE.

THE police of sixty years since deserved not the name, and the impunity of criminals was a greater encouragement to law-breaking than would be counter-veiled by the most sanguinary criminal code that even the cruelty of a Draco could devise ; yet still, instead of endeavouring to remedy the defects of the " preventive check," by increasing the number, and rewarding the efficiency of the men who were employed to detect crime, our " state tinkers " they went on botching and botching at the laws, and making them still more savage and bloody, never trying the more humane and enlightened expedients of educating and improving the lower orders, or rendering the commission of felony more difficult, by multiplying the chances of detection. 'Tis true that the " collective wisdom " marvellously lacked instruction itself, nevertheless the " country party "—the men of broad acres and of fat bullocks—found it easier and simpler to their limited comprehensions to go on in the brutal and ignorant track of increasing punishments and their severity, till at last the reaction came, and finally the good spirit and enlightenment out of doors penetrated the cruel darkness of the " honourable house," and hares, pheasants, horses, and sheep, became less valuable in the eyes of the law than an immortal soul. Previous to this, however, a brutal and bloody code, with its brutal and bloody punishments, had made a class of people worthy of the laws under which they lived, to the great credit of the good "old patrons" of the "good old times"—past, let us hope, never to be championed again. But this is digression.

At the close of the twenty-fifth chapter, we left Bob Walpole and Leary Joe in the hands of the "Philistines," and Jerry, shoeless, hatless, and half-fainting, the sole scathless escaper from the hot pursuit of the officers. As for Black Sam, the last sooty life-drops oozing from his side, he was left at the ferry-house, until a "crowner's quest" should meet to go through a *pro forma* investigation of his death. The next day the worthy coroner made out an order on the parish authorities for the interment of the disfigured corpse; the twelve honest men and true, by direction of the official (nine of them made ✗'s), signed their names to a verdict of "Justifiable Homicide," which, as one of their number learnedly remarked, meant "as he should be buried in the cross-roads;" though another, who had been present at another inquest, where suicide had caused the death of the subject, concluded, with equal learning, that it was only where a verdict of "fell in d'ye see" was awarded, that the denial of Christian burial was insisted on.

"But Sam's no more—so now no more of Sam,"

and we will turn to the living rascals. As one living thief is more interesting than a leash of dead ones, we shall not excuse ourselves for looking after the breathing trio : and first of Walpole and his fellow-captive, Leary Joe.

We have said that Walpole had brought down Jerry to the fatal spot, for the purpose of recovering certain plate, the produce of a burglary, which he had been compelled by circumstances to conceal at that place; and we have seen how they fared in this unfortunate adventure. The plate, much of which was easily identifiable, was now in the hands of his captors, and as his apprehension had been too public for him to hope anything from any attempt to bribe the officers who had him in custody, he resigned himself apparently to his fate; keeping, however, a sharp look-out for anything the chapter of accidents might throw in his way. As for Leary Joe, he retained his usual equanimity; nay, before they had reached Limehouse Hole, he had so far recovered his usual patter, as to exchange a slang jest or two with the thieftakers and the crew of the boat, in the stern-sheets of which he and Walpole were handcuffed together. Thus they rowed on until they arrived opposite Billingsgate, where (the two officers objecting to go through the narrow and dangerous arches of old London-bridge, it being then half-tide), they were landed on the Surrey shore, and thence led through divers lanes and alleys by Kent-street, to the prison in Horsemonger-lane; to occupy the quarters whence his pal, Jerry Abershaw, through the agency of Rebekah, had so cleverly made his exit a few weeks previous.

The owners of the property recovered by the officers speedily made their appearance; the preliminary proceedings were taken before two justices of the peace, at the gaol; the proofs were clear, the evidence unimpeachable, and Walpole stood clearly committed for a burglary, attended with violence, at the house of a Mr. Pewtress, a retired tradesman, residing near Camberwell, then a small, retired, and rural village.

Leary Joe, however, was destined to other adventures. Nevertheless, though not shown to be a participator in Walpole's burglary, they brought home to him a charge of "sneaking" a valuable set of harness from the inn-yard of one of the old-fashioned hostelries in the Borough High-street.

As the trial of Leary Joe came on before that of his fellow-captive, Walpole, we shall take notice of a few of what Joe expressively termed, in after days, the "hunfair and prejudiced conclusyuns as the court comed to in his little consarn."

We shall pass over the preliminaries of the trial; suffice it to say, that the indictment duly set forth the stealing of the set of harness in question, with all the puzzling phraseology and confused iteration common to such documents. Three witnesses were called: the owner of the property, who swore to his harness; the ostler to having hung it in a particular spot, where a stable-boy had cleaned it, not ten minutes before it was missed; that Leary Joe had been seen lurking about the yard; and that a pal of his (as it had since been ascertained) had seduced the said

ostler to "gaff" for certain beer, to partake of which said stable-boy had been invited; and that, during the interval of their absence, to use the expressive phrase
of the younger witness, the whole set of harness "valked its chalks, and vas
never more seen until the fast trotter of Leary Joe was nabbed a-grinnin' through
the collar on it, in Ratcliff-highvay."

The case thus far seemed pretty clear, and the judge, in the usual form, called on
the prisoner for his defence; for the humane law allowing counsel to criminals
was not then enacted.

Joe's spirit rose with the occasion, and placing his fore-knuckles on the ledge in
front of the felon's dock, and steadying himself by forming a support with his un-
bent thumbs against the perpendicular front of it, he thus delivered himself—

" Vell, my lordship, and genelmen o' the jury, yer don't think for vun moment
as the hevidence you've heerd this day vill be con-sidered sufficient to take avay a
Hinglishman's buthright, trial by jury—no, genelmen, you hears vot these false-
svearin' varmints (the judge here requested the prisoner to confine himself to his
defence, and not to assail the characters of the witnesses). Thank'ee, my lordship," continued Joe, ducking his head like a Chinese Joss on a chimney-piece;
" thank'ee, but if so be yer lordship had had the misfortin to be charged vith prig-
gin a hole bundle o' pigskin, vot vould yer lordship's feelins be (his lordship
smiled) at such er himpertation on yer charackter? Vell, yer lordship, put yer
lordship's self in *my* place, and see a skulkin' vagerbone as yer lordship has treated
to beer, times out o' mind, come up cos he vant's to get out o' lending the loan of
another pusson's harness to a friend, and saccryfice his friend to the last hextremity
of the lor, sooner nor svear to the truth, cos, d'yer see, genelmen o' the jury and
my lordship, he'd get the sack from his place ——"

" Get the *what*, prisoner ?" inquired his lordship, raising his eyes from his notes,
for he was a judge like the late Sir James Allan Parke, whose researches had not
extended far into the Slang Dictionary.

" Get the *sack*, my lordship," repeated Joe, with emphasis; " vhich means, in
Hinglish, as his master or missus 'ud give him the bullet."

" The what ?" repeated the unlearned judge.*

" Lord bless your lordship's hinnocence; they'd tell him to valk his chalks (his
lordship again applied his ear-trumpet to his ear, and looked with puzzled aspect
at Leary Joe), they'd tell him to shove his trunk, nammus, bolt, mizzle, hop the
tvig (his lordship seemed as amazed as though the court had been addressed in the
Ojibbeway language, and Joe, getting impatient, amid the tittering of the jury-box
and bar, and the laughter of the officers in court, became yet more impressive).
Yes, my lordship, I stands here hinnocent as the babby vot's unborn, the wictim
o' circumstances, a hunfort'nate prisoner as carn't get heerd for the vant o' book
larning, and so I s'pose I'm to be hanged vithout benefit o' clargy—yes, my lordship, I've been falsely svorn agen ——"

" Really, prisoner, your language is so strange, and your defence is so irrelevant,
that I cannot allow it—you must be *brief*, if not, I shall proceed, on the first devia-
tion, to charge the jury."

" Thank'ee, thank'ee humbly, my lordship, but I arn't no brief, though the
counsellor for the persecution had von. I'm a poor man, my lordship, or I could ha'
had fifty witnesses to character, out of the most 'spectablest consarns in the Burrer Market; but, my lordship, I'd no blunt to pay their 'spenses. And now, my
lordship, and genelmen of the jury, this here's my defence :—

" On last Vitsun Monday vas a veek, as I and Jem Tramper vos a going down
High-street, Burrer, he vith a donkey vot he had jest bort, and I vith my light
cart—he'd svear to jest the same as I'm telling yer, if he vos only here—vot I
deals in fruit, and hegs, and poultry, and the like vith, 'cording to seasons, the
trace-hook of my harness kims clean out of the collar. 'Here's a pretty consarn,'
ses I; so I unharnesses him, and goes up the Half-moon yard to the tap, and ses
Tramper, ses he, ' I knows a cove as is about the stable here, and,' ses he, ' he'll
lend yer a collar, ses he, ' till yourn's mended.' So vith that, Jem hassails this
very mountain covet as yer lordship has seed this very day, vith your own blessed
spectacles, a svearing falser nor many a gloak as has grinned through a Norvay

---

* At the trial of Thurtell, Hunt, and Probert, for the murder of Weare, Mr. Justice Park[e]
inquired of a witness the meaning of the words " wide awake," a proof that the learned judge had
been sleeping a good portion of his life.
          † Witness ; so called from the elevated position of the witness-box.

neckcloth,* and axes him to do us a good turn by lending us a collar, though it vos never so old a vun, and ve agreed to leave mine till it could be mended. Vell, he ses he'd see vot he could do ; so Jem stands fust vun pot o' heavy, then a flash o' lightning, and then I stands a yard o' tape apiece, and then ve goes the hodd man for half-a-pint o' strip-me-naked, till, I'm blessed, my lordship, if ve could e'er a vun on us see a cart-horse's drag-chains from the Lord Mayor's goolden harness. Well, now, my lordship, see vot comes o' all this. This here ostler offers Jem his pick o' all the harness, and Jem comes out vith me, vereby I takes my choice of a set, and I leaves my own—vell, the vitnesses vos afeared to own as they'd lent it us permiscuously, and so they comes down here to svear avay a poor feller's life, and that's the whole truth of the haffair—so help me, my lordship and genelmen of the jury."

The witnesses were ordered to be recalled ; but, lo ! the elder of them, supposing he was done with, had departed the neighbourhood of the court, and was without the reach of the lungs of the crier. The stable-boy, however, on cross-examination, admitted the " soft impeachment " of the " blue-ruin and heavy," said to have been taken on the day of the theft, by Jem Tramper aforesaid, the ostler, and the prisoner. So fatal was this admission deemed, that the jury would at once have let loose Leary Joe upon society, with the full concurrence of his lordship, had not one of the officers reminded the court that the prisoner at the bar was a companion of the notorious burglar Walpole, captured in his company, and by no means the innocent which his cunning rhetoric had almost blinded the judge and jury into supposing him.

His lordship, therefore, like a judicial weathercock, at once veered about ; and, as he was one of those judges who are always most positive when least assured, the fair gale of his breath in the prisoner's favour instantly blew directly adverse, and he so furiously dwelt on the known bad character of Joe, his infamous associates, his artful villany, &c.—though none of this was proven—that the jury, at the end of ten minutes, with clear consciences, found him guilty of " stealing under the value of forty shillings ;" a verdict which Leary Joe ever repudiated as most atrocious and unjust, seeing " as he made such a hout-and-hout defence, supported by evidence." Nevertheless, as he profoundly remarked—a remark which an extensive experience in the practice of criminal courts will fully warrant—" Vot's the huse of the best case in the vorld, and the clearest evidence, either for persecution or defence, if so be the judge von't have it at no price—vich depends hentirely vether the counsel's got the hear o' the court."

The judge's vexation at the fact that he had been so nearly cajoled, by the seeming artlessness of Joe's defence, into an act of clemency, further peeped out in the sentence ; inasmuch as the man he was a few minutes before within an ace of liberating, was now doomed to " twenty-one years' transportation to the Island of Antigua, or such colony beyond sea as his majesty's government should think fit."

The trial of Walpole for burglary succeeded. Unlike the usage of the fictitious drama, where the comedy follows the tragedy, in this theatre of real life, the serious performance followed the lighter one ; but, as the fortunes of so important a personage as Gentleman Bob deserve a better place than the fag-end of a chapter, we will take scope in chapter twenty-seven for the narration of what befel him in his present critical position.

CHAPTER XXVII.

THE ASSIZES FOR SURREY—TRIAL OF ROBERT WALPOLE CHAMBERLAIN—CORRUPT MINISTERS OF THE LAW—A CURIOSITY IN CRIMINAL RECORDS—" PLATE SIN WITH GOLD," &c.—THIEF-TAKERS OF THE LAST CENTURY.

THE morning of February the 26th, 1791, saw the court-house of the county of Surrey, situate in the town of Guildford, crowded with an extraordinary multitude of idle spectators, to witness the trial of Robert Walpole Chamberlain, the housebreaker, and comrade of the notorious and desperate Lewis Jeremiah Abershaw,

* The pillory (then the usual punishment for perjurers), so called from the deal boards through which the prisoner's head was exposed, the aperture embracing his neck.

who as yet had escaped justice, and the retribution of his many daring and desperate crimes.

It is curious to reflect how much we are the creatures of feeling, habit, and surrounding circumstances; and how few of us can " realise" any state of society but that in which we live and move. " Times change, and *we* change *in* them," was true when the Roman satirist wrote, and is as true, more strikingly so, at this hour, than when he penned the thought. Times, indeed, do change; and nine hundred and ninety-nine of the *non*-thinkers are as unaware of the fact that they *do* change, save by the mutations of that span of existence wherein their own point of life is circumscribed, than if the world had not lived before them.

Not so the reading man; not so he who, adding to his own limited view the strengthening glasses of days gone by, conjures them up in their recorded deeds, to bear testimony of *how* they lived; who, siezing in the cave of the past, the lamp of experience and of history (which is ever burning for those who search for it), turns its rays on another people and another world from that which we now see. These may be strong words, but they are true; thousands of thousands of people think there is no romance except in the far-fetched scenes, farther-fetched sentiments, and farthest-fetched absurdity.

" Truth is strange—stranger than fiction," said the first of poets of the nineteenth century; and what we are about to relate, though lacking the trap-door, the stiletto, the mask, or the supernatural, which form the staple commodity of romance, is as true, and at the same time as improbable, as aught that Oriental dreamer has feigned 'neath the stimulus of opium.

Gentle reader—readers are always gentle—we have told you that Robert Walpole was taken; and hence springs a question of identity, to which the changing of the colt begot by Gladiator for the Irish Goneaway, or *vice versa*, or the substitution of the former for Running-rein, is mere child's play.

Robert Walpole Chamberlain, the iniquitous confederate of Jerry Abershaw, is in custody, doubtless. But what then? A man *was* executed on the 8th of March, 1791 : was that man Robert Walpole Chamberlain? History says " No !" and now to our story.

'Twould puzzle a modern penny-a-liner—a man accustomed to the almost military precision of the modern police—to suppose that a substitute man could be hung ! Indeed, *he* would laugh, impregnable in his own narrow conceit of knowing *how* these things are done. We will enlighten him, and show him that there are more things

" 'Twixt heaven and earth,
Than are dreamt of in his philosophy."

Robert Walpole was taken, we have said before; Robert Walpole was committed to Horsemonger-lane gaol; Robert Walpole was tried; but Robert Walpole was *not* executed !

" Prisoner at the bar, hold up your head; how say you—Guilty, or not Guilty ?" said the clerk of the arraigns.

" Not Guilty, my lord, and gentlemen of the jury !" was the reply.

The next question was put, and the prisoner threw himself upon a jury of his country.

The case was clear. An atrocious and cruel robbery had been committed at the house of a tradesman, Mr. Pewtress, at Camberwell, whereat a murder had been committed; for, although no murder was charged in the indictment, the sister of Mr. Pewtress, who was supposed to have hoarded up a large amount of money, in the shape of Queen Anne guineas, Spanish dollars, &c. was so terrified at the robbers, that she died four days after the robbery, having previously been in a weak state of health. The reader will hereafter see how this saved a scoundrel from his hempen cravat; at present we return to the trial of Walpole.

The evidence was clear, the case conclusive, and the jury having returned their verdict, the judge, as was the custom in those days, donned the black cap, and passed the extreme sentence of the law :—

" Robert Walpole Chamberlain, you have this day been found guilty, after a painful and deliberate investigation by a jury of your countrymen, of a crime whereto the law has properly attached the punishment of death. If such crimes as yours were not visited with the severest penalty, if such offenders were not removed by the sharpest method from society, it would be impossible that the honest and well-conducted part of the world could exist. How dreadful the idea that the couch of repose is not safe from the midnight robber or assassin! The sentence of the court is, that you be taken to the place from whence you came, and thence to the place of execution, and that you be hung by the neck until you are dead!"

And this solemn foolery went down for a couple of centuries with Englishmen as the remedy, the countercheck, the antidote to crime! It is lucky, for the credit of human intellect, that fooleries in philosophy, in medicine, in chemistry, and in every other pursuit wherein man's reasoning faculties were concerned, presented parallel absurdities. We have not *yet* grown out of half of them. The next generation will view us—such, at least, as do not minutely investigate what is our real state of mind—as antediluvian blockheads, and deservedly so. Judges in horse-hair wigs are, generally, like the majority of lawyers, *behind* their age. We are heterodox; but it is so upon compulsion. And now let us return.

Robert Walpole was found guilty; and, *of course*, was to be hung. Re-conveying him to prison seemed a simple operation; but how simple, we will now proceed to relate.

In the private room of the principal turnkey of the county gaol, at the hour of midnight, following on the very day of Walpole's conviction and sentence, sat four persons in close and confidential converse. Their consultations, for such they seemed, were carried on in a low tone of voice, and the very method of their meeting, and the personal appearance of the parties, might almost have marked them for conspirators; for their speech was confined to low murmurings, and each suggestion and reply was made and given in a tone that rarely elevated itself above a loud whisper. The one was the governor of the prison; a second, the reader's whilom acquaintance, Mr. Briggs, the vigilant head-turnkey, who had been so completely outwitted by Rebekah; the third, a sharp-eyed, parchment-visaged little man in black, the every line in whose inquisitive face bespoke the lawyer; while the fourth, a man of mature years, who was enveloped in a richly-furred travelling-cloak, and wore powder, gold shoe-buckles, and a satin queue, was evidently of a higher station of life than those with whom he was thus mysteriously closeted.

" Five hundred pounds, Mr. ———, will be paid down," said the little lawyer; " and for this you have the word of Sir William, the instant advice is received that he is safe in the Low Countries. He is here to give his assent and conditional draft for the amount, which will be a pretty sum to divide."

" I do not doubt the word of Sir William Chamberlain," replied the party addressed, in a slow manner, and as if speaking in perplexity; " and I would risk much to serve him, as well as to earn his liberal offer—but—but—I have a regard for my character, which stands unimpeached, Mr. Sharp; and, moreover, my present position is, with the fees from prisoners, and the traders allowed to sell their commodities within the prison, hard on £500 a year, and this I should risk, as well as ——"

" He's my brother's son, Mr. Governor; and, although that brother was a gambler and a spendthrift, and he is unworthy, yet," observed the elderly gentleman, in a feeling tone, " I would sacrifice much to preserve him from this ignominious fate. I know that there is no hope in a petition to the Secretary of State. The notoriety of his association with the desperate Jeremiah Abershaw alone forbids the hope of mercy; and if, as I have promised my sister I will do my utmost, he is to be saved, devise but the means, and I will double the sum Mr. Sharp has just named. Moreover, I will give you a bond shall save you harmless, should an exposure follow."

" You're 'xactly right," mumbled Mr. Briggs, who had winced a trifle at the mention of Jerry Abershaw; " your worship have hit the right nail o' the head there, anyways; for his being apprehended vith that hawful scapegallers is qvite enow to hang any man vithout no other hevidence at all. But raley it seems to me entirely desp'rate to manage this; howsever, money vill do a good deal, that's sartin, even in the most difficult cases, and I thinks, purvising I and Mister —— here, had a bit o' consultation like, as some device might be hit on. He'll be here, you see, to-morrow, Sir Villam, so there ain't no time to lose; and if so be it carn't be done vithout others being let into it, ve shall lose great part o' the stakes—not that I vouldn't do much vithout the hobject of the lucre of money in view, to hoblige Sir Villam Chamberlain; but here your vorship sees as ve risks everything, and if so be as others is necessary—mind yer, I don't say as they vill be ——."

" They shall be rewarded liberally, exclusive of what I have now promised, in proportion to their services, and the risks they run; and Mr. Sharp here shall be authorised to arrange for the payment of whatever you may think needful."

" It isn't exactly for that," observed the governor, with an air of self-denial, when he saw that the golden fish which his confederate was playing, was safely hooked; " it is not on that account, Sir William, that Mr. Briggs spoke. We will serve you if we can possibly do it; but meantime 'tis necessary, as Mr. Briggs has very properly remarked, that he and I should hold a little private conversation as to the praticability of this dangerous exploit: we will therefore retire, and in a few minutes let you know whether we will attempt the liberation of this young man, for whom, as a relation of yours, Sir William, I must confess I feel a great interest."

So saying, the governor beckoned the trusty Mr. Briggs into an adjoining apartment, where we will just follow them.

No sooner was the door closed, than down sat the precious pair; Mr. Briggs rubbing his hands with unfeigned satisfaction, his green gooseberry eyes twinkling with delight; and the scoundrelly governor, chuckling, but more quietly, over the prospect of the guineas of Sir William Chamberlain.

" This 'll be a good thing, Mr. ——, if so be as ve only manages it righteously," said Briggs, stirring the fire with great glee. " I has it all as plain as my hand afore me; see vot it is to have a head for these things. Vy, this 'ill be better nor a year's fees from all the scaly debtors as comes into the stone jug! Five hundred guineas for each on us, Mr. ——, and I knows how to manage easier, a precious sight, than that last escape; 'cos, d'ye see, we mustn't never let him come back vithin these four walls. I sees it, and ve'll have a man hung too, and no mistake, and then who'll blow the gaff,* I'd like to know?"

" Substitute a man at his execution, Mr. Briggs ! ha, ha ! You've been drinking a little, I'm afraid."

" Drinking—drinking !" retorted the red-nosed Mr. Briggs, who, from being cognisant of the vile venality of the governor, was upon the level with him which a partnership in infamy creates; " I don't drink—and if I do, I can't see what you should have to say to it."

The governor remonstrated.

" Well, if you meant nothink, you couldn't mean less; but I mean vot I say. Ve'll have him *supposed* to be hung, and the mob none the viser; and that 'ill save a precious sight o' difficulty in all quarters—eh?"

" You're a sharp fellow, Briggs," said the keeper of the gaol, willing to pacify his confidant; " but surely you're making yourself merry with this affair. We must earn the £1,000, that's flat, and take our chance of the after-claps. But how the deuce you'll get somebody hanged for him, passes my guessing."

" Leave that to me: I'm to have my £500—is that agreed?"

" It is," replied his confederate.

" Then book it as done," replied Briggs, and he then proceeded to disclose his plan.

" The governor highly approved of it; and the worthy pair of officials returned to the parlour, where Sir William Chamberlain and his legal adviser awaited them.

The plan was readily explained; and its very boldness and novelty marked its probable success. Is was thus contrived :—

At that very assizes there was a man of the name of Drewett, who had been tried and convicted of the then capital felony of horse-stealing. His day of execution was fixed for the following week; he was to be executed on the top of the prison, in the usual manner. This criminal was a fellow of no particular note, mark, or likelihood; and Mr. Briggs's plan thus proposed to make him the willing dupe of their ingenious scheme. At that time Drewett was still at Guilfordd, and on the following day, he, as well as Walpole, would be brought in custody to the prison, whence they had both been taken, but we will leave Mr. Briggs to explain for himself.

" You see, Sir Villam, my notion's this. Saving your presence, although your

* Expose the secret.

offer is very lib'ral, this here Valpole's too notorious a cracksman for us to be able
to smooth over his escape, and get ourselves kept in our places—no, no, Sir Villam,
the risk 's too great for us, as responsible hofficers, to run, at any price vatever.
So ve'll let him cut and run in such a vay as to make believe as this here Drewett
have escaped: and I'll stick close to him, so as nobody but Ben Pearce, the
hofficer, as has got 'em both in custody, shan't be a bit the viser. Vell, this is the
vay I'll do it, Sir Villam——"

Sir William declared his satisfaction, and his readiness to pay the heavy reward
of their treachery to public justice, and £100 additional to the Ben Pearce aforesaid, and the bargain being duly struck, Sir William Chamberlain was ushered
out by the back gate; and no sooner had the door closed, than Mr. Briggs proceeded to equip himself for his expedition to Guildford, where the adventures we
are about to relate, and by which the public were to be so completely mystified,
came off in the following manner:

And here we will pause, lest the reader should suppose we are misusing the privilege of romance writers, and asking his belief of a wild and improbable invention. We will not quote the hackneyed truism, that

" Truth is strange—stranger than fiction,"

but to give it a slight illustration.

In the present day, with the improved state of our police, our magistracy, and the management of our prisons, we can hardly be expected to gain credence for what we are about to relate, except by placing before him facts to the full as extravagant as the circumstances we are now about to relate, concerning the escape of the daring burglar of whom we have thus far traced the audacious career of crime.

In the year 1763, in consequence of the trial of M'Donald, Berry, Egan, and Salmon, four noted thieftakers (or runners, as they were then called), an inquiry took place, wherein it was stated to the House of Commons, that "the practice of corruption by *trading* justices had rendered the appointment of justice of the peace so odious in Westminster and the suburbs of London, that no *respectable man of substance* would covet the office." The reason assigned for this was, that " the gaolers, turnkeys, thieftakers, and others, connived for bribes at the escape of offenders, and the screening from justice of all such as could bribe them. That the justices' appointments (they receiving no salary) were sought only by adventurers and disreputable persons, in order to make a profit of the *fees* paid to them by delinquents ; and that those only who were too poor to satisfy their avaricious demands were brought to justice." It was further shown before a committee of the House, that the system of paying gaolers " by fees *exacted from the prisoners,* and a premium for *liquors, tobacco,* &c., &c., sold in the prisons at enhanced rates, had made the keepers of prisons venal and extortionate :" and cases were produced and proved, wherein capital felons had " eluded justice through the connivance of the authorities," to " say nothing," adds the Annual Register, " of the dreadful sufferings inflicted on those who were both poor and criminal."

The case of Berry and his confederates may be cited as a sample of the police system which then prevailed. We quote verbatim from " Wade's Compendium of British History," p. 444. " This year were tried, Stephen M'Donald, John Berry, James Egan, and James Salmon, four thieftakers, as accessories before the fact, in procuring James Salmon to be robbed by Peter Kelly and John Ellis, in the county of Kent (for which they were both convicted at the last assizes at Maidstone), with intent to get the reward on their conviction. These wretches had received £1720 from the Treasury, for persons taken by them, and convicted on their evidence at the Old Bailey only, and they had ensnared, there and elsewhere, upwards of seventy men !"—Need the reader, after perusing this, marvel at the adventure we are about to relate ?

CHAPTER XXVIII.

BEN PEARCE'S PLANS — HIS PATHETIC ADDRESS TO HIS PRISONER — SYMPATHY — OBTAINING A SUBSTITUTE TO BE HANGED — WALPOLE ESCAPES TO HOLLAND — THE RESULTS.

THE officer of Union-hall, known as Ben Pearce, and mentioned in the last chapter, was commissioned by the sheriff of Surrey, in whose official custody the prisoners tried at Guildford then were, by course of law, to escort and be responsible for their safe delivery at the gaol from which they had been brought, and to which, by the sentence of the judge, " to be taken from whence they came," they now stood recommitted until the short period of time should elapse between their conviction and the last dreadful penalty of the law.

Now, Mr. Benjamin Pearce, having duly received Walpole and his companion in misery, Ned Drewett aforesaid, from the gaoler in whose safe custody they had hitherto been, was, as a matter of course, responsible for the re-delivery of the bodies of those individuals, after the verdict of the jury and the sentence of the judge: and hence arose the necessity of making Mr. Ben Pearce a confidant in the plot which the last chapter partially opened to the reader.

Ben Pearce was a shrewd fellow, or he would not have become a thieftaker, and a scoundrel, or he would never have thriven at such a trade, where " starving honesty " took the kicks, and the sanguinary, merciless villany the " halfpence " and the praise.

Well, Mr. Pearce, having with him an understrapper, and both armed with pistols, took their seats on the roof of the four-horse stage-coach, which then occupied nearly an entire day between Guildford and London, putting up at an inn in the Borough High-street. Between them sate their two prisoners, Walpole and Drewett, each handcuffed, and additionally secured by a chain reaching from the lamp-iron, on one side of the coach to that on the other, and passing through the connecting chain of a pair of fetterlocks fixed on their ankles. Thus manacled, there seemed little chance of escape. But treachery makes bolts and bars of little avail, and " where there is a will there is a way " to villany as well as to good actions. On arriving at the Elephant and Castle, Mr. Briggs made his appearance, and, hailing Pearce, desired speech with him. The subordinate was then left in charge of the prisoners. Their conversation was so long, that the coachman became impatient, whereon Briggs observed that he did not doubt that the prisoners would like a liquor before they entered the walls, and that as they had but a short distance further to convey them, they should alight at that place. The coachman had no voice in the matter; indeed, he was rather glad, as well as the other passengers, to get rid of the disreputable party, which with their chains and guard attracted much more notice than was pleasant, as the vehicle arrived in a more densely-peopled neighbourhood.

The chain was now unfastened, and the prisoners, stiff with their constrained positions and cold bracelets, assisted from the roof. The coach drove off, and the party entered the Elephant and Castle.

" Here, lassie," exclaimed Briggs, to a red-elbowed servant, " show us a private room."

The girl indicated one by opening the door, and the five men entered.

" Now, ve have a little bit o' bisness to settle," said Mr. Briggs, with an air of consequence. " First of all, who's got any mopusses; for it's clear onpossible to settle such a matter as this entirely dry."

" Shall it be brandy, rum, or Geneva?" asked Walpole, who knew the importance of keeping the goodwill of the runners.

" Oh, eyther 'ill do. I've no choice," chimed in Pearce.

" Well, then," continued Briggs, turning to Pearce's assistant, " first and foremost, Jem Hodges here shall take his drop, as I've a bit o' bisness for him to do, to carry a letter for the guv'nor to Bow-street, which requires despatch. Bisness must be attended to, Ben, and then ve'll toddle to the lumber ken* with these two gemmen here, at our leysure—eh, Ben?"

Ben seemed to have a shrewd suspicion that there was something more meant than as yet met the ear or eye, in this newly-sprung friendship and business of Mr. Briggs; but he held his tongue, and the liquor having been ordered, consisting of two tumblers of mixed liquor, and half-a-pint of neat rum, he awaited the departure of his understrapper to leave the coast clear for some important communication.

The fellow having tossed off his dram, and received the letter which Briggs carried prepared in his pocket for the purpose, the door was closed, and Briggs, beckoning Pearce and the two prisoners to lean towards him, thus delivered himself:

" This here matter as I'm a goin' to perpose, is attended vith danger, you see, to every vun 'xcept them as is to get the best on't, so that it becomes you to con-sider as it's just as much to sarve trumps as is in misfortune, as for the lucre of gain, as ve are chancing all this to give yer another sqveak for your precious lives."

Having delivered himself of this artful exordium, the head turnkey went on, while the felons hung on his words and looks with an eager interest that seemed to amuse him in a strange degree.

" I dessay as yer thinks I'm chaffing in part of vot I says; but no, strike me if ever I laughs at a cove ven he's in for it, 'cos it ain't fair nor right to my thinkings, seeing as the trouble may fall on the best on us. But that's nothing to the purpose. Here's Ned Drewett's safe to be scragged as a tater is to get salted; he ha'n't a

* Prison.

friend nor a pal in the vide vorld as vould either ile the hinges o' the prison doors nor try on the buffing-suit for a *hallybi*, vich might ha' been done, purvising poor Ned could have found the coryanders. But that's by the vay. Vell, now, see vot a different thing it is vith our friend Valpole here : here's a petition gone up to the Home Seckertary, and although the judge have put on the black cap, he ha'n't fixed no day for his scragging. Now vot do you take it *that* argues, Mister Ben ?"

" I carn't say as I sees which way the bull runs as yet," replied the thieftaker ; " what's it to me whether one or t'other of 'em's pardoned, 'xcept as I don't like to see spirity chaps cut off in the prime of their pluck ; otherways, what is it to us, provising we does *our* duty, what others as is above us does ?"

" Right, Mister Pearce, right," returned Briggs ; " provising, as you say, *ve* does *our* duty. A vord in your ear, Ben, and then, perhaps, you'll see the case more clearer."

They moved from their seats, and stood whispering near the door.

" The thing's a reg'lar gift, you see," concluded Briggs, still whispering ; " there's a hundred goldfish* for you, for jest making a report to the guv'nor as Ned Drewett's escaped ; vich I'll hanser for his taking in vithout axing no unpleasant qvestions. You'll have to be suspended, to be sure, but couldn't you con-sole yerself for three month's rustication vith the company of a hundred likenesses of Qveen Anne ? 'cos, by the time as next qvarter comes off, Sir Villam says he'll do summat for yer as shall be as good as vot you've got, through his power vith the beaks at the Town-hall, South'ark ?"

" The thing looks likely, I must say," replied Pearce ; " but it 'll all break down, provising Ned Drewett von't come into the plan."

" Hark here," said Briggs, and he drew the other thieftaker farther off ; " a vord in yer ear agen—Ned Drewett shall be scragged instead o' Valpole, and not a soul in the vorld none the viser !" and Mr. Briggs grinned, chuckled, and distorted his visage, as though in an agony of delight at his own cleverness.

" And now," said Mr. Briggs, again approaching the table where the hand-cuffed prisoners had sat, watching with eager eyes the conduct of the officers, " I'll hexplain to yer what good luck's lying jest now ready-made in both o' yer vays. Fust, Mister Drewett, you're booked for a ride on the hos as vos foaled by a hacorn, onless you listens to the only plan as can slip your neck out o' the hempen-framed vinder. You see, Mister Valpole have very good interest at court, and vith the quality ; and jest now a petition have gone up vith upvards of a thousand clergymen's names at the bottom on it, besides the corporation of London, the Lord Mayor, the justices o' the county, and the judge as tried him ; now, if any-think 'ill save a man's life that ere vill, I should say."

Mr. Briggs, after this thumping lie, buried his face in a pot of ale, and washed it down with best part of the contents. Walpole stared at his audacious lying, but remained silent, to see what would come next.

" Vell, as I said, this here petition's gone up, but my Lady Chamberlin (Walpole stared still more, for he had never, since he betook himself to his career of infamy, either mentioned or applied to his wealthy relatives) is still all over tirrits and frights, and poor Sir Villam—a vorthy man he is, to be sure—is vell nigh as bad. I vos sore at heart to see how he did take on ven I told him o' the hunfortunate accident of yer being sentenced to die." Again Mr. Briggs's red nose disappeared in the quart, to hide his sympathetic feeling. " Vell, now, yer see, ses I to Sir Villam, ses I—it's a dreadful thing to die, more 'specially agen yer vill ; so I agreed as how, if it vere anyvays possible—more for the matter of the shocking-ness of cutting off a young feller of good family and prospects, and sparing of the feelings of poor Lady Chamberlin—as I'd try my best to persvade Ben here to take three vinks, vile you, friend Bob, jist slips out o' this here vinder." Pearce here left the room. " But now comes the tightest part o' the job : I'd be loth to see any vun hanged ; but it strikes me forcibly as a good thing might be made o' this here, and the vay's this : Ned Drewett here shall change toggery vith you, and then ve'll carry him inter the prison as Mister Valpole ; I'll keep near him, and in 'tendance on him, and nobody none the viser. Then the cry 'll be as Ned Drewett is escaped ; and, d'yer see, Ned, you'll have the benefit of this here pertition, and all the hinterest o' Sir Villam Chamberlin, and the corporation, and the clargy, and the judges, vereby no doubt ve'll see a free pardon come down, or at the vurst a commytation of the sentence."

Ned Drewett looked grave and considerate at the proposition of Mister Briggs, and certainly seemed as if he would prefer to escape in his own proper person, rather than by proxy ; yet a minute's thought convinced him that there was a vista of hope in the high interest said to be possessed by Walpole, which offered advantages not to be expected from his own friendless condition. He, accordingly, expressed himself satisfied with the arrangement, and promised to conduct himself entirely as might be directed by Mr. Briggs.

" Now then," observed that personage, " is the time for doing business. I'll call Ben in, though, afore I loosens yer ruffles, and vun at a time vill be as many as it vill be convenient to undress."

He stepped to the door where Ben was keeping watch, who entered. They first unlocked the handcuffs of Walpole, and Mr. Briggs, producing a cold chisel and a small hammer, the iron ring on Bob's ankle was soon cut through, and that individual proceeded to undress. Having stripped to his shirt, Pearce holding the handle of the door on the inside, Drewett's handcuffs were unlocked, and his upper man adorned with the coat, waistcoat, and hat of Walpole, who quickly dressed himself in that part of Ned Drewett's attire. Drewett's handcuffs were again fastened on, and his trousers drawn off over the link of his long leg-fetter, the silk stockings and breeches of Walpole being easily put on in the same way. Walpole, entirely at liberty, then slipped out at the window, which was within three feet of the ground, previously receiving directions that he should repair to a certain field in Lambeth, near the archbishop's garden wall, where, by nightfall, he should be joined by Pearce.

The thieftakers now waited a good ten minutes.

" He must be pretty well cleared out o' this nayberhood by this time, I should think," observed Pearce.

" There's no hurry votsumever," replied Mr. Briggs ; " and these things is best done vith due decorum and carefulness. It vould never do to have him grabbed agen, d'ye see, 'cos that'll spile us all. Ned, my covey, vy you looks down in the mouth ; vy, if so be I vas in your fix, and got sich a chance as this here, ven there's nothink like half a sqveak between yer and a hinvitation to the sheriff's ball, I should book myself for as good as tventy years more fun in the vurld. Now mind yer, Ned, it 'ill all depend entirely on how yer does yer part in this bisness, vether yer not scragged : and I can tell yer as the gemmen as makes the laws, and tries the prisoners, keeps hosses, and that's the reason as those as steals 'em never git's half a chance of any mercy vatsumever. Lor' love yer, I've knowed a dozen get off for killing of men, in my little experience. Some cos they vos in a passion, some cos they vas gentlemen, and some cos they got doctors to svear as they didn't think they vos qvite *compos menties*, and some cos there vos a *halibi* svorn for 'em, and a lot of other reasons, but I never knowed of any cove as got off for hoss-stealing, except by scragging. Lord love ye, it's the most dangerousest thing as a man can do. Vile here you are, Mister Valpole, a gemmen as *may*, like other gemmen have done afore him, jest told some vun to " stand and deliver !" though that ain't proved, and at last is convicted of using the wrong door-key, vereby he vas supposed to be found in somebody's else's crib. Vy, yer chance is Newgate agen the parish stocks better nor it vos afore."

Ned Drewett appeared both convinced and cheered by Mr. Briggs's logic, in which, indeed, there was much practical truth ; he brightened up, and gladly expressed his determination to abide the chance of Walpole's fate, inwardly resolving, when the worst came to the worst, to object to being executed as another person, should such an event ensue.

By this time it had become sufficiently dusk, in the opinion of Briggs, for the execution of their plan.

" And now ve'll do it, Ben," said Mr. Briggs ; " do you get outside the vinder, ready for a start, as soon as I sings out ' Murder,' and smashes these here vinders and frames vith my foot."

Ben Pearce got outside, and the window was shut down, and Mr. Briggs, mounting on a settle, asked if he was ready.

Pearce replied in the affirmative ; whereon Mr. Briggs, with one well-directed thrust of his foot in the centre of four squares, sent the frames and glass outwards into the back-garden, and following it instantly with another, he cleared the whole lower sash ; skipping, with surprising agility for one of his bulk, on to the floor, he, in the twinkling of an eye, overturned a long heavy table crash against the door, so as to block immediate ingress, at the same time firing one of his pistols. At the same moment the voice of Ben Pearce was heard outside, as he scrambled over a fence—

" Stop him—stop thief ! An escape ! Stop him !" and another pistol report resounded in the gardens at the rear of the house. Mr. Briggs seized on Drewett with the action of a clown in a pantomime ; and that individual, being helpless from his fetters, could not help rolling on the floor with the officer, who kept him under with a perfectly friendly gripe, roaring all the while for help most lustily.

The crash of the windows, the report of the pistols, and the outcries both within and without the house, at first paralysed the inmates. Boots and the ostler rushed out at the front-door, and so round to the rear of the house, where they arrived just in time to catch a glimpse of the nether end of Ben Pearce, as he rolled, rather than vaulted, over the fence, and disappeared on the other side in a dry ditch. The roaring in-doors was yet more vociferous than ever, Ned Drewett lending his lungs for a screech or two, while the heavy fall of tables and chairs gave token of a dire struggle, and the female voice of the serving-wench augmented the clamour.

" They're at it like a pitful o' bull-dogs inside there," suggested the ostler ; " *that* cove as is over the fence there is Ben Pearce, of Union-hall. Bad scran to him, ses I ; I hopes he'll not ketch the feller, whosever he is—good luck to 'im, ses I, and every cove as can queer a trap."

" But hadn't ve better see vot mischief's up in the little room there ; sum vun must pay for the dammage, and master von't like it if ve don't ——"

" Help ! murder ! thieves ! fire !" shouted the landlady, as cunning old Briggs fired off another pistol, and screaming at the top of his voice, sent another table on its side, thereby producing a compound-fracture of two of its legs.

Boots and the ostler now entered the passage, and rapping lustily at the door, demanded what was the cause of the uproar. Mr. Briggs replied by roaring out, in a half-throttled voice, to them to give him assistance in the king's name.

With some difficulty they forced away the heavy table, and getting admission, discovered Mr. Briggs and his prisoner rolling over each other, in a style that might have served as a lesson to old Barnes and Tom Matthews. They soon separated the struggling combatants, when Mr. Briggs having, after many pantings to recover breath, informed them of the escape of the " howdacious hosstealer," and his superhuman exertions in detaining the " desperatest housebreaker as ever was tackled ; but never mind," added he, " though you wasn't quite soon enough, I'm all the same obliged to you ; and Ben Pearce 'ill have him, if so be he's above-ground, and no mistake."

The fellows did not say " Amen" to this wish ; and the landlord being called in, Mr. Briggs informed him, " as the damage vos committed by a felonious escape from lawful hofficers, he vos of opinion as the county-rate vos hanserable ; but howsomever that might come off, he vould bear him harmless ;" with which assurance Boniface was compelled, will he, nil he, to be satisfied.

We will now turn to Ben Pearce, whom we left careering across the fields after his imaginary chase. Having got across the waste grounds to the end of Newington Causeway, he turned back, and at a slow and deliberate pace made his way towards the prison. Arrived there, he was ushered into the governor's private room, to whom he reported in detail the circumstances with which the reader is already acquainted. The governor presented him with twenty guineas.

" And now, Pearce," said he, " much will depend on your fidelity and secrecy in this matter. Here" (and he produced a handsome valise) " is a change of clothes necessary for the person" (this was the only phrase by which the governor designated Walpole) " whom you will meet, as you say, behind the palace at Lambeth. This will become him better than the apparel he wears, besides removing all danger of his apprehension for Drewett, whose person and clothes I must instantly describe in a circular letter to all constables and justices. When you have seen the person you speak of into a boat, which you will find waiting near Vauxhall, at the Mill-stairs, you will accompany him to Gravesend, where you will leave him on board ship, and return here ; whereon fifty guineas more will be ready for you, and a further thirty when he is ascertained to be in Holland, besides the good offices and patronage of one who *can* and *will* serve you."

Ben Pearce took the twenty guineas, and bowed his thanks. In another hour he was at his rendezvous, where Walpole, having once more shifted his attire, and thrown the clothes of Drewett into a field, where they might easily be found by some passer-by, the thieftaker and his charge stepped into a wherry, and, before midnight, darted on the foaming tide through the centre arch of old London Bridge, on their way to Gravesend.

Mr. Briggs, meanwhile, arrived at the gaol with his suppositious prisoner, and having safely deposited him in the strong-room, forbade any of his subordinates to attend to his wants, or unlock his door; declaring that "the late most howdacious escape had determined him never to trust this here desperate Valpole out of his sight, till he handed him over to Mister Ketch." The turnkeys laughed at the old-un's mishap, and his deputy calculated that his dismissal would lead to his own promotion. But how were they astonished when, next day, Sir William Chamberlain and another magistrate of the county, having arrived at the prison to form a sort of court of inquiry into the conduct of the officers in the late affair (the governor, to whom no blame personally attached, being the *third*, to form a *quorum*) after a patient sitting with closed doors—whereat the immaculate Mr. Briggs underwent, as he styled it, "a most tortering cross-egsamination, and made the most hout-and-hout satisfactory hexplanation as ever vos given of a werry orkhard-looking bisness"—the investigation terminated by Mr. Briggs being declared honourably acquitted of all blame; and Mister Ben Pearce was merely ordered to be suspended for a month, his "subsequent activity and courageous conduct being the moving causes of the leniency of his sentence."

CHAPTER XXIX.

NED DREWETT'S QUEER POSITION—ANXIOUS ATTENTIONS OF MR. BRIGGS THE GAOLER—KENNINGTON COMMON—THE WRONG MAN EXECUTED—HOW THE RULERS INSTRUCTED THE PEOPLE.

ALL the skill and tact of Mr. Briggs were now fully called out to prevent any awkward discovery from marring their all-but completed plot. As to the governor, he was more than uneasy — not having the bold and daring genius for plotting fraud possessed by his more illiterate underling; he was haunted by all sorts of apprehensions lest some misadventure should blow the fabric of their contrivances to atoms, and expose the secret artifices of its construction to the public eye. This fear increased with him as the time appointed for Ned Drewett's execution drew near, and as the weeks diminished to days he got so nervous and fidgetty, that, what between visits to Sir William Chamberlain, to consult about nothing, and continual messages to Briggs to report to him everything that happened, down to almost every wink of the prisoner's eye, that important personage became daily of more consequence, and, as several of the understrappers remarked, "it seemed as though the guv'nor had fallen in love with old Briggs, since the hos-stealer's escape: formerly, hofficers used to get discharged, but now, the vay to favour and permotion seemed to be quite t'other;" and one or two conjectured that, as the guv'nor was ill, "prehaps he might be a-going to adopt old Briggs as his heir."

The reader knows better than to share their conjectures, therefore we will hasten on to the

"last scene of all,
Which ends this strange eventful history."

Bob Walpole, under the assumed name of Mr. Marchmont, reached the Low Countries, after a favourable passage, being accompanied by Mister Ben Pearce, who, aware of his probable "rustication," thought he could not do better than embrace the offer of Walpole, and sail with him to Flushing; inasmuch as he could thus see a little of the world, have a pleasant and cheap trip, and bring back at once, in his own possession, the vouchers of his executed commission.

Three days took them there, and by the end of the week (before the substituted wretch's appointed day of execution) he returned, and claimed, at the hands of his employers, the promised reward of his services. This was a great relief to the governor's mind, as it assured him that Walpole, at any rate, was out of the reach of identification.

In the interval, most assiduous were the attentions of Mr. Briggs to the supposed Walpole ; no other individual of the prison conveyed him food, conversed with him, or sat with him, but Mr. Briggs ; and when a clergyman proposed to pray with the condemned man, he, at the prompting of Mr. Briggs, refused all spiritual comfort.   Even the condemned sermon, then a scene of some attraction to the morbid curiosity of the public, was shorn of its interest, in consequence of the absence of the principal performer in the solemn scene ; for Mr. Briggs, with most sagacious foresight, introduced a surgeon, to whom the person of Walpole was unknown, who readily and unsuspectingly earned a fee, by writing a certificate of the dangerous state of the prisoner's health ; whereby Ned Drewett, to his own no small satisfaction, was spared the infliction of an hour's sustainment of the character of a living target, whereat the eager and indecent stare of some hundred pairs of eyes, and the snuffling, droning exhortations of the worthy chaplain, who, on these occasions, drawled his commonplace against time, in order that his conscience might be at ease when he pocketed the silver contents of the box at the chapel door, wherein each visitor was compelled to drop a sixpence or more, as the charge for admission to this edifying spectacle of a fellow-creature often in the possession of full strength and life, standing, in full consciousness, on the very threshold of death.

"Time and tide"—the proverb is somewhat musty, though not the less true ; Kennington-common was crowded with eager, dense, and noisy masses of human beings.   Here and there, where some more open patch of ground offered the opportunity, were to be seen the upright sticks, each placed in the centre of a cup-shaped hole, and surmounted by bran-stuffed pincushions, brass tobacco-boxes, and wooden pears and lemons, whereat the proprietor vociferously invited all and several to have " three shies a penny" with the stout oaken sticks held under his arm.   On the skirt of the common were several canvass tents, and the small travelling houses of itinerant showmen: one with a monstrous pig, a second displaying a pictured giant outside—" as large as life"—to be seen within, the said painting giving the palpable lie to its inscription, by extending nearly from the ground to some ten feet above the roof of the supposed residence of this surpassing Goliah: nor was a " wild Indian " or two wanting; who, had they been Christian-born vagabonds, might have surely learnt, from the scene on that day presented, that boasted England was not much more civilized, and to the full as brutally cruel as the people they affect to style " savages."   They only slay their enemies; but here was an assemblage of self-styled Christians, in the heart of a great and civilised community, boasting some thousands of parsons and paid public instructors, met to gloat on the dying struggles of a fellow-man, and amuse themselves with gazing on the forcible thrusting forth of an immortal soul on its dark and eternal voyage; because, forsooth, six-bottle legislators and learned judges had decided upon the expediency of affording them an " example," which they thought indispensably necessary to protect sheep and horses on roads, commons, or in fields : nor is it long since gentlemen of broad acres, and clergymen not a few, upheld and maintained the " necessity" of public murder as the only " efficacious" preventive of such audacious invasions of the " rights of property !" Well, " the mob," as it is termed, roared and bellowed, and drank, and swore, and fought, and danced, as their several humours led them, until the disgusting show appointed for their edification should, for a time, absorb general attention : meanwhile we will turn from this scene of drunkenness, obscenity, filth, and uproar, to the condemned cell of Ned Drewett.

Mr. Briggs, who was still in close attendance upon the prisoner, had never ceased to buoy him up with hopes that, even at the last moment, a reprieve would most certainly save him from the gaping grave ; nevertheless, the poor devil had occasional twinges of doubt and distrust: but, as he argued to himself, what was the use of them : whether as Drewett or as Walpole, hanged he must be; and so far as his old mother and relatives down in the country were concerned, it would be better that there should be a doubt as to his ever being executed, than a certainty of that event having taken place ; and as this thought of home, and friends, and happier, because more innocent days, obtruded itself, Ned Drewett, for the first time, recalled that his assumed character had, of course, cut him off from the last sad consolation of bidding farewell to his relatives.

" Mister Briggs," said the countryman, " I dessay as my old moother ha' bin up to town, and ha' heard o' my escape ; and mayhap feyther, too, thof he wor

sore bitter agen I, when I boalted from whoam. Now doan't 'ee think as I mought have a sight on 'em, and nobody none the wiser ——''

"Vy, you must be a goin' stark starin' mad, all at vunce," replied Mr. Briggs, "to think o' such a thing. Vy, that 'ud blow the gaff* in a minnit. You'll have plenty o' time arter you've got yer reprieve—vich I vunder ain't come yet—ven you've bin discharged by proclamation, as Mister Valpole—to call on yer old dad and yer mother. Lor' love yer, that 'ud spile yer chance entirely. Vell, this is surely a hout-and-hout suit o' togs, these here green and silver; vot helegant buckles: and I shouldn't vunder if these here breeches ain't the most 'spensive Genoey velvet. Jack Ketch's mouth is a vaterin' for these, I should say, but he'll be disappinted on 'em yet."

"Be I to dress myself, then, i' all they foine clothes? There bean't no hurry, I s'pose?"

" Oh no ! only as it's ten o'clock,* maybe the sheriff might come, and, yer see, ve might as vell be ready for him. Here, I'll help yer. It's strange as there ain't no messenger yet. I shouldn't vunder now, Ned—indeed, I thinks it remarkable likely, seeing as the sheriff have been this werry mornin' up to the Seckertary of State, as the guv'ner have jest told me—as he have got the pardon in his pocket along vith him. On vich occasions, it ain't never usual to bring it out until sich times as the prisoner is about to be turned off."

Drewett stared half-incredulously on Briggs, but the latter never moved a muscle of his countenance, but busied himself in dressing his victim. The doomed man grew paler and more ghastly ; something foreboding the worst seemed to whisper to him that his hour was come, and he earnestly besought Briggs to tell him whether, in truth, there were any hopes of his life being spared.

" Vy, I never seed sich a feller in my blessed born days," replied the turnkey : "it's enough to make a parson svear to see any vun so chicken-hearted. You'll spile yerself entirely, it's my belief. Vy, you're ten times vorse nor half the coves as I've seen dance on nothink at the sheriff's ball, as hadn't a single chance left 'em on the cards. I tell yer as there's every likelihood as the reprieve 'ill be here, or leastvays, as it is already in possession of the proper authorities, and here you keeps on axing the same qvestions a score o' times ——"

" But wouldn't the sheriff tell me the truth, and put me out of my misery, if ——"

" Vorser nor all ; vy, you're the greatest yokel I ever heard. Hofficial person-ages never answers no qvestions 'xcept them as isn't axed at all—that's alvays the rule ; vereby they often escapes exposing their hignorance of most things as it's their bisness to know." And having delivered himself of this axiom (by acting on which, many dunderheads and knaves have passed for sagacious statesmen) Mister Briggs offered a dram of brandy (procured on the sly), to revive the droop-ing spirits of Ned Drewett.

The latter was again about to address another question on the subject uppermost in his mind, when the bell of the prison clanged loudly and frightfully to poor Drewett—it sounded like a death-knell, and he sunk on the seat with his face buried in his fettered hands.

In a few seconds the governor entered the condemned cell, and addressing the prisoner as though he himself was one of the dupes, inquired if he wished any message conveyed to his relatives. Briggs, who took upon himself the office of spokesman, at once expressed the strong hopes of the prisoner, that a reprieve would be obtained by the interest of his influential friends, and completely lulled, for a time, the suspicious nervousness of Drewett, by requesting the governor, on the part of the condemned, that he would interpose with the sheriff for an hour's delay ; at the same time hinting (in a stage whisper) at the probability of the sheriff being in possession of the important fact of the unhappy man's safety from the last dread penalty of the law.

" It's very likely—very likely, I should say, Mr. Briggs, that it may be so ; nevertheless, it would be very wrong, in our situation, to buoy up this unfortunate man with hopes, whatever may be our own private opinions. Mr. Walpole, the sheriff will shortly be here, and upon my surrender of your person into his custody, in due course of law, my power over you ceases ; I can but wish you, sir, a happy deliverance, for I really feel interested in your situation."

Having said thus much, the governor, who, though a corrupt, was not a hard-hearted man, retired, and shortly after introduced the sheriff. Mr. Briggs took especial care to duly impress on Drewett the importance of attending to his directions ; and, therefore, the sheriff seeing a well-clad man in a dress-suit, who sat with his face in his spread hands, offered to him, together with a warrant for the hanging of a certain Robert Walpole Chamberlain " by the neck, until he, the said Robert Walpole Chamberlain, should be dead," he received the counterfeit without much misgiving ; and Mr. Briggs being recommended by the governor as the most fitting escort for the prisoner, the sheriff further acquiesced ; for, being a man of feeling, he went through this most unpleasant portion of his functions in a most official and automaton-like manner.

The cart was now brought to the prison-gate, and Drewett, escorted by Briggs and the clergyman, stepped into it ; the executioner riding on the coffin, which was placed across the copse of the cart, while the driver walked beside the horse's

* The executions often took place at noonday ; occasionally, in the afternoon.

head, the vehicle being surrounded on both sides by the sheriff's javelin-men, and preceded and followed by a strong *posse* of special constables. They were quickly on Kennington-common, where the disorderly mob we have for some time lost sight of, awaited their coming. A roar of many voices greeted the appearance of the cavalcade, at the head of which rode the sheriff and several subordinate officials.

Drewett gazed around; nought met his view but a rolling sea of upturned faces, on which were expressed almost every passion of which the human countenance is susceptible, except sympathy. The multitude roared, groaned, and cheered; and the wretched horsestealer felt his brain grow dizzy, and his eyes swim at the confused sounds and sights before him.

Where was the reprieve? It was not here; but there stood, black and ominous, " the triple tree." He felt faint, and turned inquiringly to Briggs.

" Would yer like to pray a bit?" asked this officer, in reply to his question about the reprieve.

" Noa, I doan't want to pray—God forgi'e me my sins—I han't committed many; and this last—stealin' o' Farmer Thusby's geldin'—wor through bitter poverty. Oh, Mister Clergyman! thof I——"

" His mind's a-vandering, yer reverence," said Briggs, nudging Drewett; " prehaps if you was to begin a-reading summat out o' the Prayer-book——"

The clergyman began reading the prayer appointed for these sad occasions, and Drewett, groaning heavily, responded the " Amens."

Thus they came to the gallows' foot. The hangman now mounted a ladder, brought in the cart; and, having placed the loop over the beam, proceeded to adjust the noose round poor Drewett's neck, with the hardened *nonchalance* of a practised man-butcher. The clergyman asked if he had anything to say to the crowd, and Drewett replied in the negative. The executioner was about to pull down the cap, when Drewett begged he might be allowed to speak to the sheriff.

" I'll make it all right for yer," said Briggs; " keep a good heart—and, d'ye hear," added he, with a wink at Jack Ketch, " don't turn him off, as yer vally yer life, till I returns, cos I more than suspecs as the sheriff have got a reprieve for him."

At these words Mr. Briggs thrust his tongue into his cheek, and darted his right thumb smartly over his left shoulder, unseen by the wretched man, who now stood with his heels on the last round of the ladder. Jack Ketch gave a grin of intelligence, and Mr. Briggs had scarcely set foot on the ground, when the hangman suddenly dragged the cap over the nose of poor Drewett; the driver gave the horse a smart flank with the whip, and away swung the struggling dupe, like a trembling tassel at the end of a gigantic bell-pull; while the well-instructed multitude stretched their throats, and tore the air with yells and roars of brutal exultation at the delightful and exciting exhibition provided for their improvement and enlightenment by lawn-sleeved prelates and hereditary possessors of titles and Christian virtues—men whose intellect and legislatorial capacity comes to them in an exact ratio with the acres they possess by the robbery or thrift of their ancestors.

CHAPTER XXX.

MEDITATIONS IN A MARSH—A BOLD STROKE FOR A SUPPER—A ROBBERY— AN INTERRUPTION.

DOUBTLESS the reader by this time is beginning to inquire whether the author of this chequered story has entirely lost sight of the hero of the piece, while burying himself in detailing the break-up of the hopeful gang of which he was the most desperate and distinguished member. Truth to say, what with the death of Black Sam, the transportation of Leary Joe, and the escape of Walpole, and his execution by proxy, we have certainly for some half-dozen of chapters left our hero in a rather questionable state of suspense; yet these divergings are necessary to the due progress of the story. So, like a waggoner who has left behind some travellers by his vehicle, that they might pedestrianise up the steep of some heartbreaking hill, and at the top pauses to allow them time to rejoin, he here turns a backward glance to trace the approaching steps of Jerry, who was left knee-deep in the marshes on the coast of Essex, on the day fraught with such disastrous results to his companions.

The shades of evening grew deeper and deeper as he yet crouched in his reedy lair, listening, with beating heart, to every sound wafted by the wind to his damp and uncomfortable hiding-place. With the going down of the sun the wind arose, and sweeping, with a rushing sound, over the wide beds of osiers and tall reeds, produced to him a welcome agitation of their slender stems.

"This is a good thing for me," thought Jerry; "though surely it is now too dark, even if they have left any watchers, for them to see my movements. The noise and shaking of the sallows will prevent all alarm; so, by all that's desperate, I'll have a peep, if I die for it."

He scrambled a few yards, and, raising himself, saw that the coast was clear. A fishing-boat or two, tacking under close-reefed sails, dimly specked the river's surface, where the reflected clouds tinged it with coloured light. Shoreward all was still. He painfully dragged his numbed limbs after him, and crawled on to the causeway. There was a light at the Ferry-house, but there he considered it unsafe to present himself; so he determined to wait till darkness should shroud all objects, when he doubted not he should be able to steal a boat, and therewith transport himself to the Kentish side.

"Once there, I can surely make Blackheath, where I shall procure tidings of Rebekah and the Patrico. Sam's got *his* dose, that's sartin; and the next turn's mine, for there flies *one* black crow!" and Jerry spat in the direction of the ominous bird. "No, it's all right; there's two, three on 'em," added he, in a more cheerful tone. "My mammy's curse is a long time coming, if it's to come at all. Poor old woman, how she did rave about her 'darling Tom,' as she called him. Well, luck's all! and it was his'n to get his jemmy cracked for gettin' in my way. What must be, must be; and if he hadn't been so fast, maybe he wouldn't have got into trouble. Those darn'd river sharks, they've nailed all the swag as we reckoned on, and I reckon it 'ill be a case o' tightness of breath with Bob and the Leary one. Well, as I said afore, luck's all, and I am pretty well in for my share this turn, in having given the traps another slip. So here goes for a peep in at that little winder, where they've lighted the glim at the Ferry-house."

Stealthily creeping along the deep drain which bordered the roadway, Jerry approached the lonely wooden erection, and entered the wood-yard adjoining the house. Here he paused awhile under shadow of the fence. It soon grew totally dark, and he peeped, by noiselessly mounting on a sawed log, into the lighted room within.

On a clean, well-scoured deal table were displayed a few homely preparations for a frugal supper. A brown stone pitcher, covered with a napkin and cup, to keep the beer therein contained from becoming stale; a large knife and fork beside a wooden platter, and on a brown delf dish, a tempting piece of cold salt pork, flanked by a large brown loaf. Beside a just-kindling fire sate an elderly female, blowing the smoking sticks with a pair of asthmatic bellows, and opposite to her, on a low stool, was a boy of some ten years old, busied in cutting a rude miniature of a ship's hull from a block of deal held between his knees. Jerry took a rapid survey of these preparations for an expected guest to a hearty supper. He had not tasted food for many hours, and the cravings of hunger awoke at the sight of this homely but substantial fare.

Jerry approached the small casement.

"Granny," said the youngster, in a loud tone, which satisfied Abershaw that a good ear was not among the faculties which time had spared to the old woman; "won't father be home to-night at all?"

The withered crone raised her hand in curved form to her ear, as an extemporary ear-trumpet, and the child repeated his question in a louder voice.

"How can I tell, child," replied the old woman; "p'r'aps he's gone to Lunnon with the naughty men as has been took in the mashes; but your mother ought to have come from Barking afore this—I can't think what's a keeping of her," and again she puffed away with the broken-winded bellows.

There was a long pause before the juvenile resumed his cross-examination.

"But where's uncle Ben, granny? He han't gone to Lunnon too, have he?"

"Hold your tongue, boy; children shouldn't be so full of peart questions: I s'pose he's along of your father, and if one goes t'other will."

The child whittled away at his wood in silence.

" If this is to be my hot-el for supper, I'd better look sharp," thought Jerry, " or maybe it will be eat up for me by some one else. I could easily knock that old cat on the head, and I don't think there'd be any one handy afore I silenced the kinchen. But that 'ud kick up a rare bobbery, and mayhap I could get the eatables without the trouble."

He looked about the yard, and very soon discovered a broad axe, placed in a small penthouse.

" This'll do," muttered he, " if so be any one should step in, for one don't like to be disturbed at meals. Here goes — there's nothing like taking time by the forelock."

Jerry rapped at the door.

" There's mother, granny," cried the boy.

" I didn't hear no knock," replied the old woman ; " but your ears be quicker than mine, and your legs be younger, so go to the door, can't yer ?"

The boy laid by his specimen of naval architecture, and proceeded with some difficulty to release the door-pin from its fastening. Jerry, at no time remarkably prepossessing in his appearance, now smothered with black and half-dried mud, and holding in his hand the formidable axe, presented himself at the opening, and stepped in. The boy gave a cry of alarm, and rushed to his grandmother for protection.

" Why, what the dickens ails the brat ?" said the old woman, shading her feeble eyes with her withered hand, and looking at Jerry, whom, at the first moment, she took to be her son, the ferryman. " What, home so soon, Joseph ?" said she.

" Oh, granny," cried the child, " it ain't father, it's ——"

" Hold yer tongue, yer young varmint," said Jerry, in a gruff tone, " or I'll crack yer little skull for yer. You see, Mistress What's-yer-name, I'm a traveller, and have lost my way ; and, being benighted, I jest looked in, seein' a light, to know if I could have a bed here ?"

" Anan, sir ?" said the old woman, transferring her hand to her ear ; " I'm very hard o' hearin'."

" Can I have a bed and supper here ?" asked Jerry, in a louder tone.

" There's no 'commodation here for travellers," said the old woman ; " nor none nearer than the end o' the Level, at the ——"

" Then," interposed Jerry, " as you're so churlish, I'll help myself ; and look you, old Mother Midnight," added he, ostentatiously, laying down the broad axe across the table, " if you try for to hinterrupt me, you'll jest have to cook yer next supper in t'other world."

Jerry seated himself without more ceremony, and began helping himself plentifully to the eatables and drinkables.

" Oh, granny," exclaimed the boy, " the man's eating all father's supper. You shan't eat all daddy's pork !" screamed the little fellow, and he ran to the table to secure the dish.

Jerry lifted the broad axe.

" Look here, you old hag," cried he, with a menacing gesture ; " if you don't keep that young imp away, I'll just stop his fun myself."

The boy cowered behind the old woman.

" You wouldn't go to rob such poor people as we ?" urged the dame.

Jerry paid no attention to this remonstrance but by lifting the axe with one hand, without rising from his seat, and flourishing it across the table with a pantomimic twist.

The old woman muttered, but Jerry continued to satisfy the cravings of his inward man. Having emptied the jug of beer, and nearly cleared the dish, he paused, and, wiping his mouth, arose.

" And now, old Belzebub," cried he, in a menacing voice, " have you any money in the house, for I've a long way to go, and lack the needful."

" Money ! Lor' bless you, sir," said the old woman, now really alarmed ; " we be poor people ——"

But Jerry, without more ado, had began to pass his hands down the sides of the helpless crone, in search of pockets.

" Oh, Lord, save us," shrieked she, as Jerry seized a large sack of ticking, which might have served a cockney sportsman for a game-bag.

" You sha'n't hurt granny !" blubbered the boy, laying hold of Jerry's arm.

The ruffian, with a back-handed blow, knocked the poor child senseless in the corner, and went on with his inspection of the capacious pocket, by turning it out on the table. A housewife, a set of knitting-needles, a thimble, a snuff-box, and a small leathern purse, were among its contents. From the brass box Jerry took a pinch, and opening the purse amid the lamentations of the old woman, he poured into his palm two new half-crowns of the reign of Anne, and a Spanish dollar, wrapped in paper, together with half-a-dozen of the current shillings and six-pences of the Georges.

The objurgations of the old woman became louder.

" Hold your infernal clack," vociferated Abershaw.

At that moment a knock was heard at the door, which Jerry had fastened be-hind him ere he sat down to table.

" There's no time to be lost," thought he ; so, extinguishing the candle, he placed himself, with the raised axe in his hand, beside the door jamb, and with-drew the pin. Luckily for the ferryman it was not him, or that moment would most probably have been his last. Jerry saw it was a solitary woman, and, push-ing by her, he made his way down the causeway. He listened, but no noises came from the cottage, and, loosing the headfast of a small skiff, he pushed her off into the tide. Here Jerry, with the practised arm of an old waterman, soon gave his little shallop way, and, by the time the poor ferryman's wife had relighted the candle, examined the contused head of her offspring, questioned the deaf old woman, and made herself mistress of the circumstances of the case, their unin-vited and unwelcome guest was a good half-way down the Reach.

CHAPTER XXXI.

A CHASE—A SHOT IN THE DARK—AN ARREST, AND AN ECLAIRCISSEMENT.

" Yoi-ho, there! boat, a-hoy!" cried a hoarse brattling voice, which seemed to come from a throat that had swallowed nothing but cutting north-easters till its lining hung in fluttering shreds, which rattled with every attempt at speech. " Yo-o-oi, there—bo-o-oat, a-hoy!" but Jerry had no taste for being overhauled, and felt rather doubtful whether the party hailing might be exactly friendly, so he sculled away with the down-tide, easing off his left, and pulling for the point of land.

The boat's crew, for it was a four-oared galley, with one or more men in its stern-sheets, did not seem inclined to part with him in this unsociable manner, for directly after the second hail, he heard the hoarse voice again raised—

" Give way, give way, lads! Halloo, there, you sneaking long-shore lubber, are you deaf! Lay-to, or I'll drop a leaden messenger aboard you!"

Jerry redoubled his efforts, for by this time the preventive boat had changed its course, and was following right in his wake.

" He lays out well," grumbled the coxswain to the lieutenant ; " he's arter no good, sir, I'm thinking, else he'd stay to be questioned."

" Give way, lads, give way!" was the urgent command of the officer, not noting the observation. " Hail him again, Mr. Buntline, for you've a most alarming voice," added the officer, laughing.

" Boat a-ho-o-oy! D—n my eyes, but he's deaf, your honour. Boat a-ho-o-oy ! P'raps he'd hear a musket, sir ? Boat a-ho-o-oy!"

" Give him a salute with blank," said the officer, as Jerry, by this time within a few yards of shore, rowed into the black shadow of the river bank : " he can't get away from us, Mr. Buntline, for we've cut off the point there, and he can't double it. If he's a prize, we shall get his boat and whatever is contraband aboard of her, and the fellow himself may go to the devil."

In this sentiment Mr. Buntline fully concurred, for he had no taste for kicking his heels at the court-house of an assize town, or at a trial at an Admiralty court, and, provided they got hold of the goods and vessel, would much rather not be bothered with the smugglers.

" Ay, ay, sir," said he ; " he's no good, or he'd answer our hail. Shall I speak to him, sir, with the *pipe*."

So saying, Mr. Buntline significantly presented the musket, which he had loaded with a blank cartridge.

The lieutenant replied in the affirmative, and in an instant the bright flash of the piece was followed by a dozen reverberations from the steep-scarped lime-quarries on the Kentish shore.

"Boat a-hoy!" repeated Buntline; "the devil's in't, but he heard *that!*"

"Hold hard, all!" cried the officer, placing a night-glass to his eye, as the boat, by the set of the tide, now emerged into the partial light. "Damme, Buntline, you've shot the fellow. There's one scull unshipped, and t'other's hanging in the rullock!"

"Unpossible!" exclaimed that personage, dropping his nether jaw, and shading his eyes with his hand, he peered curiously towards the skiff, now but a few yards distant.

"Pull up to her, lads," said the officer, quietly.

They did so: there was no one on board. Mr. Buntline looked rather blank.

"You've shot him, Barney, to a certainty, and he's gone over the side," said the bow-oarsman, rising from his thwart, and catching hold of the gunwale of the empty boat.

"Unpossible! it's unpossible, I say," retorted Barney Buntline, appealing to his officer; "see here's the hidentical bullet as I bit out o' the cartridge. If I've done any mischief to the poor fellow, I'm sorry for it; but it's all owing to these here new army cartridges, instead of using powder and shot by the old rule o' thumb. I don't see nuffen on him," added the rough old tar, dubiously, "onless maybe, your honour, he's among they alder-bushes yonder."

Their boat was close in-shore, and while thus Mr. Barney was speculating on the probability of having committed homicide by misadventure, his fears were still further augmented by one of the seamen, who had got on board the skiff, remarking—

"Why, I'm blest, yer honour, if this here ain't old uncle Ben's skiff, at the ferry-house yonder; ay, ay, and here's his name, or I'm much mistaken, though I didn't larn to read painted letters where I went to school."

The officer stepped from his own boat to the skiff, and Mister Barney's concern assumed a ludicrous intensity (for although as brave a sailor as ever trod deck, old Barney Buntline would not intentionally have hurt a worm), when the lieutenant, stooping down, spelt out on the back-board:—

"Benjamin Trawlnet, Licensed Thames Fisherman, Rainham Ferry."

"Old Ben's skiff, sure enow," said the fellow who had before spoken; "and I'm darned if I don't b'lieve, by the pulling, as 'twor old Uncle Ben hisself; he handles a stiffish oar, and was unkimmon deaf, surely, owing, as they say, to his being in the dreadful siege of Giberalter, with Sir Gilbert Elliott, when they burnt all they floating batteries as the Spanishers had been so long a time a build-ing, with the red-hot shot—and by the same token I wor precious near being at that ere thundering consarn myself, as a boy, cos, d'ye see, I wor on board the Bellyruffian, as wor a-going to jine my Lord Hood, to relieve the fortyress, when ——"

"Silence, Jack Stiffyarn, and keep your galley-stories for Saturday night," said the lieutenant, in a tone of authority: "this is a matter that we may all hear of another day. Buntline, you're an old and trusty bo'sen, and your character, I hope, will clear you of this ugly piece of business. My opinion, Barney—is—of course—my own—but if a helping hand can be of service, you shall have it. Not another word, Buntline—you are under arrest. I shall take no other measure, because I'm sure you know your duty to the service too well to put me under the necessity of adopting harsher measures."

"Why, your honour must do your own pleasure in that matter—but ——"

"Enough, Buntline," said his commander: "'tis an awkward affair, and must be answered another day. Make the boat fast, lads, and tow her to the sloop."

The mirth of the seamen was checked at the thought of their old messmate's trouble, and the habits of discipline imposed by the service held their tongues mute. As for poor Barney, he heaved a sigh, as much of commiseration for the object of his supposed manslaughter as for his own predicament. Silently and sadly the galley held its way, slowly labouring against the tide, across the river to Rainham, in order to shorten their "ground," and save distance, every now and then a half-expressed murmur of pity for "Old Barney" escaping from the lips of the oarsmen. Their commander meanwhile preserved a most dignified silence.

"Might I ax a favour, yer honour?" inquired Buntline, respectfully, as the galley laboured past the ferry-point. "I ain't fearin' for myself, but *they'll* be expecting of Ben at the house—and—and—your honour—when a comrade *is* popped off by the fortin' o' war, or falls overboard, or sich like misfortune"—and Barney heaved a sigh—"it's al'ays a kindness to let them as belongs to him know the worsest."

"Right, Buntline, right," replied the lieutenant, who was himself a humane man: "give way, lads, to the caus'ey."

"Hillo! hillo! ahoy, there!" cried a voice from the causeway; beside which, for it was by this time nearly low water, lay a large black boat.

"A man-o'-war's boat, sir," said the bow-oarsman, looking over his shoulder.

"What ship?" shouted the lieutenant.

"The Dart."

"Our own men and the jolly-boat," said the bowsman; and they pulled in smartly.

Arrived, all preserved silence until they landed; a silence which not a little perplexed the other boat's crew; and their perplexity was increased when the lieutenant, with a cool authoritative tone, commanded Buntline to be taken as prisoner under arrest. The fellows stared in the half-darkness, but spoke not.

"He's shot poor old Uncle Ben, by mistake," said one, in a rough whisper. "I hope as it won't go hard with him."

"Shot who?" inquired the other.

"Old Uncle Ben. He wor so deaf as he didn't hear us hail him; and taking him for a longshore sneak,* or a smuggler, and he shot him wi' a blank, as he thought it wor, no doubt, but there must ha' been lead in the cartridge, and ——"

"Shot yer grandmother," replied the seaman aloud. "Why, Uncle Ben, as you calls him, is up at the ferry-house, swearing great guns at some loping varment as have prigged his skift. Hillo, ho! house a-hoy! Uncle Ben! bear a hand, and show yer figure-head; here's one o' the right sort, old Barney Buntline, in the bilboes for killing yer!" and the jolly Jack-tar ran hallooing at the top of his voice towards the house.

Uncle Ben was not long in making his appearance with his "nevy," the ferryman; and the lieutenant was right glad when light broke in upon the mystifying occurrences of the last two hours. He shook the hand of Barney; and, in recompense of the painful position he had placed him in, treated all hands to a flash of lightning at the ferry-house: Uncle Ben following it up by standing his "round." Accordingly all matters being made plain, and the *lost* boat thus happily recovered, a bottle of brandy was produced, which the lieutenant would not recognise as French, from which all present took a farewell "thimbleful," and both boats rowed from the ferry-house, laughing heartily at the story of the unknown thief's consumption of the ferryman's supper, the supposed shot at Old Ben, the arrest of their comrade, and the harmless sequel of the night's adventures.

We will now turn to the performances of Abershaw, whose chances and fortunes shall progress in the next chapter.

CHAPTER XXXII.

A MARAUDING COMMUNITY—A NEW CHARACTER—BILL HOUSEMAN—HIS PECULIARITIES AND FAILINGS.

JERRY's aquatic skill had served him at a shrewd pinch, or he must have cut short this story and his own career. Having pulled cleverly, as we saw in the last chapter, under shadow of the river bank, he was enabled to watch, himself unobserved, the motions of his pursuers. The clearly-defined line of the man-of-war's boat and its crew, as they pulled eastward, made their every movement visible; and as soon as he saw the redoubtable Barney's musket at "present," he made up his mind—lest the next moment might be too late to make it up, except as a consignment for the next world—tumbled at once into the shoal water, and made for the rushes, rolling like a stranded porpoise. Here he did not think himself safe, so, having felt *terra firma* with his feet, he commenced wading, keeping his body chin

* River-thief. The regular Thames-police were not then existent; and the men-of-war's boats down the river were the only water-watch.

deep up stream. He had soon the satisfaction of seeing that his enemies kept down tide in pursuit of his empty skiff; and, having taken an observation, which convinced him that they were out of the angle of vision, he pushed in shore, and in ten minutes was, with no other inconvenience than a wet jacket, making the best of his way, on all-fours, across a meadow to some chalk pits, the white gleam of which he could see in the imperfect light. From this position he watched the man-of-war's boat take possession of the skiff in which he had escaped from the ferry-house, and it was not till they had rowed a good five hundred yards on their return, that he ventured from his lurking-place, and betook himself further inland. Having made good some five or six miles in the direction of Chatham, he betook himself to a barn, where he slept without disturbance for a few hours. Here he met with a travelling tinker of the gipsy tribe, and from him he obtained information which induced him to take the road in the direction of Penshurst, where he told him there was a gipsy encampment which could give him tidings of Rebekah and the Patrico.

The fellow's words proved true ; for these singular people, though proverbially liars, cheats, and thieves, to all beyond the pale of their wandering community, are strictly honourable to each other ; and Jerry found his old father-in-law (according to their lax social ideas), who welcomed him roughly but heartily. The old ruffian had, by the death of his elder cousin, become king of this strange commonwealth ; hence his camp had increased in numbers, and his worldly wealth in a proportionate degree. Several wandering families, forming a portion of his subjects, were at this time located in the neighbourhood of Tunbridge Wells, then in the height of its fame and fashion, as a resort for the idle and the affluent, who crowded thither to drink the waters. The gipsies found this situation an eligible one for the exercise of their varied vocations ; for while the black-eyed women in dell and dingle, and under the " greenwood tree," read to maid, wife, or widow, the riddle of life's dark or bright destiny, the men traversed the neighbourhood carrying spoons, clothes-props, lines, cabbage-nets, and exercising the peculiar gipsy callings of razor and knife-grinding, or mending pots and kettles, and the like ; and, as may be supposed, seldom left much behind, that was not too hot, too heavy, or out of their reach.

Nor were the rising generation of these wanderers unprofitably engaged. Some stood with donkeys for hire on the high-road near the " Wells," where they reaped a tolerable profit from the bones and hides of their miserable and patient drudges, whose galled and wrung withers and rumps bore testimony to the thoughtless cruelty of the fifteen-stone fools, both male and female, who occasionally took a turn, with the more appropriate children, on the backs of these miserable quadrupeds. Other bare-legged urchins, who had not arrived at the proprietorship of one or more of these Jerusalem cavalry, also picked up the stray coppers, by turning somersaults and catherine-wheels alongside and before the numerous stage-coaches and private carriages which rattled along the roads in the vicinity of this fashionable watering-place. Thus were the daily wants of this erratic community well provided for ; and as the parks and woods of Penshurst and Edridge Castle were abundantly stocked with game of every description, these, with an occasional visit to the hen-roosts, goose-greens, kitchen-gardens, and orchards of the neighbourhood, so well provided for the creature comforts of the Patrico and his subjects, that they had little temptation to stray from the prosperous little Kentish Goshen where Jerry found them thus snugly situated.

As for Rebekah, she was not with the party, for since her separation with Jerry she had refused to leave the immediate neighbourhood of London, where she expected to find him, and had consequently not accompanied the Patrico and his party on their breaking-up camp at Norwood, but remained on that spot with the next-coming tribe, who had fixed themselves in that once-favourite resort of the sibylline sisterhood.

There is little doubt but that the devoted Rebekah would at once have taken the road and made her way to Penshurst, had she known that Jerry was lurking in its neighbourhood ; but it may be conjectured that Jerry, whose intense and hardened selfishness we have often noticed, by no means displayed such eagerness as the female who had made this unworthy choice.

Women are more self-denying than men ; but we are not going to indite a rigmarole on so trite a subject ; suffice it to say, that Jerry, after detailing to the Patrico the whole circumstances of his escape, of the death of Black Sam, and the capture of Walpole, they mutually agreed that it would not be at all safe for Jerry to approach nearer either to London or the river Thames than he was at that moment, and that even a communication with Rebekah as to his whereabout might be attended with risk of discovery. Jerry was therefore to lie concealed by day, and it was only by night that he thought it prudent to stir out in search of profitable exercise for his ingenuity, in snaring pheasants, wiring hares and rabbits, or even occasionally twisting the neck of a fine Dorking fowl, which might temptingly come in his way.

Thus passed drearily several weeks, during which he grew almost as savagely sulky as a chained bear, although the necessity of concealment was still manifest, from the general attention which the case of Walpole, already detailed, excited among all classes. Of his execution, and of the transportation of Leary Joe, Abershaw had no doubt ; and no sooner had the public talk a little subsided than Jerry once more took to the field of plunder, in partnership with a new pal, a swell-mobsman, who had been obliged to make himself scarce from London, in consequence of being concerned in the daring robbery at the house of Mrs. Abercrombie, in Rathbone-place.*

With this pal, who was "up, fly, down and awake," to every move on the chequered board of London life, Jerry was soon on terms of the closest intimacy. Like will to like, and birds of a feather flock together; hence Jerry and Bill Houseman were soon sworn companions, and indissolubly united by all the hidden sympathies of villany.

Bill Houseman, Jerry's newly-found comrade, deserves a few lines of introduction. Born in the purlieus of Saffron-hill, he had early become initiated into all the "Mysteries of London," of which, had he possessed the ready pen of an Eugene Sue, he might have written a much better account, because a more faithful one, than the fiction which that imaginative rhapsodizer of "young France" has foisted on the world as a disclosure of the "Mysteries of Paris." From "gaffing the pieman" for his smoking delicacies, up or *down* to "hocussing a barney,†" and easing him of his moveables, Bill Houseman was *nulli secundus* in that glorious region of bandannas, burglary, and burking. From this university Bill emerged, and betook himself, at the age of nineteen, to the highway, where he levied taxes on his own account, as a footpad, in the vicinity of Islington-fields, until his robberies becoming too numerous and noticeable, he was compelled to decamp, to avoid coming in contact with a sort of volunteer watch, formed by several able-bodied inhabitants of the neighbourhood. To trace his subsequent exploits on Hounslow, Bagshot, Finchley, &c., would be beside our purpose; suffice it to say, his last exploit had made too much noise to render London safe, at least for a time, and he had moved down towards Tunbridge, in the exercise of his vocation, where he figured by day in good clothes in the Pump-room and at the Concert—of course with an eye to the valuables of the company—and at night walked out of town, just to see whether he could not profitably cultivate an acquaintance with some chance traveller on the road.

Between Bill and Abershaw a close intimacy soon grew up; Jerry saw how usefully such a pal might supply the place of those who had been cut off in the very bloom and flower of their villany, and Bill admired Jerry for his unscrupulous recklessness and fierce courage. The robberies about "the Wells" in the ensuing months became annoyingly frequent, and at length the fears of the valetudinarian old gentlemen and nervous ladies, old and young, became so excited, that none dared to take lonely walks; and Jerry and his pal almost found this source of revenue dried up, from the panic occasioned by their successful buccaneering.

But it is time we should notice another affair, as its result exercised some influence over the fortunes of both Abershaw and Houseman.

Among the gifts of nature to Bill, was that rather dangerous one for an adventurer, in polite circles entitled "an enthusiastic admiration for the fair sex,"—in those in which Bill was born and bred, as "a hankerin' arter the gals." This was always a failing, an idiosyncrasy, or whatever you please to term it, of Bill Houseman's, and his "tinder" heart was continually the depository of a smouldering fire, which required only the excitement of some feminine object to fan its embers into a flame. Hence, when he "nammussed," as he termed it, from Islington-fields, he left in different parts three or four Mistress Bill Housemans, to weep in lonely widowhood his enforced exile: to say nothing of some half-dozen demireps of Chick-lane, who were constantly ready to do battle on the question of a right to

* This outrage may serve to give the reader some slight idea of the state of police sixty years since; it is thus recorded in the "Gentleman's Magazine," for March, 1785.—"Seven ruffians, about eight o'clock on the night of the 7th (February), knocked at the door of Mrs. Abercrombie's mansion, in Charlotte-street, Rathbone-place, calling out '*The Post!*' The door being opened, supposing it to be the coming of letters, they rushed in, and took from Mrs. A. all her jewels, fifty or sixty guineas in money, and all the clothes and linen they could get. The neighbourhood was alarmed by the servants, and a great crowd assembled; but, nevertheless, the robbers sallied forth, and, with swords drawn and pistols presented, threatened destruction to any that should oppose them. The mob tamely suffered them to march off with their booty, without offering resistance, and none of the villains have yet been apprehended." Volumes could not add to this plain statement of the peril of property and life, under the paternal protection "of the good old King" George the Third!

† Tossing for halfpenny meat pies (of the contents we say nothing) "a penny or nothing," was a lively and flourishing trade, in these neighbourhoods, in times when the police were unknown: the second phrase expresses the atrocious crime, then by no means uncommon, of administering narcotic drugs in beer or spirits, for the purpose of robbery, and, occasionally, of murder. The bodies recently discovered beneath the house in West-street—once the "Red Lion," a resort of scamps, pads, and divers"—are, probably, the mute evidence of some such deed of darkness.

the honour of the title of Bill Houseman's "fancy woman." Thus we see there are favoured *cavalieri serventi*—"ladies men"—in all grades, and foreigners and fashionables have by no means the monopoly even of these vices. Bill, however, was fickle as he was fond, and, like a jolly jack-tar, very much inclined to find "in every port a wife." With this susceptible temperament, Bill, about the period at which we have arrived, met with what proved to be a most unlucky adventure.

CHAPTER XXXIV.

A SYLVAN SCENE—OLD NORRIS THE GAMEKEEPER—FANNY NORRIS—THE PERIL OF BEAUTY—A PUGILISTIC CONTEST—A MURDER.

WE shall not detain the reader with a description of the beautiful scenery which surrounds the picturesque mansion of Penshurst, once the favoured seat of the chivalrous Sir Philip Sidney, the author of "Arcadia," and the retreat, in a later day, of the smooth and sweet poet Waller. But it is not with the gallantry of the hero of Zutphen, nor the woes suffered by the rhymester from the scorn of the haughty "Saccharissa," that we have here to do, but with "Old Norris," as he was called in the neighbourhood, and who held the post of head keeper and ranger of the woodlands and preserves, at this time in the occupancy of a branch of the noble family of the Howards.

Old Norris was well respected in the vicinity, and, truly, not more so than he deserved; for, although his office of gamekeeper might seem an invidious one, the neighbourhood contained but few of the dissolute fraternity of poachers, indeed too few to render their depredations worthy of note. Moreover, the lord of the soil was not one of those dog-in-the-manger proprietors who think that the county-gaol was built for nothing but to "protect" his

> "Nut-brown partridges and brilliant pheasants
> From ever steaming on the boards of peasants."

Indeed, as the Honourable Mr. Howard once observed at a rent-audit—

"Nature is liberal enough in her increase, and to spare; and, provided *unfair* means are not resorted to, such as robbing the nests, or destroying the eggs or young brood, I am not afraid of falling short of amusement on the few occasions I beat over my acres. You support the game greatly, my tenants; and as, for your own sakes, you will keep *foreigners* and *strangers* from my broad lands, I am sure I cannot do better than thus make it your interest and duty to act, all of you, as a corps of gamekeepers on my estate; for where there is no *unfair* destruction or poaching, I hold the game to be your right, who feed and who support it, confident you will not abuse the privilege."

With such a master it was not to be supposed that the head ranger's was an odious office. It was, therefore, rather from ancient habits, and from a sense of duty towards an indulgent and liberal master, that Old Norris twice or thrice in the twenty-four hours made a tour of the woodlands of the estate. On these occasions he was often accompanied by his daughter Fanny Norris, a buxom, cherry-cheeked, white-toothed, laughing, country wench, the pride of her old parent, and the coveted prize of many a rustic suitor in that pleasant neighbourhood.

Now, it so happened that about the period at which Jerry and his comrade, Bill Houseman, were levying contributions on the purses of the visitors at the Wells, that the encampment of the gipseys was at no very great distance from the snug little thatched abode of Old Norris and his plump and pretty daughter; and it further chanced that upon one of his furtive visits to the encampment aforesaid, that Mr. Bill Houseman, in the gay garb of a somewhat overdressed gentleman, encountered the smiling Fanny. This rencontre happened at an unusually early hour, as the damsel "brushed the dew from off the upland lawn," in search of some water-cresses which fringed the mouth of a spring hard-by, and with which she had determined to garnish the frugal breakfast of herself and father. The sight of a gentleman strolling in the grounds so soon after sunrise was no surprise to Fanny; besides she, like every woman, sophisticate or savage, admired a scarlet coat—and in that martial colour was the swell-thief just now arrayed. At a watering-place of such fashion as Tunbridge, the broad-flapped coat with its court-collar, and the laced waistcoat, the satin queue, buckles, and breeches, were worn at all times by those who could afford such extravagances; and therefore Fanny Norris merely made a slight survey of the gallant's finery as she tripped by him, and showed her ivory teeth in a most gracious smile; the natural carnation of her cheeks meanwhile showing its genuineness by instantly spreading over her forehead and neck, as the stranger, raising a gold eye-glass about the size of a cheese-plate to the height of his cheek-bone, stared at her *over* its rim, with a gaze of admiration and effrontery that would have done honour to " Cornet Count Carmine of the Tenth or lady-killing Hussars!"

Now, why did Fanny Norris show her teeth? or, rather, why did she smile in order to do so? and why did she blush when *he* started at her? Here are nuts for your metaphysicians to crack! Did she ———? No, not a bit of it, censorious reader. She was pretty, and she knew it. Jacques says, that the " fool i' the forest," (who, by the bye, was no fool) affirmed that

> " If ladies be but young and fair,
> They have the gift to know it;"

and he was right. Fanny knew she was pretty, and she liked to display her charms and observe their effect, more especially upon males who might wear fine clothes; though, if these were lacking, she would practise a little coquetry on the rustic swains. Pope says,

> " Every woman is at heart a rake."

The sentence is too strong; and in the present case we really believe all these rather questionable doings of the pretty Fanny sprung from nothing more than a lively disposition and a cheerful temperament; and that there was no more thought of harm in her bosom at that moment, than in that of the month-old lambkin which frisked at its mother's foot a few yards before her.

But " imprudences," says a bombastic French moralist, " are often worse than crimes :"* from which, if his ethics be worth a rush, we take it that it is no worse to commit a murder than to go out on a wet day without your great coat. However, in the perplexing contingencies of this world, it was fated that this little levity should cost Fanny dear, as will appear by the sequel.

Bill Houseman, we have already said, was a philogynist, we believe that is the Penny Mag. Greek for a petticoat-hunter. In the circle of Bill's female acquaintance, it need hardly be said that he had experienced few impediments in the shape of scruples prompted by delicacy, modesty, pre-occupation of affections, or even coquetry; he never calculated on any of these important ingredients in the minds of most women who have not forfeited all title to the best sense of the name. Bill's coarse mind, therefore, prompted as coarse thoughts; and he did not for a moment doubt but that the girl who would smile, show her teeth, and blush when rudely stared at, was at his, handsome Bill's, most entire command. Acting upon this, he made a leg, and stepping up to the now somewhat astonished girl, he placed his left arm around her waist, then, raising his cocked hat in his right hand, he *favoured* her, despite her struggles, with, what he thought, a most courteous salute. This was rather too strong for Fanny Norris's notions of propriety, so she struggled hard, and endeavoured to unwind the stranger's hands from her waist. She was a strong, powerful-limbed wench, and Bill had his best strength to put out to hold her.

" Nay, nay, my lass," panted he, attributing her well-meant resistance to a desire to be won by what the French call *empressement;* " I'll have another kiss —fairly if you like, if not, why, so—come, come, those cherry lips have not been all this time ripening, without any o' the young chaps hereabouts tasting 'em; oh, no! else they're a queer set o' hobnails, and ought to be ashamed o' theirselves—there, then—don't pant so—come, another buss, and then I'll let yer go, provising you tell me when I shall see you agen."

" Help, help! Harry—oh, oh!" cried Fanny, by main strength forcing herself from the rude embrace of Handsome Bill, and running towards a young man, who, attired in the green dress of a verderer, sprung actively towards them.

The youth in " Lincoln-green" had seen the last part of the encounter, and without more ado, made up, stick in hand, towards Fanny's assailant. Bill was not a whit behind, and running in upon him as he made his blow, rendered the ash-plant he held in his hand of no avail. They closed, and a fierce struggle

* Lamartine.

instantly ensued.   Bill quickly found that his new customer was an ugly one, he was heavier and a better wrestler, and after a brief but hard try for the throw, the rescuer got the crook and brought Bill to the earth—an ugly fall.   Our swell-mobsman, however, was a first-rate tactician, and rightly judging that though his master at close quarters, perhaps there might be another game at which he could not so well play, he ceased to waste his strength, and lay quiet.

"You scoundrel—you villain!" gasped the out-of-breath Harry, "how dare you——"

"Keep your knee off my breast, will yer," panted Bill ; "let me up, and I'll fight like a man."

Harry Hunt was an Englishman, and the request was one which he would have despised himself for ever had he refused.   He would have let him up, had it been a common quarrel—but now that his spirit of gallantry was roused by insult to his mistress, he did not hesitate an instant.

"Fight fair, you cowardly villain! that I will.   I'ze tackle ye, I'ze warrant," and suiting the action to the word, Harry Hunt rose from his prostrate antagonist's body, and pulling off his coat, dashed it on the ground.

Bill was not long in following his example, while Fanny, who had too hastily concluded that the affair was over, when her rescuer had thrown his man, ran off, in a fright, to bring somebody to part them.

The scene was now a little altered : Bill had not been a pupil of the scientific Dan Mendoza for nothing ; he had activity, a pretty good stamina, and such a knowledge of the fistic art, improved by natural genius, as falls to the lot of few commoners, and had his fortune led him that way, might have been enrolled in the pages of " Fistiana," as one of the stars in the temple of pugilistic fame.   But Bill betook himself to prigging instead of professional pugilism, and instead of robbing on the *cross*, by letting in those outsiders who might bet on him, took to robbing on the *cross*-roads—a calling, to the full as respectable, and quite as courageous as that of a *dishonest* prizefighter.   Bill's natural fistic talent had often shone ; and Petticoat-lane, Chick-lane, Chequer-alley, and Copenhagen-fields, had rung with applauses, extorted by his science in hitting, stopping, getting away, and "all the occurrents of a heady fight;" the result of a contest with a mere "rural rough," with nought but pluck and average strength to back him, could not, there-fore, be long doubtful.

No sooner were they opposite, than Fanny's favoured swain made play and rushed in with so much zeal and so little discretion, that, ere he could very well make out what was the matter, Bill had jobbed him so severely and scientifically with his one, two, and ditto repeated, stepping back after each delivery, that poor Harry, astonished as much as hurt, paused in the midst of his shower of blows, wondering what sort of antagonist he had caught hold of.   Bill, who had gone back some half-dozen yards, as if yielding to the keeper's furious onslaught, though fighting all the while sharply on the retreat, saw, with the eye of a tactician, the turn of tide, and as Harry came to a stand-still, he stepped in in turn, feinted with his right-hand, and, as his antagonist instinctively lowered his left arm to guard his ribs against the pretended blow, Bill's formidable left shot out straight as a dart from his shoulder, and catching poor Harry flush between the eyes, floored him as if shot.   For an instant fireflies seemed to illumine the atmosphere, and the verderer, who thus unexpectedly found himself on the grass, was so utterly flabber-gasted, that it seemed to him as though the earth rolled like the sea, and that it was no easy thing to lie on the ground without holding.   His faculties, however, quickly returned at the sound of Bill's voice, who inquired in a chaffing tone, whether he had "got a recipe in full, or 'ud like a little more of it?"   The thought of defeat in the presence of his flame brought him to his feet again, and again he rushed at Bill.   "Ge-e-ently—ge-e-e-nt-ly," sneered the scientific and cautious Bill, as he retreated step by step, throwing off right and left the furious lunges of his adversary's fists, without attempting a return.   "Ge-e-e-ntly, young feller; why, if yer fight often, and go on this way you'll kill all your men and get lagged for manslaughter."

Again the young gamekeeper paused an instant, not for lack of courage, but for lack of wind.

"Why, you couldn't hit me once all over a forty-acre field!" sneered Bill, put-ting his tongue in his cheek at the countryman.

Fired at the insult, Harry made a desperate plunge, his shifty opponent stepped aside without dropping his hands, and, popping his foot before him, sent Harry staggering, face foremost, with a blow on the neck : he turned, foaming with vexation, and mad with rage ; this impetuosity was his ruin. Bill knew, like a first-rate tactician, that his opponent was still formidable from his strength and courage, he therefore relaxed no precaution, but jobbed, pinked, and drew his man, until poor Harry, baffled, blown, stupefied, half-blinded, but still undaunted, rolled, " like a sailor three sheets in the wind."

At this moment Fanny re-appeared, accompanied by a man she had met.

" Oh, mercy !" exclaimed she, terrified at the sanguinary appearance of her sweetheart's battered visnomy, which, certainly, was rapidly growing more like a sheep's head, than a human one. " Oh !" and she placed her hand on her heart, which seemed about to leap to her throat.

" Leave 'em alone ; don't spile sport !" cried the fellow, on whom she had vainly reckoned for assistance. It was Jerry Abershaw !

" Go it, my tulip ! Tap his sneezur ! That's yer sort ; now yer left—upper cut him—he's nodding at yer, cos his head's a shaking ; there's a beautiful nobber ; what weaving ! now, another little-'un for *me*, Bill. That's yer sort. Take him avay, he's no use !"

Such were the exclamations which poor Fanny, half distracted, was doomed to hear, while held with a fast grip in Jerry's arms. She was not, however, of the fainting sort ; so she tried to set up a scream, which Jerry suppressed by placing his hand over her mouth. As for her sweetheart, he was scarcely conscious ; though he still tried to turn the tide of battle by fierce struggles.

" He's down to my weight, now, and a little below it," said Bill, panting a bit. " Now, I'll *polish him off !*"

And, in an instant he drew on his man, and delivering one, two, three, with the whole force of his arm, seconded by a pile-driving spring of his body forward, poor Harry's head rolled from side to side on its pedestal ; and a fourth " wisty-caster" in the throat " sent him to dorse"* so soundly, that a whole college of mesmerisers couldn't have woke him.

Jerry seeing clearly that his pal's antagonist would not come again, now released Fanny from her imprisonment in his rude embrace ; and the first use she made of her liberty was to rush to the care of her defeated champion. As for Bill Houseman, with the exception of a little contusion of his sinister daddle, he had suffered little damage from the encounter ; so, hastily adjusting his dress, during the flattering encomiums of Jerry upon his fistic prowess, he donned his coat ; but before he had completed his hasty toilet, Old Norris approached the scene, accompanied by another gamekeeper. Jerry and his comrade accordingly hurried off, and putting best foot foremost, were out of sight before the state of affairs could be well explained. The explanation was, of course, a one-sided one ; and Old Norris, indignant at the insult to his daughter, and the misadventure of Young Hunt, hastened to the Hall, and waited till his master should become visible, in order to apply for redress. The assault, upon their *ex parte* statement, appeared so wanton and brutal, that a warrant was immediately issued (for the Hon. Mr. Howard was in the commission of the peace for the county) against Mr. John Wilson (the travelling name of Bill Houseman), and another person, name unknown, for two aggravated assaults, the one on Fanny, the other on Henry Hunt. With these documents Old Norris hastened to the constable of Penshurst. Their search in the village of Tunbridge was, however, fruitless, for a reason which we will now proceed to state to the reader.

It had been already arranged between Jerry and Houseman, who began to think that the visitors of Tunbridge were getting too particularly acquainted with his person—and in consequence, moreover, of a footpad robbery, which they had perpetrated in conjunction, the very night before this chance medley—that Bill should show himself in the town on that occasion only. At the time, therefore, of his encounter with Fanny Norris, Houseman was proceeding to a rendezvous with Jerry, which will fully account for that personage appearing so suddenly on the scene of action. They, therefore, took an opposite direction to that of Tunbridge, so soon as they had got out of view of Norris and his daughter, and wending their way toward Edridge Wood, there resolved to lie perdu till nightfall, and then take the road for Horsham, in Sussex, near which place was an encampment of another tribe of Patrico's kindred.

* To sleep.

"The old un's advice is generally pretty right'us in these here matters," observed Jerry, "cos, d'ye see, he's an old fox, and up to the safest earths in a'most every county. There's few on 'em as he's not bin wanted* in, at one time or other; and he says, as Sussex is much more out o' the line o' the grabbers† than Kent, and I've no doubt he's reason. But what 'ill you do, Bill?"

"I'm for London," replied Bill; "my genius don't find a fair swing in these out o' the way parts. Why, man, for foiling the dogs and throwing 'em off scent, there's no place like London. I'd like to take that wench wi' me, though; she makes my mouth water to think on her. It's my belief too, Jerry, spite of all her squalling this morning, that if she hadn't known the young fellow I polished off so was likely to come by that very time, she wouldn't have give me so much trouble. I'll see her agen, Jerry, if I get nailed for it."

Jerry remonstrated, but Handsome Bill was resolved: and to make his determination appear the more reasonable, he went on to give a highly-coloured representation of what he called "the encouragement" Fanny had given him, concluding by declaring that Old Norris's daughter had just reciprocated his kiss, and they were getting on the best possible terms when the "spoil-sport yokel," as he called him, broke in on them.

Jerry, whose notions of the female character were not a whit more exalted than those of the speaker, saw nothing improbable in all this, and was easily won over to Bill's way of thinking. Still he did not see how it could be safe to stay longer in the neighbourhood.

"Faint heart never won fair lady," said Bill; "you'll stick by me, won't you? The cove I served out to-day won't be fit to show a head for a day or two, let alone courting. Besides, he lives a good half mile off Old Norris's."

"And I can tell you more, since your thoughts are that way," said Jerry; "the ould 'un, so they say about here, has a store of shiners by him. Mightn't we just make a crack‡ 'fore we leave here? His crib stands all alone, out o' call of any one; and if we eased him of his savings, who knows but Fanny, as I see you're bent on her, mightn't be brought down a peg or two by that pull?"

"The very thing I was turning over in my mind," returned Bill. "There's nothing like want o' tin to bring down a gal's pride. They all love fine clothes better than father, or sweetheart, or even their own selves, for that matter; and if Old Norris wasn't well to do, there'd been fewer flies round his treacle-pot. So we may kill two birds with one stone. Make him poor, and then, maybe, I could get Fanny up to the long village,§ upon some suit or other; and once there, I'd pound it, I manage the rest."

"It must be done, then, to-night," said Jerry.

"Of course," replied Houseman; "but shall we try it by ourselves?"

"No; we'll have Patrico as a scout, while you and I does the in-door work," suggested his companion. "As soon as it's dusk, I'll drop in on him; he's a sure card for any game."

Their further converse we shall refrain from reporting. Evening came, and the shades of twilight were rapidly closing into night, when Jerry, accompanied by the Patrico, made their way across the park to the wood, by a circuitous route, keeping carefully in the shadow of the trees. About a stone's throw from the ranger's dwelling, the old man ensconced himself, and Jerry proceeded on his journey alone. He had just crossed a bit of open grass-land, when he heard a rustling; in another instant he was surprised by the sound of a voice; and, as he turned towards the direction of the sound, a man issued from the underwood and seized him by the collar, crying aloud—

"Hoy! hoy! halloo! Here, Ned; here's one of them! Help!"

Jerry, in turn, grasped his opponent by the throat, and threw him, with little difficulty, to the ground; his ready knife was drawn from the side sheath beneath the breast of his coat, and he drove it twice into his assailant's body. A cry of anguish, and a heavy groan, and the victim writhed on the grass. Jerry rose, and gave him another stab.

"Well done 's twice done!" growled the savage, striking him once more in the neck.

A faint gurgling rattle followed, and the old man's eyes rolled fearfully. The moon was rising, and as Jerry gazed at the features, he saw it was Old Norris.

---

* Sought for by the officers of justice.   + Thief-takers.
‡ A Burglary.   § London.

" You cussed old fool!" muttered he. " D'ye think the like of *you* can take
Jerry Abershaw?   Life's dear, old boy; and the man that gets me once in limbo,
'ill make mine a short one—so it's mine agen yours—and you're the loser. It's no
fault o' mine, you *would* come across me—I'd rayther not ha' done it, though.
Hark! What's that?"

Jerry turned—the bleeding knife yet reeking in his hand—and saw a man making
with all speed towards the mansion, which was a short quarter of a mile distant.
It was the old man's companion, a quiet labourer of the neighbourhood, who had
been accompanying him to his humble home, there to enjoy a friendly glass, and
who had been scarce ten yards distant, when Old Norris, whose practised ear detected footsteps, had desired him to stand aloof for a minute, while he passed into
the thicket to see who it was lurking in the park—a natural movement on the part
of an old game-watcher.   What followed we have seen.

The man was about to make one, when the old man cried out for assistance; but
so sudden was the desperate defence of Jerry, that before he came up he was para-

lysed with horror at beholding his aged friend weltering in his blood, and an assassin, with gleaming knife, standing over him ! Terror chained his tongue, and he, as we have seen, fled from the spot, instinctively taking the direction of the mansion.

"By the Lord Harry ! but the game's up," said Jerry, looking after him ; and he too rushed off in the opposite direction.

"Patrico ! Patrico !" cried he in a stage whisper, as he approached the clump where he had left his watcher ; "back to camp, for your life, or the Philistines will be down on ye !"

The old scoundrel stayed for no question, and in five minutes he was huddled under his tilt along with his progeny and his quean.

Jerry, desperate ruffian as he was, prided himself on being what he called "a trump ;" he therefore crossed the park, and hastening to the spot from where Bill awaited his coming, he briefly desired him also to abscond ; then, setting off as fast as they could walk on the London road, they, after doing about ten miles across country, sheltered themselves in a wood near Rochester, where, footsore and weary after their fatiguing flight, we will leave the murderer and his companion to such rest as guilty consciences will permit.

CHAPTER XXXV.

A REFLECTION—THE "ROYAL METEOR"—COACH-TRAVELLING IN 1789—A BOOTY—AN UGLY POSITION—AN ESCAPE.

MAN proposes, but a higher power disposes ; and even when short-seeing mortals judge, from the microscopic view of the world and its unaccountable vicissitudes and chances, that vice triumphs and virtue suffers, the inscrutable and just Arbiter of events holds the poise of good and evil, so that the "poor reasoning dirt-pies" which walk the earth in the pride of reasoning, cannot see the evenness of the scale. The murder of Old Norris was the salvation of his daughter. Lady Howard took the orphan girl under her own protection, and, after the lapse of a year or two, young Hunt was promoted to the post of headkeeper, and Fanny married him.

We have said Jerry and his companion were lurking in a wood near Rochester ; but as their intended plunder at the house of Old Norris had been thwarted by the melancholy catastrophe of the old man's murder, they had failed in that enterprise. Disguising themselves as sailors, Jerry, from his salt-water experience, performing the part of spokesman on all occasions when Bill Houseman's London slang might lead strangers to suspect their assumed character, they travelled on to the Dover road, occasionally lurking in woods by the wayside whenever they saw suspicious company approaching, and sleeping at night in barns or sheds. Arrived near Dartford, they spied a solitary alehouse, near the foot of the hill, on the Canterbury side.

"There isn't likely to be many people at that little crib," observed Jerry ; "leastwise, not enow to take two sich fellers as you and me ; and what do you say to a good supper and a draught of ale ? I'm confoundedly hungry."

Bill agreed that they need not fear, so they walked in and were soon seated, and busily engaged at the gratifying labour of masticating and swallowing a piece of cold salt beef, with mustard and etceteras, with which the talkative landlady supplied them.

"Not long from sea, I suppose?" observed she, by way of a feeler, so soon as the sharp edge of their appetite was blunted.

"No," replied Jerry, carelessly ; "paid off from the Wasp o' Thursday, from the coast of Afrikey."

The woman made an observation about her horror of "black negurs," as she called them, and, after expressing her surprise and gratification that her two guests had arrived safe at home to eat beef, instead of being themselves roasted and eaten by "they horrid cannibals," she proceeded to inform them that the Dover coach changed horses at the foot of that hill, that the house in which they then sat was principally established with a view to change the horses of the New Royal Meteor light coaches, which *ran* between London and Dover *three times a week !* i. e. started on the Monday morning, and arrived in Dover on the Tuesday afternoon; from Dover on the Wednesday morning, and in London on the Thursday, returning to Dover by the Saturday night. A feat which was performed by means of *two* coaches, and one set of relays throughout the line, at stages of sixteen miles. This wonderful stride in locomotion seemed so entirely to absorb the loquacious dame's wonderment, that she seemed never to tire on this theme : Jerry and his comrade therefore found no difficulty in drawing from her every minute particular relating to the movements of this astonishing Meteor, which thus performed some six miles per hour *when* on the road ; and by allowing a comfortable half-hour for breakfast, a ditto hour for dinner, another half for tea, and stopping at night at Canterbury, for the profit of the innkeeper, and the sleep of the passengers, got over the ground, as we have stated, in something under two days.*

Jerry looked at Houseman, who returned his wink, as the woman, finding her marvels were acceptable, continued to dilate on her favourite theme.

" The first of quality, you say, sail by this here new craft, eh ?" said Jerry. " Well, it's a poor heart as never rejoices ; I've some new yellowboys that never was spent yet, and shiver my timbers if I don't stay here till to-morrow, and go up to Lunnon a-top o' this here flying Meter. What say, my hearty ?"

" I'm with yer, my out-an-outer, blow high, blow low," replied the cockney-sailor ; " we'll never let go the painter while there's e'er a shot in the locker, till we sink to Davy Jones."

Jerry laughed, it was seldom he did so, shook Bill by the hand, and ordered another jug of ale, for the rubbish which Bill passed off on the woman for salt-water lingo, tickled his fancy marvellously.

" Didn't I do it right ?" whispered Bill.

Jerry replied with a laugh.

" Well," continued Bill, who rather conceited his own skill in what he called ' patter,' " if I ain't sailor enow to queer an old man-of-war's man, let me alone for taking in a petticoat when I chooses to hang out false colours : but what were you winking about when the landlady was chattering away about the new coach ? I think I reckoned you up then—eh ?" and Bill put his forefinger beside his nose significantly.

" 'Xactly so !" replied Jerry ; " you heerd her say none but quality go by this Meter, or whatever they calls it, becos the fares is so high, the commoner sort goes by the fly-waggon, and the poor people by the broad-wheeled 'un. Well, if so be these people be such nobs as she says, maybe they wouldn't be worth plucking a bit—eh, Bill ?"

" My thoughts to a T. Jerry ; but how the deuce are we to get the necessary arms ? It won't do for two of us to stop this coach, with eighteen passengers, maybe, and some of 'em with pops, without ——"

" Pooh, pooh !" replied Jerry. " I have a pair of as good brass-barrelled persuaders as man need carry;" and he put his hand on the stock of a pistol he always kept under his clothes; " and I'll get yonder gun on some pretence." He pointed towards a fowling-piece, about the weight and size of a modern Tower-musket, which rested in the rack over the mantel-shelf.

This obstacle disposed of, they proceeded to lay their plans. That night they agreed to sleep where they then were, and the following day, either by stratagem or pretence, possess themselves of the gun, and stop the coach.

" Did you ever try a spec o' this kind afore ?" inquired Bill, as they sauntered a few yards away from the house, to avoid being overheard.

Jerry replied in the negative.

" Well, then, it just strikes me, that if we try to do it a-foot, as we shall make a mull of it somehow or other — perhaps the coachman may whip on and floor one on us, and we should find it hard to catch him agen, and many other things which require reckoning up in these little affairs."

" It's my belief you're a-funking at it," returned the desperate Jerry ; " if so be *that's* the case, why, in course, we shan't be able to do it ——"

" Afraid !" retorted Bill, " show me who's afraid ! I'm not — no, not afraid of *you*, and you ain't the handsomest man I ever seed to fall out with."

Jerry glared murderously, for an instant, at his chaffing companion, then con-

* See Wade's British Chronologer, p. 567, under the head " Roads and Travelling in 1760-84," he will find that *this* was about the *fastest* coach in England.

quering his rising savageness with an effort, he held out his hand — the placable
Bill took it.

"I didn't exactly mean you was afraid," growled Jerry, in what he meant to be
a tone of apology; "not afeard—but I thought you was making objections. If
you don't jine me in this, why I shall lose a chance, that's all, but if we're to do
the thing rightus, I don't see ——"

"Well, never mind, Jerry, I'll have a horse and saddle; and to show you I
ain't afeard, *I'll* stop the coach, and you shall take the gun and do the roadside
part of the business."

"Oh, I've no objection to your riding, if you're above collecting your gravel-
tax a-foot," observed Jerry; "so no more about it."

They returned to the house. Here Bill quickly spied out a horse among the
relays, for which he struck a bargain with the ostler, for an hour's ride—a bargain which that personage was ready to make, seeing that it was what he called
"shoulder-money," and fell into his own pocket.

All was now arranged. Time wore on, and the hour approached for the arrival
of the vehicle. The shortening days were now drawing in,

> "And sober suns did set at six o'clock."

Jerry and his comrade Bill (who had lifted the gun from its resting-place, by
permission of the dame, just, as he said, "to knock over a few sparrows in the
hedges") hastened along the road by which they expected the lumbering vehicle
to come. Nor were they long in suspense, for scarcely had they crowned the
summit of the next hill, when they saw the huge coach moving along at a snail-
like pace.

"Now, Billy, my boy," said Jerry, "if you and I rifle all those fat-headed
swells, there'll be a summut to spend jolly, and a summut to brag about—
eh ?"

Bill replied by desiring Jerry to keep in the ditch until such time as he should
commence operations, and not to show himself till he whistled.

Jerry accordingly crouched down; Bill walked his horse backward and forward a few paces on the sward, taking care to keep out of sight of the advancing
coach-passengers. They soon came, and when within about a dozen yards of the
deepest part of the hollow between the descent they had just made and the rise
they were coming to, Bill rode from his concealment like a knight of old (not a
few of whom were mere highwaymen in armour), and with levelled pistol commanded the coachman to drop his reins. The man certainly pulled up at the
salute; but if Bill had understood his profession better, he would not have run
such a foolish risk, for this action of Mister Jehu was merely with the intention
of allowing the guard, who sat in the basket behind, and was armed with a short
gun or blunderbuss, time and opportunity to take a comfortable aim, and just
knock the single audacious highwayman, who thus attempted to stop the
"Meteor," out of his saddle. Nothing, indeed, was farther from coachee's mind
than to drop his reins.

It has often been observed that there are a great many individuals in this world
who occupy situations and thrust themselves into places for which they are peculiarly unfitted, and this was the case with one of the appointments of the
"Meteor." Doubtless the clicking of a pistol is unpleasant,

> "When you know
> A minute more will bring the same to bear
> Upon your person ;"

but, in this case, though the pistol was *not* pointed at him, the guard was certainly much more *nervous* (we suppose that's the term) than the coachman. Perhaps this great charge and responsibility weighed upon his faculties; be that as it
may, he fumbled most tremulously at the long box wherein his fire-arms lay.
Bill again called to coachee to drop his rein, or he'd fire, when, amid the squalls
of half-a-dozen female passengers, and a cry of "Guard!" from three or four
male ones, a bang like the explosion of a maroon proceeded from the dickey,
where the valorous guard was seated. A cry of pain and a shriek followed.

"He's shot the rascal, thank God!" observed a pious old gentleman, coolly
looking out of the coach window.

"Amen!" ejaculated his pious old lady. "What a deliverance!"

" Whe-e-e-ew !" sounded Bill's whistle; and in a cheerful voice he cried, as Jerry appeared in the road, gun in hand —

" All right, my boy, all right !" and he discharged one of his pistols towards the coachman. " Old red-coat* there has busted his blunderbuss, and now it's all our own way — come, down with yer ribbons, or ——" and Bill presented his remaining pistol, while Jerry, who was near the fore-horse's head, added additional force to the request by levelling his longer and more formidable fire-arm. Meantime, the unfortunate guard, whose right thumb was completely shattered, added by his groans to the general consternation.

" Spare our lives !" was the cry of the old gentleman and his lady, who had just before thanked heaven for the supposed homicide, and consequent salvation of their shillings and pounds. " Oh, *good, dear, merciful, kind* Mister Highwayman, take all we have, but spare our precious lives."

As to Mister Coachee, he said nothing ; but making a virtue of necessity, sullenly set himself to observe the persons of the two scoundrels ; making up his mind that, if he should see them again under other circumstances, it might be his turn to claim acquaintance. The plunder now went on unopposed ; and Jerry and his pal having possessed themselves of about fifty pounds in money, and upwards of a hundred pounds'-worth more in jewellery, watches, and snuff-boxes, took their departure, after cutting every trace of the harness through, and casting loose the horses from the carriage, upon two of which they rode six or eight miles through a bye-road, when they dispensed also with their services, and struck off towards Eltham.†

CHAPTER XXXVI.

A TRIP TO TOWN—A DEN IN CHICK-LANE—ITS FREQUENTERS—A VICTIM—AN ENGAGEMENT—THE PLOT THICKENS.

THERE was trouble and dismay at the Jolly Waggoners at Dartford, when, about an hour after the departure of Jerry and Bill Houseman, two of the passengers, bolder than the rest, arrived ; one was mounted on the horse which Bill had borrowed for the exploit, and cast loose by the road-side, and the other on one of the wheelers of the heavy vehicle. Of course, even had the traces not been cut, this ponderous specimen of a " light coach " could not have travelled on in the hilly country of Kent with two horses, for, as we have seen, the robbers had rode off with the two leaders. There had been, too, a sad delay, for it was some time before any one would volunteer to part company from the fast-stuck vehicle. The guard was sorely wounded, and incapable of horsemanship, from the shattered state of his right hand, and no one would hear of the coachman's deserting his box. Indeed, he was the boldest of the party, and they were unanimous in refusing him permission to go forward, as night was rapidly closing in, and their terrors made them fancy every straggling tree a mounted robber.

In this state of affairs, two of the " outsides " volunteered to ride on, the short three miles, to the next post-house ; and this was the very hostelry which Jerry and his comrade had but a short time previous quitted. The delay in the arrival of the vehicle had occasioned numerous conjectures, and when the brace of horsemen rode up, they found the ostler, the landlady, and all the inmates of the Jolly Waggoners, in the middle of the highway, in dire anxiety, looking out for the Meteor. The full extent of the calamity was soon explained, and the relay of horses ordered out, with such harness as could be laid hands on ; for the reader must not suppose that, according to more modern custom, each fresh set of horses stood waiting ready harnessed at the several stages—no such extravagance had then entered the heads of coach-proprietors : on the contrary, when the coach arrived at each changing-place, the coachman dismounted, and, assisted by the ostler, detached his nags, led them to stable, and unharnessed them ; then betaking himself to creature-comforts until the other four had received the trans-

---

* The guards of long coaches then wore red coats, although that military colour was afterwards peculiarly appropriated to the mail-coachmen and Post-office guards.

† The Dover coach was robbed by two highwaymen, the traces cut, and the passengers detained nearly four hours on the road, in October, 1789. This exploit I have attributed to Abershaw. The guard also was wounded under similar circumstances to those related in the text.

ferred harness on their backs, left not his pipe or his stingo until he was summoned to lend a hand, "and put them to." Hence a change of cattle often cost an hour's delay; subsequently this was shortened to a half hour, till, by various gradations of improvement, a relay was ordinarily completed on our fast coaches in the astonishing period of three minutes and a half from the arrival of the drag opposite the inn-door.

But this was not the style of the Dover Meteor, and as the harness was, as the reader is aware, so damaged as to render its repair a work of time and skill, there was sore perplexity in stable and yard, and after sundry cursings and contrivings, the ostler, the two passengers, a stable-boy, and a volunteer at the inn, returned leading the four nags to the impatient and terrified passengers. It was nearly eleven before the coach was conveyed to the yard of the Jolly Waggoners, and as none of the travellers would consent to go farther that night (a resolution extremely acceptable to the landlady), the next day was pretty well consumed ere the authorities in mighty Babylon learned anything about the audacious robbery of the "Flying Meteor."

But it is time we should return to Jerry and his brother thief. Arrived at Eltham, they concealed themselves in the deserted "pleasuance," in days of old the scene of royal revelries and pageants. There in the magnificent Gothic hall of the palace of England's monarchs they deposited the spoils of their robbery, beneath the heaps of rubbish which had accumulated in that scene of departed revelry and splendour. It was at this time used as a barn for the produce of the neighbouring fields, and from its vast dimensions and solid structure formed an admirable shelter for the hay and grain of the neighbour farmers. Here, then, they secreted their ill-gotten booty, and taking with them merely the gold and silver (which was not identifiable), they changed their sailor's disguise for that of harvest labourers, and set out for London.

By the guidance of Bill, and at his suggestion, they avoided Westminster, and, crossing by a small boat from the field near the Halfpenny-hatch (where now Waterloo-bridge stands), they landed at Strand-lane. Traversing the Strand, and striking into the innumerable crooked courts which then lay between Clement's-inn and Fleet-market, they crossed Holborn just above the bridge, dived into that avenue of burglary and bandannas, known as Field-lane, made a short turn to the right in lieu of ascending the odourously-named Hill of Saffron, and, in another dozen of strides, were safely housed in the recesses of the Red Lion; the head-quarters of the Solomons, the Dudfields, the Holloways, the Haggertys, the Ranns, and a host of law-breakers, whose names, famous in felony, shine with lurid brilliancy, and whose deeds

"Damned to everlasting fame,"

"point a moral" in the pages of the "NEWGATE CALENDAR."

*   *   *   *   *

"'Ansome Bill! s'help me Bob!" exclaimed a voice, as that personage, followed by Jerry, entered the dingy passage of the Red Lion; "vy, here's a go! Vere *have* you been a hidin' of yerself, my toolip? A rightius vun, I hopes?" added he, with a knowing wink, as he turned his curved thumb backwards over his shoulder, and nodded his head towards Jerry Abershaw.

Handsome Bill, as he was called, laughed an affirmative.

"Vell, then, you *aire* jist in the nick of it," continued the speaker, whom Jerry had now time to scan.

He was a smart and undeniable specimen of a London prig. A short dark green velveteen jacket, adorned with a countless number of small mother-of-pearl buttons of the size of fourpenny pieces, with large open pockets in each of its front flaps, stuffed with two silk handkerchiefs of brilliant yellow and red colours, while a third, a "bird's-eye blue," was carelessly twisted round his throat, clothed his upper man. Waistcoat he had none: the breast of a checked-shirt, with many plaits, being fully displayed upon his chest. Cord "kickseys" (set off with a bunch of flaunting ribbons of a light colour fluttering from the outside of each knee) embraced his "nether-bulk;" and from these the eye passed to an unexceptionable pair of calves, encased in ribbed white cotton stockings, terminating in a pair of resplendent "ankle-jacks," secured up the front of the foot and instep in a beautiful style of diagonal interlacing, which was curious for its symmetrical regularity. This style of "chaussure," as our fashion-mongers would call it, admirably adapted for running in the ill-paved streets of London, and for scrambling *over* or *through* anything, in the event of hot pursuit, was much in vogue with the thieves of times gone by; inasmuch as it was light, gave support and steadiness to the ankles, and never could come down at heels, or slip off, in gutter, in plug-hole, or "roof-scrambling." But we had forgot his head: this was crowned by a "lily tile" of indescribable form, inasmuch as, although a hat,

> " It was not all a hat—
> Part of the brim was torn away,"

to say nothing of sundry fissures, dints, and corresponding projections occasioned by the careless usage of its master, or an indulgence in the sportive pastime of "bonnetting" on the part of his companions. This dilapidated and limp-looking "castor" was nevertheless set on the fellow's head with a knowing cock, which spoke plainly that even in that part of his apparel, seedy as it was, he affected a certain degree of nattiness. Yet even in this awful "tile" and the flabby rope of black crape, which looked as though it kept its shattered particles together, there was a fine strain of practical philosophy. The wearer well knew that this was the part of his apparel least defensible from injury, and most exposed to loss in his hazardous profession : inasmuch as, to say nothing of the common salutes on its crown, it would be the first thing to fall off in a scuffle or a chase, and the most likely thing to be left behind in a hurry. Finally, long slender corkscrew ringlets of black hair, greased to a glossiness, and twisted round a warm tobacco-pipe with a care and neatness which might excite the envy of many a feminine coquette "on conquest bent," dangled on either side his knowing countenance.

All this, which it has taken us so long to write down in words, was perceived by Jerry in a few seconds, as the fellow withdrew his pipe from his mouth, twisted one of his love-locks on its stem, and squirted the saliva through his teeth, with a dexterous aim, at a savage-looking bull-terrier which followed him, giving at the same time a chirrup like a June grasshopper.

"Vell, the sight on you *is* good for sore-eyes," continued he characteristically— "but as you're jest in luck's vay, I'll interduce yer."

"Thank'ee, Dick Downey—or, rather Downey Dick," replied Bill; "but I'll introduce myself."

"Vell, as yer likes, and the rest in ha'pence," ejaculated Dick; and pushing open the door, which swung to with a rope attached to a lump of lead in the toe of an old shoe, the trio stood in the "parlour" of the Red Lion, in Chick-lane, since dignified by modern refinement, under the name of West-street, West-Smithfield.

"Now then—go it, yer cripples!" exclaimed a sturdy, unshaved, unwashed, perspiring, grim-looking individual, a curious cross-breed of cadger, poacher, and footpad, who stood up in the centre of the room, opposite a muscular virago of some five-and-thirty or forty, with a face carbuncled with the effects of coarse paint and gin. "Go it, Nantz! rozum away, old Cat-gut!" and *at it* they went indeed : she stamping and reeling like an infuriated Bacchante, and he jumping and shouting like a wild Indian in a war-dance, to the shrieking and squeaking of a fiddle, the catgut of the strings of which must have been surely selected from a race of kittens, suckled upon vinegar, and fed on sour-krout, for such excruciating, teeth-rasping sound, never could have been torn from ordinary viscera.

"Go it, Nantz! Bravo, Black'un!" mingled with the laughter of the company; and Bill, detaining Jerry by the arm, both stood amused spectators of the scene.

> " As thus they gazed, amazed and curious,
> The mirth and fun grew fast and furious;
> The ' screeching' loud and louder grew,
> The dancers quick and quicker flew,
> Until ane caper syne anither."

Nantz, fairly exhausted—or to use the phrase of the spectators *done up*—by the combined powers of gin, tobacco, a close atmosphere, and violent exertions, reeled from the perpendicular, and as she staggered into the arms of two or three half-drunken blackguards, and fell upon the table sick, giddy, and drunk, a shout of applause hailed the victor in this Terpsichorean contest, wherein the strength of the stamp and the suddenness of the whirl, and the odd jerks of the legs could only find a resemblance in the hornpipe of the erst celebrated Dusty Bob, or the vulgarisms of the fashionable Polka.

"Brayvo! brayvo! brayvo! Gipsy Jack's done her up! Now, my kiddy, I'll thank yer for the qvartern o' strip-me-naked, as I bet yer on Jack," said one of the numerous company, staggering up to Downey Dick.

"Valker!" responded that personage; "the artful von't fit here, Mister Ned, so don't be trying it on too strong—I took Jack for choice."

"Oh, vos it that vay?" replied Ned, with affected innocence; "vell, I b'lieve it vos, now I comes to think on it. Can't ve mix it up for half-a-pint, tho', vith those friends o' yourn. Vhich *three* vill go odd man, and *I'll* take the conk'rer?" added Nimming Ned (for in that cognomen he rejoiced), giving a sign to Dick.

"Oh, I'm qvite hindiff'rent," replied Dick, with carelessness; "here's Bill's friend, and me, and you 'ill go odd man, and then, vichever stands *out*, 'ill see Bill for 'tother qvarten—eh, vot d'yer say?"

"Say," retorted Bill, laughing, "say that you must think that I've bin gitten pretty considerable green by going into the mackery,* to be picked up on so soft a lay. No, if I stands a qvartern so; if I don't, why I don't. But, as you're so nutty on your gaffing, *I'll* see you for a half-pint—sudden death;† perhaps *that'll* suit you?"

It did not seem, however, that this was by any means suited to Nimming Ned; he therefore backed out, under cover of a sharp fire of chaff and small talk, which it would be beside our purpose to detail. We shall, therefore, in lieu, give a brief description of the apartment, and the company in and among which Jerry and his guide now found themselves.

The room was large and oblong, and at the farther end yawned a wide chimney-place, within which, round an unset grate, clustered a disgusting group of filthy, unkempt, shoeless children of both sexes, engaged in roasting and toasting pig-potatoes, slices of bacon, chesnuts, or bits of meat of the most questionable colour and form. Some of these looked diseased, cadaverous, and wretched; others, cunning or desperate. These were the street population, the reserve from which the ranks of thievery and prostitution were principally recruited and supplied.

Some of the girls, when out, carried a bunch of lavender or a cheap pincushion; the boys, a cabbage-net, a small sieve of apples, or in parties of two or three cried firewood, and other cheap commodities with a joint-stock donkey. This, however, was only among the elder of the juvenile fraternity: the greater proportion were sent out by their protectors or parents on the "area," or "morning sneak," or made use of as spies and touters, to give warning of the approach of danger; or, when of a small and stunted growth, became valuable aids in burglaries or shoplifting, from the ease with which their little bodies could be thrust through apertures, and concealed in spots where the hiding of a man of ordinary stature might be impossible.

Cries, imprecations, and the most horrible indecencies and blasphemies proceeded from the mouths of these abandoned little wretches, unnoticed and unheeded by the adult part of the company, except when their treble cursings and threats took the form of blows or scratchings, when one or other of the assemblage would interfere, either as assailant of the uppermost or defender of the undermost, in which case a kick and a curse or two settled the affair between these God and man-abandoned specimens of forlorn and debased humanity. I know that some who may read these pages will condemn this picture as exaggerated—they know little of the vices and miseries which may be seen by all who have the patience and the courage to study human nature in its lowest phases of civilization. There is ignorance as "crass" (to use the language of the Schoolmaster) within half a mile of Exeter Hall, as on the banks of the Niger, or beneath the cocoa trees of the Pacific; ay, and ignorance ten times more vicious, because it combines the corruptions, the temptations, and the miseries of a highly artificial state of society, in the blessings, the elevating and softening influences of which these wretches have no share. But these sin-devoted Ishmaelites of a pseudo-pious community, have detained us too long—suffice it to say, that a commissionary-shipping, nigger-

---

* Mackery—country.—See Jon Bee's *Lexicon Balatronicum.*
† *i. e.* First toss up; since distinguished as "Newmarket."

evangelizing community of self-satisfied Pharisees, whose sympathy only becomes active as the distance and difficulty of its objects are increased, left this moral ulcer to fester and mortify under its very nose, while they exported tracts and worsted nightcaps to St. Domingo, and Scriptures and skates to Sierra Leone.

"Here's a go!" exclaimed a stumpy little fellow, with his black hair curled in long ringlets, and a sailor's jacket, as he slipped into the room, and closed the door suddenly and quietly behind him. "Here's Hirish Poll and Sqvinting Sall, vith a reg'lar lushy svell in tow, a-kimming down from Smiff'eld. Kious* a bit, carn't yer now; cos they've tipped me the hoffice as he's vell lined in the gropers."†

The intelligence of the sham sailor seemed to act as a sudden sedative. The fiddle was silenced, Downy Dick placed his back against the door, and all was

* Keep still.   † Got money in his pocket.

PUBLISHER'S NOTE

pp.131-134 are missing.

pretty nearly quiet, inasmuch as the thievish crew abated their loud chaffing to moderate tones.

" It must be a reg'lar thing among the lot of us," observed Bill Houseman, " if there's any business done."

" Vy, yes, in course," responded another of the thieves ; " alvays 'xcepting them as isn't svorn in o' the lot : this here svell, as you ses is a trump, han't paid his reg'lars yet, nor bin made vun on us."

" And what of that ?" replied Handsome Bill, who was evidently a thief of authority and influence in this law-breaking assemblage. " S'pose he isn't ; so long as he's a friend o' mine, and one in the haul,* why shouldn't he have his reg'lars ? As for his Spanishers† for garnish,‡ I'll go bail for that."

A slight murmur arose, which Jerry instantly checked, by exclaiming—

" Oh, if that's what stands in the way, don't trouble yerselves ; there's the five hog, and ——"

" Brayvo !" said Nimming Ned, as Jerry threw five shillings on the table ; " that's yer sort, more gatter‖ and a flash o' lightning§ round. It never rains but it pours. Let's have it in—— Vere's the trezurer ? Call in the cove o' the ken,¶ ve invests all the inkem in the sinking fund here, and no mistake. Jest knock vith the qvartern agen the venscot there, vill yer, mister ?"

This request was speedily complied with, by one of the thieves nearest the partition which divided the end of the room from the place where the liquor counter (for it could not be called a bar) of this filthy den of crime and drunkenness was situated. The landlord himself—a returned convict from the plantations—quickly entered in reply to the summons. As he came in, he also made a sign for quietness, by turning his thumb backward over his shoulder, and then placing his forefinger beside his nose.

" Ve knows all about it, old covey," replied the facetious Dick. " A cove as vonts easing of his yack and inguns,** and he couldn't ha' come to a more conwenient crib to be accommydated. It's all right, old buck, ony you shouldn't hurry no man's cattle, as you may vun day have a donkey of your own. Now, then, you see, these gemmen vonts a jack o' vash,†† a dowzer o' trump's blood,‡‡ and, let's see, whose for strip-me-naked‖‖—vun, two, three, four. S'help me, but I vos goin' to say as I vos a-counting *noses,* but I'm blest if Vistlin' Billy there han't lost his nose through skrimmagin' with the ladies—oh, you're for max, too, *are* yer ? Vell, then, jest hadd a halderman o' blue ruin, old Bung, and that'll make out the five bob ; and ven ve're out o' licker ve'll take into our royal considyration vot ve'll club, not to let the new member's garnish go bare ——d."

A general laugh testified the gratification with which the eloquent proposition of the facetious speaker was received. This the landlord again checked by a pantomimic gesture.

" Are they there ?" asked Ned.

The landlord nodded his head in assent

" Have you any of *the right sort o' ginger ?*" asked Downey Dick, in a whisper, as the landlord was about to retire after collecting a few measures and pots from the tables.

The reply was again a nod of intelligence, and the ruffian disappeared.

" How do I look, Jerry ?" asked Handsome Bill, turning round, and showing that personage his back ; " pass pretty tidy muster for a swell—eh ?"

Jerry, as Bill was neatly and well dressed, replied in the affirmative.

" Well, then," replied that personage, " *I'll* do the trick. Some one on yer just step out and twig which o' the molls the swell's most nutty on, cos I musn't *spoil* her, and then give the office to the other one. Jerry, you slip out, too, and don't come in till I give you a signal. It's all right, Ned, you needn't stare. I'll draw the cull§§ as nice as ninepence ; but if so be *that* suit won't fit, why then we'll splice his nightcap¶¶ for him. I don't want no more than us two in it, and all of you keep kious unless the cove's rusty—these things are best done quietly."

* Robbery.   † Dollar, five shillings ; so called.   ‡ Entrance money.   ‖ Beer.
     § A glass of gin.   ¶ Landlord.   ** Watch and seals.
†† A gallon o' beer ; so called from the ancient leathern hooped vessel, which contained four quarts.
‡‡ A quart of rum ; so called, because for many years the convicts were transported to work in the plantations.   ‖ Gin.   §§ Rob the simpleton.   ¶¶ Drug some warm liquor.

CHAPTER XXXVIII.

A REFLECTION ON THE FRENCH SCHOOL OF ROMANCE — A FRIENDLY AMBUSH — A VALUATION, AND A DISAPPOINTMENT—AN UNEXPECTED RENCONTRE.

WE left the scoundrel-quartette indulging in the smuggled Hollands of mine host of the Red Lion in Chick-lane; of their converse we can but give an outline, such as may convey to the reader some idea of the tendency and character of their discourse, rather than its actual phraseology. To do this would pollute the vilest pages of a French romance, and, thank heaven (as Sterne said of English swearing as compared with that of our Gallic neighbours), if we *do* swear, we yet do it with *cleanliness*.

Not so the modern romance-writers on the other side of *La Manche;* they scruple not to depict common street-walkers as amiable characters ; adultresses as happy and uncensured members of society ; ruffians as " good fellows" in their cups ; and men of "high feeling and honour" as "introducing" their acquaintance to *experiment* on the virtue of their wives—just to see if they (the females) possess the "virtue of resistance;" regarding their wives' fidelity, for aught that appears to the contrary, as legitimate a subject for trial as a filly's paces, or the steadiness of a pointer! Thank heaven, we say, then, that we have not yet arrived at these and a thousand other of the social *refinements* of the land to which English *gobemouches* seem just now to look for the importation of *literature* in addition to *pantaloons*,* and that the land-marks and distinctions between virtue and vice are not yet so confounded and blended in English literature as in that which ephemeral folly or fashion has, for the time being, placed in the ascendant. Holding, therefore, the privilege of "calling a spade a spade," we shall not colour the thieves and strumpets, the *stabbers* and assassins of our story, into mere "creatures of circumstance," and extenuate every crime which can degrade humanity and deform society, by surrounding the circumstances of its perpetration with a fog of predestinarianism, nor shall we soften down the harshness and truth of the picture we present by a cunning admixture of ambiguous *couleur de rose* ("that's neither white nor scarlet").

The result of this style, which we lament to see becoming daily more prevalent, is to demoralise those weak minds which have little depth of experience and thought, and to excite in many an admiration rather than a detestation of the characters placed before them by the imaginative but unfaithful writer.

It has been said that highwaymen have been made by witnessing the performance of Macheath; shall we, then, doubt that a boy of strong passions and little tenderness may find strange chords of sympathy awaken, and desire of imitation rise in his mind, when his fancy is possessed with the idea of the *valour of ruffianism*, when the library and the stage combine to show him what a " good fellow " an habitual stabber and murderer can be "when you once come to know him." We would ask, is it desirable that fornication and adultery should be elaborately set before the rising generation of females, as not only venial offences, but marks of *esprit* on the side of either the men or the women ? nay, further, that conjugal fidelity is rather *vulgar* than otherwise ? Yet upon the illicit commerce of the sexes, as upon a hinge, and upon the guilty fruits of that connexion, or upon the libertinism of some married man, or upon the acquiesence of some avaricious and contentedly cornuted husband, do each and every of these "interesting," "absorbing," "most original," "romantic" fictions turn. Truly, if it were with no other object than to check the influx of this insiduously-polluting current of miscalled literature, it would be worth while to enact a law of International Copyright.

Byron satirically apostrophises this favourite and almost exclusive source of French romance as the *teterrima causa* of all *belli;* and really, judging from the

---

* *Hudibras :*—

> " And as the French we conquered once,
> Now give us laws for pantaloons,
> The length of breeches and the gathers,
> Port-cannons, perriwigs and feathers."

filthy histories of whoredom in disguise, called "interesting romances," with which the cheap press now teems, it would appear that it was also the sole spring of every movement and derivation of imaginative literature. This vile school cannot long prevail; it is not that of the Scotts, the Galts, and the Dickenses; we do not find the web of their delightful and healthy fiction worked from such materials; no! demireps, dastards, and adulteresses do not form their representatives of the upper classes, and stabbers, street-walkers, and ruffians the mass of the lower. Yet we should be sorry to compare the interest of their life-like narratives with the extravagant and indecent farrago which for a time seems to throw their merits into eclipse, even in the meridian of their birth-place. But enough of this; we wash no moral negroes, and return at once to the den of sin, sorrow and suffering, whence we have so long digressed.

The plunder of the unfortunate victim who now stark cold was rolling in the tide of the Thames, was produced upon the table, over which swung a flaring train-oil lamp. The money was first divided, the papers and silver snuff-box being handed over to Black Ben. The division of the spoil effected, the party, as we have seen, fell to drinking; for it was the routine of that den to lie buried in sleep during the earlier hours of the forenoon, and waken up to activity as the shades of night approached, which theft and crime make their harvest-hours.

It was already past three o'clock, when Ben grumbled out—

"Come, lads and lasses, it's a gettin' late; I shouldn't a bin sittin' up here a toasting my shins, and sluicing my ivories all the blessed darkmans, only I've bin expecting o' company. I say, Bill, you're a cove what knows a thing or two about womenkind, and gen'rally haves vot I calls a pretty tidy taste in flesh in regard o' sporting a fancy mot; I've bin this hour or two thinking as there'd bin a arrival here of that sort o' commodity. Old Patrico, as they calls him, is out on the lay somewheres near Holloway, and he chalked it out that his wench should be here with the swag, if the thing comed off right. Two o'clock, or thereaway, was the figure fixed; I hopes as there han't bin no accident with the wedge, for the crib was one worth cracking, else he was out in his reckoning."

Bill looked at Jerry, who suddenly roused himself at the words of the landlord. "Rebekah Morse is her name?" asked he.

"'Xactly," replied Black Ben; "she as was lib* to Jerry Abershaw, as was spiflicated by the coast-guard, down in the Mashes, when they copped spicy Bob Walpole and Leary Joe. They do say as he and Black Sam both got their gruel there, but owin' to the high tides shortly arterwards, they never could find Jerry's body. I never seed him, but I heerd from 'Bekah as he was a hout-an-houter. She hasn't took up with noboby, as I hear, since she was made a grass-widder, and she's about as tidy a bit o' meat as ever I clapped my eyes on, and 'ud be a hornament to any flash cove's crib: and if any vun can fix her that vay, why I should say as Han'sum Bill 'ud be the kiddy, and no mistake!"

Bill Houseman laughed at Jerry, but as Black Ben was surly, and not of a temper to endure patiently a secret from which he was excluded, he burst out—

"What the blazes are you sniggerin' at, grinning like a Cheshire cat there? She won't come this darkmans, so the game's up for to-night. Come, boys, mop up yer lush." (Ben knocked out the ashes from his pipe, and placed it upright on the hob, in the chimney-corner). "Now, Nell, it's time to morris! shove yer trunk; d—n the woman, she's asleep; here Bill, lend a hand, and we'll lay her on along a bench in the tap-room, she'll snooze herself sober on a soft plank. Now Mister What's-yer-name——" and he turned to Jerry. A cautious but sharp rap at the side door interrupted Ben's speech; all voices were instantly hushed, and every ear open, while the keeper of the den stole softly to the entrance, and applied his ear to a listening hole. The lamp was growing dim for want of oil, and the streets were silent and dark; again a smart tap of the knuckle was given. "Miao-uw-o-u-w," said Black Ben, in admirable imitation of a strayed kitten. The reply was instantaneous.

"That'll do, old caterwauler," replied a cheerful whisper; "steek the flap;† look alive about it! The coast is clear, and I'm shaking with cold."

"That's her voice, by ——!" exclaimed Jerry, grasping Bill's arm.

---

* Paramour, left-handed wife.   † Open the door.

"Now for a lark!" added that facetious personage; "slip in here, and come out when I whistle."

Jerry instantly slid into a small cupboard which opened beside the chimney, and which extended (after rising two steps) entirely behind it; this was one of the many hiding-places and contrivances with which this den of crime was furnished, and which recent search has brought to light. Meantime, Black Ben had cautiously unfastened the door, and in another minute Rebekah Morse had deposited a small canvass sack, which she carried beneath her cloak, on the table. Ben, in the interval, proceeded, as he said, "to throw a light on the subject," by trimming and replenishing the lamp. Rebekah looked round, and only Bill Houseman and the sleeping woman.

"She's safe enow," said Ben, observing the direction of her glance; "b make sure of her, lend a hand, Bill. We was just goin' to put her to bed on a Norway mattrass* with sawdust blankets, as you guv the signal."

The drunken outcast was carried to her sleeping-place, and Ben returned. But where the devil's your pal nammused to ?" asked the landlord.

Handsome Bill placed his finger on his lips in signal of silence, and Rebekah proceeded to unfold her treasures, consisting of various articles, in the appraisement of which the scoundrelly Ben seemed to be as completely *au fait* as though he had served a long apprenticeship in the shop of a first-rate pawnbroker.

The first article produced by Rebekah was of gorgeous appearance, although its two sides had been crushed together for the convenience of carriage in the small sack which, suspended by a cord round her neck, hung down beneath her gown, giving her the appearance of being *enciente*, although partially concealed by her gipsy-cloak. It was a tall standing cup of parcel-gilt, with engraven shields of silver, and its cover, which she next drew out, bore a tastefully-chased figure of a race-horse in dead gold.

"Right'us wedge,† by jingo," muttered Ben, directing his eager gaze towards the sack of precious metals, as the gipsy pulled out three tankards and several spoons and forks ; a snuff-box and other minor articles quickly followed.

"Brayvo! any more on it ?"

"That's all." replied the gipsy. "Patrico says I'm to stay here to-night, and he'll come hisself in the morning ; the wedge he'll leave you to ding,‡ and knows you'll do the thing as is right. Oh! I'd 'most forgot—here's a pictur, and he ses as he thinks they're di'monds round it, an' if so, old Barney the broker's a judge on 'em, and ——"

Her speech was interrupted by a sudden exclamation as she held the miniature in her hand obliquely under the light, in full view of Bill Houseman. She stopped and stared at the utterer. His features were pale, and he looked sick.

"Some brandy, Ben !" and he caught up the hollands'-bottle and gulped down a mouthful. "It's all right—only a little qualmishness—that 'ill do !"

"Why, what the devil ails you !" asked Ben.

Bill pulled him aside, and whispered hoarsely: "It's him ! his pictur! him as we ——" and he pointed mysteriously to the floor.

"Stuff an' nonsense !" grumbled Ben ; and taking the portrait, decorated round its edge with a row of large bright Bristol stones, which the gipsies had mistaken for diamonds, he closely inspected it. "Yes," said he, coolly, "I dessay as it mought be *him*—it's like him, perhaps. Why, what a silly cove you *aire*," continued he, looking at the miniature ; " 'spose it is, what does it magnify —eh ?"

"Oh, nothing !" replied Bill, who did not seem, thief as he was, at all seasoned to deeds of blood ; "nothing ! *That's* vallyble, I should think !" added he, by way of turning the unpleasant subject, and taking up the battered cup we first mentioned.

Alas! that truth should compel us to say it, but there were, even in the good old times, "knaves" who dressed in broad-cloth and wore civic chains of gold, as well as those clad in fustian or frieze. "All is not gold that glitters," is an old proverb, but not more musty than true. Rascal gold and silversmiths, as many a modern refiner can bear testimony, were villanously prone to work in other metals than those implied by the names of their occupations, and the battering to which this grand piece of plate had been subjected, had exposed several secrets which the "cunnynge artificer" had never meant to be known. These peculiar features were now undergoing a rigid scrutiny from the ferret-eyes which twinkled in the bullet-head of Black Ben.

"Whe-e-a-w !" whistled he in a low tone, as he continued his scrutiny. "Abram-work‖—rascally Abram work ! so help me ——! Look'ee here ! and

    * A deal board, so called from the country whence they were principally imported.
       † Valuable plate.   ‡ Dispose of, make away with.
  ‖ Counterfeit, sham. The term "shamming Abraham" was derived from the "Abram-men," as poor lunatics were anciently called, the melancholy infirmity of loss of reason being a favourite fraud of the olden beggars, ere asylums were generally founded. The writer lately saw at a city refiner's a magnificent piece of plate, consisting of a candelabrum and epergne, each bearing pompous inscriptions of their presentation to a member of a noble house, by "the grateful, &c., &c., corporation of the town of, &c., &c.," in consideration of the "distinguished services of, &c." to the borough of ———. These tokens of gratitude had been knocked down at a sale of plate, at per oz.,

here! and here!" added Ben, pointing out at each break the base metal which formed the body and pedestal of the cup.

It was indeed disappointingly manifest that nothing but the shields and raised figures had any pretensions to intrinsic value.

"I shouldn't wonder," said Ben, "if this here's the same;" and producing a pair of pliers from a cupboard, he quickly forced off two nuts on the inside of the cover, and disclosed the knavery of the manufacture—the horse was a mere lump of copper, coated with silver and then gilt!

Rebekah looked somewhat blank.

"I'm blowed if this airn't a mare's nest," said Ben, pursuing his scrutiny; "the tankards is Sheffield too, though werry good uns — o' *the sort*. Well, this do beat cockfighting; crikey, what a haul!" and he grinned facetiously.

"What, ain't it silver, Mr. Benjamin?" inquired Rebekah. "You don't say so!"

"I'll show you, my blackeyed 'un," replied Ben; and, stepping to his closet again, he produced a small glass-stoppered bottle containing nitric acid.

"Now, supposin' as this wor goold, this here stuff would lay as quiet on it as though it wor a drop o' water, but 'stead o' that, you'll see it 'ill turn as green as cabbage—look here."

The test was applied, the metallic fume arose, the biting liquor boiled and bubbled as the copper was eaten by the aquafortis.

"There *may* be a trifle on it," resumed Ben, "as is a little better nor they makes tea-kittles with. I'm sorry for Patrico, though; the spoons and forks is wedge, in course;" and he took them up and bent one of the table-spoons with his powerful hands. "Playted on soft hiron, by the living——!" and indignant at knavery which was not in his own line, Ben, with beautiful consistency, proceeded to curse every separate corporeal particle of the manufacturers' and owners' souls to the bottomless pit. "These must ha' bin a pretty set o' *would-if-they-could* people, wherevers they hanged out, as belonged to sich household stuff as this. Well, if so be as I do use hiron prongs and chivs,* I lets my wisiters know what they aire a-eating with."

Rebekah looked terribly chapfallen.

"And these here sparklers," for Ben's shrewdness awakened as he went through with the lot; "this nick-nackery's no go as it stands: so we'll just knock out the pictur;" and he forced the little ivory oval (with some hair wrought in a seed-pearl cipher at the back) from its frame.

Rebekah desired him not to throw the painting in the fire, which he was about to do, so he handed it to her, and she deposited it in her bosom.

"I'll just see in no time if these is stones or paste," said Ben; and starting one from its setting by twisting the frame, he applied its point to a spotted bit of dingy looking-glass on the wall. "Soft as Hirish butter!" was his exclamation, as he surveyed the damaged facet. "Oh, Bekky, Bekky, how the Patrico will swear, and cuss, and drink when he comes to——"

An undeniable sneeze echoed from the chimney-back. Rebekah turned a little pale, and clasped her hands in silence; Ben turned to whence the noise proceeded, and Bill Houseman laughed.

"Didn't you hear that?" inquired Rebekah.

"Hear what?" answered Bill, quietly tipping the wink to the landlord.

"It was only the cat," said Ben.

"No," replied Rebekah, "it was a man."

"Nonsense," replied Bill, in a bantering tone; "how can you tell as it wasn't a woman's sneeze; does a man sneeze different?"

"It sounded from the chimney," persisted Rebekah.

"Maybe," said Ben; "there's rum noises in these houses, Bekka. But come, this is a cussed bad job; it's a rigler do, and no mistake. 'Bad luck now, and vorse next time,' as Phil Pickpurse used to say; he's gone to 'Tigguee† these nine

and one of them, weighing *nominally* 200 ounces, contained barely *thirty-five* of fine silver! There were more utterers of "base metal" than the poor smashers, even in those days of what my Lord Maidstone calls "simple faith in trade."—*Query:* Does his lordship apply this phrase to the *venders* or the *purchasers?* it is rather ambiguous. The plate was made upwards of eighty years ago. The application of the term to cheats, impostors, and base metal, gilt or plated, was easy and manifest. * Knives and forks.

† An elegant alias for Antigua, formerly a spot for transported felons.

years. Come, take a sup o' gin, wench; we wor a going to roost, but your comin' put the stop on us. I s'pose you wouldn't like me to hop the twig and leave you here wi' 'Ansome Bill, till the Patrico comes in, eh? If so, say the word, and I'm dumb as a door-post. He's good company, I can tell yer!" Here Black Ben tried on a laugh, which fitted his surly and ferocious muzzle as a smile would a bull-dog's. Rebekah, so far from approving of this arrangement, declared that if he was about to go, she should return to the Patrico's squatting place; whereon the landlord, with unusual complaisance, for reasons we shall here-after see, decided on sitting up; "though," as he said, "if he should go off into a snooze in the harm-chair, they must kiss pretty loudish afore he'd wake." The fire was now stirred, three tumblers produced, and in each of them Bill proceeded to put some sugar and spirits, Ben declining any further liquor.

"Then *who* is the *third* glass for?" inquired Rebekah.

"That's for the *cat!*" replied Bill.

Rebekah smiled, though she did not see the joke; then, as if a sudden thought struck her, she went on:

"Oh, Mr. Benjamin, speaking of the absent, have you heard whether Jerry, *my* Jerry, has been seen anywhere in Lon'on?"

"How the devil should he be seen," replied Ben, "onless it be his ghost. I'm thinkin', pretty Bekka, as bein' too long a widder is muddlin' yer brains."

"Oh, no; Patrico saw him down in Kent, a dozen times since that, along with a spicy swell cracksman from town; and I think, from what he said," and she turned with a woman's natural shrewdness to Bill, "as this pal o' yours here can't be *much* unlike the very man."

"Blown agen, by G—d!" laughed Bill, his vanity tickled by the compliment (for there is pride of a sort in the breasts of burglars as well as barons), "and all along o' my good looks!"

"Ah, they'll hang you, some day, them aggrawating curls o' yours," said the landlord, mollified by the combined influence of Rebekah's smiles and the liquor he had imbibed.

"And what 'ud you give me, 'spose I was to tell you where Jerry is?" inquired Bill; "a kiss, o' course?"

"If you're his pal, you wouldn't ask it—and if you ain't, you don't know," replied the gipsy, shrewdly.

Jerry waited to hear no more, but, gently pushing open the door, came out from his hiding-place.

"The *cat*, by goles!" cried Bill; and, the next moment, the blood-stained burglar was folded in the arms of the pretty Rebekah.

> "Why did she love him? Curious fool, be still!
> Is human love the growth of human will?"

CHAPTER XXXIX.

THE ARCANA OF THIEVERY—FLASH HOUSES—A RESPECTABLE TRADESMAN—REFLEC-TIONS—A PLOT—SHOPLIFTING—A MISTAKE—A PURSUIT AND CAPTURE.

JERRY and his newly-found *bona roba* now became dwellers in the flash hostelrie of Black Ben. A shambling, extensive building was that queer old house; a complete rookery of nests for thieves in hiding, and offering in its numerous stair-cases, its concealed communications, its under and above-ground trap-doors, its spouts,* false-floorings and panels, contrivances for the concealment of law-breakers and their booty, of which but few traces remained when the hand of improvement tore down its walls, and levelled its foundations for the inspection of the idle and the curious of the present day.

* Among the contrivances lately exposed in the old houses in West-street (formerly Chick-lane), was a *spout*, or long wooden trunk, similar to those in use at pawnbrokers', for the purpose of letting down articles from the upper warehouse to the shop. This apparatus was artfully concealed in the bottom of a recessed cupboard, which, when lifted up, disclosed a long passage, lined with planks, and once possessing a sack fastened to a cord and pulley: the stolen property placed herein was lowered into a pit in the cellar, behind a strong brick wall, where it might safely lie until time and opportunity should come round for its withdrawal.

The Red Lion itself, a large tenement, had other outlets : one to the rear of the neighbouring houses, another by a trap opening on to the river Fleet, up the course of which felons might escape to Turnmill-street and the lawless region of " Half-hatch," as it was then called. Add to this, that the vile character of the neighbourhood, its filthy wretchedness, and its viler inhabitants, offered no attraction to visitors. Brothels, low liquor-shops, tripe-dressers, bone-boilers, manufacturers of vitriol (or aquafortis), and the like offensive callings, seemed to have made this region their favoured station, and therefore we cannot wonder that this degraded Alsatia was an eligible lurking-place for such a one as Jerry Abershaw.

Tired of the country, he now sought the "peopled wilderness" of town, and, in company with Bill Houseman and one or two other pals, betook himself regularly to the avocations of a professional thief. Numerous were the purses filched daily by them at *buz* and *cover*,* and the property procured by *dragging* ;† nor did the arts of *sneaking*‡ and *hoisting* § lack in them fine practical professors, while, in the last-named branches, Rebekah proved an admirable auxiliar.

Emboldened by success, they gradually flew at higher game, and there seemed at one period a probability that the promising and prosperous firm of Abershaw, Houseman, Morse, and Co. might attain the rank of *receivers*, and deal in the goods which others had stolen, instead of risking their necks in the more active service of daily rapine.

But all the hopes of Jerry and Bill becoming *family-men*‖ were dissipated, smashed, scattered, floored, and frustrated by one of those unlucky *contr'etemps*, which, sooner or later, seem to fall to the lot of every recorded practitioner of the art of felonious appropriation, whatever may have been his talents, his daring, and his temporary success.

On the right hand of the Strand, as you progressed westward, stood, in days of yore, the Old Exeter Change, once a covered arcade for the sale of Sheffield cutlery, scissors, penknives, knotted teapot stands, many-coloured rugs, razor-strops, pincushions, gloves, scent-bottles, brushes, and all those nicknackeries of the toilet, devised to—

" Make dames killing, or to leave them neat."

If less lofty in its architectural pretensions, and less brilliant in its lighting—

" For in those days we had not got to gas"—

than its modern successor, hight " The Lowther," and less classically decorated with coloured frescoes and wreathed panels than the pigmy diagonal descendant —the short passage of some thrice three shops—which has usurped its historic name,¶ Old Exeter Change was far more solid, valuable, and bazaar-like, in the

---

* In thieves' *patois*, a *buzman* was the pickpocket who performed the theft, and his *cover* a confederate who stood beside the victim, in such a position as to screen the thief, while operating, from the observation of passers or bystanders. His office, also, when the principal was detected, was to receive and *ding* (or make away with) the property, or obstruct (*accidentally*, of course) the person robbed from making pursuit. Street robbers, even within these thirty or forty years (see the " Life of Hardy Vaux"), frequently pursued their nefarious calling in parties of three or more, whereof one or two of the least skilful in the manual practice of their *profession* baffled pursuit, by running *before* the real robber, and shouting " Stop thief;" or, as occasion required, taking up a fictitious pursuit in a wrong direction, bawling lustily, and misleading the cry.

† *Dragging* signified robbing carts, carriages, &c. while standing at warehouses, wharfs, shops, or waiting at the doors of their owners' houses.

‡ *Sneaking* was entering shops, areas, &c. unperceived, during early morning, and making-off with such valuables as were easily comeatable.

§ *Hoisting* was a name for shoplifting, practised by well-dressed thieves, and often female confederates.

‖ *A family-man*—do not start reader—in thieves' slang, meant neither more nor less than one who dealt in stolen goods. See John Bee's " Lexicon Balatronicon," and " the like o' that."

¶ There is no slight danger that this curious little upstart " Exchange" may altogether escape the notice of the public, unless formally introduced. Be it known, then, to all men, by these presents, that " *New* Exeter 'Change" is a small court in Catherine and Wellington streets, Strand, which the curious in corners may discover in the following manner: coming from the westward you turn to the left up Wellington-street North (an agreeable spot for " noontide-contemplation made," and much frequented by actors " in collar," for studying parts and open-air rehearsals), pass on until you have cleared the pillars of the portico of the Lyceum (miscalled the English Opera-house, because what few English Operas *there are* are never, by any chance, performed there), you will find, on the steep ascent, a well-placarded, rotten range of planks (known as the Exeter cascades), on your left hand ; make a three-quarter turn to your right, and you will perceive two iron gates at the upper extremity of the office of the *Morning Post;* perhaps they *may* be open, if so, slip through them, and behold, 'tis two to one that you are *first* on 'Change. N.B.—This assertion will hold good for any hour in the four-and-twenty. Should the enthusiastic explorer of this

wares presented for sale, than the piles of toys, jars, baskets, flowers, mosaics, and French trumpery, which now obstruct the public nuisances called " Arcades." The upper floors of this celebrated lounge, where Colley Cibber gossiped with the " pretty glove-maker," and the bucks and bloods of the reigns of the three first Georges made assignations with citizens' wives (as we see in the comedies of Cibber, Vanbrugh, Wycherly, and others), was for many years occupied by a col-lection of birds, beasts, and reptiles, known as Polito's, subsequently as Cross's, and, at the period of the final demolition of the Exchange, removed from the crowded thoroughfares of London to the delightful lakes and grounds of the Surrey Zoological Gardens.

On the Strand side of the projecting block of houses forming the "Exchange," which here narrowed that " artery of London's living tide" to choking fulness; were several shops richly furnished with valuable goods, and which opened at their rear into Exeter Change, where they did a supplementary sort of business, during certain "fashionable" hours, in nicknacks and baubles, *etui-cases*, fans, and the cheaper sorts of jewellery. One of these shops was rented by Gabriel Garnet, a sleek, well-to-do denizen of the precinct of the Savoy.

Gabriel was a snug "respectable" sort of man, who, with a good shop, a good stock, and a thriving trade, kept up a comfortable character ; he had thrice been chosen churchwarden, and though as hollow a knave as ever smiled over a counter while he stabbed a customer to the very bottom of his breeches pocket, had so many of those outward and visible signs of what people call " a respectable tradesmen," that they care not to inquire whether there is any inward and spiritual grace under the solemn pretence. Mr. Garnet had got rich, however, and that alone, like charity, will cover a multitude of sins. He was overseer of the poor, and he *overlooked* them ; he was churchwarden, and he took especial good care that the *cash* of the church should not be wasted. In short, Gabriel Garnet was a very worthy man ; he went to church twice every Sunday, wore a bushy brown wig, a pair of silver-rimmed spectacles, and square-toed shoes ; carried a large family Bible under his arm (which he never read) ; slept during sermon in a well-padded pew ; never failed to return a seven-shilling piece into the plate at the quarterly charity ser-mons, out of the hundreds he robbed the poor of annually ; and, if it *had* been his luck to have been born and to have thriven a few hundred yards further to the east, who knows but he might have been the chairman and governor of half-a-dozen charities, a guardian of the poor, a churchwarden, an alderman, a trustee and treasurer of a sea-bathing infirmary, nay, by some of the *unaccountable* accidents of life, a lord mayor ?

Now Mr. Garnet's shop had, by its position and contrivance, and from the valu-ables contained therein, for some time attracted the particular attention of Bill Houseman ; and as it was the winter season, when the town was full, and the days short, several consultations were held at the Punch Bowl, near Temple Bar,* as to the best mode of easing the cosy Gabriel Garnet of some of his plate and jewels. As a private watchman was kept within the Exchange, while another *slept* in a small moveable box, which was placed every night at Mr. Garnet's front door, in the Strand, " cracking the crib" was voted both perilous and unwise, and at last a combination of the *sneak* and the *lift* was unanimously agreed on, as the most feasible method, by these proficients in the art of unlawful appropriation.

Rebekah was at once called in to council, as on her, of necessity, must the exe-cution of a part of their scheme devolve. The *modus operandi* (the mode of *doing*), in both senses of the word, was carefully arranged, and the following Wednesday fixed for the affair to " come off."

> " But he that prigs wot isn't his'n,
> Doth oft get cotch'd and lodged in prison,"

says some moralizing poet of priggery, whose name we cannot quote, inasmuch as we never remember to have heard it ; and Jerry, as regarded the silver plate of

---

curiously-named passage be determined to push his discoveries, he may walk through in nineteen good paces, and find himself at the terminus—the pavement of Catherine-street—in a line with Thurston's shop-window.

* This house, as well as the Swan (in New Church-court, near St. Mary's, in the Strand), were for many years noted nests of thieves and swell-mobsmen. The latter was long known as " The Shandy Gaff," an untranslateable title, which we must leave to future commentators, with the mere remark, that the term is now applied to a commixture of ale and ginger-beer. The Punch Bowl lost its license some years since, and is now Cann's Eating-house.

Mister Garnet, was doomed to add another to the thousand exemplifications of the ancient truism, that—

> " There's many a slip
> 'Twixt the cup and the lip."

*　　　　　*　　　　　*　　　　　*

" Hist! hist! Jerry!" whispered a female voice, amid the crowd of idle loungers who thronged the avenue of Exeter Change. " Hist, Jerry, not so fast! I'll step round into Garnet's now—you see his boy has left the shop—and while I price a pair of earrings in the Strand concern, you and Bill can watch your chance in the 'Change."

" That 'ill never do," replied Bill, after a moment's consideration. " No, no; you and Downy Dick shall go in, and we'll pipe the bloak;* but don't be too fast, or we mayn't get a good chance."

But we must give the reader some notion of the whispering party of marauders, and their personal appearance on the evening in question, which was a dark and cheerless one in the gloomy month of November. It was scarcely six o'clock, and many people were yet crowding the sheltered arcade. Rebekah, whose slender and *petite* figure, to use a theatrical phrase, well adapted for " making up " a character, was attired in a long but scanty riding-pelisse of pale blue cloth, while Dick, whose person was none of the thinnest, was costumed in a style of vulgar finery. A laced coat, with huge cuffs and embroidered pockets, a pudding-like cravat, and a three-cocked hat, adorned his upper man, while velvet inexpressibles, with watered silk continuations, and a pair of huge paste-buckled square-toed shoes, indued his nether limbs. Jerry was habited like a sober Methodist preacher, and Bill was glittering in the gay apparel of a man about town. Agreeably to the arrangement, the *lady* stepped into the Strand, with her *soi-disant* uncle, and in two minutes they had entered the shop, and engaged the attention of Master Garnet.

" I don't think, niece," observed Dick, as he stood with an air of constrained consequence at the counter, " that them topazes at all become your complexion; becos', d'yer see, yeller stones isn't altogether suitable to a brown countingance : and you ain't very fair, you gipsy, you ain't," added he, for the purpose of showing his degree of familiar consanguinity with the lady.

Mr. Garnet thought the gentleman's phraseology somewhat coarse ; but, blinded by his eager cupidity, he attributed it to rustic breeding ; and hugging himself mightily upon the notion that he had a delightful pair of rural *greens*, proceeded to exhibit various necklaces and jewellery, recommending them with all the plausible flattery of which he was master.

" You don't think yellow stones, sir, are suitable to the lady's complexion. Upon my word sir, I admire your taste and judgment. Rubies, sir, for a warm clear skin, such as the lady's—a-hem—or emeralds, perhaps. Now, here's a suite of emeralds—a Sevigné, sir, with three drops—unique, though I say it, and not to be matched in London ; which, with the necklace to correspond, is only thirty guineas. I'm really almost ashamed to name such a price, sir—except in hopes of future favours, I could not. These emeralds, sir, I refused thirty-eight guineas for, last week, from the Dowager Duchess of Longwind ; it was on *credit*, though, ha ! ha ! And, though the money's sure, *some day*, yet I'd rather do business with a small profit, sir, and a quick return, than keep names long upon my ledger. That's my maxim, sir—prompt payment, and low profit, sir. What does the lady think of them ?"

" I saw," said Rebekah, carelessly turning over the valuables with which the counter was becoming strewed ; " I saw some pale blue stones, with pearls among them, at Mr. Gem's in the City, which——"

" Oh, madam, I beg you'll not mention Mr. Gem ; I know what you mean, madam, a set of turquoises, Persian or French turquoise ; I never, madam, never say a word in disparagement of a brother tradesman, that's my rule ; but—a-hem! Mr. Gem, madam, has no such suite or turquoise in his shop as I have. Or pink topaz, madam, which perhaps would harmonize—excuse me an instant !"

Mr. Garnet turned round and sought an iron safe with numerous drawers, and

---

* Watch the old man.

Downy Dick hesitated not a moment. A necklace was "dinged"* by Rebekah, and found its way, together with a diamond ring to which he helped himself, into Dick's capacious coat pocket.

The thing was neatly done, and when Mr. Garnet again turned, the gentleman was sucking the end of his gold cane, and his brunette niece attentively examining the emerald necklace. Jerry had in the mean time entered the back shop, and sneaking thence, while Bill Houseman watched the Exchange entrance, possessed himself adroitly of a tray of valuables.

Success is sometimes dangerous. Garnet had no suspicion of his customers, and Dick abstracted another ring. But if Garnet was off his guard, another person was not. His better half, finding him engaged with some genteel customers, had silently stepped down to the top of the stairs which led from the house into the front shop, with a laudable interest in the trading, in which she was much more than a sleeping partner, as most of her neighbours could testify. Here, elevated some dozen feet above the people below, she had an ample opportunity of seeing without being seen, and the first thing she spied was the last act of Downy Dick, as he appropriated the second ring.

She descended; but imagine her surprise and horror at perceiving Jerry, who at that very moment was in the act of making his exit from the back-door with the tray of precious stones. Alarm kept her silent one instant, the next she burst into a piercing shriek.

"Murder! robbers! rape! thieves!" screamed the bereaved Mrs. Garnet, rushing frantically towards the back-door.

"God bless me! what ails the woman?" exclaimed Garnet, who saw nothing to excite this dreadful outburst. Instinctively, however, he began hustling up the valuables before him. It was now his turn to cry out. Snatching a necklace from the counter, Rebekah, at a wink from Dick, darted from the front door, and Dick made good use of his time; he threw the contents of a large box of high-dried Scotch snuff into the face of Mr. Garnet, with one hand, while with the other he clawed up in his extensive paw sundry smaller articles, such as brooches, earrings, and head-ornaments. Poor Garnet howled with pain; blinded and agonised with the pungent dust, he for a few seconds forgot even his darling property; and Dick was ensconced in the back parlour of Black Ben—nay, Rebekah, who had made the circuit of Skinner-street and Cow-lane, and thence passed through Back-court, was housed, or nearly so, before their unfortunate victim had recovered the imperfect use of his organs of vision.

But we must turn to see how Jerry and his comrade fared in the vigorous pursuit which was made after them by the active Mrs. Garnet.

CHAPTER XL.

"STOP THIEF !"—BOUNCING IT OUT—DAVE TURNER—AN AWKWARD FIX—AN INTER-
VIEW WITH HIS WORSHIP.

THE distracted appearance of Mrs. Garnet, as she rushed into the avenue of Exeter 'Change, occasioned a general commotion amid the crowd of loungers, which might have been expected to prove favourable to the escape of Jerry and his pal, Bill Houseman; but daring expedients, though often crowned with success, have no patent or privilege in their favour; nevertheless, the exception may be taken, when they do fail, merely as a proof of the rule.

Mrs. Garnet, screaming at the top of her voice, "Thieves! murder! robbery!"—we are not sure that in her distraction she did not use another outcry, usual with females of mature age in all cases of dreadful alarm—achieved no other end than that of drawing upon her the attention of the loungers then and there assembled. But if her interjections were incoherent, her actions exhibited remarkable method and singleness of purpose. She had spied Jerry as he made his exit, and she took care not to lose sight of him—no, not at the moment when, with rare dexterity, he passed the valuables to Bill Houseman, by a momentary action, unperceived by all but her. Jerry was but a few yards from her, so he at once darted out at the gate-

---

* Passed from the thief to the confederate.

way of the Exchange. Mrs. Garnet, with all her apparent bewilderment, detected
this pass of legerdemain, and bustling through the people in pursuit of Handsome
Bill, who was swaggering up the arcade with perfect nonchalance, threading his
way quickly and cleverly among the crowd, she seized him by the coat. Bill,
however, was an old stager, and in the few seconds which had elapsed, had thrown
the small morocco-covered jewel-case under a projecting bulk, on which was displayed a heap of goods, and transferred its contents to his broad salt-box pocket.
He turned, with well-affected surprise and perfect self-possession, on Mrs. Garnet.

"'Pon honour, madam, but you astonish me, demme! To what am I to attribute this ex——"

"Oh," gasped Mrs. Garnet, "good people, pray hold him!" Bill had gently,
but forcibly shifted her grasp from his lappels. "Pray secure him; he's the
thief--he's got the jewels somewheres!—oh! oh! oh!—hold him! hold him."

"Split me, but this is the most unaccountable—— Really, madam!—'pon my veracity, I believe the woman's a little crazy. Does any body here know this person—will somebody take care of her—demme!" added he, trying to walk off.

The astonished bystanders were too much confused to attempt the detention of so mohock-looking a personage, but the jeweller's wife rushed after him, and again seized him.

"Help! help!" screamed she; "he's a thief! he's a thief!"

At this moment several shopkeepers, male and female, issued from their stalls in this old-world bazaar, and, unluckily for Handsome Bill, recognising Mrs. Garnet as a neighbour, interposed.

"Step in here, sir, if you please," said a man to the well-dressed accused, who, but for the virtue which resides in a good coat, would have met with no such courtesy. "Step into my shop; if you have not the articles about you, I'm sure Mr. Garnet will apologise, but really I cannot let you go without your address, and ——"

His speech was left unfinished, for Bill, as if resenting his unmannerly attempt at capturing him, exclaimed—

"Demnition, sir, do you mean to——" and suiting the action to the word, dealt the interposer such a blow in the breast, as extricated himself and sent his would-be captor sprawling. It was of no avail; half-a-dozen bystanders collared him, or rather made good their hold on all parts of his upper garment; but even for this contingency Bill was prepared—quickly slipping his arms from the capacious sleeves, he stooped, and making a well-meant rush, was clear of the immediate crowd.

> "As darts the dolphin from the shark,
> Or the hare before the hounds,"

Bill vanished by the western entrance, leaving behind him the proceeds of their spoil. That hour was a black one in his horoscope. Close by the gate, and at that moment entering, was the noted Dave Turner the thieftaker; though late on the scent, he came in time for the death. At the Brown Bear, in Bow-street, he had gathered an inkling that there was "a plant" laid that very evening in Exeter 'Change, and with one of his lurchers was hastening to the spot when his ears were greeted with the outcry, and the next instant he saw the half-stripped Bill emerge like a hunted fox from a well-beaten cover.

"Tally ho!" cried he to his follower, and in twenty seconds Bill was run into by these staunch hounds of the law. He struggled, but it was in vain.

"Soho! soho!" cried Dave Turner, as the pursuers came up; "'Ansome Bill! I knows him, werry good, werry good! We'll jist walk back, my good people, and see what fun he's bin arter."

"Robbed Garnet, the jeweller's shop!" exclaimed a half-dozen of voices.

"Oh, werry well!" then the thieftaker added to Bill, *sotto voce:* "is it a plant for *forty*, or can you manage a *scrape** for an extra ten *quid?* If so, it's all right; if not—q-q-q-k!" The latter inarticulate sound intelligibly mimicking the sharp jerk of the rope which begins the process of strangulation.

"All right!" panted Bill.

"Werry well;" and then Dave added aloud, "Now then, good people, stand aside, while we conveys our pris'ner back to the shop where this here robbery was committed."

The crowd gave way, and the officers, one on each side of the prisoner, made the best of their way to Garnet's shop. Short as the distance was, the following whispered converse passed between the officer and his captive.

"Actyal robber, Bill? can they hidentify yer?" asked Dave.

"No," curtly replied Bill.

"Werry good; I arn't inquisitive, but is the goods found?"

"There'll be no sweetmeats,"† rejoined Bill, "for they've nailed the swag,‡ leastways, best part on it."

"Wus luck," grumbled the admirable guardian of the public's property; "wus luck!"

By this time, escorted by a dense crowd, the officers and their prisoner had arrived at Garnet's shop; the door was closed, and to prevent further danger to the

---

* Shall I be compelled to earn the amount of blood-money given by the crown on conviction, or can you give £50 to get off?
    † Reward offered.   ‡ Recovered the booty.

stock of valuables by the momentarily increasing assemblage, some neighbours kindly cleared away the people, and put up the shutters, thus obstructing the view of the idle curious. Mister Turner, too, repelled the inquisitiveness of several immediate neighbours, and, for reasons of his own, ejected them from the premises, under pretence of the prisoner being crowded on.

Poor Garnet, as well as the smarting state of his blinded eyes would permit, detailed, with aggravations, the particulars of the robbery, during which Dave Turner exchanged peculiar looks of intelligence with the thief.

Indeed, as yet, the affair seemed pretty favourable for Bill, but Mrs. Garnet quite changed the complexion of the case. She first related the robbery of the case of jewels (of which old Garnet was entirely ignorant), then described the appearance of Jerry in a manner that would have done credit to a *Hue and Cry* advertisement, and lastly, stated clearly that she had seen the transfer of the property from the unknown thief to the prisoner, whom she identified, and finally produced his coat and the stolen jewels.

Dave looked perplexed and serious. " In course, in course," said he ; " that there's clear, you knows the man as took the case o' val'ables ; well, maybe, so does I for that matter, werry well. *He dings* 'em to this here swell, werry well, you seed that, marm ? there' no doubting the hevidence of one's own eyes, marm. And this here's his coat ? Werry well ; these here things, marm, you'll have to conwince a jury on—to me, they seems, werry clear : so if you means to press the case, marm, I'll take the prisoner afore their worships in Bow-street, where your attendance, and that of yer husband will be necessary ; and I hopes, marm, as you won't forgit to say a good word or two to his worship, about my wigilance in this here ugly and unfortnit affair."

In ten minutes Bill was before the magistrate at his house, under the piazzas in Covent Garden (for there were no evening sittings), and in an hour afterwards he was conveyed by Dave Turner and his runner, to the prison in Tothill-fields.

CHAPTER XLI.

A THRIFTY TRADESMAN—A SLAVE-OWNER—THE PERILS OF WEALTH—A PAIR OF ORPHANS—TEMPTATIONS—WORLDLY HYPOCRISY.

THE escape of the hero of our story and that of his astute companion, Downy Dick, together with the safe keeping of Handsome Bill in the prison of Tothill-fields, gives us leisure to breathe awhile from the oppressive *malaria* of crime, misery, and low debauchery. Let us turn, then, from the dense mass of corrupted civilization, which forms the substratum of a vast metropolis, to other scenes of contrasted manners and habits of life. This we the more gladly do, inasmuch as the personages and adventures we are about to introduce, materially influenced the career and fortunes of Jerry Abershaw and his confederates.

In one of the most stirring, industrious, and therefore the most thriving, provincial towns of Lancashire, dwelt Ebenezer Lazenby, an honest, pains-taking tradesman, who, by the careful management of a business left by his father (an intelligent and ingenious watch manufacturer for the London and export markets), had succeeded in amassing what, in the ancient borough of Preston, was considered a handsome independence. Until the age of thirty-eight, the " worthy watchmaker," as his well-to-do townsmen did not scruple to designate him, had been so totally absorbed in what our more volatile neighbours across channel have called an Englishman's end of existence—namely, making money—that he had never allowed himself to think of that expensive luxury—a wife. Such an addendum to a household was considered by the thrifty Ebenezer, albeit he was not a mean man in some respects, as one who would take from his hands the reins of domestic expenditure ; which the scrupulous integrity and over cautiousness with which he had been home-educated told him must ever be regulated at a rate far beneath the income of the disburser, or prospective ruin must inevitably await him. These maxims Ebenezer had imbibed from his parent, a strait-laced presbyterian ; hence he had always, carrying prudence to an extreme, shrunk from ideas matrimonial, and quelled (occasionally with difficulty) his rising preference for one or other of the " Lancashire witches," with which Preston and the neighbouring hamlets abounded. The establishment of Ebenezer, therefore, consisted of a brace of apprentices to his craft, a sour old housekeeper, "frae north o' Tweed," and a red-elbowed female servant of all-work. These were his home companions; in his counting-house and factory he found employment for a clerk and some twenty workmen; to these his mornings and afternoons were devoted; his evenings, to reading and sometimes prayers (a habit acquired by long drill in his father's life-time), and expounding (as he termed perverting torturing) scripture texts—a solemn chat with some prosaic chapel-going neighbour—and an early retirement to bed. These regular habits, joined to a precise studied manner and a delibera-tive mode of speech, gained for the well-to-do watchmaker the character of an eminently pious man. The general deference, too, with which he found his person and opinion regarded among the elders of the small congregation to which he belonged, combined with the spiritual pride and self-sufficiency too easily engendered in narrow minds by the peculiar doctrines of election and predestina-tion prevalent in his sect, persuaded Ebenezer Lazenby that he was indeed a shining light, and one whose steps were guided from above; hence, in his case, as in so many others, the dangerous doctrine of fatalism, as he called it, " a state of grace," was a direct road to the backslidings which he fancied could not befal one who was " a chosen vessel."

We have said Ebenezer was thirty-eight; his abstemious self-denying life, and an originally hale constitution, had preserved his vigour of body, and in all proba-bility he might have still gone on slowly accumulating wealth and keeping a fair worldly outside; but circumstances were combining to place him above the secure station he had hitherto occupied, and to develop his true character; too often a secret to a man himself, until a disturbance of the even tenor of his exist-ence throws him into new and unaccustomed positions as regards his fellow-men.

This event was the return to his native country of an elder brother, Edward Lazenby, who had quitted Liverpool in his boyhood, volunteering on board a slave-ship to the coast of Africa; one of those manstealing barques of misery, crime, and death, known at that time as " Guinea traders." A strong constitution and an iron determination of purpose, a cruel and stony heart, and the cool perse-vering courage for which Edward Lazenby was conspicuous, raised him, on the death of the captain and mate of the vessel in which he served, to the rank of its commander. The produce of two or three trips to the Gold, Ivory and Slave Coasts, placed him in a position to purchase a vessel, in which he quickly amassed money by the accursed traffic in human flesh and blood; a traffic which, thanks to the in-defatigable exertions of a Clarkson, a Wilberforce and a Buxton, no longer dis-graces us as a Christian people. It would be beside the purpose of our story to detail the horrors and atrocities by which Edward Lazenby acquired his wealth; suffice it to say, that therewith he purchased an extensive estate in the island of Grenada, in 1763. Here fortune still undeservedly prospered him, and, after a marriage with a " brown lady," of French extraction, the daughter of an opulent planter, he returned, at the period of which we now write, to Liverpool, bringing with him two children, the innocent heirs of his ill-gotten riches.

In a commercial country, and more especially in a city owing its rise to com-merce alone, wealth assumes an undue preponderance in the social scale; and Mammon, the god of the six days' worship, and too often of the whole seven, deposes Him who is peculiarly "Lord of the Sabbath." " God's nobility and Nature's" are almost unknown; and a gilded idol, with its heart of stone, its brain of lead, and its feet of clay, is exclusively bowed down to and worshipped. " Get money—honestly if you can—but get money," is the axiom, and its posses-sion is conceded as making " the man," irrespective of philanthropy, patriotism, generosity, wisdom, and all those virtues which alone entitle him to the respect and esteem of his fellow-creatures. The gold of Edward Lazenby plated over every personal defect. He bought a handsome mansion in the vicinity of Liver-pool, gave gorgeous and vulgar entertainments; the splendour of his equipages and the beauty of his illiterate though elegant wife were universally extolled; his name shone in gold letters on the boards of the public institutions and hospitals, and he was spoken of as " a liberal, high-minded merchant, of princely fortune." A liver-complaint, however, was insidiously undermining his once sound constitu-tion, and the physicians recommended the air of Naples or Nice, as indispensable during the second winter after he had reached his native shores. On this voyage it was decided that Mrs. Lazenby should accompany her husband, while the two children should be placed under the care of their uncle, the Preston watchmaker, of whom we spoke in the opening of this chapter.

From this excursion it was fated that the wealthy slave-owner should not return. The city of Marseilles, to which the vessel that conveyed the health-seeking party was bound, was that autumn visited by one of those pestilential scourges so common in the Mediterranean seaports. A vessel from Smyrna brought thither the devastating plague, and among the earliest of its thousand victims were the parents of Walter and Eugenia Lazenby—at that time under the protection of the thrifty Ebenezer. The arrival of the sad intelligence aroused the first evil thoughts in the avaricious uncle's bosom. So sudden was the stroke of death, that the same day's post brought to Ebenezer a letter from his brother, exulting in the anticipation of renovated health, and the probability (for no certain intelligence of the fact had reached England) that the scourge had broken out in Marseilles.

Ebenezer rightly surmised that "a wealthy English merchant and his wife" mentioned in a Marseilles gazette as having fallen victims to the visitation, were no other than his brother and sister-in-law. He hastened to Liverpool, privately ransacked his brother's papers, and discovered a rough draft, or copy of his will. It firstly bequeathed to his wife Eugenia the bulk of his wealth, in trust for his infant children. Then came some liberal donations to public charities (for those whose consciences tell them their unworthiness, often seek to compound with heaven by restoring a part, after death, of what they have amassed by crime and cruelty during life), and the document closed by a scanty appropriation of £500 to his brother Ebenezer, in consideration of his trouble in executing the trusts therein contained, in the event of the decease of his said wife. The greedy Ebenezer persuaded himself that he was an injured man : his brother's wealth had excited his envy, although he had hypocritically been among the first to congratulate him on its possession, and now, by a safe and a short cut, this coveted dross seemed within his grasp.

Strange thoughts arose in the predestinarian's bosom as he paced the gilded saloon of his deceased brother's spacious and gorgeous mansion; he almost persuaded himself that the wealth which, he knew, had been earned by crime, had been accumulated by his brother—"a vessel of wrath"—that it should come to him, one of the "elect." He "jumped" the consideration that he was at that moment scheming the spoliation of two helpless orphans, whom he was bound by every tie of blood and of religion to protect and foster; and saw one of "the stern necessities," as he termed it, of his peculiar position. Besides, with him the wealth would at once be available for a number of excellent purposes; was he not in a fair way, he argued, provided he had the capital, to make this property yet larger, and at last bequeath it to the very infants from whom he should merely withhold it—with noble interest for its use ?

Ebenezer argued but with himself, and his cupidity pleaded eloquently. Then arose the thought that the law would place this fine estate, and the thirty or forty thousand pounds which was appended thereto, in the hands of the chancellor, and he (Ebenezer) should thenceforth be excluded from gratifying his itching palm with the clutch of his brother's gold. At length his resolves took form and method. Hastily examining his brother's escritoir, he was satisfied there was no farther testamentary document; the single one above-mentioned was accordingly committed to the flames, and another carefully prepared, in which Ebenezer closely counterfeited his brother's hand. In this his property was duly left to his wife (whom Ebenezer knew to have shared his brother's fate), and, failing her survival, to Ebenezer himself—merely providing for the annual payment of certain small sums; next leaving to his children, Walter and Eugenia, two several West India estates, to their absolute possession, on their arrival at years of discretion; in the mean time, out of love to his dear wife, and his well-beloved brother Ebenezer Lazenby, he bequeathed to them, or the survivor of them, the precious charge of their care and education.

To Ebenezer's delight the original document was witnessed in the island of Grenada, by *three* French domestics; their marks and signatures were quickly forged, and, to crown the whole, the crafty uncle left by a sham codicil a snug legacy to the very witnesses above-mentioned, on a separate codicil made in England. This he reasonably concluded would silence the signers, and so it proved.

All these things duly contrived, Ebenezer placed the supposititious document in the place whence he had withdrawn the real one, and retired, after giving several unimportant directions to the household, of whom he was, in the absence of their master, the nominal head. The heart of Ebenezer beat painfully loud that evening on his return to Preston. He was new in crime, and scarcely dared to face the innocent unconscious creatures he had been so cruelly plundering. He retired early, on the plea of indisposition, and spent his first sleepless night in perplexing speculations and vain surmises as to his future career as a wealthy man.

Strange that so oft the consummation of our desires should bring with them a severe rebuke to our misjudging anticipations! Ebenezer had all his life yearned for riches as the means of happiness, yet now they were attained was he happier? No! uneasy dreams disturbed his sleep, and he started from a disordered bed, feverish, nervous, and miserable. Yet the farthest thing from his thoughts was a relinquishment of his ill-gotten plunder. Day after day elapsed—for at that time fast-ploughing steam-ships had not made communication rapid and punctual—still, beyond the general accounts of the ravages of the plague in the Levant, on the shores of Italy, Greece, and Southern France, no special communication spoke of the death of Edward Lazenby and his wife—a fact easily accounted for by the circumstance that the only confidential domestic who attended them had shared their fate. Ebenezer, therefore, wrote, after the lapse of a month, a letter of inquiry to the mercantile house at Nice, to which his brother had desired all letters to be addressed, inquiring after his health, expressing satisfaction at his last communication from Marseilles, and hoping for a happy reunion in the Spring of the ensuing year. The reply may be guessed: inquiries were set afoot, and shortly after an official return from the British Consul certified the death and burial of Mr. Lazenby, his wife and servant, at Marseilles, in the English cemetery.

The grief of Ebenezer was well feigned; he lavished caresses on his little nephew and niece, wore an extra-sour aspect and one of the deepest of hatbands, and cautiously abstained from going near "Lazenby Lodge," for so, with "the pride that apes humility," had the defunct slave-dealer named his imposing seat.

The death of Mr. Edward Lazenby, "the opulent West India merchant," was duly trumpeted in paid paragraphs, and the virtues and beneficence of a hard-hearted trafficker in blood received the grovelling laudations of all the servile tribe who adore wealth for its own sake. To Ebenezer, who knew his brother's natural disposition well (for he was the ruffian and scapegrace of the family, and many a time had he heard his father hold this very Edward up as a warning beacon to youth), these mercenary praises taught another lesson—that money could not only conceal vices, but was the source of many imputed virtues. So money Ebenezer resolved to have, as the best key to the good opinion of the world—a thing his cold pride much aspired to.

The testamentary paper was found, even as Ebenezer intended, and the *ci-devant* Preston watchmaker entered, with the congratulations of many friends, on the possession of Lazenby Lodge, five thousand pounds per annum, and large estates in the West India islands, productively cultivated in sugar, rum, and coffee, and well-stocked with the sable brethren of their pale-faced oppressors.

If Ebenezer Lazenby had any misgivings, while pursuing the craft of watch-making, of the lawfulness of mere dealing with his fellow-creatures as with the beasts that perish, it quickly wore off when he himself became a slave-owner. We easily persuade ourselves of what we wish to be persuaded: Ebenezer comforted himself with the reflection that, as he was predestined to be a slave-owner—and that, as a logical *sequitur*, there must be slaves, or their owners could not exist—it was part of the grand scheme of Providence, that he should continue to oppress the helpless and torture the unresisting. In the enjoyment of this comfortable creed we leave him, and beg the reader to leap over two years of his life, till we find the whilom watchmaker a greater man than he ever expected to be.

See how wealth's attended! Troops of smiling friends
Obsequious crowd around high Mammon's throne.
Can worth or virtue, wit or genius bright
Command such homage! No; and thus
It ever has been, and so long as man
Will not upturn his eye from grovelling earth,
And seek the higher ends for which heaven formed him,
Crime and oppression still shall dog his steps.
Racked with uneasy thirst for sordid dross,
Its gain shall bring him no satiety,
And still the craving demon urge him on
To deeds which humble Virtue weeps to see.

Ebenezer Lazenby was soon waited on by many men, who, worshipping his wealth and not its possessor, offered their humble services to raise him in the social scale, well contented with their hire for so doing. Among the foremost of these we must reckon a skilful, unscrupulous, and intriguing attorney. This fellow soon wormed himself into Lazenby's family secrets, and without ever disclosing how much he really knew, hinted at so much as gave Ebenezer firstly great uneasiness, and ultimately a very considerable apprehension of him; indeed, Mr. Ferdinand Lynx was one of those men who, when they once get a footing, soon show that they may be exceedingly useful or ruinously mischievous. Mr. Lynx was a compound of cunning and worldly wisdom, and to the most fawning obsequiousness of general manner united a daring insolence and a decisive tyranny, when occasion served, that made him far more to be feared than relied on. This Ebenezer soon found, to his cost of pocket and peace of mind. In the first instance he had employed Lynx on the affair of the will; Mr. Ferdinand carried out the business, with the assistance of a proctor, in the most zealous and satisfactory manner, as he also did several other affairs entrusted to his charge. No sooner, however, were these settled, and Ebenezer installed securely in his ill-gotten position, than Mr. Lynx, fearing that he might possibly be superseded by some higher and more respectable practitioner, resolved on a bold stroke, in order to retain the extensive legal business which Ebenezer Lazenby could now bestow. His mode of effecting this will best be shown by a slight sketch of a conversation which took place, at the period we have now arrived at, between the sharp attorney and his client.

It was nine o'clock, and Ebenezer, retaining his early habits, had seated himself in the small but splendid library of Lazenby Lodge—where it was his custom to read his correspondence and transact the business of the day—when Mr. Lynx was announced. He entered with a lowly bow, and a salutation of mock humility; Ebenezer politely motioned him to a seat, for he dreaded and disliked the man.

"A fine morning, dear sir," said Lynx, in an oily tone, fixing at the same time his keen eye on Ebenezer; "I fear, however, that I interrupt you?"

Ebenezer laid down his pen, and leaning back in his chair, replied in the negative.

"I trust I shall not be deemed intrusive," said the man of law; "but a *rather* singular application has reached me, respecting a matter that concerns *us both* nearly."

"Proceed," said Ebenezer, coolly.

"I have received a letter from Grenada, a-hem," proceeded Lynx, "by which it appears that a certain Louis de Monnier, an attorney of that island, is commissioned to make inquiries on the part of one Monsieur Lagrenue, respecting the counterpart, or rather the original of a will, of which Le Monnier holds a copy, duly attested; and in which he further requests an attested copy of the will proven at the decease of the late Edward Lazenby. Perhaps I ought to state that this Mons. Legrenue is the father-in-law of your deceased brother. Now, as *I* am the attorney thus applied to, I resolved, respected sir, previously to transmitting the copy required from the will-office, to wait upon you and make you cognizant of this matter; a proceeding which my high respect for your character, and my deep gratitude for past favours, commanded me as a duty." As he said these words Ferdinand Lynx, though inclining his head almost reverentially, darted a glance of such keen scrutiny at Ebenezer, that he felt almost pained, and involuntarily started. The next moment, Lynx looked as imperturbable as ever, and assumed an inquiring but deferential aspect, as if awaiting a reply to a mere commonplace query.

Ebenezer hesitated an instant, and then coolly entered upon the subject with the caution of his temperament.

"A-hem, Mr. Lynx, you see this is an affair upon which I must confess I do not exactly see the drift and bearing of your speech. Of course I am interested, as their guardian, natural and appointed, in all that concerns my infant nephew and niece, yet I cannot exactly divine *why* you so press upon me the importance of this application to you; you will, of course, as an attorney, furnish the information required, and ——"

"Exactly so," interposed Lynx, "exactly so, but the instrument made and executed in Grenada was witnessed by ——"

"Two or three persons, domestic servants of the deceased, and I presume that they are forthcoming, if necessary, to prove their handwriting as witnesses?"

"Of course," replied the finessing scoundrel, "they *are* forthcoming if required; but I believe, nay, I am *certain*, that the document here proven as the will, is not exactly *identical* in its provisions with the paper deposited with the clerk of the peace, or prothonotary rather, in that island." And again Lynx stared—this time almost insolently—in Ebenezer's pallid face.

"Who says so?" asked Ebenezer, his voice involuntarily faltering as he spoke.

Lynx replied by producing a copy of a testamentary paper, accompanied by a letter, and silently handed them to his patron without a word of comment.

Ebenezer saw the gulf before him; he scanned the documents: the date, the witnesses' names, were all in duplicate, like the very paper he had destroyed on the night he had falsified his deceased brother's bequests; and these he had transferred to the forgery of which Lynx had duly taken out probate in the ecclesiastical court of Doctors' Commons! Ruin stared him in the face. The wily Lynx saw how his game stood, and played it accordingly.

He coughed briefly twice, to attract the attention of Ebenezer, and then proceeded thus: "There are two courses to adopt, my dear sir; the one to brave certain exposure by allowing the real truth to reach that distant colony; the other——" and again the scoundrel coughed hesitatingly; Ebenezer motioned him to go on; "the other rests with *me*. I can transmit a *duly attested* copy of the will of Edward Lazenby—but the *date*, my dear sir, the *place*, and the *witnesses* must be changed. The risk, my dear sir, the peril, will be as great to *me* as to *you*: yet, the regard, the gratitude I have," and the rascally orphan robber assumed a tone of whining pathos; "yes, the admiration I feel for so liberal, kind and enlightened a patron, would impel me to venture—provided—I ——" and here Ferdinand Lynx cast down his eyes as though modesty would not permit him to name a recompense.

"Name your terms, Mr. Lynx," said Ebenezer, firmly.

"Provided I might be allowed to become your steward, agent, and legal confidential adviser."

"Is that all? are you not so already?" asked the disconcerted rich man.

"Why—yes, to be sure, sir; but—but—I have of late been sounding several of my friends and yours, who think that dignity—say a baronetcy, or at least knighthood, should accompany and add lustre to your wealth. Rank, sir, is necessary to give riches their due importance. Sir Christopher Cottonwool, the great manufacturer, owes much of his good fortune with the people of the borough of Guzzledown to his title: now, I think—nay, I am certain—that if you would empower me to ask for you, I could secure the representation of Pocketburgh—a snug borough, with a sleepy constituency—and, once in parliament, a baronetcy, my dear sir, is secure, and thenceforward your re-election would be a matter of course."

"But this will, Mr. Lynxeye?" suggested Ebenezer, so soon as he could get in a word edgeways.

"Oh, dismiss that from your mind, my dear sir, don't bestow another thought on that affair. 'Tis all arranged sir, for a new will, dated subsequently to that transmitted to me, and even that is not all—you see, my dear sir, how careful I am of your reputation. I have this morning confirmed a rumour, which has already taken the form of a paragraph in the county paper, to this effect." Mr. Lynx here drew a local newspaper from his pocket, and handed it to Ebenezer, who read therein as follows:

"POCKETBURGH.—Much interest has been excited in this town, by a report that the well-known wealthy merchant Mr. Ebenezer Lazenby, the staunch and enlightened representative of the interests of our African trade, will shortly offer himself for the suffrages of the free and independent electors of the borough. The principles of the gentleman above alluded to are well known to be those of an ardent and uncompromising supporter of the venerable constitution in church and state, which has raised this glorious country to be the envy and admiration of surrounding nations; but which constitution is at this time sorely menaced by canting saints and loud-mouthed jacobins, atheists, and infidels, who, themselves possessing nothing, seek to effect a general scramble. We need hardly say that this merchant-prince has too large a stake in the country to become one of these, and that therefore in him the West India interest will find an uncompromising

defender. We congratulate the electors of Pocketburgh on the probability of
securing such a representative. Sir Plausible Pliant, it is said, will accept the
Chiltern Hundreds, for the purpose of strengthening the commercial and colonial
interest in the Commons' House."

Ebenezer was too cunning a casuist not to perceive what lurked under this fine
show of words, and although perplexed by the audacious assumption of Mr. Lynx,
saw that he was in his power.   The canting roundabout phrases which alluded to
the slave-trade, here disguised under the unmeaning phrases of " constitution,"
" the West India interest," " the African trade," and the like, almost extorted a
smile. He laid down the paper, not without a flutter of pride at the adroit
flattery of Lynx ; for already ambition had awakened in his selfish bosom, and he
coveted greatness, doubtless because riches had failed to confer happiness—that
aim of being which silly men pursue by such mistaken paths. " And so," said
the slave-owner, coldly, " you think Sir Ebenezer Lazenby, Bart. and M. P.,

would sound better in the ear of the multitude than plain Mister—good—and that it becomes me as the *proprietor*" (and he laid an emphasis on the word proprietor), " of extensive West India estates, to stem the tide of pretended philanthropy and liberality, of a class with whom philanthropy means a love for another man's goods, and whose liberality is most shown by giving away their neighbours' property, almost invariably having none of their own."

"Excellently expressed, admirably put, *Sir* Ebenezer," said the sycophantic Lynx; " ha! ha! capital! *we* must have you in parliament, the nation cannot do without you—indeed it won't, sir. Such men as you, my worthy sir, are wanted in these times to stem the tide of innovation and anarchy. But there is one thing: Sir Plausible Pliant, who has professed himself ready to act according to the wishes of the peer who nominates to the borough, must have a consideration—you understand me—eh? I do not mean the price of the seat itself, that I well know through the earl's agent; in fact, my lord's man of business told me that Cullender Castle being mortgaged, five thousand pounds *must* be had to prevent a foreclosure, and that Pocketburgh was at my service, provided I would find a candidate; and where could I look for one," said Lynx, " but in the person of my esteemed patron?"

"And so," thought Ebenezer, " this Lynx is prepared to falsify the copy of the will he is about to transmit, provided I make him my legal agent—cunning rascal! he will take no direct bribe, as that might commit himself. But he has wormed himself too far into my secrets for me to dare to break with him: I must dissemble; and affect, as well as he himself does, to consider him honest and myself uncompromised."

The Roman poet has asked " *how* two augurs could look each other in the face without laughing?" the thing is every day done in the busy world. Here were two consummate scoundrels, concocting villany, yet actually agreeing to conceal it from each other and themselves!

"And now, my kind sir," said Lynx, " I may consider the matter of Pocketburgh as arranged, and *you* need give yourself no further disquiet about the attested copy of that document which gave rise to this conversation?" Ebenezer nodded assent, and Mr. Lynx, rising, bowed servilely and retired.

CHAPTER XLII.

THE PERILS OF THE ORPHANS THICKEN—MR. LYNX IS YET FARTHER SEEN INTO— A MATRIMONIAL SPEC.—A DANGEROUS PLOT AND ITS ISSUE.

LET us now view Sir Ebenezer Lazenby a member of parliament, a baronet, a ministerial supporter, and a man of patronage; his morning levees crowded with the " little great," and all the corrupt spawn of a corrupt social system. With a change of life came a change of manners. The once frugal and steady tradesman had ill-exchanged his self-control and independence for the gilded servility of a place-hunter, and (by an infraction of the law) a government contractor for rum, sugar and molasses, the produce of his estates. It may be necessary to observe that Mr. Ferdinand Lynx was the ostensible agent in these transactions. According to law no member of the House of Commons could be a government contractor, or a holder of a patent grant from the crown; yet, strange to say, in the unreformed house, a very large number of ministerial supporters were known covertly to receive their bribes from the ministry in the shape of plunder of the soldiers and sailors, under the pretence of sealed contracts for supplies, in which they were frequently preferred over fair traders. In this class we may now rank Sir Ebenezer Lazenby, whose fortune, somewhat impaired by electioneering expenditure, required this method of repairing the loss.

In short, as Sir Ebenezer's ambition had mounted, and his fortune increased, so had his expenditure in a yet greater ratio; and hence the wealthy man with five-hundred a year (for such he really was two short years before), had risen—sunk we should rather say—into the titled pauper with thirty thousand. Mr. Lynx watched all this well; each successive phase of his patron's fortunes not only " brought grist to his mill," as he privately expressed it, but made Sir Ebenezer yet more his bond-slave, and the factor of his gains. The master-stroke was now to be achieved.

The Earl of Cullender, the nominal patron of Sir Ebenezer, was, like many a lord of high station, needy, greedy, and mean spirited, yet proud. He had one daughter, the sole heiress to his family shield and his many mortgages; she, of course, at his decease, would become a peeress in her own right; she, too, was proud—as became a lady of sixteen descents—yet mean and avaricious as her father. All this Mr. Lynx duly weighed, and his next scheme was a matrimonial one for Sir Ebenezer. At first he began by obscure hints at a peerage; the change of a family name by a special act of parliament, he observed, was a mere question of expense, and that was not one for such a man as Sir Ebenezer. He next made his approaches to the old earl, well knowing that the Lady Caroline Montrevor De Fitzroy would need little or no courtship, provided papa did not obstruct the affair. The Lady Caroline was one of those artificial and soulless creatures of fashion who place the summit of human happiness in a West-end mansion, with tall powdered footmen, a box at the opera, a gilded equipage, squeezed routes, and the entreé of the royal drawing-room during "the season." She was not, therefore, likely to refuse a husband who would bring them. We shall not dwell on the ease with which Lynx secured the old earl to his views; this point gained, he, by circuitous methods, contrived, by the confederacy of the earl, to throw Sir Ebenezer and Lady Caroline together. The young lady, who, to tell the truth, was not deficient either in superficial accomplishments or personal attractions, quickly perceived her game. She had passed five-and-twenty summers; and immediately upon this new prospect discarded a captain of the Guards, with whom she had flirted through three seasons, as well as a barrister of high expectations but scanty means, who had just accepted "a shabby colonial judgeship, and a paltry knighthood," as she termed them. These "sacrifices" she took good care Sir Ebenezer should hear of, even if he had not observed them. Moreover, the astute Lady Caroline took or made numberless opportunities to meet Sir Ebenezer (by accident, of course), and in several mere friendly tête-à-têtes artfully contrived to make him a sort of confidant in what she called her little "affaires du cœur."

The baronet had, as we have already said, placed a rigid rein upon his desires in the spring of his life, and was accordingly unused to female society. The effect of these curious disclosures may be guessed; for the wily young lady most ingeniously impressed him with a most favourable opinion of her piety, simplicity, sincerity, disinterestedness, and warmth of heart. To such an extent did this disturb the equanimity and heat the blood of Ebenezer, that one evening, as he rolled home in his chariot from a party at the earl's, whereat another of these agreeable coquettings had taken place, he found himself exclaiming: "I must have her! she is too lovely, too excellent a creature to be lost upon some idle butterfly of fashion, who cannot appreciate her worth! Yes, she would adorn a palace or a cottage; and—and—I think—nay, I am sure, I am not wholly indifferent to her; else why this confidence in which she lays open her whole spotless and affectionate soul? True, the men she has discarded are younger, but then— and now I think of it she almost, nay, she positively said, that 'she preferred a man old enough to advise and counsel'—ay, those were the words, 'old enough for a friend, and such a one, she thought, no woman of sense and mind would find too old for a lover.' Yes! I'll see the earl—he owes me some favours—and sound him on the subject of his daughter's affections. If he approves, I will offer myself and fortune to his inestimable daughter!" Such were the resolves of Sir Ebenezer Lazenby, who, keen as he was in many things, had little suspicion of the mean intrigue, the sordid selfishness, and the dirty scheming of that portion of society which those beneath them envy and admire as "the fashionable world."

The finessing game of the precious trio, the lawyer, the needy earl and his manœuvring daughter, was soon played up to the winning trick; and Sir Ebenezer, who thought himself the happiest man alive, and a clever one to boot, as the reader may suppose, attributed to himself all the merit of bringing a matrimonial scheme to conclusion, which, had he been aware of the deep-laid plans of those who had already contrived it, he might possibly have shrunk from as a snare.

The fashionable newspapers soon made known that " a marriage was on the tapis between Sir E——r L——y, the wealthy representative of P——h, and the accomplished and lovely Lady C—— F——y, only daughter of the E—— of C——;" and shortly afterwards the bells of St. George's, and a long line of carriages, attracted the gaping crowd in Hanover-square, and the public—who never had a conjecture on the subject—perceived the accuracy of the intelligence from the announcement of the name of the "happy couple," with the titles of the noble giver away of the "lovely bride," who "were made one by the Right Rev. the Bishop of Lawnsleeve, after which the distinguished pair left London for Cullender Castle, where it is supposed they will spend the honeymoon."

Due time elapsed, another announcement followed: " On Saturday last, at Lazenby Park, near Richmond, the Lady Caroline Fitzroy Lazenby, of a son and heir." And here we will pause awhile, to see what effect this event had on the fortunes of the orphans, Walter and Eugenia.

CHAPTER. XLIV.

THE ORPHANS—A NEW SCHEME OF MR. LYNX—ITS FRUSTRATION—A HIHGHWAY ROBBERY AND A DILEMMA.

WHEN a man takes the first step from the straight path of rectitude, let him not say, thus far will I deviate and no further: thenceforth his progress is no longer under his own control, and Sir Ebenezer Lazenby formed no exception to this general rule. But we have too long lost sight of the infant children of the deceased slave-owner, whose ill-gotten gold had been the moving cause of all this studied villany.

With an ardency of temperament suited to the tropical clime which had given him birth, Walter Lazenby inherited the wayward disposition of his father. His generosity and high spirit of honour he derived from his mother, for assuredly his other parent had little of those qualities. He was now six years of age, and his sister four, and they had been placed, from a period at which they could know little, under the care of a matron, who kept a select school in a retired village in Kent, as completely secluded from all ties of home, as though they had never possessed parent or guardian. The stipend for their support was duly paid from the office of Mr. Ferdinand Lynx, and once in each half year he had condescendingly visited the small establishment, and reported to Sir Ebenezer on the health and position of his ill-used wards. The birth of a child, as has been already noticed, opened new views to Sir Ebenezer, and shortly after a bill passed the legislature without notice or comment, whereby he changed his name to Fitzroy, having already quartered the arms of that ancient but decayed house, with those "found" for him by the accommodating College of Heralds.

All now seemed attained, yet was the future of Sir Ebenezer Fitzroy clouded with doubt and misgivings. The vision of the dark-eyed West Indian boy, who might in some after year arise to trouble himself or his noble offspring, often rose in the watches of the night. The eventful eve when he falsified his brother's last will; the error he had committed in transcribing the signatures of the foreign witnesses; the dangerous exposure which must follow a discovery of the fraud practised by the rascally Lynx—who had, as we have seen, transmitted as an authenticated copy, a will to which fictitious English names were affixed, utterly at variance with the copy in the archives at Doctors' Commons—all these, and a thousand other conjectures, probable and improbable, haunted him. A fellowship in knavery levels the distinctions of rank. Though cold and difficult of access to others, the embryo peer—for such he already esteemed himself, if not in his own person, certainly in that of his child—was but an equal when in conference with the knave, who, in helping him to become what he was, had enriched himself; to him, therefore, he resolved to unburthen himself; and from what the reader has already seen, he may guess that Ferdinand Lynx was no stranger to what his patron's hopes and fears must be on this delicate point. His course was quickly resolved on. Entering his patron's library one morning at the usual hour, he found Sir Ebenezer, seated in a position of deep abstraction, his head buried in his hands. He raised his eyes one moment as the man of law entered smilingly on tiptoe, with a velvety tread, soft as the cat-like animal whence his patronymic was derived, the next he cast them down again, sunk his temples between his palms, his elbows still resting on the splendid morocco covering of the writing-table before him. Mr. Lynx cast one furtive glance at the papers thereon lying, and instantaneously saw, amidst numerous ship letters of dates long-past, and miscellaneous documents, a miniature portrait of the deceased mother of the orphans, a locket, and some other trinkets. The sharp-eyed practitioner needed no other cue to his patron's reflections. Approaching him closely, he whispered, at a glance towards the door of the apartment, in a tone of almost familiar confidence, " *We* are not safe, my dear sir, *we* can *never* be safe while ——" The baronet raised his hand and gazed eagerly, almost imploringly, into the speaker's face. Mr. Lynx stopt short, and assuming a look of perfect simplicity, went on—" while *we* decline to do justice in some way to these children"—the baronet looked astonished and alarmed—" I mean precisely what I say, my dear sir," resumed Lynx, in a repentant tone—" *we* must find some way of severing these children from all former and present ties. They are scarcely yet of an age to know their true position. The remembrances of their earlier years, on which I have carefully and kindly questioned them, are excessively vague and imperfect ; nay, such as I will venture to say *I* could so far confuse in their youthful minds as to prevent the most acute stranger, with whom they may hereafter come in contact, from tracing their identity." Sir Ebenezer breathed again.

" See here, my dear sir," continued Lynx ; "here are the only mementos these disturbers of our peace possess of their already almost forgotten parents. This locket bears the counterpart portrait of the one lying before you. Would it not be easy, my dear sir, to *provide* for these children somewhere in the West Indies, far distant from Grenada, and deal with them, after a discreet interval, as the *offspring of a slave-mother?*" Sir Ebenezer started, and Lynx checked himself for a few seconds, as if to let his proposition sink well into the mind of his auditor.

" As the children of a slave-mother," resumed Mr. Lynx, slowly, as if delivering himself of some profound legal axiom, " they, of course, are not entitled to inherit, even supposing any difficulty should, which is by no means probable, arise. They would, by that very fact alone, be cut off. Again, my dear sir, to render assurance doubly sure, *we* might supply ourselves with documents" (Sir Ebenezer winced once or twice at this repetition of the plural pronoun), " which would prove that Walter and Eugenia were but the adopted children of Rose Clermont and her husband Edward Lazenby. The proof of these things, if ever called for, which is far from likely, cannot be wanted for some ten or twelve years, at soonest. Leave all to me, sir, and long, long ere that time, both these troublesome infants shall have forgotten you, their parents, their claims, and, unless otherwise disposed of, even *themselves.*"

Sir Ebenezer raised his head, and looked steadily at the face of Lynx ; nought was legible there but an expression of deferential respect and attachment, akin to that of a faithful dog ; but, alas ! how libelled is the sincere quadruped by the comparison !

" Mr. Lynx," said Sir Ebenezer, with an affected calmness, " this conversation has lasted too long. You have already the control of these children, and to you I commit their affairs and mine. I have no doubt your attachment to *my* house will prompt you to do your utmost to serve its interests."

Mr. Lynx placed his hand upon the spot where the heart is supposed to be placed by nature : we say "*supposed*," because, in the structure of such a lawyer, a heart could not exist without serious hindrance to his successful career of life. He followed this gesture with a slight bow and a hyena-like smirk, hemmed twice, as if to clear his throat, and went on.

" It is that very attachment—ahem—I may say *devotion* to the service of Sir Ebenezer Fitzroy, of which he has just made such flattering mention, that prompts me, nay, impels me to proceed with this delicate subject in the frank and candid manner I now do. This boy, Sir Ebenezer, must be removed, and the damsel consigned to some safe keeping. The youth I would recommend to be shipped off to sea : I can find a captain who will take him off my hands some two or three years hence, as a destitute orphan, dependent on my charity ; till then a sojourn in Spain, where he shall learn the language, and be duly impressed with the idea that his mother was a quadroon slave, the chance favourite of his father, and not within the pale of lawful wedlock. The girl I shall place with a female friend, and, as I think she will prove handsome, I will moderately portion her, and marry her in humble life."

" Good !" responded the half-reluctant and conscience-pricked baronet, with a half-groan; for he felt he had no power to gainsay the Mephistophilean limb of Satan, who held him enmeshed in his toils.   But

> " The best-laid schemes of mice and men
>   Oft gang a-glie,"

sings Robert Burns, and so it will be seen, by the sequel, did those of Mr. Ferdinand Lynx.

It was no part of that worthy's plan to lose sight of the orphan Walter; on the contrary, despite his proposals to Sir Ebenezer, the crafty villain meant so to hold this disturber of the baronet's quiet enjoyment of his estates in reserve and within reach, that his patron would not dare to dispense with his forced services; for he saw well he was both feared and hated.   A week or two after this conversation, Mr. Lynx made his appearance at the preparatory-school where the young Walter and his sister were placed, with a long visage, and told a canting, hypocritical tale, to the school-mistress, of what he called " sad intelligence from the West Indies," being no less than the discovery of the illegitimacy of Walter and Eugenia.   This fact, of which Mr. Lynx asserted he had not the slightest previous idea, he went on to say, should, however, make no difference in his determination to support, clothe, and educate the deserted and bereaved little children.   However, as they had never any title to the name of Lazenby, they must in future be called only by the name of Girardin; that being, as he said, the maiden name of their mother, an unemancipated slave, promoted to the "honour" (as he, with upturned eyes of horror, explained it to be considered in the wicked West Indies) of becoming the mother of her master and owner's children!   The plausible, moralising, edifying reflections, and generous resolves of Mr. Lynx, quite convinced Mrs. Edwards, for that was the name of the single-minded lady, of the excellence of his head and heart.   The children were called in, and the good lady, with great regret, and almost tears, parted with her young charges, who, Mr. Lynx informed her, were about to depart for their native island by an early sailing ship.

Having thus cut off the possibility of tracing them out, should any one feel interested in so doing, Mr. Lynx paid the account of Mrs. Edwards, she inserting therein the names of Walter and Eugenia Girardin, as those of the children for a time under her care.

As the carriage which conveyed the lawyer and his victims rolled away from the door of Minerva House, Mr. Lynx chuckled inwardly as he looked on his infant prey.   Walter was a high-spirited and intelligent boy; and as the antipathies of children often seem intuitive instincts, so was it in this case.   He detested, nay, so far as one of such tender years was capable, despised the fawning kindness, the overacted affection of Mr. Lynx.   This the lawyer did not fail to perceive, and it embittered his malice; for though he seldom did mischief without the motive of gain, yet he loved it better than doing good.   Walter, he saw, shrunk from his caresses, and almost repulsed his advances.   Indeed, there was no cordiality or confidence between them.   They agreed no more than an acid and an alkali, nor could any mental chemistry force their quiet amalgamation.   Mr. Lynx, therefore, perceiving that mildness would be thrown away, plucked off the mask, and sternly and harshly told the boy, with much exaggeration of the importance of the communication, that his birth was illegitimate.   The force of this was, of course, unintelligible to young Walter; but that his mother, whom he tenderly loved, although he had but a childish recollection of her person, was insultingly and deprecatingly spoken of, he perfectly understood, and his indignation almost burst his little bosom.   After a flood of bitter tears—he scarcely knew wherefore they flowed—he felt so violent an aversion for Mr. Lynx, that he inwardly resolved to fly from his protection; and although whither he should betake himself he had no idea, the resolve momentarily gathered force.   The only hesitation he felt, was that of leaving his dear Eugenia; yet, as Mr. Lynx had already told him roundly that their separation was about to follow, the boy, in his despair, determined to abscond.   Thus the party travelled till London was reached, and they put up at a great coaching inn, the Golden Cross, at Charing Cross.   At night the orphans were placed in a separate bed-room, and here, with tears and embraces, young Walter disclosed to his sister his intention of running away, he knew not whither.   His sister's entreaties prevented him, quite as much as want of opportunity, from immediately carrying out his wild and almost purposeless scheme; but when, on the following day, Mr. Lynx departed for a short time, during which he placed the female child in charge of a woman, who was the tool of his designs, Walter's determination became fixed, and he awaited eagerly the time when he should be enabled to put his project in execution. This came sooner than he expected.

The next morning Mr. Lynx took his departure for Bristol, carrying Walter with him, with the intention of placing him in a school in Gloucestershire, whence it was his design to send him, after a year's sojourn, to the East Indies. They had travelled within ten miles of Reading, that being the intended extent of their first day's journey, and there for the night it was the intention of Mr. Lynx to stop.

The post-chaise in which they journeyed was overtaken by darkness as they changed horses near Maidenhead; the lawyer, who was enjoying a doze, lay reclined in one corner of the vehicle, in the other sat poor Walter, silently weeping his hapless lot. The harshness of Lynx, and the cruel things he had said of his beloved mother, preyed on the boy's mind, aroused his fierce indignation, and lacerated his young heart, though he by no means understood the motives of their designing utterer. It was enough for him that they were injurious to the only being he had ever loved, and rage and hatred swelled his little bosom almost to bursting.

Thus they rode for a mile or two, till the carriage entered a narrow way through a gloomy hollow, where the over-arching elms excluded even the feeble light of a young crescent moon. They had not proceeded far when an unusual disturbance attracted the attention of young Walter: some loud imprecations were followed by a violent jerk or two, and the next moment the chaise fell over on one side against a grassy bank. Mr. Lynx awoke at the concussion; but before he could arrive at a clear perception of the state of affairs, the door on the off-side opened, and a man's voice shouted—

"Stir hand or foot, and you are a dead man!"

The threat was enforced by the pointing of a large brass-barrelled blunderbuss in at the opening. Walter sat still, fixed with astonishment and alarm, and Mr. Lynx, for villains of his stamp are often personal cowards, trembled from head to foot; his teeth chattered with fright, and on the words being repeated, this time with the addition of a fearful oath, he faltered forth a prayer for his worthless life. The ruffian gruffly replied—

"Don't sit whining there, you old humbug, but fork over the ready, and be d—d to you. Come, look smart, d'ye hear? and don't keep your betters waiting."

Mr. Lynx fumbled in his pockets, and produced a small green silk purse; the fellow clutched it, and deposited the coin in his pocket without examination.

"Your ticker, old chap. Come, don't lose time."

Mr. Lynx groaned, but made no motion of compliance.

"Here, Dick, bear a hand," cried the robber, and he transferred the blunderbuss to a coadjutor, who kept it pointed at Lynx; while the footpad, leaning into the carriage, seized the lawyer by the ankle, and dragging him from the seat into the bottom of the vehicle, by one vigorous pull brought him on his back into the roadway. Mr. Lynx gave one loud cry; his second was stopped by the hands of his assailant, who, placing a cloth round his mouth, secured it to the back of his head, uttering all the while the most blasphemous threats. Walter now saw that their assailants were three in number; the man who first appeared, a tall, athletic person, being busy in rifling the pockets of Lynx, while the others assisted in holding him.

We have said that the carriage lay partially overturned, with its two wheels in a drain, and its side resting against a tolerably high bank, at the top of which was a small hedgerow. The thieves, dreading nothing from so small a boy, had left Walter unguarded; desperation lent him strength and agility, and, unnoticed by the busily-engaged robbers, he scrambled through the open window, reached the top of the bank, crouched through a gap, slid down on the opposite side, and crept along a drain, under shelter of some tangled briars. After going about a hundred yards the voices grew fainter, and he sat down to consider what next he should do. True, he had escaped; but, certainly, he had not calculated beyond that. His first idea was, that he would seek for some house, and beg shelter; which, poor innocent, so little did he know of the realities of life, he imagined would not be refused him. Leaving him in this position, let us return to look after Mr. Lynx and his unpleasant companions.

Their search was soon over; a gold watch, a pocket-book, and a few guineas rewarded their labour, so after bestowing a cuff and a kick or two on his prostrate carcass, they went off, leaving the postboy with his hands tied behind his back, sitting on the roadside. They did not forget, too, to cut the traces, and liberating the horses sent them, with a hearty thwack apiece, back the very road they came, along which the sagacious old posters, well knowing it as that leading to their stable, merrily trotted, till, finding no whip or wheels behind them, they fell into a walk, and finally discovering by their noses an accessible field of clover, they got through a gate, where we will leave them luxuriating, by far the happiest of the party that had a short hour before left the Red Lion posting-house at Twyford. As for Mr. Ferdinand Lynx, his eyes being bandaged, he resorted to the use of his ears, and those organs having satisfied him of the final departure of his persecutors, he plucked off the scarf, hoping that it might hereafter prove a clue to the discovery of the robbers. It, however, proved to be the knitted comforter from the neck of the postboy, which the scoundrels had applied to this purpose, so here the object was foiled. After another thought or two of his precious self, and his abstracted valuables, Mr. Lynx hastened eagerly to the chaise to seek his youthful charge—the vehicle was empty.

"Confound the villains!" muttered he; "more mischief may come of this than the few guineas they have taken. Hillo! postillion! here, hoy!" exclaimed he. The hand-tied driver rose from his recumbent position, and came forward.

"Where's the child?" asked the anxious lawyer; "the boy, you staring dolt, who was in the chaise? Have the rascals carried him off?" The driver rubbed his eyes and peered into the carriage.

"Dang me if oi knaw," grumbled he; "I han't a-zeed un zince he got into the chay wi' you, zir."

"They blindfolded me, blockhead," cried the enraged Lynx, "but you had the use of your eyes; tell me, sirrah, for you must have seen them, did they carry him off? I'll hang you, you scoundrel, as the thieves' confederate, unless you answer me instantly and truly."

"Scoundril yoursen," muttered the *boy*, who by the bye was a wiry chap of some two and twenty, as tough as his own leather leggings; "keep a civil tongue i' yer heed—'twor best for 'ee; oi'm as honest as you any day, thof oi doan't wear zo foine a cwoat. Oi tell 'ee oi ar zeen na bwoy sin' you got in wi' un, zo you're as loikely to knaw about un as mysen."

Mr. Lynx saw the fellow was not to be bullied, so he changed his tone, and proceeded in another strain.

"Well, well, my friend, this is no time for altercation, but this boy must be found; I will give you five guineas to set me on his track, and ask no further questions. Which way did they take him? what sort of men were they?"

"As to yer money, I zuppose we're much aloike for that matter, just now," replied the surly yokel; "they ha' cleaned oi out o' four zhilling an' three ha'pence, beside a rack-comb, a 'bacco-box, and a money-bag as my Zukey worked for oi. Dang it, oi wish they had left oi Zukey's pus;" and the bumpkin scratched his shock head as he thought of a crooked sixpence it contained, which was a love-token from his rustic flame.

"All your losses shall be made good," said Mr. Lynx, persuasively; "I am rich, my good fellow, and you shall be rewarded handsomely, provided you will pursue and trace these villains, with any assistance you may be able to get in the neighbourhood. Raise the country on them, my good fellow, by hue and cry; get back this boy, and I will give you fifty guineas, nay, a hundred guineas reward."

For Mr. Lynx, terribly alarmed lest some ugly disclosures might follow young Walter's abduction, was liberal in promises; moreover, he, like most other poltroons, had no objection to send others on perilous enterprises, provided he himself could stay behind in a whole skin.

"Whoy," replied the post-boy, "to be zure, a hundred pound 'ud tempt a chap to troy purty hard—but then, d'ye see, I ha'n't noa hos, them cantankerous beastes ha' gwoan clean off. Howsever, as you seem a genelman sort o' man, oi'll push on to next varmhouse, if so be you'll stay by the chay, and——"

To this arrangement Mr. Lynx objected *in limine;* he did not relish the idea of being left alone, his fears for his precious self having not yet subsided.

"The chaise is safe enough, my friend," observed he; "it can't run away

without horses, so let us make our way back together, get help, and pursue the rascals."

The postillion assented, and off the two plundered wayfarers trudged back the way they had travelled. It being now pretty dark, for a May night, they passed the clover-feeding horses without espying them. It was past twelve o'clock, and all the inmates had retired to rest, before they reached the inn of the Red Lion. Mr. Lynx, who was a poor pedestrian, being thoroughly exhausted, worn out, and footsore, through nervous agitation, fear, anxiety for the future, and bodily fatigue.

CHAPTER XLV.

A VISION—THE YOUTHFUL OUTCAST—EAVES-DROPPING—A FRIEND—A RETURN
TO LONDON.

YOUTH and innocence sleep well; the fugitive Walter wandered by fields and hedgerows for an hour or two, until weariness of limb and heaviness of eyelid tempted him to rest. A sheltering rick of old hay, in process of cutting into trusses, offered a pleasant, convenient, and fragrant chamber ; and here, after a careful survey of the adjacent fields, in which nothing was visible or audible but a few dozen of hurdled sheep with their tinkling bellwethers, did the orphan outcast betake himself to repose. His slumber was long, but strangely interrupted by incoherent dreams. In the vision he again roamed among the citron-groves, feathery palm-trees, and tufted cocoas of the land of his birth, which came back to his mental sight with a vividness and distinctness of which his waking faculties had no idea. His mother bent over him with tender affection, and, kissing his forehead, assured him of her protecting love ; anon, he strayed among the slender acacias, or under the lofty trees of a tropical forest festooned with the gorgeous parasitical flowers of a southern clime, while at his right hand tripped his dear sister Eugenia, arrayed in a loose dress of spotless white. Suddenly his companion's beautiful features became distorted with horror, and close before them he saw, rearing its crested head amid the long flowering stems of an erica, the deadly form of a *cobra di capella*, or hooded snake, the most venomous and fearful of the sun-engendered reptiles of that sultry clime. The gleaming eyes of the horrid creature were fixed upon the pallid face of its victim, who stood transfixed and motionless with terror ; Walter threw himself between the serpent and its fascinated prey—when lo ! the face of the hideous thing changed gradually to a human countenance, its cheeks distended with a spiteful grin, and the features of the detested lawyer, Ferdinand Lynx, presented themselves to his astonished gaze ! He sprung upon the monster and clutched its slender throat with both his hands—his grasp seemed endowed with mighty strength—the face of the lawyer appeared contorted with the throes of death—his sister uttered a piercing cry—he awoke—the vision fled !

Again he slept ; this time he stood, still with Eugenia by his side, on the edge of a deep ravine, skirted by precipitous rocks. They looked together down the dizzy height into the black abyss below, at the bottom of which flowed turbidly an autumnal torrent. A rustling in the scorched herbage and a crashing of boughs behind them attracted his attention, and turning he beheld a huge panther slowly crouching, and dragging his cat-like length along the earth. The next moment he gathered up his form to pounce on them ; and again the face of his human persecutor scowled in the beast's front. Flight was hopeless : before them lay the awful precipice, behind the beast of prey, whose demoniac eyes gleamed with a cruel joy. Once more young Walter sprang to the combat ; the struggle was fierce ; he felt himself borne over the edge of the steep descent—he fell, and fell, until a sense of buoyancy pervaded his limbs ; he was caught in an embrace, he looked up and beheld, her face radiant with delight, his beloved mother ! Bright pinions extended from her shoulders, her face wore a seraphic smile, and, pointing to the gulf below, there, fathoms down, mangled, torn, and prostrate among the sharp-jagged rocks, lay the man-faced monster ! His protruded eyeballs, fixed in death, stared horribly from their blood-stained orbits, his open mouth discharging clotted gore. The dreamer turned his eyes from the fearful sight, and strove to embrace his saviour—in vain. The excess of joy, like the excess of terror, woke him ; he started to his feet, and behold it was a morning dream.

The birds carolled gaily over head, the tender green of early summer was heightened by the first golden beams of a rising sun ; the early rooks cawed cheerfully as they flapped their way in search of their morning meal ; the distant chanticleer crowed loudly as he summoned his feathered seraglio to come forth and pick up the dew-worms, or the grains he had discovered in the moist soft ground ; the lark, upspringing from the dewy lea, sung loud and clearly as he took his skyward flight, and was heard at "heaven's gate" long after his tiny form and nutbrown hue were lost to the most piercing sight ; the humming-bee buzzed from flower to flower, and all nature wore its freshest smile. Walter looked around him, not without a mingled sensation of gratitude for his escape, and of apprehension and doubt for the future. He soon after saw a curl of smoke arising from the skirts of a small wood ; the sense of hunger urged him to approach it, and he cautiously walked along the side of a hedge-row till he had neared the spot, doubting and almost fearing the result of his meditated appeal. He quickly came in sight of a tilted tent, a small cart, a donkey, and two or three ragged urchins, and a little farther on he espied the fire whence the curling wreaths arose ; it was made upon the ground, surmounted by a triangle of three hedgestakes, and over it was suspended an iron pot, in which the cookery of the encampment was going on. This was attended by an ancient crone, and while Walter watched her proceedings, himself unobserved, he perceived she was joined by a tall man in a long coat, who in his person much resembled, as Walter thought, one of the robbers who had waylaid them on the previous night. Nor was he mistaken: it was the Patrico, and, although his face had been blackened for the better execution of the exploit, Walter, whose perceptions were keen, felt almost assured of his identity. His first thought was flight; but this was quickly decided in the negative, against his will; for at the instant he turned, with the intention of putting his design into practice, he was confronted with a swarthy man, carrying a thick bludgeon in one hand, and something in the other which he concealed beneath the long tail of his slouching great coat.

"Hollo! my kinchin," cried he, "vhat brings you out so precious 'arly in the morning, eh? Come, don't funk, my young 'un, but just let's know vhy you're a-skulking hereabouts? It strikes me as you ha'n't been at home all night," added he, for his quick eye detected the disordered and soiled state of the boy's clothes, which he also observed were of a texture and workmanship that bespoke him of a respectable rank in society. "Playing at truant, eh? I see; bolted away from the old bum-brusher. Vell, I likes a lad o' pluck—but von't you catch toco for it, vhen you gets back, eh, my young gentleman?"

Though Walter perfectly comprehended the purport of this speech, he was by no means clear as to the meaning of several of the words, he therefore replied by saying "that he had escaped from a cruel man, who ill-treated him and abused his mother, and that he would gladly work and do anything to make himself useful, rather than go back to Mr. Lynx," for in his artless simplicity he thought that everybody must at once see the hardship of his case. At mention of the name of Lynx the fellow's swarthy visage lighted up, and his black eyes glistened with satisfaction.

"Here's a go," muttered he; "this is a chance mustn't be slipped. Vell, who vould ha' thought it! A fifty pound job, and no mistake. How the Patrico vill stare—and to find him so permiscous like! Vell, luck is better nor good guidance, arter all! Come along, my nut-brown lad; you're precious lucky to ha' tumbled among friends, I can tell ye." The sudden change of the fellow's manner pleased Walter exceedingly; and, doubting not that his appeal had made the stranger his friend, the artless orphan accompanied the fellow towards the fire, where the old crone and the Patrico stood. The latter stared with some surprise at the gipsy and his youthful companion; but the younger gipsy made a sign to the elder one, and, after recommending Walter to the old crone's charge, he and the Patrico stept aside to confer in private.

The mystery of how the gipsy, whose name was Joe Lovell, came to be acquainted with Mr. Lynx's name, and the loss of his charge, will soon be cleared up.

"Well, Joe," enquired the Patrico of his scout, "is all right up yonder?"

Joe replied by an affirmative nod.

"But how," said the old man, "came you to pick up that boy? he may be dangerous to us all. That's the very hidentical boy as vas in the chay last night, ven ve stopped it."

"I knows that parfeckly vell," replied Joe; "but it so happens as I didn't pick him up at all; he just now throwed hisself in my way. Hows'ever, I s'pose you vould like to hear how I got on at the Red Lion. I'll tell yer: so soon as I heerd the old bloak and the postboy was straight off arter the hosses, as supposed, I pulls foot like a good one along the bye-lanes and across the common, whereby I was so fort'nit as to get into Lion tap—arter goin' a bit of the Lunnun-road, by way of a blind—a good hour and better afore the two hove in sight or was heerd on. So in I drops vith a few turneries, wooden spoons, pegs, and clo'es lines, as Slouchin' George shared vith me, a little vays up the road I spoke on; he, likevise, goin' in vith me, and puttin' me fly to say as ve'd just come from town— vich vas also made right by a story as he pitched into 'em about a dreadful fire, as had burnt down the Royal Circus Thehater, and a precious sight o' houses, in St. George's fields. Vell, vile they vas in the midst of this yarn, in rushes a hostler, vith his mouth open, a-saying as the old genelman vith Dick the postboy vas outside, and as how they'd been robbed on the highvay, and the 'osses vas killed and they vounded, and the chay broke to pieces on the road, vith a sight more on it, as made me put my tongue in my cheek on the sly. Presently, as all but the hoskeeper vas in bed, in comes the old lawyer bloak hisself, and I takes good care to seem precious eager to larn all about it. But it seemed as if he wor so blessed frightened about losing sight of this here young kid, as a'most to forget everythink else as had happened. He offers fifty guineas out-an'-out, and no questions asked, to any vun as vould bring him back. So soon as I heerd all as vos to be got out, I and George volunteers to go in search o' the young vagerbone, and here he drops right in our vay!"

We have already, in a former part of our history, explained the absolute rule which the Patrico, or head of the family or tribe of gipsies, exercised in all matters, domestic and public, of each of these wandering communities. Joe, accordingly, awaited the decision of the old man, doubting not but it would be that the boy should at once be restored to Mr. Lynx, and the fifty guineas secured. Perplexity and doubt, however, sat on the old man's face, and at last he spoke as follows—And here we must observe that it is notorious in those days of gipsy brigandage and strength, one of the common methods of recruiting their numbers, or more often of extorting rewards, was the kidnapping of young children—

" Sartinly, fifty canaries is a tidy revard for a kinchin; but then, on the other side o' the qvestion, comes the vally on him to them as offers it. This here Mr. Lynx is one o' they la'yer coves, and they seldom offers all they mean to give at fust go off. There's a dollop o' papers too in a skin,* as I've stowed avay till I can get 'em read over by Black Ben, at the crib in Chick-lane. He's avake to these legal dockyments, and ve can't get his advice till ve gets to Lonnon. If so be as this Lawyer Lynx offers fifty so ready, depend on't the kinchin's vorth more to some vun or other—he'd never offer nothink vithout he seed the vay to make a profit out on it. Besides, who knows but the boy hisself—if so be there is any underhand vork in spiriting him avay in this here manner—mayn't be able to revard us better nor old Lynx hisself? Who, fustly, it's sartin, ain't no father of his'n; and, secondly, ain't no friend to his mother."

The Patrico delivered this with an air of such profundity and deliberation, that Joe Lovell perfectly acquiesced in its justice and truth ; indeed, he strengthened it, by relating what the boy had added—'that he had rather work or do anything, than be taken back to Lynx.'

" Vell, then," concluded the Patrico, " so soon as the young 'un has had a good breakfast—vich he must eat some distance off the camp, in the vood hereby, for fear any vun should drop in at mealtime—vich couldn't be pleasant either for us nor him—I'll have a little private convarsation vith him, and egsamine him touching his birth, parentage, and edication."

So saying, the Patrico broke off the consultation, and the two men returned to the fire. In a few short vords, in the foreign language of the gipsies, the Patrico bad the crone prepare a substantial breakfast for young Walter. Then, turning to Lovell, he ordered him to take the boy into the thicket, and there remain on watch near him till the meal was despatched. He also, in as kind a tone as he could assume, told the boy of his good intentions towards him, assuring him that, if he attended to his directions, he should not be betrayed to Lawyer Lynx. The lighthearted and courageous Walter was delighted at the reception he had experienced ; nay, he almost liked the canting old crone who watched the kettle, and who had been entertaining him with some flattering lies and compliments during the old man's absence, and thought their wandering and independent mode of life far preferable to the irksome restraints, and tedious strictness, to which he had been subjected under the discipline of Mrs. Edwards, who, though a good woman, had very different notions of how children should be managed, to what are generally entertained by children themselves.

His favourable impression of his new found friends was by no means diminished on the arrival of a chubby-cheeked brown-visaged urchin, who, in a few minutes, came from the open-air kitchen, bearing in a wooden bowl of turned sycamore, covered with a wooden lid, a portion of a boiled fowl, in some flour broth, made savory with leek and parsley, and topped by a piece of rye-bread. To Walter's taste—for he had eaten nothing from the previous afternoon, and his out-of-door couch had acutely whetted an appetite at all times of healthy sharpness—so sapid and grateful a steam had never arisen from mortal provender ; it was a dish for

---

* Pocket-book.

the gods, and he contrasted it with the scantily buttered bread, and milk and water of sky-blue colour, with which he had stayed his stomach at Minerva House, with great disparagement of the latter morning meal. As soon as he had satisfied his craving hunger his aged protector the Patrico, for such Walter had considered him, appeared.

To all his questions young Walter answered with the artless ingenuousness of his disposition; but the Patrico, though naturally shrewd, could see no guiding clue in the youth's story. He told him he had a sister, Eugenia by name; that she, as well as himself, were born in a far-off country across the sea; that they left there before he rightly knew its name, but that his mother, whose name was Lazenby, and was a lady, had told him that the country was an island, as it was surrounded by water. That it was in the West Indies he also knew, for Miss Edwards had shown it him in a map, when he was learning geography; that his father had a great deal of money, and brought them both to England; and then he knew no more till his " uncle Lazenby " came to see him and his sister, in a fine house his father lived in, and told them that their father and mother were both dead a long way off, and they should never see them more. Here the poor boy burst into a passion of grief, that for a moment moved the Patrico himself.

" And what then became of the fine house and all your father's money?" enquired the Patrico.

" I don't know," replied the boy, " and I didn't care, no more did sister, when we'd lost our dear mother. And then they dressed us in black, and uncle Lazenby and Mr. Lynx came, and Mr. Lynx said he'd take care of us, but I didn't like him, nor sister neither; at first he used to be very kind and give us things; then he put us to school, and came to see us but once a half-year at last—but we didn't mind about that—and uncle Lazenby never came near us at all. At last, a short time ago, he came down to Mrs. Edwards's, that was our schoolmistress's name, and said he was very sorry to tell us such a shocking thing, but that we must be told it, or else we might think more of what we should be when we grew up a man and woman than we ought to do; and that all we had, our pocket money, and our clothes, and our schooling, and our victuals, must be paid for with his money, for that he had found out our mother was a wicked woman; now I hated him when he said that, I knew he was a liar, a wicked liar, and I would have stamped on him, if I'd been strong enough," said the boy passionately; " for my mother was a good woman, and is now an angel in heaven, I saw her last-night," and the tearful eyes of Walter flashed fiercely with fire and passion.

The Patrico shook his head, as if he doubted the youth's sanity, and smiled incredulously; nevertheless, he was pleased at what he called " the youngster's out-and-out sperrit."

" Well done, my lad," said he, encouragingly; " and sarve the old beggar right. Go on."

" And then—and then—he said——" and the boy almost choked with rage, " he said as my mother was such a naughty woman, and was never married to my father; that we weren't his children, and our names were not Lazenby, but Girardin, and that was mother's name, and so it was ours. And he said he'd explain all that, and make it clear to us, by-and-bye, but we were too young as yet to understand it. But he was a liar there, too; for mother's name's at the back of her picture, and I've got it here." And the boy produced a small locket, with hair in it, on the back whereof, in small seed pearls, were the initials " E. C."

The Patrico took it in his hand, but could not read the interwoven cypher, for such it was.

" Well, my boy, E. C., you say; and what does that stand for?"

" Eugenia Cleremont," replied Walter, firmly; " and that was my mother's name, for my grandpapa Cleremont was her father. And Mr. Lynx is a liar—yes, a wicked wretch, to say my mother was a slave, and her name was Girardin. I had a nurse, old Cicely—she was a slave; and father and mother had slaves of their own. Old Brutus, *my* man, that carried me out when I was little, was *my* slave; but mother was a lady and a free woman."

The Patrico smiled, as he thought how early the brown boy before him must have been taught the tyrannic principles of slavery in foreign climes.

" So you had your own slaves, when father was alive?" asked he.

" Of course," replied young Walter, as if *not* to have a slave was a surprising thing ; " and so had sister Eugenia, and mother had ever so many to fan her and dress her, and father ever so many to wait on him ; so how could my mother be a-slave ?"

"True," replied the Patrico ; then he added to himself: "no, no ; this boy mustn't go for fifty. It's true as I can't make much out of his story ; but one thing's clear, as this Lynx and this here Mr. Lazenby is a-doing of these young un's out o' their rights. I can't get it back for 'em, that's sartin ; but I'll have more than fifty—ay, or a hundred, too, afore I'll find him for Mr. Lynx, sharp as he may be. Besides, if so be as he vants to keep the boy quite out o' the vay like, he von't be for hollowing very loud, for fear o' vaking them as might look too close into the consarn. Vell, this is a slice o' luck, and no mistake. I see ve shall have to take the boy to mess for the good o' the common-vealth—ha ! ha !" and the Patrico chuckled at the rich perspective.

Walter, who was pleased to see the old man in such good humour, although ignorant of its cause, thought it a favourable sign ; he therefore went on, and communicated what else he supposed his newly found friend might think interesting or important. The Patrico listened attentively, from time to time interposing a question or two. At length their converse ended, the boy having nothing further to disclose. The Patrico walked away a few paces, and gave a low chirruping sort of whistle, which was quickly replied to by the appearance of Joe Lovell.

"Joe," said the old gipsy, "we must take this boy to the 'long village ;' but, as it wouldn't be safe for him to be found in our company, we must transmogrify him a little : 'berrying'* he doesn't want ; but we'll cut his hair and change his togs, and he shall ride vith you and George in the tilt cart, along o' the door-mats and brooms—and, d'ye hear, he mustn't stir out at any time till arter dark."

"Ay, ay," was Joe's response.

And as Walter readily understood that the motive of thus disguising him was to prevent his re-capture and consignment to Mr. Lynx's guardianship, he readily submitted to the disfiguring transformation performed upon him—nay, with the love of novelty and adventure so strong in the youthful breast, he positively felt pleased, and yielded a ready acquiescence to all that was required of him.

That afternoon, ensconced among the articles of hardware, in the interior of a covered cart, driven by Joe Lovell, while George, the other gipsy, hawked wares at the houses as they passed along, the trio took the way towards the great City.

CHAPTER XLVI.

LONDON—THE DEN IN CHICK-LANE AGAIN—A HIDING-PLACE—MENTAL CORRUPTION
—WALTER'S FIRST MORAL DEBASEMENT.

THE evening shades of a summer's day closed in as the distant view of the metropolis was gained by the travelling party, as they paused by the road-side, at the Halfway House—so well known to market carts and country waggons, by half-blocking the road, near the wall of Hyde-park, between Kensington and Knights-bridge. The park wall has long since been displaced by an iron railing, surmounting a low brick parapet ; and the house itself has been, within these four years, swept away by the hand of modern improvement. At the time we write of, however, it was a much frequented hostelrie for teams and carriers on the great Western-road. Here, for the first time, young Walter left the cart ; and, as night fell, he and Joe Lovell passed the toll-gate at Hyde-park Corner, and entered upon the long line of Picadilly, its vista illumined by countless glimmering lamps of train oil. The lad felt delighted as he paced along beside his gipsy companion ; the love of adventure, mingled with a pleasing sensation of curiosity and wonder at the various sights and sounds, the busy traffic, the splendid shops, and the hurrying crowds, kept his mind fully employed, as they pushed along unheeded and unobserved ; till, striking out of the main road near Leicester-square, his conductor led him through innumerable bye-streets, alleys, and short cuts, ere they emerged into Holborn, by the narrow strait of Great Turnstile. Pursuing an eastward course, they descended

* Staining from walnut juice.

Holborn-hill, and plunged into the fishified region of Field-lane. A narrow turning on the right soon brought them—through a labyrinth of baskets and barrows, covered with coarse fish, stale vegetables, and wretched fruit—to a low door, in the front of the caravansera known already to the reader as the dwelling of Black Ben. The house was, as usual, pretty full; and Joe, opening the half-door of the counter with the familiarity of a friend, the next moment introduced his juvenile charge to the notice of the landlord and a brace of guests, who were tippling at a little table in the "snuggery," behind the bar. One of the guests was a showily-dressed young man, of determined aspect, the other a dark-complexioned damsel, in whom Walter recognised, as he thought, a likeness to Joe Lovell himself, or perhaps the Patrico. Nor was he far out in his conjecture, for Rebekah Morse was a cousin of Joe's; the other guest was our hero, Jerry Abershaw.

"Patrico will be here to-night," said Joe, as he entered; "he's sent this boy on a-head, as he wishes him kept quiet a while; he's gettin' some writin's as he ses he'll get friend Ben here to spell out, and vich he's a thinking may turn up summut in our vay."

Joe here took the landlord aside, and whispered him to the effect that the concealment of the boy was of much importance, and that he more than suspected him to be entitled to some property, which certain persons had conspired to cheat him out of. Ben, of course, felt a natural indignation at all dishonesty which brought no grist to his own mill, and, therefore, as a partner in the gipsy firm, declared his readiness to do all in his power to detect the scoundrels "as would take advantage of a hinnocent boy."

This affair settled, the party sat down to carouse; Walter being first conveyed to a small apartment, entered from an aperture in the wall of the house, and forming part of a false chimney projecting into the next tenement (also in the occupation of the host of the Red Lion), and which was so ingeniously contrived that it presented on the outside a mere projection of apparently solid brickwork, with a fire-place, evidently for many years securely blocked up with the same material.

What boy that has a spice of romance in his composition, but is pleased with novelty, be it ever so inconvenient? Young Walter saw with pleasure this snug little cabin, as his guide called it, contained a trucklebed, a mattrass and a rug, together with a washstand, a small stove, a couple of chairs, and other conveniences; for, in fact, it had more than once been occupied by fugitives from the violated laws of their country for many days, whom none dared to communicate with lest it should lead to their detection and capture. A small oil-lamp was placed on the table, consisting of a broad wick surmounting a globe-shaped cistern, standing on a small brass pot. Joe pointed to a shelf in the tiny corner cupboard, saying—

"Now, my younker, see here—this here's ile for your glim vensoever it gets low, onless you prefers the dark; you puts it in this here little hole, and screws it down, so."

Walter watched his mode of replenishing the lamp from the small-spouted tin, and expressed himself aware of the contrivance.

"There's another convenient dodge in this crib too," said his swarthy valet-de-chambre; "touch this here knob, and the panel slides back; you sees that handle? vell, then that ere's a bell, as rings to the bar, and is on the same bell as the parlour von, oney it pulls it the contr'ry vay; vereby old Ben knows vether it's his friend in this here crib, or they in the t'other room as vants him. There's a book too, though I can't say as I can read it, that maybe 'ill please yer; you'll have yer supper presently; so now, good night my lad, and keep up yer pluck, for nayther Lawyer Link nor none of his crew dare come anigh this place; so yer may think yerself precious lucky as you're got among friends."

Walter, in his simplicity, thought so too. He sat buried in a deep reverie; all the strange and unaccustomed sights he had witnessed in the three days since his escape from his persecutor crowded through his mind.

Walter was an impassioned, hasty boy, with principles as yet totally unformed—thanks to the neglect of his uncle and the misconduct of Mr. Lynx. His plastic mind remained in a ductile state, ready to take the form which circumstances might impress upon it. His youthful disposition had as yet assumed no bias, and awaited the guiding hand of an elder to give it that turn and direction which must direct its course to good or evil. His imagination was lively, his courage high, his emulation great, his passions violent, and his character contained those elements which go to make a remarkable man, whether for crime or for virtue.

What a perilous position for such a youth! By a natural progression his reverie proceeded from his past to his present position, with which, despite of some slight and transient misgivings, he was on the whole satisfied; his vehement hatred of Mr. Lynx having much more to do with this conclusion than he had the slightest suspicion of.

Walter was a creature of impulse, easily attached, capable of ardent love and of bitter hate. The former feeling lay in the grave of his mother, none since had awakened it; the latter was alive and in full vigour, for Lynx had aroused it. His reflections next took the road which a metaphysician would expect, but can no more account for than could the boy with whom our story is now occupied—they busied themselves with vain futile endeavours to pierce the misty future: this is beyond the ken of the world-experienced, how ridiculous then must be the extravagant fancies of one who knew nothing of the world and its ways! His first train of thought for the future was that of " going to sea ;" the never-forgotten turn of boyish adventure; and immediately the few books he had read, such as " Robinson Crusoe," " Anson's Voyage," and " Old Dampier's Adventures," rose vividly, and he successively attributed to himself and imaged in his own person the delights, as he thought them, of a desert island, and the joys of the company of parrots, goats, monkeys, fences of growing wood, groves of milky cocoanuts, and even yearned for the society of an amiable savage like Man-Friday rather than the to-him-inexplicable social savage, a cruel crafty lawyer. He revelled in adventures among Patagonians, in captures of rich galleons, in visits to far distant islands in the Southern Main, and all these things came more vividly and clearly to his mental vision, owing to the early recollections of his boyhood in a tropical clime, and the sea-voyage he had taken so shortly after his powers of observation and reflection were first awakened. Then he bethought himself of a soldier's life, his picture being formed solely from an old staring coloured print or two which had fallen in his way, intending to depict some event in the campaigns of the Duke of Marlborough, wherein his grace was seen prancing on a Brobdignag war horse in the foreground, as brilliant in cocked hat, curled wig, and square laced coat and bucket boots, as indigo blue, yellow ochre and vermilion could make him, while in the distance rows of infantry, marked by red and yellow lines, poured volumes of smoke from an open plain at a town so surrounded by stone walls and round flanking towers (whence protruded innumerable cannon of gigantic calibre), that it seemed a standing miracle to any contemplative mind, how they ever could have survived for five minutes so insane an exposure ; then, to add to the delightful keeping of the scene, the valiant commander who had set them " where they would get so damnably peppered," caracoled with his red face towards the spectator, and his right arm grasping a baton, appropriately pointed over his left shoulder, as who should say, " What do you think o' that for military stratagem ?" But Walter saw none of these discrepancies ; he merely fancied, poor child, that the said gallant caracoling in cocked hat, and knocking over a few dozen of the enemy, by way of breathing yourself, was the everyday performance of a soldier, and one of which the aforesaid cocked hat and yellow star on the breast was the customary reward. He therefore was divided in opinion as to whether, when of a proper age, he should give his country the benefit of his service by sea or land, although his preference leant to the former, inasmuch as he had an idea that he could enter upon shipboard at a much earlier age than he could grow to the inches requisite to form a gallant cavalier—such as he had seen in the picture aforesaid, and in a regiment of royal guards, a troop of which had once greeted his eyes as they marched through the Kentish village wherein his school was situate—a vision of martial glory he had never forgotten.

In this uncertainty of mind, the boy arose from the side of the truckle-bed we have already mentioned, seeking relief from his perplexing thoughts took up the book of which Joe Lovell had spoken, and proceeded to read, doubting not but that it would wile away time and finally produce slumber ; of which he did not feel the usual approach, owing to the feverish excitement of his brain at his new and unexpected position. The book bore the following title—" *A True and Authentick History of the Lives and Exploits of the most notorious and celebrated Robbers, Sea Pyrates, Rovers, Buccaneers, Highwaymen, Thieves, Banditti, and Murtherers of all*

Nations. Newly collected by Captain Alexander Johnson, &c.'' A more mis-
chievously attractive work, in his present situation, nor one more likely to be found
there, can hardly be imagined. It was the bane without the antidote. Unlike
such narratives as that we now indite, the work the unarmed mind of Walter had
thus encountered made heroes of its ruffians; described their atrocities with a horrible grotesqueness and coarse wit which almost left the mature reader in doubt
whether the writer considered them crimes; dealt in obscene and profane anecdote,
with a gusto that sugared over the disgusting ingredients; in a word, instead of
showing '' vice its own defeature,'' it almost went the length of carrying out the
Spartan morality—that is is not the '' crime'' but the '' detection'' which deserves
censure.

Here was a work—filled as it is with varied adventure—for the solitary study of
a mind like Walter's! Pope's axiom—

> " Vice is a monster of so frightful mien,
>   As, to be hated, needs but to be seen;
>   But seen too oft, familiar with her face,
>   We first endure, then pity, then embrace,"

is a truism to a certain extent, as is every truth in ethics. Walter began to read for the sake of the adventures, and fell, without reasoning on his emotions (how should such a child do so?), into an admiration of the boldness of the villains who were the chief actors therein. The next step was a desire to imitate them; and when at length, after a hearty meal, the boy fell asleep, the watches of the night were filled with daring exploits, wherein the dreamer led a bold crew of pirates against Spanish galleons, loaded with gold; or revelled, amid heaps of jewels and un-counted wealth, on the cave-worn shore of some distant island of the Southern Sea, while his roving barques lay at anchor in the sheltered bay: nay, so little did the *morale* of the affair affect young Walter, that, without any positive inclination to vice, and losing sight of the base sordid motive as well as the criminality of the act, he fancied himself another Du Val or Turpin, and, bestrid-ing his good steed with pistol in hand, robbed some "avaricious hunks," to bestow his wealth on "a poor deserving widow," whom he had wronged. This, the very knight-errantry of ruffianism, has, we regret to say, been too often chosen by dra-matists and romance-writers, to ornament the tissue of their fictions. This is the "matter, deep and dangerous," which we shall essay to avoid in this our history of Jerry Abershaw. Leaving young Walter in this "fool's paradise" (would it de-served no worse name), let us look below at more hardened sinners.

The Patrico had by this time arrived; and the four individuals already men-tioned, namely, the Patrico, Ben Holland the victualler, Joe Lovell, and Jerry, sat in close consultation. Before them lay several papers, a note-case, a memorandum-book, and a pocket-book with steel spring clasp. Black Ben was busied in perusing the documents, which, if one might judge from sundry "hums" and "hahs" that from time to time escaped him, were either very satisfactory or very perplexing. What their contents really were we take the privilege of storytellers to keep to ourselves till a more fitting opportunity for disclosing them; suffice it to say that the private papers, the memorandum-book, and pocket ditto of Ferdinand Lynx, gent., &c. one &c., contained rather more than that worthy limb of the law would have disclosed under cross-examination of the severest pleader that ever wore frizzled horsehair in lieu of his own natural head ornament. And now, as young Walter is fairly housed and secure from the pursuit of his hypocritical pro-tector, we will just look after the protector himself.

CHAPTER XLVII.

MR. LYNX DECIDES ON TRUSTING TO THE CHAPTER OF ACCIDENTS—WALTER REMAINS IN HIDING—HE IS MADE A FELLOW OF THE THIEVES' UNIVERSITY.

WE last heard of Mr. Lynx at the inn which he and the postboy had reached on the night of the highway robbery. That the lawyer got little sleep that night may be well supposed. He saw the awkward consequences that might ensue to himself as well as his patron, although, truth to say, he cared little about the last-named personage provided number one could escape scot-free. The next day he returned to London, and there, in the library of Sir Ebenezer, detailed the unhappy *contretemps* which had placed young Walter beyond their reach.

Sir Ebenezer Fitzroy, whose villany was but of a half-and-half order, felt by no means unhappy, under all the circumstances of the case, that the young fellow had taken himself off. For he viewed it as an advantageous incident which solved a problem that had of late disturbed his rest. He could not bring himself to the de-termination of absolutely making away with his brother's child, and he saw no other safe method of dealing with him. He was of opinion, also, that to raise a public disturbance by offering large rewards for his recovery, might attract an un-pleasant amount of notice towards the boy, and lead to enquiries. He therefore resolved to trust to the chapter of accidents, and remain quiet.

Mr. Lynx, also, to whom the boy had more than once declared his determination to run away and go to sea, hoped that he had carried his threat into effect; and as nothing could be done without publicity, he resolved to keep silently a sharp look-out, to see if chance enquiry might not, in one way or another, put him on the track of Walter, and perhaps enable him to direct his course, without even the boy himself knowing to whom he was indebted for the dilemmas in which he might find himself involved.

Thus the young West Indian, for the present in little peril of pursuit or detection, remained in hiding ; Patrico, Jerry, Rebekah, and Black Ben himself, not a little puzzled that no advertisement, offering a heavy reward, no handbill, or other public announcement, was issued, on which they might found a scheme of extortion, and net something handsome for the restoration of the lost heir, as they naturally supposed Walter to be.

" I'll tell 'ee what," said the Patrico, as he sat in consultation with Black Ben, in the snuggery already alluded to, " there's something as I can't onriddle about this youngster. Fust of all, that old la'yer, as was wi' him, offered fifty guineas, then a hundred to get the boy agen, and seemed half crazed at his loss. Now, although Joe, and myself, and Jerry, and Rebekah has all been on the tout, we carn't none of us find out this lawyer as had the boy in charge ; and, more than that, can't find nobody as knows anythink about the lad, nor his sister as he talks on. Now, one thing's sure and sartin, as, if he's nailed, they'll trace the bit of padding* to us, mayhap—that won't do. Well, the next look-out is to purvide for him. Now, as it won't do to keep the boy here idle, Jerry and Bekkah seem both of 'em to fancy him, and as he seems quite cut by them as belongs to him, he can't well be in better hands to larn a thing or two."

CHAPTER XLVIII.

A RETROSPECTIVE GLANCE—COMPOUNDING FELONY—CONSCIENTIOUS SCRUPLES, HOW QUIETED—HOUSEMAN'S RELEASE—EDUCATION—WALTER TAKES A DEGREE IN THE COLLEGE OF CRIME.

AT the close of chapter forty, Bill Houseman was left snugly lodged in the old prison of Tothill-fields, awaiting his trial for the shoplifting affair at Mr. Garnet's, in the old Exeter 'Change. It was about five in the evening of about six weeks after the attempted robbery, that a somewhat seedy-looking individual, with inflamed eyes and carbuncled nose, presented himself at the counter of that cosy dealer in precious stones, Sheffield plate, and less valuable nick-nackeries, and with a mysterious yet deferential air, requested the favour of five minutes' interview with Mr. Gabriel Garnet.

" That's *my* name, sir," replied the fussy little tradesman; " at your service, sir. I've no secrets, sir," added he, peering towards the small winding staircase, on the top step whereof he espied the silken skirt of his larger and better half, listening, as was her practice, to the business going on below; " so, sir, if you please, you may as well state your business at once. I've no secrets—no secrets." Mr. Garnet, too, having by this time scanned his visitor, and perceived, although it was candlelight, that his black coat was rusty, and his cravat yellowish, changed his tone as he uttered the last words.

Mr. Crocodile Fuddlebrain, for he it was, was not, however, to be put off. He assented, with a ready bow, to the propriety of Mr. Garnet having no secrets ; "but—nevertheless—at the same time—notwithstanding *this* affair, *his* little business was of such a strictly confidential nature, that he could only communicate it to Mr. Garnet alone, in private. Could he, therefore, request the favour of Mr. Garnet's company to a neighbouring tavern, where, in a private box, they could, without attracting attention, talk over the subject with a bowl of punch ?" Mr. Fuddlebrain concluded his mysterious proposal by handing his professional piece of pasteboard (a somewhat dingy, disreputable-looking card, printed in shabby letterpress) to Mr. Garnet. This was too much for the very small modicum of patience possessed by Mrs. Garnet. A secret—to be told her husband, too, alone ! A secret in which she was only to share at second-hand ; to be imparted, too, in a tavern, over a bowl of punch ! The ire of the portly lady not only rose at the audacity of the seedy-looking stranger's proposition, but her dignity was offended at the bare idea of her husband, as it appeared to her, almost entertaining the idea of assenting to it.

* The footpad-robbery of the post-chaise, already mentioned.

" Over a bowl of punch, too !" exclaimed the portly lady, gliding down the few steep stairs, which serpentined, corkscrew-fashion, into the shop, and, without resistance or refusal on his part, snatching, rather than receiving, Mr. Fuddlebrain's card from the fingers of her husband. The lawyer turned towards the new comer and propitiated her with a most servile bow and an obsequious grin, as she slowly spelt over his address.

We say spelt, because Mrs. Garnet's early education had been but small; her earlier years having been consumed in assisting her mother, a laundress and clear-starcher, in the less laborious parts of her business, alternated with the care of two or three younger brats, her brothers and sisters. Her transition from this was to a maid of all work; and from this position in his uncle's house Gabriel Garnet married her. A bouncing, red-faced, attractive wench, of provident habits, industrious disposition, and violent temper, she, nevertheless, proved a "good wife," in the common acceptation of the term—ruling Gabriel and her household by her violent temper, and herself by a prudent economy in worldly affairs, induced by early poverty and privation. There is nothing so soon mollifies low-bred and illiterate people as a vast show of that deference to their worldly position, which they imagine to be their due. Mrs. Garnet was, like all upstarts, marvellously impressed with a notion of her own importance. The fawning manner of the thieves' attorney quickly appeased her ire, and, not to be outdone, she positively courtesied to the man of law, in a style that approached a coarse imitation of the opening of the *Minuet de la Cour*, her rustling quilted silk petticoat adding to the effect of the formal *salute*. Mr. Fuddlebrain saw his cue in an instant. " Ay, ay," he mentally observed, "grey mare the better horse, here. I'll do it." Placing one hand on his left breast, Mr. Fuddlebrain drew back a pace.

" Madam," added he, again bowing, " so perfect a stranger am I to Mr. Garnet, that I really did not know, till now, that he was blessed with such a treasure in his household. Yet, bless me! what a head I must have —— What a memory! I owe you, madam, a thousand apologies. May I say that I am speaking to the lady who so boldly, so intrepidly—a-hem—with such presence of mind—protected her husband's property from robbers, a few weeks since? I thought so. Well, madam, the fellows who write in the newspapers, I'm sure, did great injustice to your meritorious conduct on that trying occasion. If I may judge from what I have since heard, from private sources, the villains had positively got clear off with the property, when your decision and really heroic courage frustrated their atrocious and audacious attempt, snatched their booty from them, and was the means of lodging one of the gang in gaol, where he now lies waiting his trial."

Mrs. Garnet felt herself rising, even in the high heels of her shoes, as the attorney thus volubly delivered himself; yet she held back, looked as modest as her plump and somewhat brazen face would allow, screwed up her mouth into a simper, and protested, with sundry " lauks," " dears," and " oh, las," that the gentleman was " too good," " too polite," and such like "sarsnet" phrases as she had picked up among citizens' wives of her acquaintance. Mr. Fuddlebrain's course was clear, and he went on, Gabriel remaining a mute listener to the conversation.

" Yes, my dear madam—I address you, you perceive, with the familiarity of a professional man, which I know your good sense will excuse—it was by an oversight, for which I shall not easily forgive myself, that I omitted addressing myself to you in the first instance—more especially when I recollect the prominent, the leading part you played throughout this unpleasant, and, to most females, alarming attempt. Excuse me, but when I spoke to my worthy friend here, Mr. Garnet, if he will allow me to call him so, of desiring a private interview—in fact, being engaged on a delicate mission, requiring a certain amount of secresy—I never for a moment contemplated that disclosure of the business to *you* was among the conditions of my interview; on the other hand, perhaps, as the affair is a little delicate and personal—a-hem—in fact, relates to matters which—a-hem—in some points, it is hardly right—in fact, it would be advisable—that Mr. Garnet should be able to say he knew nothing ——" (Mrs. Garnet's curiosity was raised to the highest pitch.) " It would be better, viewing the subject in all its bearings, if it could be so managed, that *you* should be the party with whom I negociate."

Mr. Garnet, who still wore a green silk shade, in consequence of the damage his optics had received from the pungent contents of Downy Dick's snuff-box, actually raised the temporary pent-house from his eyes, and stared, as well as their weakened state would permit him, at this riddling envoy. Mrs. Garnet was still more gratified. Bridling up with some dignity, she observed that, " in course, if it was not proper Mr. Garnet should know the particulars, it could not be proper for her to hear them; therefore, perhaps, the gentleman would partly explain his meaning."

Mr. Fuddlebrain readily complied.

" I presume, madam," said he, glancing round to see there were no more auditors, " that your natural good disposition and humanity would prompt you to save a fellow-creature—a young man of good connections—though he has fallen in with evil companions, from an ignominious death ?"

Mrs. Garnet by no means seemed softened by the exordium, and merely nodded her head to the speaker to proceed.

" I have received," said the rascally compounder of felony, " a letter" (and he produced one from the pocket of a well-worn red morocco case) " from the lad's mother—for he is quite a youth—expressing his parent's distracted state at hearing of the shocking position in which he has placed himself by his wickedness and folly."

Mrs. Garnet interposed something to the effect that the fellow should have thought of all that before he tried to rob honest people of their property, and coupled it with a proverb about folks having to lie in beds according to their way of making them. Mr. Crocodile Fuddlebrain bowed assent to the lady's proposition, but went on.

" True, madam, very right; this young man—I've no doubt you perceived he was a superior young man—ladies have keen eyes for that—is the only hope of a widowed mother, and his death—yes, his death, madam—will send her grey hairs with sorrow to the grave."

Mrs. Garnet grew somewhat impatient, which Mr. Fuddlebrain perceiving, changed his tack.

" Now, madam, I wouldn't, as a professional man—and, I flatter myself, a man of the world—have dreamt of obtruding myself on you with a mere appeal to your sympathy or compassion on behalf of a man who has so grossly outraged you, and one of whose confederates, not yet in custody, has inflicted so cruel an injury on this worthy man here. I should have thought it absurd to do so. But, in the first place, allow me to observe, that this young man was not the actual thief; moreover, he did not commit the wanton outrage of which the other ruffian was guilty; indeed, he himself, at an interview I had with him at the prison, deeply deplores the act. And now, madam, comes the delicate part of the proposition, which, with your permission, I will impart only to your private ear."

Mrs. Garnet, with an ill-grace, observed, " she did not see what good could possibly come of it, if they talked for a week. She was sorry the young man should come to such an end—very sorry; but it was his own seeking, and he must take the consequences. Besides which, it was their duty to protect society by prosecuting and punishing such offenders; which she should certainly urge Mr. Garnet to do, with the utmost rigour of the law."

Fuddlebrain still bowed assent, but persisted.

" Exactly so, madam; I should expect as much from your determination and decision of character. But may I observe that you have not suffered pecuniary loss; and although I should be the very last man to advise a dereliction of public duty—as you very properly observe—there are motives of action, springing peculiarly from the compassion and tenderness in the female bosom, which I should refrain from appealing to in the sterner sex. I am further instructed, and intrusted with a proposition more substantial; but that, as I before said, I would rather entrust to your own ear."

Mrs. Garnet was a greedy woman, with, as may be supposed, no very high principle; money and fine clothes were her standards of respectability; gentility she venerated, as something above her; and if there was one thing more than another she prided herself on, it was being " a woman of business."

" Oh, if it's a *business* proposal, Mr. Fuddlebrain, then there's no harm in it whatsoever. I'm often obliged, when things requires making up one's mind, to work Gabriel here up to the p'int. Gabriel, my dear, I'll just step into the back parlour, and hear what this here gent. has to propose; not that I'll do anything that isn't quite right as to this young fellow, whom I'm determined shall be prosecuted with the utmost rigour of the lor."

Having delivered herself of this set speech, Mrs. Garnet flounced into the back-parlour aforesaid, holding the inward handle of the glass-door until the lawyer had entered, and closing it without a remonstrance from the hen-pecked Gabriel, who, to say the truth, had a high reliance on the tact and natural acuteness of Mrs. G. in " business matters."

Mr. Crocodile Fuddlebrain seated himself in the arm-chair to which he was motioned; produced the morocco note-case before mentioned, hemmed, wiped his spectacles with a cotton pocket-handkerchief, and peered over them with a furtive glance at the stately Mrs. Garnet, who sat rigidly upright in a chair at the opposite side of the table, as who should say, " Now, open your credentials, the court is prepared to examine them!"   Fuddlebrain saw that pathos must be thrown away.

" Now, my dear madam," said he, " business *is* business; this young man's friends, have employed me to wait on *you*, and make an offer, which, to speak plainly, I think no sensible person could refuse.   First, there's the chance of an acquittal—I do think you do not prosecute in hope of seeing the young man's life taken : then there's the great trouble, unpleasantness, loss of time, and expense in dancing attendance at the assizes; then there's the degradation—for indeed, madam, it is degradation to such a highly respectable female as yourself, of being placed up as a gazingstock for a crowded court — principally very low, vulgar people—to give evidence, and be cross-examined.   Well then, I have a proposal to avoid all this.   Let Mr. Garnet be taken ill, go to the country, and be confined to his bed, on the 24th of next month, and remain so, until the 27th, and I, on the part of Mrs. Wilson (that's the name of the young man's mother) will guarantee to you, madam, twenty guineas per day, to be paid into your own hands for your private use!"   Mr. Fuddlebrain paused, and pretending to read with great attention a paper before him, gave Mrs. Garnet full time, like an experienced angler, to " pouch the bait."

We have said Mrs. Garnet was greedy—she had never before been tempted with money to be earned so easily—yet her good sense told her she was offered a bribe to connive at a serious offence.   She was about to reply, perhaps unfavourably, when at the first articulate sound, Mr. Fuddlebrain broke in with—

" I fear, madam, I have been somewhat precipitate in thus making an offer, forty pounds is what my client here places at my disposal; yes, forty pounds," mumbled Mr. Fuddlebrain, staring through his spectacles at the supposed letter; " nevertheless, my dear madam, if I *have* outstepped my instructions, so let it stand; and if, from that tender feeling which must dwell in so fine a form—that mercy which is ever the accompaniment and the adornment of feminine grace—this young man's life should be saved to his sorrowing mother and wretched sister, by the absence—and nothing is more easy—of your husband on the days I have mentioned, then this slight token of a mother's gratitude, and a sister's joy, will be indeed well bestowed."   As he finished this cajoling and flattering speech, Mr. Fuddlebrain produced three bank notes of twenty pounds each, and placed one of them before Mrs. Garnet; she mechanically took it up, looked at it abstractedly, and straightway fell into a brief meditation on the " lovely joseph," and the " beautiful Chantilly lace" sported the previous Sunday by Mrs. Bullock, the senior churchwarden's wife.   The like she would have bought, but prudence forbade, and lo! here was the twenty pounds, whereat she valued the coveted finery, offered to her to do nothing! could anything be more easy than that? Besides, she now began to have some compassion for the widowed mother and the only sister, which Crocodile had so cunningly invented for the nonce.   Why too should she destroy the life of a smart young fellow, for some paltry jewellery, which, moreover, she had not lost? That eloquent pleader — self-interest — had almost gained the cause, when Mr. Fuddlebrain, marking her indecision, settled the question.

" My dear madam," said he, " 'tis not only an easy, a simple, but a praise-worthy act; our best legislators, our worthiest and most enlightened lawyers, doubt the right, the religious right I mean, of a man to shed his fellow-creature's blood on the scaffold, for a paltry amount of worldly goods. Let that be as it may, here is a handsome, spirited young fellow of respectability, gets into bad company and is detected in a daring attempt—frustrated, madam, by your more than manly courage and decision; well, his life is in your hands, and I offer to bear you harmless, with a slight pecuniary acknowledgment of the mercy you extend!"

"I'll speak to Garnet," said Mrs. G.; "he shan't appear against this young man; however, if that wretch who so burnt poor Gabriel's eyes is overtaken, not all the Mint o' money shall save him from the gallows. And now, Mr. Puddle-cane, not a word to my husband as to the note, leave *that* to me. It isn't, as you very properly observe, right that he should know all about this transaction, for fear he should be questioned; and what he don't know," added the lady, with a gracious smile, "he won't tell! Trust to me, sir; the young man's blood shan't rest at *my* door, I assure ye."

Mrs. Garnet rose, rang the bell, and insisted on Mr. Fuddlebrain taking a glass of wine, which he would gladly have exchanged for the like quantity of stiff Jamaica. Mr. Garnet, too, like a child who has been kept out upon probation, was graciously invited in to partake of the port and sweet biscuit; when Mrs. Garnet communicated just so much as she thought fit. Imparting, of course, her desire, followed by her command, that Gabriel should not appear to prosecute the young man in custody; giving as her reasons therefor, charity, compassion, sorrow for his relations; indeed every motive save and except the sordid one which had first called them into existence, and without the promptings of which all Mr. Fuddlebrain's rhetoric would have been about as cogent as the Irish experiment of "whistling jigs to a milestone." Mr. Garnet, having no opinion of his own, in his wife's presence opposed nothing, and Mr. Fuddlebrain departed, highly satisfied with the prosperous issue of his negociation for the extrication of Handsome Bill's neck, from "edge of penny cord."

The following morning saw Fuddlebrain at the gaol of Tothill. His person was well known to the turnkeys, and he found no difficulty in obtaining admission.

Bill Houseman was one of the inmates of the middle or larger ward; and here, in the yard, among motley groups of criminals of all ages, debtors, vagrants, old and young thieves, and offenders of every grade—from the drunken mechanic who had assaulted a watchman, to the dashing highwayman, the desperate burglar, and the atrocious assassin—he awaited the slow process of gaol delivery by the law. He was well acquainted with the exertions being made out of doors for his release, through the agency of Jerry and old Ben; which he was duly informed of, almost day by day, by Rebekah; for Abershaw himself, did not, of course, care to show his face at a place where, if no present inconvenience should arise, he might naturally presume as little communication or recognition as possible, would be most judicious.

Time rolled on, though tediously, and at length Bill Houseman stood in the dock at the sessions, was arraigned, and pleaded "not guilty." Mr. Crocodile Fuddlebrain, as we have seen, made the way safe. There was no prosecutor to give evidence. Mrs. Garnet, it is true, was there; but she declined positively swearing to the prisoner; nay, went so far as to state, that she could not be quite sure he was the man she seized in the Exchange. Mr. Dave Turner, too, for good and solid reasons, was troubled with the like conscientious misgivings. He began his evidence in chief by stating, that, on the evening in question, as he and his comrade were coming from Southampton-street, Strand, towards Exeter 'Change, "quite permiscously," he "seed the prisoner at the bar with a lot o' people round him, as just come up; he (the prisoner) was calling 'stop thief!' and seeing nobody afore him, except a young man as was a-runnin' too, but who was out of his reach, he collared him." "Most sartinly he made no resistance" went on the thieftaker, "but said as how he was pursuin' the other man, 'cos he heerd the people a-calling out; but that, my lord, was too stale a dodge for me, so I capturs him, and takes him back. Well, my lord ——"

"Did you know the prisoner at the bar as a reputed thief?" interrupted the judge.

"Why—a-hem, my lord, I carn't exactly say as I know any bad of him, but, my lord ——"

"Gentlemen of the jury," said his lordship, "in cases involving the life of a prisoner, the law requires the clearest evidence of the offence. It would be a waste of time, gentlemen, to proceed; I shall leave the case in your hands."

Bill Houseman, here, by the advice of Mr. Fuddlebrain, enquired "whether his lordship would like to hear his witnesses to character?"

The judge replied in the negative; and the jury, without leaving the box, acquitted the prisoner, and turned Handsome Bill once more loose on society.

Things now went prosperously with the fraternity of Chick-lane. We have noted in a former chapter the disappointment the scoundrels experienced in consequence of the plated goods and valueless articles they had stolen from the house at Islington. Mercury, however, at this period seemed in the ascendant, for the star of thievery shone propitiously on their nefarious enterprises.

Young Walter, surrounded by such sights and scenes of profligacy as we have heretofore described, gradually overcame the disgust with which, at first sight, they had inspired him. He formed a particular friendship with Downy Dick and one or two other flash lads of his kidney; for whose low art, perverted ingenuity, and bold wickedness of manner, it will not surprise any one deeply read in human nature, or the world, he soon imbibed that species of admiration, which prompts to an emulative rivalry. How far poor human nature is the creature of education and early impressions, and how awful the responsibility of those to whom power, for good or for evil, is delegated by their fellow-men, seems only just beginning to be perceived, even by a small section of the statesmen and legislators of this self-sufficient age. How much of crime, how much of the vice which plunders, outrages, demoralises, infests the crowded city, the bustling mart, the gilded theatre, the clanking factory, the stifling workshop and the dark mine, which fills the sylvan preserve with bloodspilling affrays, which fires the rick and the homestead, visits with furtive design mead or fold, or bares the robber's knife and bludgeon in bye path or highway—how much of this is owing to perverted or neglected training, is a problem which few philanthropists—and how few !—have as yet striven to solve.

To say that any unit in the millions of our dense population grows up uneducated is untrue; perhaps it would be better for many if they did. They would then, at least, have no more vices than their natural ones, corrected, as they oft would be, by some of the savage virtues which man in a semi-civilised state is seldom destitute. Let us not be misunderstood : all members of the community *are* educated. Is it for *good* or *evil* is the question. The state is bound to place a sound education within reach of all—let us rest assured that it is a pernicious fallacy that the mind of youth can remain uneducated. Every human being *is* educated—that is to say, every human being derives principles of conduct, and habits of action, from the authority, the conversation, and the example of those by whom he is surrounded. The thief is educated, the poacher is educated, nay, the pickpocket is most sedulously educated. There is no school in the world where more emulative alacrity is shown by the pupils than in that where a "Fagin" is the instructor, and a *Charley Bates* the assistant. Vice has its normal schools, its colleges, its universities, in every great city. Crime has rewards and premiums for the zealous, full as tempting to corrupt natures as those of honesty, virtue, and rectitude. True they may be, and by those properly instructed are known to be, like the Dead Sea fruit—without fair to the view, and within ashes—but youth and inexperience sees only the golden outside. Let this great truth, then, be never lost sight of—that a government and a people have not to choose between education and non-education, for the simple reason that non-education does not exist. It is therefore between education and perversion, or mis-education, that we have to choose ; to decide between possible good and positive evil, and the responsibility of rulers cannot be evaded or neglected.

We have said that Walter Lazenby was of an ardent temperament, and a forward disposition ; his associates soon led him into scrapes and dilemmas which exercised both. The boy's reading, which was soon neglected for more practical pursuits, prompted him to view dishonesty rather as a proof of spirit than the reverse. He soon learned several ditties of a flash and facetious character ; and, as his voice was decidedly good, his carriage superior, and his personal advantages higher than most of the juvenile thieves which resorted to the Red Lion, he soon became an object of attraction, young as he was, to more than one of the vile little outcasts which formed the female portion of the gang.

Among these, Walter's preference (it could not be called more, for he was now but twelve years old) fell upon a pretty-looking girl, three years his senior, known as Sly Sally—for each of these juvenile thieves had, of necessity, a female partner, as a necessary coadjutor, not only in his schemes and depredations, but as an indispensable adjunct to his state of dignity as a "flash man." Such an individual, without his "fancy," would have been viewed as but half-equipped for his profession. We must confess, however, that Sly Sally, young as she was, was but a

cast-off of Mr. Richard Stubbs, already known to the reader as Downy Dick, who having transferred his attentions to another damsel, they had "agreed to differ;" and with Giovanni-like indifference, the accomplished thief had encouraged the *liaison* of Sally with his young pupil and *protégé*.

The lad's progress in this college of crime was surprising; and within three months of the time of his matriculation, he was such an adept in a variety of experimental operations, as to excite the envy and admiration of older practitioners. True that he had as yet done nothing in the way of adding to the finances of the commonwealth of knavery, yet he bade fair to become a most useful member. He had already accompanied Dick and Nimming Ned on sundry predatory excursions, and shown his quickness as a scout, or a "cover" to their operations. He could lift the skirt of a coat, hung for practice in a room, and extract a kerchief, or even a heavy pocket-book therefrom, without causing either of the several small bells thereunto affixed to give the slightest tinkle of alarm. He had practised himself in assuming several disguises; learnt the art of "dinging"* with readiness and dexterity; and, by several times threading the various interlacing alleys and

* Passing property from himself to a confederate, or receiving it from one.

narrow courts in the immediate vicinity of the great thorougfares of the City, provided himself against the mistake of falling a victim to pursuit, by turning up any *cul-de-sac*, or blocked passage. He further had been initiated, by Downy Dick and his female partner, into a knowledge of several skulking places and "fence kens;"* whereunto, in the event of its being dangerous to return to head-quarters, he could retreat for a time, till the peril was past. Indeed, it would have been difficult, so far as the *morale* of his character was concerned, to have recognised the smart young thief as the erewhile open-hearted and ingenuous youth, Walter Lazenby.

His plastic and unformed character had hitherto received no shape, and the mould it now took so readily will not surprise those who know how easily youth is corrupted. Not but Walter knew that dishonesty is criminal. To him, however, that was a mere abstract principle. In practice he viewed it as the necessity of his existence; and he pursued thievery with the same energy that, in other circumstances, would have prompted him in a praiseworthy career.

All he heard and all he saw, all his reflections and all his little reading impressed his mind with the notion that the scheme of the world was mutual plunder, and that, in a higher or lower grade, all mankind were thieves. Is such a notion to be wondered at, situated as the boy then was? His uncle, he felt assured, had robbed him of some unknown quantity of wealth—*that* he quickly learnt from the plain speaking of the Patrico, Black Ben, Jerry and Rebekah—that Mr. Lynx was his confederate in the crime, he as little doubted; and hence his mind, when he permitted himself to think, which was but seldom, took a bias of self-justification, and he viewed himself as revenging, by his own dishonesty, the plunder he had experienced at the hands of others. Hypocrisy and knavery were with him synonymes for religion and commerce; and he soon, with good reason, so far as his own experience went, believed that there was no honour in man, nor virtue in woman.

About the period we now write of, after a successful foray by himself and Dick on the pockets of his majesty's lieges, on the occasion of the king going in state to open parliament, the "pals," as they now termed themselves, returned one evening to the den, accompanied by their respective *bona robas*, and the spoil having been purchased by a Jew "fence" (who paid the landlord a per centage for the recommendation), Walter and Dick found themselves in possession of several guineas each. A treat to their less fortunate fellow-thieves followed, and that night, young Walter, for the first time, got thoroughly intoxicated. This was the work of Dick, who thus, as he declared, made "a man of him." Thenceforth Walter, who already in the spirit of imitation had indulged in the Nicotian weed, no longer declined the proffered glass of Geneva, and his debasement was completed.

Thus things went on, "bad had arrived, but worse remained behind;" and shortly after, it was Walter's fortune to be engaged in a more serious and criminal adventure, through the tutelage of more hardened offenders.

We have said that Abershaw, Joe Lovell, and the recently emancipated Bill Houseman, had of late been fortunate in their depredations. Hence they seldom visited the den in Chick-lane, except as occasional visitants. Rebekah now occupied a detached cottage in the Holloway-road, near the foot of the rise of Highgate-hill—a district then so little traversed after nightfall, that it was excellently suited to their purposes.

The new junction road of Kentish-town, and the archway leading to Finchley, were not then, or for many years subsequent, even projected; and hence all that extensive tract of fields, lying between Battle-bridge, Kentish-town, and Highgate to the south, and Hornsey, Stoke Newington, and Islington on the north and west, was, with the exception of the two lines of the great North-road, traversed only by bridle-lanes, footpaths, or narrow cart-tracks skirted by hawthorn hedges. The easiness of unobserved access after dark had directed their choice, and the trio varied their marauding exploits, at one time by stopping the carriers or graziers, and then, so soon as the public mind was alarmed, they betook themselves to the metropolis, and did a little in burglary, shoplifting, or other branches of the great trade of thievery. Chance throwing in their way what seemed an excellent opportunity, led to the adventure we are about to relate, and which once more changed the position of Walter Lazenby.

---

* Receiving places for stolen property, and retreat for thieves.

CHAPTER. XLIX.

JERRY ABERSHAW AND BILL HOUSEMAN VISIT THE RED LION AT ISLINGTON—
A NEW CONFEDERATE—AN APPOINTMENT MADE.

JERRY ABERSHAW and his comrade, Handsome Bill, were seated in the parlour of the old Red Lion at Islington; Jerry was neatly attired in a thick brown riding-coat, a broadbrimmed beaver hat (but of unquakerlike shape), broadstriped cord breeches, riding boots heeled with plated spurs, and broad leather instep-guards, which denoted them worn rather for use than ornament. His head was further furnished with a wig of a lightish brown, with whiskers to match of a yet lighter shade; his whole appearance betokened the north-country grazier, a class well known and respected on the road and in the hostelries of the vicinity. His companion, Handsome Bill, was clad for the nonce as a young farmer, yet a spice of the sporting man peeped out in his "making up," as the theatricals phrase it. From his tripe-coloured tops depended long straps, and his leathers ("kickseys," as he called them) had a bow of narrow white silk ribband hanging below the last pearl button. His coat of bright blue, with lustrous double-gilt buttons, would not now-a-days have passed muster, but it was then, worn in a careless style, esteemed the *ne plus ultra* of "buckish" costume. His hat was a compromise between the cocked hat of the gentleman, and the round shapeless one creeping into favour; its brim was wide, and looped up on each side with a piece of white (not silver) cord; its crown, moderately high, diminished gradually towards the top; a riding crop, having a fox's head for a whistle, with a strong hammer-like gate-hook a few inches lower down the handle, and a white pudding-like neckcloth, with a galloping fox in gold athwart its front tie, completed the noticeable parts of his exterior.

Their talk was such as each thought most suitable to the character he had assumed, and their object, it may be supposed, was what they termed "piping on the lay," a phrase which we can only translate by the well-known sporting phrase of "marking down" game. Many an unthinking and jovial grazier or commission-dealer let fall, in the openness of social converse, so much of his private business, the whereabouts of his residence, his periods of going and returning, and his personal property, as led to his plunder at some future safe and convenient period, and little did he suppose that he had himself furnished the intelligence required, and thus become accessory to his own plunder.

While Jerry and Houseman smoked their long clay wax-tipped "aldermen" in the parlour, or "commercial room," as it was sometimes pompously called, their "touter," Joe, occasionally picked up no less valuable information in the tap, amongst drovers, servants, carriers, and packmen. This night he thought himself peculiarly lucky.

Among the beer-drinking assemblage at the iron-edged deal tables in the tap was a discharged chairman—for the sedan was then in high favour among the nobility and gentry. This fellow, who was a rough specimen of a Yorkshire tyke, possessed much of the acuteness for which York became proverbial; this, with a love of liquor, and very imperfect perceptions of the principle of *meum* and *tuum*, whenever his own gratification or greediness was concerned, had led to his discharge without a character. He had lived a while by sponging on his fellow-servants, borrowing of others, and running scores at divers public-houses; and now, as London failed to offer him any farther resource, he was vagabondizing about, picking up a precarious existence—it could not be called subsistence—by escorting home the company who visited Sadler's Wells theatre with a flaring link, occasionally holding a horse, or even riding the miserable animals exposed for sale in Smithfield on market days, on their trial gallops (in most instances shuffles or hobbles) up and down the broad part of St. John's-street, a nuisance at that time in full vigour.

To this scamp Joe Lovell had proffered a drink of his quart of twopenny ale; and as the fellow sat down and became communicative, he, by way of raising himself in the estimation of the farmer's servant (for so he thought his companion), told him some of his "experiences" in better days, as one of the liveried retainers in the mansions of the great.

Joe listened attentively; he soon found that the fellow had an intimate and local knowledge of the interior of several houses he described; that he was destitute, and, by his own showing, an unscrupulous knave—a character he rather seemed to glory in than otherwise. All these facts he duly communicated to Jerry Abershaw and Houseman. Joe made an appointment with the fellow for the following night at a low public-house, when, under the influence of a liberal supply of liquor, and the advance of a few shillings, he gave the party so accurate an account of the situation, the back and front premises, the entrances, the plate deposits, the sleeping apartments, of the two or three mansions in which he had lived, that Jerry and Houseman not only gave him a further reward, but it was settled that the Yorkshireman should receive a share of the proceeds of their burglarious enterprise.

CHAPTER L.

OXFORD-STREET AT THE CLOSE OF THE EIGHTEENTH CENTURY—RECONNOITRING—
WALTER LAZENBY MAKES AN IMPORTANT DISCOVERY—STORY OF THE FORGED WILL
—WALTER NEVILLE'S CONFESSION—A MURDER—AWFUL DEATH OF THE MURDERER
—A BURGLARY.

A CLOUDY, chilly, dreary autumnal day had closed early in storms of driving rain. The glimmering few and far between oil-lamps of Holborn and Oxford-road, now known as Oxford-street, were slowly struggling into "darkness visible" under the manipulation of the lamplighter; not a few of them either obstinately refusing to burn at all, or expiring after a few faint sputters and flickers so soon as the ladder-bearing Prometheus had left them with his igniferent flambeau. Where they did survive in small doubtful heads of dirty-coloured light, they cast faint reflections of their tiny selves on broad brown puddles and treacherous holes in the ill-paved streets, and served only to render the dreary darkness more dismally apparent. The highways thus early, for it was scarcely six o'clock, were traversed only by a few pedestrians, whom business alone compelled to be out of doors, and the plash of boots, and the infrequent clatter of some housemaid's pattens were varied at long intervals by the rattle of a ricketty hackney-coach, or the smoother roll of an equipage of more pretension.

Such was the state of Oxford-street, in the year 1847 blazing with gas, in the "dark ages" which closed with the eighteenth century, as three men, accompanied by a boy, turned down the street named after my Lord Berners, and exploring a cross-street to the right, paused, under shelter of a high dead wall skirting the courtyard of a spacious residence.

"Hist, Bill!" said Jerry, in a low voice, "do you two stand close, while I and Rob step down the mews and take a squint at the back o' the crib. D'ye say," added Abershaw, addressing the out-of-place servant, "that the carriage comes home at six, and the sedan fetches Sir What-d'ye-call-him, from Vestminster, at eleven or twelve sometimes?"

"That be the go," replied Rob, "exact. The bwoy mun be planted afore the coach cooms in, else the geat mought be locked; an' zure enow, there'll be noa chance o' gettin' in a'ter that; vor there be Jan, the footman, forbye bouth the chairmen i' hall, e'en thof the 'omankaind be gwan to bed. My lady bees oot o' town, as I hear, so there be less o' they squallin' cattle i' the crib."

"So much the better," replied Jerry, "but suppose we take the boy with us—yes, we will; we may lose time by having to come back, if so be the coast is clear. Here, Watty," whispered Jerry, "follow me. Now then, Rob, lead the way softly, and I'll keep you in sight; you, Bill, shall stand watch here till we come back, and give us the signal if anything stirs."

Rob turned down the long stable-yard which stood at right angles with the building whereto their steps were bent, sneaking carefully along from dung-heap to dung-heap, and by each well-known stable-door, till he arrived at the one sought. Drawing from his jacket pocket a small key, he opened a little door in one of the large locked gates of the coach-house. They quickly and silently passed through an eight-stall stable, wherein three or four horses were quietly enjoying their hay and oats; at the end of this they ascended a step ladder to a loft of large dimensions, lighted by two small cabin-like sash windows. Jerry now turned the slide of his dark lantern in momentary scrutiny of the place. " Good !" said he ; " why it is but eight or ten feet to the yard at back !"

" Nobody sleaps here," returned Rob Jephson, " and cross t' yard there be a bull's-eye winder, as swings on a centerpin; that be the pantry and meat-safe, it leads into the under-ground passage o' t' kitchen, and the zarvants' stairs be straight afore ye ; up-stairs be t' 'ould gentleman's study as he calls it, a big room out o' a little un' at back here, wi' a glass door as opens into a little place wi' a flower-pot or two and a bath."

" I understand it all, just as well as if I'd hung my hat up there for a week," said Walter, sharply.

" Well, then," said Rob, " if so be you can get up they stairs into that big room and get under the sofy, or behind the screen, or out into the little glass room, beyand, thee moight live there a month, barrin' the vittals, and nobody the wiser, for he doon't use the bath there at this time o' year."

" Well, as to the rest o' the vallybles," interrupted Jerry, " *we'll* see to them ; all we want o' you, Watty, is to sleep with both eyes open till old powderhead have gone to snooze, then sneak into the hall passage, slip the front jigger,* and let me and Bill in. When once we're in the crib, we'll manage the rest on it. Meanwhile, Rob will stay here with the rope and haul you up, in case anything ugly should happen."

The boy expressed his certainty that all would be right so far as *he* was concerned; and in a minute or two after, young Walter having been lowered into the little yard, and waited a short while to see that the coast was clear, squeezed his slender body through the half of the circular window already mentioned, and found himself surrounded by sundry proofs, in the shape of butcher's meat, poultry and game, that the inmates of the mansion he was so uninvitedly visiting lived on the fat of the land. Another listening pause, and he opened the door of the small store-room; a faint light at the further end of the passage showed its extent and a flight of steps at the extremity. From within a closed black door on the left, which doubtless led to the front kitchen, he heard the rattle of loud gossip and the laugh of some merry-making domestics; he trod softly along, heard something that sounded suspiciously like a hearty kiss, then a renewed burst of romping laughter, and cries of " A forfeit ! a forfeit !" " The slaveys are pretty jolly, however," soliloquised Walter ; " so much the better, they won't hear me." So saying, the lad rapidly ascended the stair; halting one instant on the landing-turn, he mounted half a dozen more steps. The inner glass doors, intended to prevent the effluvium from the kitchens ascending to the grander apartments, were before him ; then came a long, large hall, whence, to the right, opened two doors, to as many spacious apartments. On the left the spiral curve of the grand staircase, with its gilded balustrades and scagliola columns, ascended to the drawing-room suite. Still farther forward another pair of glass doors excluded the draught from the outer street when the hall-door was opened, and through its panes Walter spied a lounging menial engaged in social converse with a huge " tun of flesh " ensconced in a bee-hive chair.

" Just as the Yorkshireman said, to a T," muttered Walter ; " they're waiting for the bos,† and there's no company. This is *my* crib then," and he opened a door to the left, nearly at the head of the kitchen stairs, and behind the pair of glazed doors first spoken of. The room was dark, save a dim light at the farther end, but there was a glowing fire in the apartment. He stealthily crept along to the farther end, but hearing at this instant one of the passage doors slam, he laid himself down and rolled sideways under a spacious sofa, near the door entering to the little bath-room which Rob had described. Here, crouched as snugly as the boy Jones of palace-haunting notoriety, he lay, while John entered the apartment, and whistling an air from the last opera of Mozart or Cimarosa, proceeded to replenish the fire with a liberal supply of Wallsend from a splendent coal-skuttle. For this, young Walter was obliged, as upon his leaving the apartment, which was of most agreeable temperature, and thickly carpeted, the dancing flames, as they roared up the narrow throat of the register stove, enabled him distinctly to scan every object in the room. Bookcases with lacquered brass latticework, containing

---

* Open the hall-door.　　　　　　† Master.

gorgeously-bound volumes in scarlet or white and gold, filled each recess, and extended, also the entire length of the lower end of the apartment, small tables on which were also books, and busts were fixed in their intervals. Several print-stands, bearing huge portfolios in their angular jaws, were scattered here and there; and facing the fireplace was a large library table, covered with crimson stamped morocco, flanked by a well-stuffed circular-backed arm-chair of the same material and colour.

There were other objects too which more excited the cupidity of the juvenile thief than gorgeous volumes or costly furniture. On the writing-table stood a massive inkstand of silver-gilt, elaborately chased, bearing pens of the same costly material, a richly engraved taper-stand, for letter-sealing, and a gold desk-seal of gigantic proportions; these, with a pearl-mounted paper-folder, and a splendid desk-knife, young Walter already reckoned as his own.

A rat-tat-tat at the front-door, of length and potency enough to awaken the Seven Sleepers, soon after followed, and put to flight his calculations, and he again rolled into the darkest recess of his hiding-place.

" The House is up," said a domestic, as he passed along the passage (the phrase was unintelligible to Walter), " and your master will not leave home again to-night. He will dine in the library, alone, Thomas," added the same voice.

" The devil he will," muttered the concealed boy; " I don't like that so well: but never mind, p'raps he'll go to bed the sooner for coming home so early."

In a few minutes, a bald man of somewhat heavy figure entered the room; his face was rosy and his head partially bare; he looked between fifty and sixty, but was possibly not quite so old as he looked. His features were harsh and lined, and his forehead and the corners of his eyes wrinkled as if with careful thought. His eyes were grey, and each overhanging bushy eyebrow, like his hair, was growing white. As he paced the room with meditative step, the fingers of his hands interlaced with each other, his countenance occasionally assumed an almost lugubrious expression, and his breathing once or twice became so painfully oppressed, that young Walter thought he heard him groan. From time to time, too, he cast suspicious glances, and looked askance at his figure as he passed one or other of the small looking-glasses placed in the panels of the splendid room. It needed but a superficial observation to see that man was ill at ease. Still, on the entrance even of a menial, his manner changed, and he gave his orders in a cheerful, firm voice, and with a briskness of manner in strong contrast with the evident melancholy into which he relapsed in each short interval of solitude.

A luxurious dinner, in costly plate, occupied a tedious time in its many removes, rather than in the quantity or number of dishes tasted by him for whom its tempting delicacies were prepared. At length the formal meal was over, and the owner of the mansion left alone, with a brilliant cut claret jug of many facets, in its costly mounting, accompanied with several slender-stemmed glasses of green and amber, on a ponderous silver tray.

" Rare crib this to crack," thought Walter, as he lay *perdu* beneath the drapery of the sofa-cover, peering out from his hiding-place with the eye next the ground, his vision being assisted by the perfect shadow in which his end of the apartment was thrown, and the back of the gentleman's arm-chair being towards him, his face, of course, turned in the direction of the door.

A solemn silence reigned in the room, interrupted only by the musical jingling tick of a complex French clock of the Louis Quatorze style, with large white oval figure-plates of enamel on its ormolu dial; and the pedestal of which represented, in bold brass-work richly gilt, the struggles of the never-dying Laocöon. Ever and anon, too, as the night progressed, a soft, mellow, gentle bell told the departure of each fifth minute, while, every quarter of an hour, eight merrier-tinkling silver ones chimed off the march of time. The ninth hour had sounded slowly from a deep-toned spring, and an old jangling Swiss air had followed it (for the horologe, like many of the time, was intended to be musical), when the elderly owner of this stately mansion, the envied proprietor of all this magnificence, rose from his seat.

It was clear he had been

" Stretched on the rack of a too easy chair,"

for he sighed heavily as he rose; walked slowly, like a man who has no purpose, to a table, took up a book, put it down again; glanced at the title of another, muttered: "Too dry;" started as he read the title-page of a third—it was a religious work—laid *that* down, and paced the room with unsteady steps. At length he, as he passed another table whereon lay some of the ephemeral literature of the period, once more stopped short, and fumbled listlessly among the paper-covered magazines.

"'The Gentleman's,'" muttered he; "prosy and verbose; 'The Carlton House Magazine,' frivolous and fashionable; 'Legends and Tales.—Volume I.;' this may beguile a weary hour. Oh, wealth and worldly honour," murmured the man, as he walked back to his seat, "how light are ye in the scale when weighed against that priceless treasure—a clear and unreproaching conscience!"

Walter was positively transfixed with wonder; he almost felt contempt for the fool, as he deemed him, who, in the midst of such luxury, could not enjoy himself. Suddenly he started once more from his seat.

"The forged will," muttered he; "who has placed this in my way? Ha! I smell some trick in this—pshaw!—I'm getting foolish. I was wont to be of a good nerve and a cool head, but I'm strangely altered. What is this idle story to do with me? I'll read it, perhaps it it will give me a shock; my brain is fevered by dwelling on one point. Come, then, let's see what this idle scribbler has to say on this unpleasant topic. Will it resemble aught in its features the history of——"

Again he glanced quickly and sharply round the chamber, then slowly seating himself, he proceeded reading, half-aloud, as follows:

The Forged Will.

It was towards the close of a raw and gusty day in the month of October, that year when the Invincible Armada of Spain threatened destruction to the religious liberties of our beloved country, that a single horseman rode rapidly up to the principal entrance of Marstoke House in Warwickshire.

"Ah! Walter!" The reader started to his feet at this coincidence of name, as though stabbed by some sharp instrument; he speedily, however, regained his composure, and resumed: "Walter, my man, right glad am I to see thee again," said the owner of the mansion; adding, in a smothered tone, aside: "A south fog rot ye! What in the name of the fiend hath brought this ill-omened hound hitherward?"

"And glad am I to see you well, good Master Oldcraft," replied the stranger, in hoarse guttural tones, getting at the same time off his wearied steed with some little effort, and all the caution and deliberation of one who had apparently ridden so far betwixt sunrise and sunset, that his legs were afflicted with a sort of cavalry cramp, and bowed outwards like those of a bandy-legged turnspit.

"You are alone here, Oldcraft, are you?" he continued, pausing after his dismount, "or have you visitors or residents in your house, besides the good lady, your wife, at the present moment?"

"Alone, man," said the host; "my wife even is absent at Warwick just now."

"*Good!*" returned the other, resigning his steed to the serving-man, and shaking his friend by the hand; "'tis best so."

"But you look pale and ill, Neville," said Oldcraft; "come in, come in; a stoup of wine will refresh and revive you. You've surely journied far to-day."

"I have done so," returned the traveller; "I have neither stopped nor stayed since daybreak, except to feed and once to change my horse at Weedon, and glad am I after my ride to find you alone here, since I have that to talk about which will scarce be fitting subject for other ears but thine and mine."

In saying this, he unstrapped the leathern belt which confined his ample riding-cloak, doffed his beaver, and, ushered by the master of the mansion, strode after him into the interior.

The two persons here introduced to the reader were good and portly figures— "good men's pictures," as Portia has it, strong-built broad-shouldered, stout-limbed fellows, and both were accoutered for the nonce, in suits which were the usual equipments of persons of condition residing in the country, in Queen Elizabeth's reign. Yet, although these men wore their doublets slashed and puffed, and embroidered after the most approved fashion, had their ruffs starched to the firmness of a deal board, and carried rapiers by their sides of more than an ell in length, yet was it easy to perceive at a single glance that neither of them were gentlemen.

The one who, by reason of his being in possession, we may suppose to be the proprietor of the house and domain we have found him in; he was clad in an embroidered doublet, slashed and puffed, with continuations to answer, wore huge rosettes in his shoes, and, as before mentioned, carried those attributes of a gentleman of his day—rapier and dagger at his girdle. His features, however, were not good, and although his physiognomy gave you the idea that he possessed a considerable share of courage, firmness, and talent, yet the face was essentially vulgar and common-looking, and his figure rather too fat and burly; there was also a want of breeding in his manner and appearance altogether, which neither his clothes nor his inches made up for; in fact, he looked more like one who had had riches thrust upon him, than one who had been born to them.

The visitor was a tall, gaunt-looking fellow with a restless eye, an aquiline nose, a long Quixotic visage, dark elf-locks, and an expression of countenance so uneasy and disturbed, that apparently he was ever on the fret lest a bailiff or an officer of justice should pounce upon him unawares; he looked haggard also, and care-worn to a degree, showing evidently, that in addition to his usual style there was now the effects of hard drinking and over fatigue. He was accoutred, like his friend, in the somewhat rich dress of a country gentleman, and, in addition to his long and curiously guarded rapier and dagger, carried horse-pistols a foot and a half long at his girdle. His wide and heavy riding-boots, which were pulled up to the middle of his thighs, were accommodated with large and most persuasive rowelled spurs.

As soon as Master Oldcraft had conducted his friend into a good-sized oak-panelled apartment, on the hearth of which glowed a comfortable wood fire, he once more bade him welcome to Marstoke House, and ringing a little silver bell which stood on the table, desired the servant who attended, to bring wine and refreshments immediately; meanwhile, his guest, after spreading his extended palms over the blazing logs, and then thrusting his heavy boots almost into the flames, in order to warm his feet, now that he was fairly housed and in a goodly arm-chair placed opposite to that in which his host had seated himself, seemed to forget his fatigue in the anxiety and misery of his mind. His brow became more contracted, his countenance even more faded, his eye was sunken, and trouble and anxiety were in his every look.

He started "like some guilty thing" when the attendant serving-man threw open the door, to bring in the wine and other refreshments, shrunk and drew off his eye as he caught the man's glance, and walking to the window of the apartment, appeared for one moment to be watching the on-coming snow-storm; then suddenly returning to the fireplace, was again lost and absorbed in deep and troublesome cogitation.

Oldcraft watched his visitor with a steady eye for some time, ere he interrupted his reverie; apparently he saw what he did not altogether like in the mood he beheld him in, and his welcome had lost half its former heartiness of tone, as he poured out a cup of wine, and bade the traveller drink to refresh himself.

Walter Neville took the proffered glass, returned the pledge of his friend, and drained it to the dregs; after which, fetching a deep and long-drawn sigh, he threw himself into the vacant seat beside the table, and shadowed his face with his hands. The host, still eyeing him with a searching and steady gaze, proceeded to a litte cross-examination.

"The wine is good, Neville, is it not?" he began. "Try another glass, man; your spirits seem somewhat clouded. I don't recollect that I ever saw you so strangely moved. Even now, you said you wished to confer with me alone; have you any of the old leaven to talk of? I thought that subject was to be for ever quiet between us, eh?"

"It *was* and *is* settled," returned the visitor; "but matter hath grown out of it that I would fain speak to thee anent; matter appertaining to myself. In short, I am in want of the comfort and consolation of your companionship and your advice—not to mention that the shelter of your roof will be more than convenient just at this time. I come to be your guest here, Master Oldcraft, for some weeks, perhaps, ere I take the western voyage. You see I am unceremonious in manner, and scruple not to invite myself. Nay, for the matter of that, we know each

other well enough for me to say it suits my purpose to enjoy the air of Warwickshire for a term, and keep close the whilst; and it *must* suit yours to say,
'Walter Neville, you're welcome.'"

"There needs no ghost come from the grave," returned the host, "so to
speak the words of our new poet of Stratford, to tell me that fact, Neville. Beat
about the bush no more, man; out with your secret, and let me see if I can do
aught to assist thee. What new villany weighs so heavily upon your conscience?"

"More than I can find words to describe to thee, Oldcraft," said the traveller;
"but it must be done, the tale must needs be told, or I shall die!"

"Curse upon the ban-dog!" muttered Oldcraft; "what a thing it is to be but
half a villain! What, that over-greed of thine," he continued, aloud, and
somewhat bitterly, "not satiated with the fortune thou hadst amassed as my
partner, sent thee again to the dice-table, and I suppose the loss of all you had—
avariciously as thou didst always pouch the uttermost farthing thou couldst

scrape together—has nearly driven thee frantic, so that now thou art come yelping here, to confide this thing to me, and ask a further share, thinking, as thou even now didst hint, that I dare not refuse thee."

"No, by heaven," returned the other, in his peculiar and deep tones, "you are safe there. I would I were steeped in poverty to the very lips, so I could undo what I have committed. I am twice, nay, three times as wealthy, Oldcraft, as when I saw thee last ; but unhappy was the hour in which I became so ; accursed the deeds which have put me in possession of it. For I have done an ugly crime to gain those riches, and the hand of heaven is upon me. Yes, Oldcraft, in me you behold a murderer !"

Dreadnought Oldcraft, who wrote himself Esquire of Marstoke House, in the county of Warwickshire, and who had risen to that estate from the calling of a London attorney, "who told the clock for many years in Bridewell dock," was what might properly be called, in every sense, a cool hand, and on this occasion he showed to advantage the imperturbable nature of his disposition. He neither started with horror at the abrupt declaration of his visitor, nor did he summon his household to secure the delinquent after so unscrupulous a confession. Perhaps he had his reasons: be that as it may, certain it is that he merely smiled as he rose from his seat, and quietly walking to the door of the apartment they were sitting in, he threw it suddenly wide open, stepped a pace or two into the hall, glanced hastily to the right and to the left, and then returning to his seat, took up the little silver bell from the table, and rang it merrily for the servant.

Walter Neville had meanwhile also started to his feet, and stood, "with cat-like watch," observing the motions of his auditor, and with his right hand grasping the butt-end of one of the pistols at his girdle, seemed apparently in doubt as to the fidelity of his friend; but as Oldcraft returned into the room, his eagle eye caught the motion, and he signed to him to relinquish the grasp upon the weapon before the servant answered to the summons.

"I have business of importance," said Oldcraft to the servant, "with my friend here, who is fatigued with long travel; get fire and a bed prepared in the guest's apartment, let the supper be served without delay, and place all we require at once upon the table; after which, leave us to ourselves, see to the security of the house, and quit us for the night. When you have refreshed yourself, Walter Neville," he continued, so soon as the serving-man withdrew to hasten the evening meal, "we will continue this matter ; meanwhile, calm yourself and compose your spirits. It is ill-talking between a full man and a fasting, as the Scot hath it."

So saying, the host arose, and locking the door, removed at the same time the pistols of his guest to the table behind where he was sitting, and taking down a huge and elaborately-carved tobacco-pipe, the bowl of which was as big as a Scotchman's mull of the present day, he proceeded, with infinite care, to fill it with the weed of Sir Walter, which had just then come into fashion, and reseating himself in his high-backed chair, puffed out such large volumes of smoke, as he prepared himself to listen to the communication of his companion, that, although the voice reached him through the fumigation he kept up, the countenance of his guest was completely hidden in the cloud.

WALTER NEVILLE'S CONFESSION.

"I must needs begin my story," said Neville, "from the time I left this place, after we succeeded in gaining possession of this estate, buried Sir William Marstoke, gained the suits you wot of, and had taken up your residence here in Warwickshire. You took the estate, I had my share in ready money. I confess the partition was just, and I am content with what you have done for me."

"There's honour among thieves, then, according to the old proverb," said Old-craft. "Come, I'm glad you give me my share in that, as I gave you yours in rose nobles. Proceed, and come to your story. Let's have less matter ; eschew compliments ; I don't want 'em—I want facts."

"When I left thee, then—as you may easily suppose, after all that had happened--I was not likely to be a settler in London. I therefore sold what few things I possessed in the old house in Bridewell dock, where we had carried on business so long, doffed my suit of sables for more gallant accoutrements, and began to cast about in my mind where I should like to live and ruffle it—since I was in condition to do so—with the gentlefolks of the land. I had never forgotten Matthew Marstoke, Sir William's brother, to whose house you used to send me sometimes during the suit between him and Sherloke, and which suit we lost some ten years agone. The kindness and hospitality of Matthew Marstoke, and the pleasant style in which he lived during the short stay I used to make at his house in Kent, made an impression on me. I remembered, too, his easy disposition, and the frequent invitations he used to give me to return and visit him ; and, more than all, I remembered the riches he was possessed of, the tales he used to tell me of the moneys he had no use for, the chests of plate in his lumber room, and the bags of gold which had lain uncounted for years beneath his bed. In short, I resolved to visit Matthew Marstoke ; and setting out for Kent, arrived at Sandwich, and found he was absent from the house he used to dwell in, and living then at another place he possessed at Wingham."

"I know the house well," said Oldcraft ; "it has a row of poplar trees before it. I've visited him myself there : I remember also his dwelling in the town of Sandwich ; it's the great house in the market-place, stands at one end, a large red brick building. Diccon Grasp, our agent, was on one side, and Master Hogsflesh, the mayor, lived on the other."

"I took that house," resumed Neville, "for Marstoke had removed from it in consequence of its being haunted, and dreadful sounds were heard all night long. I took that house after staying with Marstoke for a fortnight, and became his tenant ; meanwhile, Marstoke, I must tell you, had grown quite demented, I may say almost silly. He had fallen into bad health, and was paralytic withal. He was delighted at my coming to see him, as he was ever at war with his domestics, who, he said, were eating him up alive, and killing him by inches ; so that I became (as you may suppose), in a short time, master of his whole establishment, and lived at free quarters, kept all his relatives at a distance, cudgelled some of his domestics, kicked others out of the place, and made quite a reformation in the household, till at last the old man was fain to consult me on the subject of destroying his old and making a new will. You may easily suppose I did not lend a deaf ear to the suggestion, more especially as I naturally expected he meant to make me his heir, after all the service I had rendered him. To my surprise and anger, however, I found, when we came to be closeted together, that he had a daughter living at Ghent, whom he had long discarded for marrying after her own inclinations, and against his ; and that having cut her off whilst his resentment lasted, and which had endured full thirty years, he was now relenting, and wishing for her return before he died ; so having entrusted to me the task of writing to tell her of his forgiveness, he also gave me full instructions to make a will in her favour, never so much as naming me for a legacy therein."

"Ho ! ho !" laughed Oldcraft ; "I should like to have seen thy hatchet-face at that moment. Your finger strayed towards the poniard at your girdle, I dare be sworn."

"Not a whit, man ; I vowed a deep revenge for being thus paltered with, and resolved upon a scheme which I quickly put in practice."

"What, you filched the bags from beneath the bed, I suppose ; advertised the hungry relatives of the old man's intentions, and turned them loose upon him again, eh ?—had him regularly torn to pieces by his own kith and kin."

"Not that, either," said Neville ; "and here begins the story of my present discomfort."

"Begins !" said his auditor. "Why, man, I thought this preamble of thine was beginning, middle, and end."

"You shall hear ; but give me more wine, for the story chokes me in the utterance. I laid the plot thus :—I invited Marstoke to spend the Christmas week with me at Sandwich. The town was just then all alive. The threatened invasion of the Spaniards made folks full of preparation. Sandwich, you know, is one of the Cinque Ports, and consequently a place of some importance. Meetings were daily called ; soldiers quartered upon the inhabitants ; merchants, noblemen, and gentry vying with each other in fitting out ships at their own charge, and troops were constantly passing and repassing along the coast. I attended these meetings, entered heart and hand into all the proceedings, offered my services to join the expedition, and appeared as forward as any there. Meanwhile, *one* only thought possessed me wholly, which was how to get Marstoke's riches into my possession, and dispose safely of the old man. Murder was upon my mind day and night, and until the deed was effected, I could get neither respite nor rest. Just Heaven ! little did I dream the state of mind this deed would reduce me to, when perpetrated. In short, the invasion, as you know, was deferred ; Christmas arrived, and Marstoke was my guest, in the old house at Sandwich. Amongst the soldiers, sailors, artizans, and men-at-arms who crowded the town, I sought out and hired two servants, fellows ' out of suits with fortune,' and whom I had good reason to know were fit for any work I chose to put them to, and worthy of trust if properly treated and rewarded. On Christmas-day, I feasted several of the inhabitants of the town, and we kept up the revel till day-break next morning. You will therefore easily perceive it was not a very extraordinary circumstance that old Marstoke should be taken suddenly unwell, and confined to his bed—nay, so sick was he, that I thought it but expedient he should make his will as he had before intended ——''

"Ah ! ha !'' said Oldcraft ; " what, you drugged his posset for him, eh ? and tampered with the roast-beef and plum-pudding ? put ratsbane in the sweet-sauce ? Ah ! you are a cunning fellow, Neville, but you have no head for these matters.''

"Not so,'' said Neville ; " I gave out Marstoke was seriously ill ; and on the third night after our Christmas feast, when all the town were wrapped in slumber, I turned the two fellows I have named into his room, with directions to strangle him in bed. Accursed be the hour in which I conceived the deed ! Never shall I forget the horrors of that night ; what with wind and rain, I thought the whole town would have been levelled with the earth before morning dawned. As I watched beside the old man's chamber-door, whilst the deed was being perpetrated, I heard his struggles as the villains strangled him in his bed. With morning's dawn (I had lain upon my bed where I had first thrown myself, like some terrified urchin in the darkness), I somewhat recovered my self-possession, and reflecting that the worst act in this hideous drama was over, proceeded towards the consummation of my plot. With some little difficulty I approached Marstoke's room ; it was long ere I could muster courage to open the door ; I feared to see the old man's ghastly corps upon the floor, where I had heard him fall, and stood with my hand on the lock, like one suffering in the agony of some hideous dream, unable alike to go forward or retreat. At length, after some hours of this irresolution, I was aroused to the necessity of exertion by the sound of the two scoundrels I had thus employed knocking at the outer gate for admittance, and the opening of the maid-servant's door in a remote part of the house, as she answered to their summons. Collecting all my energies, I entered the apartment, and rushing to the bell-rope, pulled it violently, calling at the same time to the maid, to desire one of the men-servants instantly to take horse, and hurry over to Wingham for Marstoke's lawyer, as he was so much worse that he desired to make his will. Meanwhile, before the scrivener came, I conveyed Diccon Webb, the other man, into the bed with the dead body, and drawing the curtains close round them (the room at the same time being darkened), I directed him to groan, like one in great pain, and counterfeiting at the same time the old man's voice, answer any questions the lawyer might put, so as to manage to leave the bulk of his property to me, stopping any inordinate curiosity and compunctious visitings of the scrivener by a heavy legacy in his favour. We managed matters so well, that all was effected without interruption or suspicion. Webb, counterfeiting old Marstoke's voice, and seeming hardly able to give directions as to how the will should be made, disposed of his estate in my favour ; after which, desiring to repose himself from the exertion, the company assembled were requested, by desire of the apparently dying man, to leave him to his repose. Soon after this, spreading the news of his death throughout the house, and calling the servants up, I showed them the corpse, as if just departed, in his bed. But the worst is yet to come. I succeeded to the estate ; but the remorse I suffered was so great, that I could not bear to live in the neighbourhood ; my two new houses I would have been thankful to any one to have fired and burnt to the very ground. I grew nervous and frightened at my own shadow. The countenance of old Marstoke, and his cry to me for assistance, haunted me day and night. The two scoundrels, Webb and Basset, too, began to grow upon me, and the constant sight of them was as basilisks to mine eyes. I feared to part with them, and to keep them was ruinous ; they spent what money they listed, robbed me to my face, and one of them, in his cups, affirmed amongst his companions, that it was in his power to hang his master any day in the week. Basset, the other fellow, informing me of this, I became so seriously troubled that I resolved to fly the place; and in order to prevent any danger of further babbling, managed matters with Basset so as to have Webb closely made away with. To effect this, I settled with them both to precede me to London; and sending them on the night before I intended myself to set out, gave directions to Basset to deal with Webb on the road. Basset followed his orders, but did the deed somewhat earlier than I intended: he stabbed his comrade through the back, as they rode side by side along the Sandwich flats, and, dismounting, threw his body into the haven. The waters washing it up to Sandwich early next morning with the tide, to my horror and confusion, it was brought to my house just as I was about to set forward on my journey; so that I found myself obliged to attend the mayor during the inquiry about the rascal's death, and even agree with the magistrates as to the propriety of sending out a party to overtake and capture Basset for the suspected murder. This new mishap almost unsettled my wits, and the officers having luckily failed in capturing Basset, I hurried from the town two days afterwards; the whole country being just then engaged in preparations for the armada, I joined the forces assembled at Tilbury Fort under command of the Earl of Leicester. Could I have safely joined the Spaniards, I would have done so. As it was, I sought in the bustle of the camp, and the pomp and circumstance of war, to forget the horrible transactions I had been engaged in; but it would not be. That which filled the minds of all around with enthusiasm, was by me uncared for. The glorious sight of a queen heading her armies in the field, and riding through the lines to exhort the soldiery to remember their duty to their country, avowing her intention herself to lead us against the enemy, and perish rather than survive the ruin and slavery of her people, was lost upon a wretch whose nights and days were passed in agonizing remorse. The very din of the engagement, and the turmoil and bustle accompanying the destruction of the armada—the shrieks of the dying, the shouts of the victors, the thunder of the cannon—was all, I found, as nothing. I walked the deck of my own ship, and even boarded the enemies' craft, with the ghastly countenance of old Marstoke continually before me wherever I turned; so that I resolved, more than once, to surrender myself on the return of the fleet, and, confessing all the villany of my life, end my sinful career upon the gallows."

"How, then, stands the matter with you at the present moment?" said Oldcraft, now fully interested in his companion's tale. "Speak, man, quickly. You said, even now, the business was blown. What leads you to think so?"

"The news," answered Neville, "which reached me yesterday, before I left London (where I had been keeping close), of Basset's having been arrested at Faversham, and committed to jail on suspicion of Webb's murder. I fled on the instant, and behold I am here in my extremity."

The guilty man, covering his face with his hands, sobbed aloud as he finished his story, and in his agony and remorse called upon his more cool and apparently even more hardened companion for counsel and advice.

"Give me comfort, Oldcraft," he said, "for I feel the hand of Heaven is so heavy upon me, that I cannot live under the burden of my crimes. Death seems hovering at my heart, and yet I cannot die. Nay, there is the smell of death even in this apartment where we sit; methinks it is my grave."

"Prophetic are thy words," said Oldcraft, suddenly bringing round his right arm, and firing one of Neville's own pistols into his breast, shattering his lungs to pieces with the closeness of the discharge. "Prophetic are thy words, fool! for 'tis thy grave."

The wretched victim, uttering a cry of agony as the life-blood flowed out in one gushing tide, fell with his face upon the earth a ghastly corpse, as his executioner, starting to his feet, dashed his pipe to the further end of the apartment.

"'Twas time, indeed, to look to this gear," said he, as he pounced upon the quivering body, and turning it on its back, proceeded to ransack the pockets of the doublet in search of his papers, which he hurriedly thrust into the fire without examining. "'Twas time, indeed, to stop this driveller's mouth, or, by the Lord, I should have been involved in his cursed confessions up to the ears. Former transactions, as well as more recent pastimes, would have doubtless come out before he had made an end of his shrift. What, ho, there! Help! murder! help, ho! Here, Stephen, Robin, James, help here!" he continued, calling aloud, and at the same time drawing Neville's sword from the scabbard, and throwing it beside the body, after which he stepped to the door, and threw it wide open. "Help, here! Arise, I say; I am assailed in my own house! Behold," he cried, as the terrified servants, awakened by the report of the pistol and his cries, hurried half-naked from their beds, "this caitiff, not content with trying to extort money from me on this blessed night, suddenly attacked me, sword in hand, and would have murdered me, had I not luckily possessed myself of one of his pistols, and shot him dead."

A deep and awful silence, only interrupted by the occasional rattle of the snow-storm upon the casements, and the fitful gusts of the winter's wind, reigned in Marstoke House for the remainder of that night. The serving-men and maids, who had been summoned from their beds by Master Oldcraft's cries and the report of the pistol, were huddled together in the kitchen of the building, where, over the fire they had coaxed back into life, they discussed in fearful whispers the suspicions and surmises to which the strange transaction gave rise. In those days of rapier and dagger, the matter of a man slain in a country mansion was not of such rare occurrence as to cause any very great confusion or dismay; yet still, a death so oddly come by as this man's, having been shot through the lungs in the dead of the night, and on the very hearth, too, where he had so short a time before been seen draining the cup of kindness with his host, did not altogether pass current without its comment.

Meanwhile, the principal actor in this hideous drama paced up and down the ample chamber to which he had retired, after having given orders that the body of his victim should be left exactly as it had been discovered by the servants on his summoning them to his assistance.

"My star," he said, as he communed with himself upon the deed he had just perpetrated, "my star is yet in the ascendant; my good angel, or evil, if you will —for I care not though the very devil himself dispatched this miserable driveller hitherward—has this night put it in my power, by one bold stroke, to rid myself of the distrust and anxiety I have so long felt on his account; and, by putting a seal upon his lips for ever, for ever rid me also of my fears."

This self-congratulation of Master Oldcraft's was suddenly interrupted by the clatter of horse's feet, passing rapidly beneath his chamber-window. He paused in his soliloquy, and instantly extinguished the lamp which was burning upon the table beside his bed, and stepping to the window, cautiously drew back one of the sliding shutters, and gently opening the casement, looked forth. The day was just breaking, and he beheld a small party of some half-dozen horsemen turn the angle of the building as they rode into the fore-court. He was only just in time to catch a glimpse of their shining hauberts, as they disappeared round one of the flanking towers of the old mansion, on their way to the principal entrance.

Marstoke House had formerly (in the early part of Henry the Eighth's reign) been a religious establishment, and occupied by a fraternity of Carmelites. It was, at the present time, only partially inhabited. Its master, Oldcraft, and his small establishment, occupied but a part of one wing; and being much discountenanced and disliked in the neighbourhood, the place had a deserted and melancholy appearance at the best of times. On that side of the building which was occupied, at the bottom of the garden, stood a large water-mill, which had, in other times, pertained to the monastery; it was at present in the tenancy of one Jenden, a miller, who carried on business there. In the park, or meadow-land beyond this mill, were numerous fish-ponds, beautifully shadowed with overhanging branches, and intersected by innumerable narrow divisions or walks, made for the purpose of netting or draining these stews.

A something struck upon the heart of the guilty man as the horsemen drew up, and commenced a clamorous summons for admittance, that the arrival of the party had reference to Walter Neville's late misdeeds, and that he himself was not altogether uninvolved. Darting to the door of his chamber, he called to his servants not to draw bolt nor bar until he had ascertained the object of these visitors. The order, however, came too late, as the door had been readily opened, on the leader of the party demanding entry in the Queen's name, having a warrant for the apprehension of one Nichol Oldcraft, for the murder of Sir William Marstoke, of Marstoke Hall.

Master Oldcraft, hearing these awful words, stayed no farther parley, but fled with precipitation from the hall which he was about entering, and retraced his steps to his chamber. After securing the door, he hastily drew back a sliding panel, which admitted him to a small staircase leading to the garden of the hall, whence he intended to go and conceal himself in the adjoining mill. The hunt, however, was fairly up; and he found, on emerging from the passage to the garden, that the mill was in possession of several of the party who had gained admission to the hall. Still, the mill was his only chance; and creeping along a hedge-skirted walk beside the stream, he endeavoured to gain it.

The miller, who stood near the mill-door, was listening, with open mouth, to the recital of one of the men-at-arms from Warwick; and Oldcraft, seeing no other chance, quickly stepped across the wood-work, and, as the mill was not at work, concealed himself in the wheel.

" Strange news, indeed," quoth the burly miller, as he moved across the platform; " strange times, these we live in. Well, I did always say these Oldcrafts wor no good; I never liked the man in my life, and for the 'oman I ses nothing. It's no business o' mine—so I'll e'en go arter what is."

And saying this, the miller stepped up and turned the water on his mill. The next moment a piercing shriek rung out amid the rush of waters from beneath where he stood. The miller hastened back in alarm, turned off the water, and stopped the wheel. It was too late: the body of the wretched Oldcraft, severed in twain, floated out with the rushing tide."

———

" Pshaw!" exclaimed the reader, as, finishing the tale, he cast the volume on the table; " there's no analogy in the case—no parallel—no consistency. I shall never imbrue *my* hands in the blood of——" he paused. " No, no; those times of violence are gone by; fraud and finesse are more powerful now-a-days than force ——"

A gentle tap at the library door broke off the thread of the soliloquizer; the portal opened, and—wonder upon wonders—in slid, rather than walked, Walter's old aversion—Mr. Ferdinand Lynx.

The old gentleman started, but quickly composed himself; and the man of law, being motioned to a chair opposite, sat down.

" There is no intelligence obtainable," said he, slowly, "none whatever. No trace of that troublesome boy."

Walter listened eagerly. Why should the gentleman—nobleman, he thought, at least—feel interested in his welfare or discovery? It must be his uncle!—yes, the much heard of, but little seen patron of Mr. Lynx—into whose mansion he had thus unexpectedly and unwittingly intruded.

A pause of some seconds followed ere Sir Ebenezer Fitzroy—for he it was—broke silence.

" I cannot help thinking, Mr. Lynx," observed he, " that you attach undue importance to the absence of this boy. Eugenia is provided for, and in a few months, under another name, will be married to one of the under-keepers at the lodge at Richmond. He believes, as well as herself, that she is the natural daughter of my brother, and is not likely to talk much, for the sake of his wife's reputation—with whom, by the bye, I think the young fellow is hot in love—about her origin. On that point, too, she has been well impressed by Mrs. Crofton; and, from what I hear, has a proper sense of the humiliating effect of any general disclosure of her illegitimate origin. As to the boy, he will turn up, depend on't, in some low capacity of life, whence it will be easy to promote him, and send him to one of the colonies, or, perhaps, contrive his emigration to some remote district in New South Wales, or elsewhere. It is late, however, Mr. Lynx; and, if you have nothing more to communicate, as I do not feel altogether well, I think I shall retire, after writing a short letter to my lady, which must be forwarded by special messenger at early morn."

At this juncture, the jingling clock told out four quarters and the twelfth hour; Sir Ebenezer arose, and, touching a spring, prevented the interruption which would have followed from its musical performance. Mr. Lynx sat but a few moments ere a low and almost whispered converse was entered upon, opened by Sir Ebenezer, which so absorbed both parties, that they seemed forgetful of the lapse of time, and the letter spoken of by Sir Ebenezer, was in like manner cast into oblivion. Walter heard large sums of money spoken of; mortgages, loans, exchanges, contracts, debentures, title-deeds, interest, discounts, post-obits, the price of stocks, and a score of things, of which he could only comprehend the general relation they bore to money.

While they thus talked, the hidden accomplice of the burglars was on the rack ; he feared, and with good reason apparently, that the old gentleman would never leave the apartment, and in that case, how should he effect the object of his entrance—namely, opening the hall-door to the ingress of Jerry and his con·federates. His position grew more critical every minute; and his quickened hearing very shortly made it clear that some forcible means were being adopted, at the rear of the house, to obtain an entrance by the very window through which he had, five hours before, so easily slid, but which, ere the servants retired to bed, had been closed and fastened.

"Click ! click ! click !" the sounds of forcing the catch, came to Walter's ear with painful distinctness, as if almost immediately beneath the spot where he lay concealed. He thought it impossible that the baronet and his adviser, who still sat in close converse, could be much longer deaf to these unusual noises. But, no ; absorbed in their muttering converse, and the occasional inspection of written papers, they heard nothing. At length, the "cr-cr-cr-st" of a small spring-saw on the bolt of the back-passage-door was distinctly audible. Once Mr. Lynx said, as he turned his ear to the direction of the noise : "What's that ? Did you not hear it, Sir Ebenezer !"

All was silent for a few seconds, and Sir Ebenezer replied that "It must be the wind ; it often shakes the door of the little bath-room—I must remember to have that remedied to-morrow."

The next sound was the dull, dead crush of forcing the lower door with a "jemmy." Young Walter, inwardly cursing their precipitancy and impatience, gave himself up for lost.

We will now turn from the library of Sir Ebenezer, to see what had been going on outside during this long suspense. Handsome Bill, who had been twice or thrice round to the front of the mansion, in company with the Yorkshireman, had as often returned, after observing that all was still, and that the last glimmering candle, in the attic story, had been long extinguished. On the third occasion, he declared his conviction that one of two things must have occurred ; either that, worn out by watching, the youth had fallen fast asleep, or that his heart had failed him. To the latter supposition, Jerry stoutly demurred ; he at once declared Walter to be a trump, an out-an'-outer for pluck ; and that the first being the true state of the case, or, as he expressed it, "the exact size of the thing," a remedy must be sought by a forced entry.

"If they find the kinchin asleep in the libery," argued the villain, "we'll be done, so sure as the sun rises—for he's there, and no mistake ; let's crack the crib then ; there ain't no watch, excepting one crawling pauper, as they've turned out o' the parish work'us to save his keep, for a quarter of a mile round the place, I knows that ;* and he's so blessed deaf, that if you ax him the name of a street, he tells you its 'arter twelve.' Now, Mat. here says as there's ony one male in the consarn besides the baronet—and he's an ould un. What stops us then ?"

Houseman agreed to the reasoning, and in ten minutes more the burglarious trio were at the work which young Walter alone, of all the inmates of the mansion, had heard, or, if hearing, understood. The concealed boy counted their stealthy footsteps as they ascended the lower stairs ; still Sir Ebenezer and Lawyer Lynx rustled their papers and muttered on. They passed the door, and acting under the advice of the discharged servant, whose fidelity they insured by bringing him with them, mounted to the drawing-room floor, where, as he truly told them, a gorgeous service of massive plate stood exposed on the extensive sideboard. Jerry alone remained on the first landing, near the door of the apartment wherein Sir Ebenezer and Lynx were in earnest converse ; he listened at the portal while the other two went up, and judge of his surprise and momentary dismay, when he distinctly heard, by applying his ear to the keyhole, the low converse of two

* It is a fact that the nightly watch, not only westward, but in the very heart of the City, was thus made up, or "manned," as it was called, even within twenty-five years of this present time. In Ludgate-street, a "chargeable pauper," a worn-out old hobbler of seventy-five years of age, did "duty" till the week of his death, at the door of a house where the author's father dwelt, and slept nightly on a raised flap or ledge, in the recessed doorway, provided with abundance of straw, wherein to nestle his septuagenarian feet, by the occupier of the house ; the ward authorities, to enforce vigilance (! !), having deprived old men, who watched (!) eight or ten hours, of the shelter of a box.

male voices. To give a warning to the pair now busy above would be madness. "Can the young villain have played us false?" muttered he, grasping the handle of a long knife, which he carried in a breast pocket of his coat He next saw, by the faint light discernible through the same aperture, that the parties had not retired to rest; the thick carpet against which it closed, and its list-bound edge, excluded all other light, and its position prevented the parties inside from being at all within his range of vision. Internally cursing their ill-luck, he again listened. His comrades up-stairs were by no means cautious; and once or twice the chinking rattle of the heavy silver articles they were depositing in the sack they had brought with them, rung audibly on the echoing staircase. The sound of a descending footstep from the upper story met his ear, and at the same instant a voice withinside the apartment he was guarding, exclaimed: "Surely there is some one moving overhead !"

Jerry rapidly ascended the stair.

"Hist! hist! the house is alarmed," whispered he, hoarsely.

As Bill turned towards him, a glass door, which communicated by a back-stair with the conservatory at the farther end of the drawing-room, opened, and a servant, with an old-fashioned blunderbuss, appeared. Handsome Bill, who was dressed as a sword-wearing gentleman, espied the unwelcome intruder; he drew his rapier; the man's blunderbuss, as on all such critical occasions, missed fire, the harmless flint drew sparks from the hammer, and Houseman stepping quickly towards the menial with bared weapon, the latter fell on his knees, and begged for mercy.   Bill, who was not naturally ferocious, bade him lay down his weapon; the man obeyed.

"Spit him," muttered Jerry, advancing.   The fellow once more implored his life, and Houseman interposed.

"Be quiet, or you're a dead man," said Bill.

The footman needed no second bidding, he knelt already half-dead with fear.

A voice now rose from below: "Run, good Mr. Lynx, run for assistance, alarm the neighbourhood, there are robbers in the house!"

Mr. Lynx darted at the glass-door of the hall; it was fastened, and he could not unlock it.

"Stay here till I call," said Jerry, hastily; "I'll secure your retreat," and he rapidly went below.

There was a moment's silence, and then the voice of Walter Lazenby was heard.   He had crept from his hiding-place, and was crossing the library towards the door, when his exit was barred by Sir Walter, who, seizing the poker from the fireplace, had interposed himself.   The youth held in his hand a small brass-barrelled pistol, and thus, mutually armed, the relatives confronted each other.

"I shall fire, uncle, and your blood will be on your own head," said the youth, firmly.

The baronet gazed a moment on the speaker's face; the next, the weapon dropped from his powerless hand, and he staggered towards a chair, the back of which he grasped convulsively.

"My God!" he involuntarily ejaculated, as the likeness of his wronged brother glared upon him, in the face of his defrauded son, "my nephew Walter! —even as that other Walter looked, when in boyish quarrel we stood opposed forty years ago!"

"Yes, uncle, your brother's son; and he will force his way from this house, even though his path lies over *your* corpse!"

"Brayvo, my young trump," cried Jerry, as he entered.   "Come, old Bladder-pate, no snivelling—there's no help nigh, so tell us quickly where you stow your mopusses, or I'll make this bit o' steel and your ribs close acquaintance."

The ruffian looked fully capable of executing his threat, and the half-fainting baronet replied only by a groan.

The trembling lawyer, whom the darkness of the passage had caused Jerry to pass unobserved, beside himself with fear, despairingly turned the handle of the glass-door to effect an escape.   Abershaw caught the sound, and darted into the passage, dragging the unresisting coward back into the room.

"Lawyer Lynx," said Walter, pointing scornfully at him; "my uncle's accomplice in his villany."

"So, so," chuckled Jerry, looking contemptuously at the terror-stricken object; "then we're masters here, and no mistake—the cove up-stairs is disarmed, and these two we can manage nicely," and a horrid thought of a triple murder darted athwart the ruffian's visage, as he scowled around.   "Your money, old Hunks; don't let me ask twice."

"You shall have money—ay, more than you expect; but, Walter, Walter," faltered the baronet, "how happens this?—how——"

"Ask the boy no questions, you old villain, and he'll tell you no lies," interrupted Jerry.   "Keep an eye on him, my lad, one moment, I'll not leave you above a yard or two."

Jerry returned to the stairfoot, and gently called his comrade Bill.   He came down, and stood truly astonished when he beheld the scene.   Sir Ebenezer Fitzroy had sunk, pale and nervous, on a *fauteuil;* Walter, with cocked pistol in hand, stood a short three yards from him; Lynx, equally pale, knelt on the soft carpet.

"I told you he was a trump," said Jerry; "but that's neither here nor there.

This old buffer's his uncle, and he promises lots o' tin—ready down, and no trust," chuckled the ruffian, significantly pointing to his long knife; " so here we are to settle this business, and no questions asked. Now the blunt, old boy— and *then*——"

The rest of the sentence he whispered in the ear of Handsome Bill, who started, but the next moment smiled. The wretch, in that short sentence, proposed the assassination of his victims, and the burning of the house.

" You shall have all you ask," faltered the baronet; "but this boy must not leave the——"

" Ha! ha! good !" sneered Jerry; " but as we've got the upper just now, we'll make the conditions, and no mistake. Come, no loss of time, or we'll cut the throats of every mother's son of ye, and ransack the crib arterwards. Come, bustle, quick !" and the desperado, stepping towards Sir Ebenezer, brought his sharp weapon close to his throat. A slight cry escaped him, echoed by a groan from Mr. Lynx, who looked imploringly at the baronet.

" You shall have money ; nay, more, you shall never be pursued, if you will spare our lives."

" Come, that's reasonable," said Bill.

" Here are my keys," said Sir Ebenezer ; " in yonder *escritoire* you will find five hundred guineas."

Jerry's eyes gleamed; he clutched the small bunch, and hastily unlocking it, placed ten ponderous rouleaus in his capacious coat-pocket.

" Good. Have you any more of these ?"

" None, but some loose money," was the reply.

" Well, give us that to pay expenses," laughed Jerry. " And you, Mister Doleful," turning to Mr. Lynx, " just obleege us with your small change."

The lawyer promptly emptied his pockets on the floor.

" Well, Bill," said Abershaw, in a low voice, drawing his companion aside, "shall we —— or make conditions ?"

" The murder will excite pursuit," urged Bill ; " let's hold the boy over him, as a security for his silence. We know enough *now* to have him safe."

Jerry nodded assent.

" Walter," said Jerry, " I'm your protector; that old hunks and this cheating old cur shall eat humble pie. And if you ever dare," and Abershaw turned menacingly toward the baronet, " to *pipe* this concern—ay, to try even to trace us—if you dare to set the traps on our trail, mark *my* words, I'll stick *this* into your heart, if you'd the judge sitting aside of you—so beware ! There are more, too, of my mind, so breathe but a syllable of this, and I'll show you a short cut to t'other world, without a chaplain to take your confession. Besides, I've here" (and he pointed to Walter) " good bail that you daren't. Now, lads, let's be off— we give you two hours ; if, before that time, a living soul quits this house, there shall be those waiting at the door-steps who shall stop their crying out without a gag—do you understand ?"

" You shall neither be pursued nor molested, if you leave this place without in- flicting further injury."

" For the sake of this boy," said Jerry.

" And to secure *our* secresy, mind you keep your own," replied Houseman.

Mat was now called down, and in ten minutes the desperadoes, after quaffing a bottle of rich wine, which stood on the library table, left the house, by the very way they had entered it. Jerry once or twice halting and proposing a re- turn, to make, as he called it, " all safe," by taking the lives of the whole three. In this, however, the sanguinary wretch was overruled by the united opposition of Houseman, Walter, and the Yorkshireman.

Next day, the back premises of Sir Ebenezer underwent various alterations and securings, and the servant, who knew nought but the burglary, having been duly imposed on by a fabrication of Lawyer Lynx's, the precautions were attributed to an "attempt at burglary, which had the night before been made at the mansion of Sir Ebenezer Fitzroy, by three armed ruffians, whose discovery, before they had time to effect their nefarious object, was frustrated by the promptitude and courage of the baronet himself, who, assisted by a legal gentleman of the name of Lynx, at that time staying in the house, put the villains to flight, although they had already packed up various valuable articles of costly material and rare *vertu*, for the purpose of carrying them off." Such was the paragraph in the *Daily*

Advertizer, and after a few days' gossip, and some profitable jobs for blacksmiths, whitesmiths, bell-hangers, and inventors of patent alarums, no more was said about the burglary at Sir Ebenezer Fitzroy's.

CHAPTER LI.

EUGENIA LAZENBY—A MARRIAGE POSTPONED BY A DEATH—BROTHER AND SISTER —AN AWKWARD HITCH IN MR. LYNX'S CONTRIVANCES.

WHILE engaged with the more important personages who figure in the foreground of our history, we have too long overlooked the fairest flower in the rank growth of social weeds, which illustrate the gardener's ancient proverb, that—

> " Slow groweth herb of grace,
> But ill weeds thrive apace."

Eugenia Lazenby and her fortunes, ruled, so far as wicked men could control them, by the sinister influence of her uncle and his scheming coadjutor, seemed likely to find a haven of repose—and a happy one—in the bosom of humble life. Her marriage-day, with an honest, active, plain-spoken young fellow, was already fixed, and though, in a worldly point of view, it might be unsuitable to the heiress of vast property, the union offered, at least, the chance of cottage contentment, and a peace of mind, rarely dwelling in the gilded saloons and painted halls of the high and mighty of the earth. But events were in progress, which acted upon higher personages in the drama of life wherein her lot was cast.

We have already noticed the illness of Lady Fitzroy, the wife of the hitherto prosperous, though by no means happy, Sir Ebenezer. A tedious confinement, followed by a gradual sinking, and the occasional accession of puerperal fever, laid the scheming lady, the last lineal descendant of the ancient house of Fitzroy, in the family vault, there " to lie in cold obstruction, and to rot " with the air-built plans of her needy parent and grasping self. The household was thus thrown into sudden mourning, and, as a matter of course, the wedding, contrived by Sir Ebenezer and the crafty Lynx, was postponed in compliance with public decency.

Eugenia, now a lovely girl of sixteen, had as yet had but few interviews with her intended, who must have been cold and frigid indeed, had he failed to be struck with admiration of charms of so rare an order as those of his patron's adopted child.

The bridegroom elect was a young fellow of respectable origin, being the son of a reputable farmer, who, falling into pecuniary difficulties, and dying at the age of thirty, had left a young widow and six orphan children, scantily provided for. The former owner of Lazenby Park, now changed in name to Fitzroy Lodge, had respected the father, and at an early age, after giving the youth a plain education, had placed him as a sort of bailiff on the estate. Steady in his habits, and winning in his address, he had retained his situation, and was now ranger of the park and grounds, and under-steward to Sir Ebenezer, or rather to Mr. Lynx, who managed the rents and profits of the estates of his patron in Lancashire, Middlesex, and the West Indies.

During the interval here noted, Eugenia Lazenby, her mistress lying dead, remained in the house at Richmond, where she busied herself with her needle, in the mourning preparations of the melancholy mansion. The spring-tide came, with its birds and flowers, and she wandered forth one evening on a visit to the little park lodge, tenanted by her affianced and his mother—for the period of their union was now only delayed till the pompous obsequies of the heartless woman of fashion should be completed, and the formal period of full mourning of the household dependents have expired. As the dark-eyed girl, graceful as a fawn, tripped along the narrow path, shaded by lofty chesnut-trees, whose budding spikes proclaimed the advent of youthful summer, she pensively thought of her absent brother Walter, whom she so dearly loved, and who she had been told by Mr. Lynx was now at sea in one of his majesty's ships, and would doubtless return in a short period with promotion and honour. This the simple-minded, unsophisticated damsel doubted not in the least. Her heart had been hitherto unoccupied save by a sisterly love, and as she had seen no specimen of mankind, to know intimately, except her betrothed, is it surprising that, like Shakspeare's Miranda, she could truly say—

My affections
Are indeed most humble : I have no ambition
To see a goodlier man ?

Thus, then, attired in a close-fitting black dress, trimmed, as was then the fashion, with a few jet bugles, the fresh-cheeked damsel wended her way, and was already within a short distance of the ivy-covered cottage when she perceived two men approaching her; the one was a middle-aged man, of heavy step and rusty apparel; his more youthful companion gaily attired in a vulgar style of dress, consisting of a shooting-jacket of black and light blue plaid, with innumerable pockets and broad shell-buttons, a pair of light-coloured trousers of fancy cord, his head covered with a jaunty cap, and wearing round his neck what seemed at a distance a twisted coil of silken handkerchiefs of the brightest and most staring colours. Stepping aside under the umbrageous timber, she hastily sought to avoid the meeting, never for a moment supposing that their business could be with her. The younger man, however, anticipated her intent. Running across in the very direction she had taken, he hurriedly approached her, and ere she had time to utter more than a short cry of recognition, she was folded in the embrace of her brother, Walter Lazenby! A few sounds of mutual caresses, and Eugenia's neck and forehead crimsoned as she became aware that the elderly stranger stood within a yard or two, staring at her with his fishy lack-lustre grey eyes, with a look of undefinable cunning and satisfaction. Walter caught the direction of her eyes. " A friend, *my* friend, dearest Eugenia; the person to whom I owe this happy meeting. But what means this black dress, is Sir Ebenezer, our uncle——"

" No, no, dearest brother; but his wife, Lady Fitzroy is dead."

" You must leave this place, with me too, dear Eugenia, before your absence can be discovered. Our perfidious uncle has robbed us; he is rich and powerful, and ——"

" Nay," said the ingenuous girl," he has been kind to me, very kind, and has he not been so to you, Walter ? I was told that you had gone abroad as a midshipman in a ship of war; how then comes it, I meet you thus ?"

Walter's countenance grew dark, a scowl gathered on his brow, but he suppressed his rising emotion.

" There is not time now," replied he, " to tell you many things which it is fitting you should know. Suffice it, that our uncle is a villain and a robber."

Eugenia started, and for a moment thought her brother was demented, so fierce and harsh was his voice.

" Yes, Eugenia, a villain; the despoiler of our birthright, and the seeker of our ruin. Oh, what sights and deeds have I witnessed, and taken part in, since I saw you last! But if he is a villian, there is one of yet blacker dye, that incarnate fiend Lynx, with his hypocritical pretensions to interest in our welfare. Eugenia, we have indeed a hard task to perform; but, with the aid of this friend," and he pointed to Mr. Crocodile Fuddlebrain, to whom Eugenia felt an instinctive aversion, " and others, whom you shall hereafter see, we will unmask the scoundrels, expose their schemes, and vindicate the fair fame of our slandered mother !"

The single girl's large, black eyes dilated with amazement, and she trembled with fear she could not control.

" Have you not been to sea then, dear Walter ?"

The youth smiled, and bitterly added—

" Yes--no—I have been to *see* strange things—but ask me no more questions now, this is not time or place. Fly, beyond the pursuit of——"

" But, Walter, dearest Walter," interposed Eugenia, " will you not accompany me first, a few yards, to yonder cottage; there is one there who will be indeed rejoiced to see the brother of his betrothed wife; often and often have I spoken of you, and as often has he wished that before the period of our union, you should return to make one in the joyous party, and——"

Walter replied not, his brow grew so severe that his sister faltered and paused.

" *This* too," said he hoarsely to his companion; " this is the contrivance of our persecutor."

The thieves' lawyer, for the first time, broke silence—

" Not a doubt in the world of it," replied he; " a branch of the plot—a part of the scheme—I see it—yes, quite clear—this young lady here must be advised by those that are older in the ways of the world. Yes, I see—marry her, and shelf her anyhow—that's the plan—very good—but we'll baffle 'em yet. If I may be allowed to suggest, madam," continued Fuddlebrain, moving his hat slightly in a deferential manner; " no time must be lost, in leaving this neighbourhood. There will be much to do, in getting papers and documents, and witnesses, for Sir Ebenezer is powerful—as my young friend here very rightly says; and in getting up a case, every possible precaution must be taken, moreover ——"

" Dearest brother, let us speak alone," said Eugenia, hastily; " I have that for your private ear, which may remove this misunderstanding. I am perplexed and giddy; I scarcely know what to say—Oh, how little did I foresee, that our first meeting would be like this!" and, the girl embracing her brother tenderly, sunk her head on his arm, and burst into a flood of tears.

" Nay," said Mr. Fuddlebrain; " if you please, I will retire; but, pray come a little farther to the left; you are in sight of the windows of the mansion, and I perceive two men standing at one of them—there, on the drawing-room floor."

Walter looked towards the house; at the window stood two figures, evidently observing them; and, although too far off to be distinguished accurately, he had no doubt they were Sir Ebenezer, and his factotum, Lynx. " They see us, Crocky," said he; " let's be off. Come, Eugenia ——"

" Nay," said the maiden, appealingly; " I cannot go, Walter, without one farewell of ——" her voice faltered.

" Your safety—mine—that of all concerned, depends upon your instant decision."

" One instant, dearest Walter, and I will go with you; but, why am I thus to fly from *him*, even if my uncle and Mr. Lynx be all that you say. I surely can meet you at some other place—appoint it, and I give you my word, my heart will bring me thither."

" See, see," said Fuddlebrain, withdrawing himself from the line of view, his ruby nose becoming a pale blue with fear, " they have left the window, and here are several men coming from the front door. Quick, quick," and the old poltroon set the first example, by hastening off through the trees, towards the park gate, by which they had entered.

" Hasten with me, Eugenia," emphatically exclaimed Walter, impatiently, " or, my life and yours may be sacrificed, sooner or later, to their fiendish schemes!"

" It is too late," replied the girl, pointing in the direction by which old Fuddlebrain had shuffled off; " there is ——"

A young man, respectably attired, and carrying a gun in his hand, was hastening towards them; he was soon up, and gazing fiercely at Walter, who returned his look of defiance, was evidently about to resort to the summary process of the blow first, and the word afterwards.

" It is Walter—this is my brother, dear John!"

The young man's brow relaxed, a smile instantly replaced the frown, and, extending his palm frankly, he heartily shook the hand of young Lazenby, ere he had time to withdraw it.

Walter looked angry and embarrassed.

" Eugenia," said he, reproachfully, " you have delivered me into the hands of our destroyer."

The young man doubted the sanity of the speech; but the next moment, his wonder, and that of Eugenia, were at the climax; for four stout fellows, followed by Mr. Lynx and Sir Ebenezer, who brought up the rear, joined the party.

" Seize him, bind him!" cried Mr. Lynx, and Sir Ebenezer, in a breath.

" It is my bro——" The girl's speech was cut short by one of the menials, who, at a sign from Sir Ebenezer, caught the maiden by the arm, and forcibly dragged her aside. Her intended quickly resented this profanation of her person, for, in a twinkling he struck the fellow so hard a blow on the arm, that he lost his grasp, and the liberated Eugenia once more rushed to her brother's arms, where she fainted.

Walter drew a pistol from his breast pocket, and pointing it with a sweeping motion towards the bystanders, Lynx included, cried out, " Stand back ! every man of you; this is my sister, and by —— the first who stirs to take her from me, will rue the day !"

A short pause ensued.

" Unhand the maiden," urged Mr. Lynx, in a tone of remonstance " and you shall depart unharmed—you know your fate, if Sir Ebenezer were not merciful enough ——"

" Silence, you croaking wretch !" vociferated Walter, " or this bullet shall spare Jack Ketch a job, by ridding the earth of you."

Lynx shrunk back, but young John Cooper, now fully confirmed in his suspicion, that the newly-found brother of his intended, was of unsound mind, took advantage of his closeness to Walter. Seizing him from behind by both elbows, with a herculean grip, he, with as little violence as he could help, bent down the enraged stripling, by placing his knee in his back. The foaming Walter cursed fiercely in the brief struggle, and the pistol he held was exploded in the air, as he strove vainly to point it over his shoulder backward at his friendly assailant. He was quickly on the ground, and as quickly secured by cords.

" Is he mad, think you ?" enquired Mr. Lynx, in a tone of sympathetic inquiry, approaching as soon as he found that the victim was well secured. " Poor fellow," added he, turning to Sir Ebenezer, and wiping away an imaginary tear from the corner of his eye ; " I always feared, Sir Ebenezer, that it would come to this ; his mother was afflicted similarly, and——"

A blood-curdling curse broke from the pinioned Walter, and he gnashed his teeth and bit his tongue till the blood came, for further articulation was denied him. Eugenia slowly recovered from her swoon, and gazed wildly on her betrothed, who supported her beloved form on his arm.

" Where is he ?" ejaculated she. " Oh, dear John, rescue my brother Walter !"

Mr. Lynx gave a pantomimic shake of the head, and applied his forefinger to his brow to intimate to the young fellow, who was more and more bewildered by everything he heard and saw, that Walter was deranged, then, pointing towards the house, indicated that John Crofts should lead Eugenia thither. Thoroughly alarmed, however, she resolutely refused to go, and appealed to Sir Ebenezer and Lynx to release her brother.

" I have forgiven the boy's violence too often," said Sir Ebenezer, aside, in a kind tone. " He is already associated, as I have reason to know, with the basest and most desperate of society."

John Crofts, whose respect for Sir Ebenezer was great, felt both pained and astonished; and poor Eugenia, her hand on her heart, listened in terrified eagerness to every syllable, which struck to her soul.

" Yes," said Sir Ebenezer mildly, " 'tis a dreadful tale, but he has himself forced its disclosure, at a time, too, when my heart lies bleeding on my wife's bier." Sir Ebenezer, like Mr. Lynx, resorted to his kerchief. " Since that unruly boy ran away from the protecting care of Mr. Lynx, I have sought in vain, as to-day's occurrences prove, to conceal from you his desperate career of crime, by an innocent fiction of his absence at sea. Heaven forgive me for the falsehood ; it was done to spare you, my Eugenia, the painful truth. Yes, and Mr Lynx here is my witness, that youth, young in years, but an adept in crime, confederated with a gang of lawless desperadoes, midnight assassins, and housebreakers, forced his way into my town mansion, despoiled it of much property, and, but for the fear of detection, would have murdered me; yet I let him escape unharmed, for the love I bore to my brother, his father and yours, in blood, though not in the eye of human or of heavenly laws."

Mr. Lynx, who had joined the group, so soon as he saw the bound Walter led like a corded tiger to a place of security in the mansion, here lifted up his eyes in admiration of such unexampled forbearance.

" Yet now," resumed Sir Ebenezer, " he must no longer be trifled with. If I gave him up to justice he would suffer on the gibbet the penalty of his crimes. But no ; I will send him to some far distant clime, where repentance may visit him, and where the scarlet sins he has been guilty of may become white even as wool."

And the *ci-devant* Presbyterian watchmaker and preacher turned up his eyes in true conventicle fashion. The unsuspicious Eugenia and honest John Crofts were edified and convinced.

"But shall I not see him again, uncle, before he goes? Pray, let me have one interview. He was always good, kind, generous, and warm-hearted; he will hear that from me which his impatient spirit would not brook from others."

"Alas! my pretty innocent, I fear he is too much corrupted. Did you not hear the awful blasphemy, the horrid imprecations, with which he assailed my esteemed friend here?"

Eugenia did hear them, ay, and they yet rung in her ear like the death-knell of hope.

"Besides," chimed in Mr. Lynx, "although it is a dreadful and a delicate topic, I have reason to believe, from the very best information I could obtain, that a course of abandonment, debauchery and indulgence in ardent spirits, has so undermined his intellect, that when under the excitement of liquor he is dangerously insane."

To this John Crofts mentally gave his decided concurrence.

"No, no," added Sir Ebenezer, "I must be firm; your happiness, Eugenia, and that of this worthy and respectable young man, must be my charge; and though I will not lose sight of your brother, believe me, you must leave to us the care of Walter Lazenby; that so we may be enabled to protect others from his violence and madness, but above all, to protect him from himself."

Sir Ebenezer here lifted his hat condescendingly, and departed towards the mansion; while John Crofts, Eugenia, and Mr. Lynx followed at a respectful distance.

CHAPTER LII.

MISGIVINGS—MIGHT VERSUS RIGHT—REMORSE AND HARDENED VILLANY—A CONTRAST—THE LAW AND ITS ADMINISTRATORS—MR. LYNX'S SUCCESS—AN UNFORESEEN DENOUEMENT.

POOR Eugenia! the events of the last hour had bewildered her brain and crushed her heart. A dull heavy sense of woes to come weighed upon her spirit, and she felt as if her brother's shame, the report of which she doubted not, had degraded her, and rendered her unworthy of the hand of the honest young fellow beside her; nay, a something whispered ominously, as she then thought, that she should not—nay, *could* not, be his bride. In fact, she had grown years older by this her first insight into, or suspicion of, the depravity of man's nature. Like Miranda, to whom we have already likened her, she had seen nothing evil of mankind, and she, naturally, her thoughts taking the reflex of her own pure soul, supposed, if she ever had reflected on the matter, that sincerity, honesty, and kindness, formed portions of the general character of man. But the denunciations of Mr. Lynx and Sir Ebenezer by Walter would recur unbidden to her memory; his words echoed in her ear at every new turn taken by her uneasy thoughts, and pointed the finger of scorn and exposure at two persons, of whom she would fain have thought kindly and well. She tried to persuade herself, too, that they might be the ravings of a distempered brain. No; he was calm and methodical enough in all he said, till seized and bound by the myrmidons of her uncle. Again, he had touched a tender chord in her heart, when he spoke of vindicating their dear mother's fame and honour. Walter had always loved her, she argued, and could not but wish her well. True, his dress and his words were strange, but had he not said he was hunted to the death by Sir Ebenezer and Mr. Lynx, for the sake of wealth that belonged, of right, to herself and him? Walter did not lie in times past; but then the awful imprecations he used! No! she was paltering with her heart and with truth to believe ill of him. She would seek Sir Ebenezer, and implore him to grant her an interview; when, if she should find him really not in his right mind, she would dismiss from her recollection these perplexing thoughts. Poor simpleton! full of this idea, she hastened to Sir Ebenezer, who mildly and evasively avoided a direct refusal, spite of her importunity, and deferred the interview till the morrow. Meantime, let us look into the councils of the worthy pair, who were pretty nearly as much perplexed by this unexpected *contretemps*, as poor Eugenia herself.

"Awkward business, this, my good sir, ex-ceed-ing-ly embarrassing," said Mr. Lynx, as he took a chair on the opposite side of his patron's table.

"And what do you advise, my good Mr. Ferdinand?" enquired Sir Ebenezer, mildly.

"Our course is clear, Sir Ebenezer; at least I would submit to your better judgment the only line of policy which my poor contrivance can suggest. We have already paved the way to a doubt on the part of his sister and her husband, that his intellects are affected; once establish *that* as a fact, and all difficulties vanish. The strongest charges, the most circumstantial accusations he can make will fall pointless, and be addressed only to ears, whose deafness is as purchasable as their feelings are blunted by their occupation. I mean the keepers of a private madhouse. Once there on a medical certificate, which I can readily procure, I must ask, Sir Ebenezer, for my own safety as well as yours, to have the sole control of what further shall be done. As for the girl, her marriage must be concluded as soon as possible; I will have some talk with the bridegroom this evening, and I will not fail to impress upon him, and all with whom I come in contact, the melancholy circumstance of the youth's aberration of mind."

"Good, friend Ferdinand; yet it irketh me sorely thus to persecute the children of my brother; the more especially since my late sad bereavement, and the delicate health of my only hopes — the only hope of the Fitzroy line, my son, my darling Charles"—the old man's voice faltered for a moment; for the pampered, high-bred, woman of fashion, who had lately left this world and its vanities, had been too frivolous and heartless to suckle her own offspring, and the boy she had left behind her, seemed—nay, was certainly daily sinking from hereditary consumption. "I often think—yes, bitterly, in the silent watches of the night," resumed the baronet, in the tone of a man who soliloquises, rather than addresses another—"often does the idea recur to me, that my safest course had been that of honesty and fair dealing towards these helpless children. But 'tis now too late —that fatal night when first I stepped aside—first swerved from the path of virtue; yes, that night when I falsified a dead man's wishes——" Sir Ebenezer rose nervously, and paced the room, Mr. Lynx following his every motion with his keen grey eyes, and assuming a mingled look of contempt and vexation. "Yes, again I say it, that night fixed my fate; predestined me to fall, to descend lower, lower, lower, in the scale of meanness and crime, till I became the bond-slave— the instrument of evil—the tool of one, who, possessed of my secret, holds my life, and, what I valued more, my fair fame, in his hand, and urges me step by step down the fatal declivity; at the bottom of which, ay, even should I 'scape worldly exposure, yawns everlasting destruction! I, who once was esteemed a man of rigid goodness, am now, by one false step, no better than a castaway. Tell me," said the baronet, whose forehead was now crimsoned by excitement; "tell me why you urged me onward in this thorny path? Tell me, what shall hinder me from doing justice to these orphans? For, indeed, ere long I feel just Heaven will let me have no child to inherit this illgotten wealth?" And the unhappy, envied lord of slaves, mansions, parks, and equipages, sank on a gorgeous *fauteuil*, and hid his face in his hands.

Mr. Ferninand Lynx "grinned horribly a ghastly smile," and stepping to the arm of the chair, said slowly, in a grating voice, scarcely repressing the insolence of its sarcasm, "You wish me, sir, to tell you *why* I counselled you to the course you have adopted? I will do so; but, first, my worthy patron will allow me to remind him, forgetting for a moment, in this confidential colloquy, the formal courtesies of life, that when first I proffered my services—moved thereto, I admit, by the hope of professional advancement—that *I knew he was a forger!*" Sir Ebenezer's body bent forward, and his head bowed as if from excess of pain, still he did not remove his hands from before his eyes. Lynx paused: "Some gratitude, surely, is due to the man, who, cognizant of a damning and ruinous fact, instead of moving the Chancellor to protect the orphans—a matter which might have proved profitable, as well as safe, and redounded to my reputation—preferred waiting on the man, and pointing out to him the perils of his position, with the mode of avoiding them. You ask me why *I* urged you on: ask your own bosom. The labourer deserves his hire, and I have had no more. I saved the reputation of Ebenezer Lazenby; I stewarded his wealth, I served his behests, I endeavoured, at all risks, to preserve to him the riches he had acquired, and to increase them; and now he asks me, why *I* urged him? For shame, Sir Ebenezer; either give me the whole and sole disposal of this boy, or I will wash my hands of all farther share in these transactions, and, retiring to France or Italy, leave you to disentangle the web, the main and central working line of which you had yourself laid down, before I humbly offered to work out the problem of becoming rich, which you had so rashly and incompetently entered on."

Sir Ebenezer Fitzroy rose to his feet, and gazed with a countenance which slowly became pale as monumental marble, on this strange and, to him, disrespectful speech of the hitherto servile lawyer.

Mr. Lynx looked cool, deferential, and imperturbable, yet when Sir Ebenezer for a moment tried to assume a look of dignity, Lynx's lip was compressed with a sneering smile.

"Then it is even so," said the baronet; "you *are* my master, and you have the audacity to defy and threaten me."

"Nay, nay, my good sir; I never *threaten*, I always *act;* and while you act with me, Sir Ebenezer, our common interest, nay, our common safety, is a stronger bond of union, a firmer security of co-operation, than all the parchments the wit of man ever devised or executed. But I must have my way : this boy is dangerous ; yet, in deference to your scruples, I have hitherto rather let chance and the course of events direct my proceedings and his, than endeavoured to coerce circumstances—a thing, Sir Ebenezer, which I know your peculiar tenets deny the possibility of—but, sir, as occasions rise, and complications present themselves, so is the ability of the man of resources elicited, and his ingenuity stimulated. I must have have my own way with this boy, and the rest you shall hear from none but these lips."

Sir Ebenezer groaned ; then conquering a momentary compunction, he said, " You are already my master, who then shall come between you and the boy ? Do as you see fit ; but, remember, no violence, or there must be retribution."

Mr. Lynx smiled, slightly bowed, and left the apartment, after a second bend of the body at the doorway.

" He is but a poor thing, after all," muttered Mr. Lynx, as he descended the stair ; " I must coerce him, I see, even for his own good—and mine. Well, I cannot unriddle these predestinarians. Why, of all men, should they hesitate for good or for evil, seeing all is fore-ordained ? No matter ? *I* make *my* fate and shape my fortune, even though the mighty ship, the Fitzroy, should sink in this venture ; the long head of Ferdinand Lynx may save enow from the wreck in his little barque to make him comfortable for the rest of his days."

Mr. Lynx soon reached the hall, where, by inuendo and insinuation, rather than by direct speech, he made it understood that the young man taken in the park was a dangerous lunatic ; but that his unhappy state had hitherto been kept from his sister, to avoid giving her pain ; more especially in consideration of her approaching nuptials. As all the household really loved Eugenia Lazenby, the story excited sympathy, and acquired belief; and this was strengthened by Mr. Lynx straightway visiting the prisoner, who was firmly bound, and placed in a strong brick cellar, in the basement of the mansion, used as a depository for firewood.

Here the unlucky Walter (little thinking of the curious ears listening, and goaded by the pretended sympathy of Lynx for his unhappy condition) burst, as might be expected, and his tormentor intended he should, into the most furious revilings, to all of which the lawyer replied in speeches replete with forbearance and pity.

" Poor young man," said the coachman, as the group returned to the servants' hall ; " he's mad as a March hare—he oughtn't to be let loose. I hear as he was just about to do a mischief to poor Miss Eugeny, when John Crofts stopt him. Well, it's just as well as he comed here at once in day-time, when he 'scaped from the 'sylum, or he might ha' done some mischief to some o' us, or leastways to master or Mr. Lynx."

The other menials acquiesced ; and before the household retired, all had perceived, or imagined they had, something insane in the tones, gestures, or looks of Walter Lazenby.

By early morn, Mr. Lynx had visited a neighbouring clerical magistrate, before whom he laid his own version of the affair. The dignitary, who had a profound veneration for wealth, and yet more for a man who held several presentations, was of opinion that the young Creole ought to be placed " in some place of security," and offered his signature to an order for that purpose, being " perfectly satisfied," as he said, " with the statement of Sir Ebenezer Fitzroy, and anxious to spare so excellent a family the pain of any public exposure. Thus armed, Mr. Lynx proceeded to another of the worshipful unpaid, another parsonic magistrate, who was equally facile in the cause of a rich man, sheltering himself under the observation that, " as Dr. Tithem, his brother in the commission, had signed, he could not have the least hesitation in following so good an example." The family physician of Sir Ebenezer also flourished his name a-foot of the document ; and thus, without either party seeing the supposed lunatic, or even having proof of his existence, three guardians of the law, and protectors of the unprotected, consigned a young man to the most dreadful incarceration that can be imagined.

Such deeds, thirty or forty years ago, were of frequent perpetration, as is shown by the blue books of parliament, in the inquiry which preceded the establishment of public commissioners of lunacy, and a vigilant inspection of public madhouses.

Arrived at Fitzroy Park, Mr. Lynx, having provided himself with two sturdy keepers, and certain cords, proceeded to carry his designs into effect ; yet, fearing that the young man's manner, or some earnest circumstantiality in his explanations might raise a doubt as to his sanity, he resolved on a diabolical scheme to effect the object he had in view; this was neither more nor less than mixing the food he gave the prisoner with an intoxicating drug. This, of course, he dared not entrust to other hands than his own. Having provided himself with a moderate quantity of strychnine, he administered it to the unfortunate young man, who quickly displayed its stupefying effects in the strange expression of his eyes, the incoherence of his speech, and an occasional drowsiness which he continually strove to overcome. Mr. Lynx, satisfied with the effects of his experiment, now introduced his myrmidons, and poor Walter, who after a little raving fell backward in a half comatose state, was carried to a post-chaise, with Mr. Lynx and one of the keepers, the other riding on the bar; and in a short hour Walter was chained, still half unconscious, to the side bar of a stout low oaken bedstead, strewed with straw, in a white-washed den, with a flag-stone floor, an iron-plated door, a grated unglazed window, having for food a pitcher of water and a loaf. Such being the "refractory" room of the "private lunatic asylum" of Smooth-tongue Doubleface, M.D., which in this case really meant Mad-Doctor, seeing that the higher honours of medicine were not very likely to have been his.

The career of Dr. Doubleface had been as follows:

First—an apothecary's boy, then a footman, then a valetudinarian gentleman's gentleman, subsequently a bankrupt innkeeper, afterwards a ditto schoolmaster, now the proprietor of a mad-house and a self-dubbed "Doctor."* Here then was Walter fixed, and as he is now fast-chained, we may safely look after some other personages of the story.

CHAPTER LIII.

A CONFERENCE—A LOVER'S FEARS AND SUSPICIONS—SUCCESSFUL SEARCH, AND IMPORTANT RESULTS.

A CHANCE sown seed scattered by the wayside oft grows to a spreading and robust tree. The random accusations of Walter against Sir Ebenezer and Lynx, had had a strange effect on more then one of the auditory. If the servants of the hall were easily satisfied, John Crofts was not, and his ideas took their tone from those of Eugenia. The night of the imprisonment of Walter, they had a lengthened conference, in which so absorbed were they, that they scarcely for a moment disported in those little dalliances and tendernesses so common to lovers. Both seemed to feel the serious difficulties of their position, and the young man, prone to believe all that was good of Eugenia, doubted not her truth when she artlessly described to him the position in society she enjoyed in her childhood, during her father and mother's life. John Crofts indeed, he knew not why, began to treat her with a species of respectful deference, as though she were his superior; and as they conversed confidentially, for the first time, on the parentage of Eugenia and her brother, he felt convinced, though he did not give expression to his conviction, that there was foul play somewhere. He had seen something of the world, a false friend and a rascally lawyer had ruined his father and brought him to a premature grave, and often in early childhood had he heard his mother dilate on the perfidy of mankind, and the villany to which the love of lucre would prompt unscrupulous men.

"And what," thought he, "if this beloved girl should be indeed the rightful mistress of a half even of Sir Ebenezer's uncounted riches? Can I then aspire to her hand?"

The thought was indeed bitter, for the young fellow loved Eugenia, for herself, and the idea of her being wealthy seemed to him a bar to happiness.

"Eugenia," said he, his voice trembling with emotion, "it is needless now to tell you how I love you; that, I hope your heart is assured of. But—but—alas! Eugenia, strange suspicions are haunting me—I fear—I dread that some of the words your brother spoke are too well based on truth; and, though I almost doubt his being right in his mind, yet—yet—I cannot tell you, Eugenia; I love you,

---

* This is precisely the history of one of the "doctors" who kept an extensive and celebrated "private asylum," near London, in the year 1816!

and tremble lest a higher station, and one more worthy of you, should place a gulf, an impassable gulf between us."

The ingenuous girl's hand returned the pressure of his.

"Never, John, never; no change—and I *fear* one—for I am not greedy of wealth —shall make me other than I now am. But, John dearest, I feel convinced that my brother is not insane, but merely enraged ; for there was a repulsive-looking man with him, when I first met him, who said, I think, that he was a lawyer, and that what Walter asserted with regard to Mr. Lynx and Sir Ebenezer was no more than truth."

"Could we not find that man?" suggested the lover, who, recovered from his first surprise, had now positively become a partizan of Walter's. "What was he like ? Where did he go to?"

"He left the park, I know not whither," replied Eugenia.

"Perhaps he is at some public-house in the town," suggested the young man; "I'll go and seek him."

To this proposition the anxious Eugenia immediately assented, and the lover quickly set forth in search of Mr. Crocodile Fuddlebrain ; nor was his search of long continuance. That worthy, drouthy soul had cast anchor at the Ship, and there, in the tap-room, was in full converse with Jerry Abershaw, Bill Houseman, and Joe Lovell, the gipsy, when honest John Crofts looked in upon his voyage of discovery.

Eugenia's description—women have a talent for description unapproachable by the male sex—was enough. Mr. Fuddlebrain's seedy black, empurpled proboscis, wrinkled gaiters, baggy neckcloth of questionable whiteness, cobbled shoes, and fishy eyes, struck young Crofts with the effect of a speaking portrait when one is already intimate with the original. He saluted Mr. Crocodile, who returned his nod with the solemn courtesy of a man who thought, "here's a new customer, and a likely one." A further inspection of Mr. Fuddlebrain's associates was not so satisfactory. Crofts was a young fellow who knew a thing or two, and he fancied he could read "felon" branded on each forehead of the *quartette*, save Mr. Fuddlebrain's, where swindling and poltroonery appeared more legible. He paused an instant ere he seated himself at the end of an inner bench, between which and the table a passage was made for a time by the rising of Handsome Bill, who, with grinning courtesy, motioned him to a place beside the lawyer. Young Crofts declined the proffered accommodation, and asked Fuddlebrain whether he could have a minute's private converse with him.

"Certainly, my good sir," hiccupped the lawyer, "cer-tain-ly. My time, sir, 's the public's. I've no time of my own—none, sir. What with attending the courts, getting up cases, writing out briefs, assembling witnesses, proving *alibis*, indicting people that perjure themselves in their evidence against my respectable clients, and ceterer, and ceterer, and ceterer, I've no time to myself at all. But at your service, sir—at your service. Hope it's something heavy, for the worse a case the better I like to show my professional skill in it."

"I merely wish a word apart," replied John Crofts. And Mr. Fuddlebrain, on whom drink, though it apparently stupefied him, really acted only on his bodily functions, never affecting seriously his nervous system, which yet defied the potency of alcohol, shuffled out from behind the iron-edged deal table. It was a peculiarity in Mr. Fuddlebrain's constitution, that when he seemed very drunk in the legs and eyes, his mental perception was quite as acute, nay, more so than when the horrors of perfect sobriety had full hold of him. Then he termed himself as "unscrewed," "shaky," "only half himself," and, pursuing his figurative phraseology, "could only be cured by a hair of the dog that bit him overnight"—this metaphor implying that a renewed application to liquor was requisite to "wake up the dead stuff inside of him." John Crofts considered the man drunk, and he was to some extent right, but he quickly found, when they got into conversation, that Mr. Fuddlebrain was "wide awake." He began by "pumping" John Crofts, as he termed it, as to the object of his mission; then, explaining to him that he was a "professional man," and never gave an "opinion" unless feed in advance, he obtained a crown of him; nor, despite John's hurry and anxiety, would Crocodile stir a step further in the affair until rum, grog, and lemons, to the amount of another two shillings—for which he left the young man to pay—were placed on the table in the next room, with a couple of sixpennyworth's for themselves, because "talking was dry work."

Eugenia's lover now entered upon a statement of the events at the lodge, so far as he knew them; and he was pleased, on account of Eugenia, yet pained on account of his patron, when his worst fears received a confirmation from the statements of the strange lawyer. Jerry and Houseman, too, were called in; and although John Crofts disliked them, he knew not why, his antipathy was much abated when he found they were zealous partizans of the imprisoned youth, intimately acquainted with his ill-usage, and expressed their resolve to run any risks for his deliverance.

The reader is already aware of Mr. Lynx's successful plan for the confinement of Walter. This was unknown to John Crofts, who supposed him still to be confined at the hall, in the basement cellar. He therefore acurately described the spot, and that same evening was fixed for the liberation.

We need hardly say that, aided by John Crofts, the ruffianly Jerry and his companion, Handsome Bill, gained easy access by a back-door, and that this was effected with the full knowledge and approval of Eugenia herself.

Poor John Crofts little knew the extent of his newly-found associates' villany. He had watched till all the servants had retired, then slily abstracting the key of the outer back-door from its nail in the "housekeeper's room," he transferred it to his pocket, and awaited till the last candle was extinguished. He then, not without a misgiving that "the end scarcely justified the means," stole like a felon to the entrance, and gave admission to the burglars.

The way to Walter's supposed place of confinement was quickly shown, and John Crofts certainly stood amazed at the celerity and ease with which the fastenings of the door were disposed of by his new-found coadjutors. They entered; the place was empty; the young man looked amazed and disappointed, not so Jerry and his comrade.

"They've moved him off, by goles," said Bill.

"Well, it can't be help'd," rejoined Jerry; "but surely, mister," and he turned to John Crofts, "you don't think as we're to run all this here risk for nuffin—to go away from such a slap-up crib as this without some token o' remembrance. I see several little things as I passed along, as seem light enow for carryin', but as you're a friend o' Walter's sister, in course, we don't want you to 'stand in;' so, p'raps, all things considered, it would be just as well for you to go to bed, or somewheres out of the way, while we does 'the professional;' it 'ill save all questions, and pervent your knowing anything about it, if curious people should ax you."

John Crofts had but an indistinct perception of the meaning of this speech; its cool audacity quite confounded him. He felt inclined to look upon Jerry as one of those coarse wags, who delight in what they call "chaffing a yokel." He tried a laugh: "You're trying to astonish me, I suppose," said he; "this has been an anxious job for me, and the sooner we all leave the house, and I return the key to its proper nail, the better pleased I shall be. If any one should see us, or hear us, we are ruined for ever."

"Maybe," replied Jerry, coolly; "maybe. But I don't mean to go without taking something with me for my trouble. What little crib was that," added he, his practised eye having caught sight of an iron-plated door, near the great dining-parlour; "the one, I mean, with a lot o' smith's work and nail-heads about it? you know; a narrowish black door?" and he stared at Crofts with a threatening scowl.

Eugenia's lover saw the full extent of his danger. "You shall take nothing from here," said he, firmly; "'tis my master's house, and worthy or unworthy, I am his entrusted servant. I have some little money of my own—that I will cheerfully sacrifice, but——"

"Nonsense, my good fellow," interfered Houseman; "these high-fangled notions won't fit. By fair or foul means, we'll have a little something. All you're asked to do is easy enough. It's only to keep out of our way. But we can't afford to waste time!"

"You shall touch nothing in this place, while I live," said Crofts, firmly.

"Bah," retorted Jerry; "look here!" and he bared a knife from his breast-pocket, with his right hand, and produced a double-barrelled pistol in his left. Bill seconded him by showing similar arms.

"Now," said Jerry, as he saw the young fellow turn pale—what man would not do so under such circumstances, for he was totally unarmed, though his agitation arose as much from fear of the wreck of his character, as from bodily apprehension. " You see we don't come without the needful tools. We're loath to harm you—but if we must, we must—for ——" and the desperado swore a fearful oath. " We don't mean to go empty handed. We want you to make yourself scarce, that's all ; for if any rumpus do take place, we'll 'peach on you—*you* let us in, and who'll believe it was for any other purpose, than that we've come for, seein' as the first cover's drawn a blank and our fox is gone ?"

" Again, I tell you, if twenty guineas——"

" Can't take your gilt, nohow," interrupted Handsome Bill ; " you're in for this job with us, and no mistake, so behave like a sensible man, and make the best of a job, as you didn't quite see the bearin's of when you began it."

" Let's have no more patter," added Jerry abruptly ; " time's precious, as I said afore. Here, Bill, this way ; and keep a still tongue in your head, else it'll be worse for all on us—yourself among the rest."

John Crofts was about to leave them and hasten to Eugenia, who was listening with anxious trepidation near her own room-door, but Jerry stopped his movement.

" Excuse me," said he, sneeringly, " but perhaps you're going to ' blow the consarn,' and chance it. That raly wont suit our book at all."

" I am not about to give any alarm, on my word," said Crofts, earnestly.

" I'll take it," said Jerry ; " but mind, false play, and ——" he pointed significantly to his keen knife ; " and she, though she was twenty times Walter's sister, shall try the sharpness of *this*."

The young man's blood ran cold as he almost shrunk from the murderous gleam which flashed from the assassin's eyes as he said this, accompanying the threat with a gesture more expressive than words.

" I will be silent ; but she—she—must not be harmed."

" Who'd hurt her except yourself, with your foolishness," rejoined Houseman.

Crofts heaved a sigh, and hurried gently along a passsge and up a flight of stairs, where he met the trembling Eugenia.

" He's gone," were his first words.

" Who ? Walter ?" enquired the agitated girl, scarcely suppressing her delight.

" Yes, Walter ; he has been spirited away by that infernal Lynx : but worse, much worse remains to be told."

" Oh, don't spare me ; tell me all—anything but suspense," whispered she.

" The men I have brought here, and admitted to the house, are—are— robbers."

" Merciful heavens ! Will you not alarm the people ?"

" I dare not ; I let them in, I procured the key, they are armed, are desperate, and have threatened, if I do so, that they will denounce me as their confederate. One ruffian told me so ; and they will be as good as their word."

" Alas ! dearest, and I—I—am the cause of this ; I urged you to ——"

" Hist ! hush ! hark !" whispered the young man; " they are now rifling the place."

Listening from where they stood, they could plainly hear peculiar yet slight noises, which the operations of the burglars occasioned from time to time. Ten to twenty minutes elapsed ere they heard, to their unspeakable relief, the outer back entrance slowly and carefully closed. The young man yet held his affianced, who was almost fainting from terror at the complicated horrors of the situation in which her slight imprudence had placed her, when she suddenly remembered the danger of her lover.

" Fly, hasten, quit this place, and hurry to your cottage, dearest—oh ! what ruin if you were found here. Fear not for me, I can support myself. Fly, John, fly. Hark ! what is that ?"

Eugenia and Crofts were on the first landing of the great central spiral staircase of the hall ; in a few seconds they became convinced that by some means the servants had been awakened. Steps were approaching by a back-stair, used for the attendants from the kitchen and offices, and leading thence upwards to the servant's dormitories. It communicated with the spot they then stood on, which was far from any sleeping-rooms but those kept for distinguished visitors, by an ante-chamber with two doors, one communicating with each staircase, and wherein, on grand occasions, the lacqueys mustered, and things for the immediate use of the grand tables in the banquetting-room were placed. Through this Eugenia had come, and thitherward flight was impossible.

"Hasten up-stairs, hasten," urged Eugenia.

"Nay, do you depart and leave me here," remonstrated her lover.

"If you will not go," said Eugenia, "we will stay here together, and meet the worst."

They had small time to reconsider their resolution, for almost at the moment of the girl's last loud whisper, the door of the corridor opened, and first came the gardener with a musket, behind him the coachman and a stable-helper with a poker and a pitchfork, while the rear was brought up by three or four other men and boys, and as many of the younger serving-wenches, who coquettishly declared they couldn't stay in their bed-rooms till the house was searched, and who, with shawls half wrapped round their buxom persons, and occasionally *accidentally* exposing what they thought the prettiest parts of their person, either ankles, bosoms, shoulders, arms, or dishevelled locks, as the case might be, were intermixed with the four footmen, who carried on sundry little gallantries during this exploring of the premises, which may be more properly left to the imagination of the reader than recorded in sober prose.

At sight of John Crofts, in his usual day dress, with Eugenia, similarly attired, leaning on his shoulder, the foremost of the group stood dumbfounded with amazement. The coachman stammered a question as to how they came there, which was echoed by the head groom.

"Stand back there in front," cried some of those behind; "here's Sir Ebenezer!"

And, sure enough, the next moment the astonished baronet formed one of the surprised lookers-on.

John Crofts now found his tongue. "I'm aware, my good sir, that appearances are against me, yet, Sir Ebenezer, let your displeasure visit me alone. Impelled by a desire to free the youth you yesterday placed in confinement, I joined with others, whom I will not betray, in an endeavour to effect his liberation."

Sir Ebenezer stood amazed. "And how, sir, came you to join in so mad, so un-grateful a scheme? Have I ever behaved to you or yours in a manner to call for such treachery? Who, I demand to know, urged you to this disgraceful deed? who prompted you to this treachery? For well assured am I there are some enemies of mine, and of my family, who have prompted these deeds. Where, then, are they, young man? I insist upon knowing their names."

"I know them not," replied John Crofts, earnestly, "on my soul I do not. I met them in the town last night, where I imparted to them the fact of young Walter's confinement. They proposed immediately to set him at liberty, and I— I alone—am to blame for their admission to this house, and its ruinous consequences to me."

"Nay, Sir Ebenezer, 'tis not so," interposed the girl, raising her swollen red eyes from young Croft's shoulder; "it was I who, desiring my brother's escape, first suggested to my lover" (and the girl blushed proudly) "this bold and unfortunate attempt. He is innocent of everything but the wish to serve me. It is I, my good sir, who am guilty."

The panic-stricken butler now joined the group, announcing in a few brief words the loss of the most valuable of the silver plate under his charge, by the forcing of his pantry and plate chest.

"Was this, too, part of your scheme?" said Sir Ebenezer, coldly; the unhappy young man hung his head.

"Take him into custody, and keep him safe," added the baronet; "lead this girl to her bedchamber, and place with her some trusty female. We will investigate this matter thoroughly in the morning. Meantime, you may see to all the outward fastenings, and all retire to rest."

"Sha'n't we pursue the robbers, Sir Ebenezer?" cried half-a-dozen voices, for the sense of numerical strength had made the domestics valorous.

"No," replied the baronet, curtly; "it would be of no avail. We shall soon get a clue to these villains, and doubt not they shall be brought to condign punishment."

The unresisting John Crofts was led slowly away, and Eugenia, after a farewell embrace, in silent grief, followed the housekeeper to her own apartment, amid the sympathy of all but her uncle, for her goodness of heart had made her a

general favourite with all except the man who had so deeply injured her, and who had therefore as much cause to fear as to hate her.

Mr. Lynx had not yet returned, and Sir Ebenezer resolved to wait till next day, and consult with his cunning adviser, before he took further steps in this perplexing crisis of affairs.

———

CHAPTER LIV.

THE MAD-HOUSE—MIDNIGHT REFLECTIONS—AN ESCAPE—A RENCONTRE—JERRY ABERSHAW AGAIN—A CAPTURE, AND A MURDER.

THE chilly damp of the night air fanned the fevered temples of young Walter, as recovering slowly from the stupefying effects of the potent drug, he returned to a clear perception of the events of the last two hours. He recalled to mind the repeated assertions of Mr. Lynx, as to his insanity, and soon perceived the exact position he was placed in.

"Oh, I'm mad, am I?" laughed he; "well, I don't feel quite right in the head—that old scoundrel has hocussed me, has he? I'll be revenged though," and he gnashed his teeth with bitter rage. He next examined his chain; it was a clear moonlight night, and the silver rays streaming in at the narrow window, made every object perfectly visible. "Pretty stout bit of iron; but what's this? A snap-shackel and spring-key—ha, ha! If I was quite mad, dear uncle, and still dearer guardian, this trumpery might keep me; but I've learned something more than you taught me, since I set up for myself." As he said this, the youth, applying his thumb to the secret stop, and pressing outward the half-hoop of the shackel at the same instant, released the cross-piece from one end, and the chain was detached from the rings on the stout leathern strap which encircled his waist.

"So far so good; I wish I had a knife though," muttered he. "This pitcher, if broken, might cut leather—but no, breaking that would make too much noise; so I'll e'en wear this waistband for a while, as a remembrancer of their kindness."

He mounted the bedstead and tried the single bar of the narrow window; it was set in an oaken sill, and, if removed, would give sufficient room for the egress of his slender person. At this juncture he espied a small holdfast in the wall, having a flat thin head; to extract it was a brief process, the mortar offering little resistance. Ten minutes' careful and industrious rubbing against a smooth stone in the floor ground this to a very tolerable substitute for a screw-driver, and in a half-an-hour the four screws which held the bar-plate to the sill were all dexterously extracted from their holes. Walter listened attentively; all was still, except the low moaning of some idiot prisoner, or the blood-chilling clank of chains, as some persecuted maniac turned on his miserable pallet in search of some more easy position for his aching limbs, while the master of this mansion of misery snored heedlessly on his bed of down. It was but a short drop from the cell into the garden, and skirting the wall and the hedges on the side thrown in shadow by the brilliant luminary of night, in a few minutes more young Walter had agilely climbed an angle of the high wall, by the assistance of an overhanging fruit-tree, dropped on the outer side, and was hastening along the high road. He resolved to strike into some wood or thicket when day should dawn, and lying there till evening take his chance of reaching by next night the great city, which he felt sure lay at no very great distance. He had not walked an hour, when the silent river, gleaming like a silver serpent, disclosed its tortuous windings among wood and grove, dotted here and there with verdant islands, looking like tranquil abodes of the blest, as they lay bathed in the liquid light. But Walter's was a guilty mind, and the guilty have no just appreciation of the milder glories of nature. He rejoiced at sight of the river, 'tis true, and quickly perceived that he and its stream were journeying one way; but his satisfaction arose from the fact that he felt assured he was in the right direction for the spot where he had left his comrades.

As two o'clock chimed from the ivy-covered tower of the old church, he reached Richmond, little suspecting what had occurred during his brief absence. As he descended the hill towards the town-end, he heard the rattle of light wheels; he stood aside in the shadow of a tree to avoid observation, when what should greet his eyes but the spring "tumbler," as its proprietors termed it, owned by the partnership of Abershaw, Houseman, and Co.; it contained Jerry and his two comrades well armed, together with the booty so audaciously abstracted a few minutes previously from Fitzroy Park. A low whistle of peculiar cadence, sufficed to check the fast trotter.

"That's Walter's whistle, by G——!" said Bill; and he said right, for the youth instantly presented himself to his surprised comrades. "Come, tumble up, lad," said he, "and tell us how the devil all this happened, as we shove along tow'rds town. Hang me, but I think they deal with Old Nick hereabouts. We've been to-night and cracked a crib up yonder, just to get you out o' quod, and they'd spirited you off through the key-hole or somewheres. Howsever, we paid ourselves for the trouble by easing 'em of some heavy-wedge.* I say, Jerry, I'm thinkin' that young cove up there at the house, as is arter our pal's sister here,

* Silver-plate.

won't be in a very particular nice mess in the mornin'. They'll be sure to pipe*
him, even if he don't nose† hisself. How he did take on, surely, when we told
him as we never left nothing behind when we went out visiting, as wasn't either
too hot or too heavy to carry, or else was out of our reach—ha, ha!" and Handsome Bill laughed approvingly at his own wit.

" You've not done any harm beyond helping yourselves?" asked Walter.

" Not a bit," replied Jerry, to whom the question was principally addressed;
" there might have been though, for that young feller as is your sister's sweetheart was precious bumptious, and talked about kicking up a bobbery, and callin'
the servants up, but I put a stopper on him; and there's no harm, except as
p'rhaps he'll have a awk'ard examination to go through to-morrow, seein' as he
prigged the blacksmith's daughter, and dubbed the jigger‡ for us, just to make the
visit smooth and pleasant."

Walter felt rather satisfied than otherwise that it was so; for he entertained
no kindly feeling towards John Crofts; firstly, on account of his position with
regard to Eugenia, and secondly, for the energetic grasp and ugly fall given by
his hand, which led to Walter's capture and bondage.

Thus they trotted on through Mortlake, preferring the Surrey roads as least frequented, till Barnes Common appeared in sight. Here Jerry became aware of the
distant whirr of wheels on the flinty road, and the fast trotter was stopped for a
few moments, and drawn across the greensward behind some fir-trees, near a turn
of the road. The sounds approached.

" We're in luck's way," observed Jerry Abershaw, who had an insatiable thirst
for plunder and violence. " I'll pound it this is some late swell. It isn't our old
friend, Sir Ebenezer, 'cos he's at home, as we well know. The drag, howsever, is
on the road towards many other topping cribs besides his'n. I s'pose, Bill, as
you're ready?"

Bill suggested that, after the style in which they had raised that neighbourhood
about their ears, they should do no more that night.

" Pooh! stuff!" replied Jerry; " in for a penny, in for a pound. We'll just
stop the rattler.‖ It's a private drag, in course, at this time o' night—eh, Watty?"

Walter neither concurred nor dissented.

The party, consisting of Walter, Jerry, and Houseman, alighted from the cart,
tied the nag to a tree, and planted themselves by the roadside, in the shadow of a
spreading elm. In a few minutes the travelling carriage came up to where they
were standing in ambush. It was quickly stopped; and Walter was not a little
surprised to find the voice proceeding from the interior was that of Mr. Lynx.
He had with him a male companion—a miserable, seedy-looking personage, in a
black coat as rusty as that of Mr. Fuddlebrain. His figure, however, was in striking
contrast to that ponderous, bloated, empurpled professional; being as meagre, pale,
attenuated, and woe-begone as his prototype, the starved apothecary of Mantua.
This individual, as we shall hereafter see, was upon a mission somewhat akin to
that of Shakspeare's poison-vendor, to which also " his poverty but not his will
consented."

Jerry was as much surprised at this *contretemps* as Walter himself; he took the
youth aside a moment, while their comrades rifled the carriage.

" This *must* be a *finishing* job, Watty," whispered the ruffian; " it won't do to
let them go again; that Lynx will hang us all."

" I fear so. But can't we take him alive, secure him, and make him useful to
us?" urged Walter, with ready wit, and moreover anxious to avoid blood-spilling.

" You've hit it, by G—d!" replied Jerry, clapping him on the shoulder. " We'll
nail 'em both, box 'em up at Ben's crib, make the old scamp tell us all we wants
to know, and sarve him out at our leisure. But halves, you know, Watty, pervising
I helps you to your own!"

" Agreed," replied the youth.

The ruffians quickly gagged and blindfolded Mr. Lynx, who expected nought
but instant death; and having served his companion the same, they were
deposited, fast bound hand and foot, in the bottom of the chaise-cart—which was
driven off by Houseman and Joe Lovell, while Jerry preferred walking another
road with Walter, as so many in the vehicle might excite more observation
when they arrived in the neighbourhood of the metropolis.

---

* Discover him. † Betray. ‡ Stole the key and opened the outer door. ‖ Coach.

Lynx and his companion in bondage were covered with sundry green boughs, laid crosswise, and on these were placed three sieve baskets, packed over with leaves, to resemble those carried to the London markets by gardeners' carts. The prisoners being clear off, Jerry desired Walter to take a cross road on the common, telling him he should quickly join him.

Walter walked off at a smart pace, and in a few brief moments a fearful deed was done. Approaching the postillion, who stood by his horses' heads as he had been commanded to do, Jerry asked him, in an indifferent tone, where he was about to drive those gentlemen when he stopped the carriage.

The trembling lad answered : "To his measter's, Sir Ebenezer Fitzroy's !"

The ruffian, stepping slightly behind the youth, seized him by the throat with his left hand, and as suddenly plunged his long knife into his side, near the fifth rib ; he withdrew the weapon, and as the boy fell, again drove it into his body. One gurgling groan and the spirit of the murdered youth had fled. Abershaw leant over the corpse, and thrice repeated the blow ; then dragging the body to the road-side, cast it into a bramble-covered ditch.

" Safe bind, safe find," said he, drawing a long breath. " These hanimals can't go far."

And he cut one trace on each side of the chariot, and hurried after Walter at his best pace. He quickly overtook him, and in reply to his questions as to whether the boy might not cause pursuit to be made, said that he had bound him, and placed him in a dyke, whence, " he'd pound it, he wouldn't stir till after day-light !"

With this explanation Walter was perforce satisfied ; and leaving the twain on the road, we will turn to Fitzroy Park and its inmates.

———

CHAPTER LV.

FITZROY PARK—THE PLOT THICKENS—JOHN CROFTS IN TROUBLE—A PARTING.

SIR EBENEZER FITZROY'S perplexity may easily be imagined when—for ill-news flies apace—he was disturbed at early morn by a rapping at the door of his bed-room. His reply of " come in !" was followed by the appearance of his valet, who, with a pale and affrighted aspect, advanced to his bed-foot ; and behind him —for in his consternation he left the door open—several of the male servants were visible, all equally terror-stricken.

" Oh, sir ! I have have hardly words to tell you what has happened—it is so dreadful. The postillion James, sir, Mr. Lynx—and maybe somebody else—is all murdered on Barnes Common. As yet, sir, they've only found James's body, stone dead, sir, and he lies below in the hall. Perhaps you'd like to see the men as have brought him ? The horses and chariot is safe ; and they've not been able to find the other bodies. What had we better do, sir ?"

" Mr. Lynx murdered, say you !" cried the affrighted baronet ; " murdered almost at my very threshold ! My dressing-gown, Jennings, my dressing-gown ! Send the men here. Gracious heavens ! this must be followed up. Are the wretches in custody ?—is there any trace of them ?"

Jennings hastily helped his master to dress ; and another of the domestics, within hearing of the order, ushered the countrymen who had found the carriage in the position of which the reader is already aware, up-stairs to the baronet's presence.

" Send immediately for the nearest magistrate ; I must have assistance in the investigation of this horrid business. Go, as many of you as can, and leave no place unsearched for the unfortunate Mr. Lynx. He may be sore wounded and helpless ; hasten ! leave no means untried to gain traces of the villains. The man who first brings information shall be handsomely rewarded."

These hurried orders were given as the fellows, three in number, were shown into the room. They were labouring men, working in the market-gardens, with which the district abounded, and could throw no further light on the affair than that, as they were going to their daily toil at the hour of five, they found the horses grazing on a bank near a hedgerow, just at the point where three roads from different points of the common unite together, and form the main Surrey highway towards Barnes and Richmond ; that, after tying together the cut harness, they made search for the driver of the vehicle; that they quickly came upon a quantity of blood, and tracing the drops, they shortly found the murdered postillion.

Leaving one of their party with the carriage, they went and gave an alarm at the nearest inn; and having found out that the vehicle was the property of Sir Ebenezer Fitzroy, they had brought it home. The baronet committed the statement, and while putting questions to the men, his brother magistrate, a neighbouring clergyman, arrived. After some expressions of horror and indignation at the audacity of the murder and robbery, the examination was repeated; and the fellows, having received a small gratuity from Sir Ebenezer, were sent below to refresh themselves with meat and ale, where they were subjected to incessant and eager questionings by the female servants, who in return for their fearful intelligence kept them so largely supplied with good things and humming ale, that the fellows became immensely communicative, and each going beyond the other in horrible details, they gave such a highly-coloured version of the affair, that the horror-struck wenches gathered round open-mouthed, and felt almost annoyed when the bumpkins had no more fearful lies to tell about the present murder, and half-a-dozen others which they had heard of, and now jumbled together and attributed to the same gang as had infested that 'ere road for many a year. At length, their appetites having been appeased, and their auditors' curiosity keenly whetted, they were again called up, their names and addresses taken in writing, their "marks" made to their depositions, and having been warned that they must attend to give evidence when called on, they were sent about their business; Sir Ebenezer first informing them, that a reward of one hundred guineas would be paid by him "upon receiving such information of the murderers as might lead to their conviction."

The clerical magistrate having departed, Sir Ebenezer fell into a painful state of distraction; he had several times been on the point of disclosing to the clergyman the occurrences of the previous night; but a dread of opening up an enquiry which must lead to an acknowledgment of the relationship of Eugenia to himself, which must make public the existence of Walter, and consequently his claims, which might also lead to bringing that young man prominently into notice, of whose violence and his associates Sir Ebenezer had already had fearful proof, and whose present supposed position in a madhouse might consequently be exchanged for gaol, deterred him; then, too, the absence of Lynx paralysed him.

We have said that Sir Ebenezer was but second villain in this domestic drama, and like that personage in Surrey plays, his half-faced villany was ever suggesting doubts, fears, and middle courses, in contrast with the thorough-paced, unscrupulous rascality which marked all the doings of his coadjutor, Mr. Ferdinand Lynx. He, therefore, desired John Crofts to be brought before him, and privately questioned him upon his knowledge of the mysterious events of the previous night.

The young man, who had been confined to his room in a sort of parole imprisonment, was candid in his confession. He related to Sir Ebenezer, without concealment, the motives which had involved him in the enterprize for the release of Walter, and warming with his subject, when he came to speak of Eugenia's declaration of her disbelief of Walter's insanity, disclosed the communication which had been made to him by the unknown lawyer, and by Walter's companions, as to that youth's claims to large property; he further avowed his "criminality," as he himself termed it, in having given admission to two villains, whose names he did not even know, with the mistaken notion that they designed merely the liberation of the brother of his betrothed bride.

Sir Ebenezer listened to the disclosures with an ill-suppressed agony; every remark of the young man seemed to give another shattering blow to the edifice of crime he had so painfully built, and any one who could have read the feelings of the two men would have said that the master was the conscious criminal, and his servant the unintentional accuser.

Sir Ebenezer saw that more victims must be made ere he could sit easy in the bad eminence to which his first crime had led him; yet he lacked the energy to resort to extreme measures. Accordingly, he made a merit of his forbearance; and after pointing out to Crofts his extreme leniency in refraining from prosecuting him as an accessory to a felony—a charge which, however true, the conscious innocence of the young man impelled him to repudiate, he told him that he should send him for a time away from that neighbourhood, to his house in Lancashire; where, if his silence, discretion, and good behaviour warranted it, he should be, after a time, followed by his intended, towards whom and himself, despite this heavy offence (which he fully believed, or pretended to believe, was an unintentional one), his good feeling was unaltered. Suspicion, however, had taken strong hold of the young fellow's mind ; he saw he was in the power of Sir Ebenezer, but he distrusted his professions, and more than ever suspected the villany of lawyer Lynx. "Why this extreme leniency ?" thought he, "unless there was something more in this affair than the baronet chooses to disclose ?" He therefore dissembled, and after some awkward protestations of his gratitude, Sir Ebenezer cut him short by telling him that he must for some time take leave of Eugenia, as it would be out of the question, after such a stigma on his character, that he could remain in his household ; and moreover, that the farewell interview must take place in his (Sir Ebenezer's) presence. Hypocrisy, like other vices, is contagious. John Crofts saw that Sir Ebenezer was dissembling, so he met him by dissembling too. He prayed Sir Ebenezer to reconsider his decision, but by no means with such zeal as he would have done, had he not intended to carry out a counter-scheme of his own in frustration of the sentence. Of this, the main present features were escape. As soon as he should get beyond Sir Ebenezer's grasp, and making Eugenia the partner of his flight—for he inwardly resolved not to leave her whom he valued more than his own safety to the machinations of two men, who he now firmly believed to be her secret enemies. Eugenia was soon after sent for, and the weeping and somewhat indignant girl was at a loss to interpret the almost cool facility with which her lover bowed to the decision of Sir Ebenezer ; indeed, her awakened pride at what she almost thought indifference on the part of her intended rendered the parting so painful, that her mingled emotion made her shorten the leave-taking, and hasten from the presence of both her lover and her uncle, to find solace in the privacy of her own apartment in a flood of indignant tears. Crofts did not dare to undeceive her as to his departure, so narrowly was he watched by the suspicious and fearful baronet.

That night John Crofts left the mansion, but his adventures will more properly fall in a future chapter ; for the present we will turn to look after the fate of Mr. Ferdinand Lynx and his companion, the needy apothecary.

CHAPTER LVI.

THE BITER BIT—MR. LYNX'S UNPLEASANT JOURNEY, AND YET MORE UNPLEASANT LODGINGS—DISCLOSURES, AND A CONSULTATION.

'Tis but a few years since a somewhat parallel case to that we are about to narrate occurred in this metropolis, in the vicinity of that bustling thoroughfare the City-road ; the position, therefore, in which Lawyer Lynx found himself, is no wild coinage of the fancy. Blindfold and bound, he was driven and jolted over the vile pavement of Snow-hill, West Smithfield, and Chick-lane, unable to give even a guess at his whereabout, save that by the grunting of swine and the bleating of sheep, and the lowing of oxen, he was sure that he was slowly passing through the crowded cattle market of Smithfield. His silence and that of his comrade was effectually secured, for Joe Lovell had laid himself down between them with a drawn knife, which, he fully explained to the trembling lawyer and no less horrified apothecary, would be sheathed in the body of the first of them which should cry out.

The vehicle passed under a narrow archway on the right of Chick-lane, near the stinking thoroughfare known as Pickled-egg-alley, and entered a dilapidated shed. Here the driver and his companions dismounted from their seats, Joe still preserving his recumbent guard. Handsome Bill departed for a short time, and on his return a low and fearful whispering took place in a corner of the stable. Mr. Lynx gave an awful groan, and broke into a profound sweat ; he thought his hour was come, and muttered a sort of witch's prayer backwards, which, like Macbeth's "amen !" stuck in his throat.

Poor Mr. Pestle, too, his companion in misery, presuming some new horror had arrived, echoed the groan ; whereon Joe, although he was wellnigh bursting with laughter, gave utterance to a sanguinary and deep-toned threat, whereof the burden expressed his intent to "cut loose their soul-bolts, and let daylight through their respective ribs," unless the strictest silence was observed.

Mr. Lynx ventured, in a most piteous, faltering whisper, to beg his life, as did also his companion; to which their sentinel replied, "that their lives depended on their keeping their —— tongues still, an injunction they were fain to obey.

In a short time the arrangements of the rascally trio appeared to be completed, for Joe, slipping from the cart, proceeded to loosen the bonds of Mr. Lynx; and that personage, having been helped from the vehicle, was led by one hand, while Houseman took his arm, through a quantity of loose straw; thence, after ascending a step-ladder, into a loft, from which place, after traversing a few paces among trusses of hay, &c., he again descended, and was led to the back door of Black Ben's hostelrie, by means of a narrow passage between two high walls, which was contrived as a means of egress and ingress to the house, in case of exit by the front door being prevented by any casualty.

Arrived at a damp, dark, dismal, and foul-smelling room, the bandage was removed from his eyes, and so long had he been in partial darkness, the objects were tolerably visible to him, even in that imperfect light. The floor was of moist, greasy brickwork, except a large square trap-door of rough boards, through which exhaled a most fetid odour, and beneath which the rush of water was distinctly audible. A seat of brickwork extended along one side of the wretched dungeon, and as they entered a number of enormous water-rats squeezed themselves through a small drain at the lower corner of the den, squeaking and gibbering as they escaped from the presence of the intruders on their play-ground.

Poor Lynx's blood ran cold at these disgusting vermin. He was naturally a coward, and the thought of being left alone and in darkness in such a place, bathed him in a cold sweat; his teeth chattered audibly, his knees tottered under him, and he sunk on the cold brick seat.

"Yo-o-o-u don't mean to leave me alone in this horrid cave?" expostulated the lawyer; "you can't—you must not! Pray stay with me, for the sake of mercy, or leave me a light. I will pay—I will reward you; ay, and will never betray a word of what you have done, on my soul I will not, if you will release me from this horrid place. Oh! be merciful—give me some other prison, I care not where, so as it is not here, and I will submit cheerfully to any conditions you may require of me."

"You don't like the saloon, then, old Six-and-eightpence?" said Joe, in a chaffing tone. "Vy, there's bin better men nor you lodged here at odd times, on'y most on 'em aint had much chance of a change, onless it was to go down stairs there vithout the convenience of a ladder." And the ruffian grinned to see the livid horror which spread over the lawyer's face.

The wretched Lynx, his fears aggravated by his position, at once comprehended the term of the jest, and the extent of his own helplessness.

"Take my life then at once," urged he, desperately; "I shall not survive the night."

"Pooh! stuff-o'-nonsense," replied Joe; "you'll get used to it in time. It ain't none o' the sveetest o' lodgings, 'specially arter rain, 'cos that drives a little stink down, and a good lot o' rats up, and the varmint is then rayther troublesome. But there's some questions as you'll have to answer, vich other people 'ill put, and ven they've done vith yer, p'raps, they'll let yer go—I say p'raps, 'cos maybe they mayn't think it safe to let yer go at all, 'xcept so as yer can't split about vot you've seen or heard; no matter. I dessay you're peckish, though. Here, Bill, get some bees'-vax, a buster, and some gatter* for the svell; ve mustn't starve our prisoners."

Mr. Lynx protested he had no appetite.

"Nonsense; you'll be hungry afore the morning. Good day, sir, and I hopes ven next you lock a person up in a mad-house, you'll remember how kindly you vos treated ven you vere clapped in limbo at the suit of them as you meant to rob, but as vos sharp enow to turn the tables even on the knowin' Lawyer Lynx. Good *day*, sir, and a good appetite for yer breakfast."

As he said these last words, Joe deposited a jug of beer, a small loaf, and a slice of cheese on the brick bench before mentioned, and nodding his head, retired with a grin, the rusty bolts and lock of the door grating horribly as he fastened them on the outside.

* A loaf, cheese, and porter.

The wretched man was in darkness, and alone. The gurgling splash of water, the damp, cold, foul-smelling vault, the dreadful fate which he feared awited him, all rushed on his mind. He groaned aloud in the anguish of his soul. His brain became dizzy; his very heart seemed sick with the stench which impregnated the air. For a long time he sate in a state of mental stupor; at length he became conscious that a cooler and a fresher air came from an aperture in the brickwork at the farther end of the arched vault, and that at the same point a dim hazy light was visible, doubtless occasioned by the striking of the sun's beams at an acute angle on some distant spot. He arose, sick and giddy with mental and bodily exhaustion; he groped along the slimy wall in the direction of the glimmer.

The cellar in which he was confined was so low at the spring of the arch, that frequently he struck his head against the brickwork. On arriving at the aperture, a gush of fresh air, rivalling, in his estimation, the breath of a May morn in sweetness, albeit it came only from the ale-cellar of Black Ben, saluted his olfactories. Mr. Lynx, too, could perceive, as his eyes became accustomed to the imperfect light, that divers puncheons and barrels were ranged around, and that the cellar was reached like the one he occupied, and that the blessed streak of daylight at the further end fell through a door or grate of iron bars, by which ingress to the cellar was obtained, down a flight of earth steps, faced with rough stones on the front edge. Here, then, the poor devil took his post, first for the sake of purer breathing, and secondly to feast his eyes on the apology for daylight which gleamed at that distant spot.

There is an Arabian proverb, that when the well is dry man knows the worth of water, and Lynx was an exemplification of its truth. In a long life he had never felt one spark of gratitude to the Great Giver of light and life; his muckworm soul had never expanded in joyous praise when he saw " the sun in its majesty, and the moon walking the heavens in her brightness;" not he. For him the orb of day was to light him to profit, and the chicanery and roguery which he called " business;" and the moon as the occasional lamp to show his meditative mood the way to other men's coffers, thence to plunder, by mean stratagems and quirks, the money they had earned by honourable toil.

The orphan-robber and man-despoiler sate alone in his misery; the dirty deeds of his hours of liberty rose in accusation against his craven soul. How he yearned for the open day, and half-formed resolves of amendment awakened in his despicable heart.

Hour after hour went by; the streak of light grew dim, then dimmer, then went out gradually, and he was left alone—alone with darkness, horror, and a guilty conscience. Still he strained his eyeballs towards the spot where the blessed outer world—for so he now thought it—held its only communication with his imprisoned wretchedness; he gazed till those dirty, dilapidated steps reproduced themselves on his eager eyes—ay, even when covered with their lids—in the guise of stairs of red-hot iron. Though they seared his very sight, he could not banish them; nay, he joyed in the painful contemplation. To him they seemed, like the ladder in the patriarch's dream, as steps whereby man might ascend to heaven, for Lynx, indeed, was " of the earth earthy," and the world was his elysium.

Anon he became aware of the hum and murmur of distant voices in conversation. No music to his ear had ever sounded so sweet. They spoke, as he thought, of society, and to such a wretch as he solitude was indeed death. A faint glimmer, too, evidently proceeding from an artificial light, brought the lowermost step in dim outline to his view. It proceeded from the small apartment behind the bar of the Red Lion, which communicated with the staircase of the cellar into which he was thus furtively peeping. He feared lest, if he should be discovered, that the wretches in whose power he was, might cut off this little consolation by stopping up the hole which communicated this little comfort.

Thus hour after hour passed away, yet he took no food; his very soul shuddered at the idea of eating in that loathsome place; he felt sick, faint, but not hungry. Resting his chin upon his hands, which grasped convulsively the crumbled bricks, his knees on the ledge already mentioned, he from time to time fell into a doze of mere mental exhaustion. From these brief minutes of oblivion he awoke to the stern realities of his horrid fate. At one time he slept—yes, slept—he knew not how long; and awakening, his burning thirst led him across the den in search of the stale beer which his gaolers had left behind them. He clutched it: the

draught seemed life to his parched throat.   He felt for the food, too, in the darkness.   The rats had forestalled him ; that grieved him not, for he loathed victual. Returning refreshed, he again took his stand at the aperture.

His faculties quickened by anxiety, he after a time heard a small clock strike the hour of ten. In a few minutes after, a heavy step descended ; the man bore a light—it was no other than Ben Holland, and as he came down, Lynx caught these words :

" Well, I agrees to it. If so be this la'yer won't do what we wants of him, mum's the word.   I'll let no one out o' here to tell tales out o' school.   Here, Dick, bear a hand ; I can't tap the cask and fix the pipe too !"

Lynx saw that one of his captors followed the speaker, and while they busied themselves in detaching a pipe from an empty cask, and screwing it to a full one, he heard the following converse, in bated breath, with many interruptions.

" That 'ere portrait, mark my words, is this here Walter's mother; them papers is relatin' to a queer job as has been done about his father's will—let me alone for smelling a rat! Well, this here Lynx, and Sir Ebenezer What-d'ye-call-him—for he seems to have a couple o' names—is in the job, and they go shares. Now, if so be as we can make this la'yer sign his name to a written confession o' the facts, as the Patrico purposes, I don't see how we can do anythink to prove it's right'us, and his own handwriting, unless we brings him for'ard. That game won't never do for us; we mustn't meddle wi' the law, else, depend on't, sooner or later, it 'ill meddle wi' us. It's all wery well for people to talk, but we must look to ourselves. I don't see as there's any pull in rightin' others and gettin' all wrong yerself. Well, here stands the game, as I take it: Young Walter's bin done—so has many a better man; we can't do more for him than we can—that's plain. It's wery fine for old Crocodile Fuddlebrain to prate about gettin' estates for him, and all that sort o' stuff, but he won't help us when he's got 'em; and how we're to be the better for shoving ourselves into a fix, I don't know. Old Lynx here can't be let out, that's sartin; he'll twist the necks of the whole of us if ever he do. I wish he hadn't been brought here at all; but as he's here, why, whatever old Crocodile says, he mustn't go, onless we all on us cut first; and if we do that, where's the recompense? I means to have five hundred down on the nail, and no mistake, if I'm to hop the twig from this crib, and no mistake. Promises from that young feller is all very fine, but they may scrag the lot on us afore we sees the shine of his gilt. So, as I said afore, we must do what we can with this la'yer, and then ——"

The rest of the sentence was lost in an indistinct whisper, and after a few more commonplace remarks, the precious pair quitted the cellar.

Unhappy Lynx! The grating of the gate, as the host fastened it behind him on his departure, grated harshly as those of Milton's hell. He was, then, to be sacrificed, inhumanly murdered, to allay those villians' fears! The horror of the thought overpowered him, and he fell helpless and insensible on the cold and slimy ground.

How long he lay there, he knew not. He was aroused to consciousness by a keen sense of stinging pain ; a sharp instrument seemed to pierce his face. He raised his hand in horror ; a huge water-rat had fixed its fangs in his cheek; his cold hands were bloody, and the damp loathsome weight of a hundred of these disgusting reptiles was upon his person. They had begun their attack on his prostrate body. Fierce burning bites assailed his hands and face, and the filthy wretches, as he rose into a semi-recumbent position, fiercely fought for their prey, hanging to every part of his apparel, portions of which they had already torn, and fixed upon the exposed flesh.

The wretched man started to his feet ; the noxious reptiles squeaked, gibbered, and showed fight, fixing on his fingers as he strove to tear them from his person. In the madness of despair, he screamed aloud ; echo alone replied. He rushed from side to side of his narrow prison, beating himself against the walls, in vain ! The pain of his bleeding wounds seemed like renewed bites of his innumerable assailants. He stamped upon their soft bodies at every step ; they shrieked, but returned to the attack. Nerved by despair, he rushed to the small aperture already mentioned, and giving a howl like that of a fire-encompassed tiger, implored a rescue from this horrid death.

Suddenly a confused sound of voices and footsteps was heard near the door of his dungeon ; he rushed towards it, and struck heavily against the woodwork with his lacerated limbs. It opened, but the first man who entered bore a light and a weapon; the latter he aimed at the head of Lynx: one bright flash, and the bullet had sped on its mission, and Mr. Lynx lay weltering, senseless, in his gore.

" You'll not tell they as comes arter us much, I'm thinking," panted Jerry Abershaw, for 'twas he who was the foremost of several men and a female, who almost simultaneously burst into that horrid hole. "Here, bear a hand, Bill. Come, Bekka, now then!" and the ponderous trap already mentioned was heaved up. " There, make fast the door behind us, some one—here's enow on us ! Have a care there—here's a light."

And the ruffian turned the bull's-eye of a dark-lantern full on the aperture of the trap, where, on one side, a number of stout wooden projections, each about a foot below the other, were visible, set in the brickwork which formed the wall or side of the vast culvert, at the bottom of which the black stream of the sewer—once dignified by the name of the river Fleet—rolled rapidly.

"Keep your pluck up, Bekka, and mind your foothold," said Jerry. "Ladies fust is manners."

And taking Rebekah Morse by the elbow, on whose bronzed face fear rather for his safety than her own, was legibly written, he partially helped her down, till, by an agile bound, she landed herself on a projection of brickwork, or earth, formed alongside, and above the ordinary level of the centre.

"Keep your left hand agen the wall, and hold the rope you'll find in the staples there. Now, Ben, you're heavy carcased, and shall follow me. Come, Bill, down with ye."

The villains needed no second bidding; all were soon below, and Jerry had scarcely closed the trap behind him, which he carefully did, before voices were demanding admittance at the outside door; and in a few seconds the stout sloping plank with which its inside was wedged, fell as the door broke from its hinges, prised away by a strong adze wielded by a vigorous arm.

"Why, who the devil have we here? A stiff 'un, by goles!" exclaimed Dave Turner, lifting the head of Mr. Lynx from the ground; then, spying the bleeding state of his hands and face, he continued: "That murdering varmint Jerry Abershaw's cut the poor old cove all to pieces."

"May I drink p'ison if it ain't Lawyer Lynx!" rejoined one of his comrades. "The very man we were looking for; and here he is, as safe a corpse as ever walked into a dissectin' room on another man's shoulders. Well, strike me, but——"

"Hold your clatter," responded Turner; "he breathes."

And, sure enough, next moment Mr. Lynx gave a heavy groan, and opened his corpse-like eyes with the stolid stare of a stale codfish.

"He's worth a dozen dead 'uns yet," said another. "Come, let's take him up into the fresh air—faugh! how the place stinks."

Mr. Lynx was speedily carried to the upper world, where leaving him in the hands of a surgeon who was immediately called in, we will turn just to see how this almost miraculous deliverance has been brought about.

———

CHAPTER LVII.

AN ELOPEMENT—THE PERPLEXITIES OF SIR EBENEZER FITZROY THICKEN—AN UNINTENTIONAL BETRAYAL.

JOHN CROFTS, as we have seen, left the mansion of Sir Ebenezer with a heavy heart. He dared not trust any one with his secret resolve, yet it was necessary that he should have a coadjutor in his enterprise, which was no less than conveying to Eugenia the true state of his feelings and intentions, and proposing to her to do that with him which he had, with the best of motives, prevented her from doing with her brother—namely, elope from the dangerous protection of the baronet. His brain was busy with the thought, as the carriage which conveyed him from Fitzroy Park rolled down the long avenue, and no sooner had it passed the boundaries of the park, than he hailed the postillion, who was an old friend, and thus addressed him:

"You know, Bob, that I was going to be married," said he, in a cheerful tone. The youth replied in the affirmative.

"Well, that's all over now, I suppose; but it's rather hard for a young fellow to leave his wife that ought to be, without a token to remember him by." The lad seemed to agree fully with the proposition.

"I wouldn't get you into any trouble on my account," said Crofts, "but if you will give this letter to my old mother, at the lodge, now directly, you will serve me; and to show you I'm not ungrateful, here's a crown for you."

"I'll do it for your sake and Miss Eugenia's," said the boy, "let alone your crown."

Crofts gave him the letter, and in a few minutes the lad returned, having safely delivered it to the widow Crofts.

The letter entreated his mother would, without delay, put the sealed enclosure into the hands of Eugenia Lazenby; and ere the afternoon was old, the aged woman, not doubting but it was merely an affectionate farewell, placed it safely in possession of her to whom it was addressed.

The agitation of Eugenia may be easily conceived when she read as follows :

" My dearest, my only love,—How much I was pained at being compelled to dissemble my feelings this morning, in presence of Sir Ebenezer, words cannot express. That my seeming indifference sprung from the hope of effecting our mutual deliverance from the meshes of two perfidious men, must plead my excuse for inflicting a temporary pain on her whose happiness is my only end in life, I trust you will believe when you receive this assurance. At the hour of ten I shall be at my mother's cottage—but of this breathe a syllable to no one. At eleven I shall be in the chesnut avenue, where, should you be unable to meet me, I will wait till twelve o'clock; at that hour, I will be beneath your window, and if all is quiet within doors, let your signal be three taps on your window-frame. I will come provided with the means of your escape. When we are beyond reach of your and my persecutor, I will more fully explain the urgent necessity for this step on the part of yourself and

" Your devoted lover,
" JOHN CROFTS."

Poor Eugenia hardly knew whether pain or pleasure had the mastery of her feelings on reading this strangely-worded letter. It was clear—for love persuaded her of the truth and honour of the writer—that the worst suspicions of her guardian and Lynx were but too true. She therefore hesitated not, but imbibing the spirit of her betrothed, determined not to place him in unnecessary peril, and, if possible, to meet him at the earliest hour named, so as to prevent his dangerous approach to the mansion. She therefore feigned, or rather did not feign, although she concealed her ulterior views, an intense anxiety to condole with the old widow; and in order to lend plausibility to her scheme, she requested the female who attended on her to ask Tomlinson, the steward, whether she might not visit the mother of her lover, without infringing on the rules Sir Ebenezer might have laid down for her conduct, during the time she was under the kind of surveillance to which Sir Ebenezer had sentenced her.

The worthy man, knowing of the departure of John Crofts, immediately declared that he saw no reason why she should not visit the old lady; nay, he himself offered his services to escort her. This she adroitly evaded, by saying that, should he accompany her, displeasure might fall on him; while, on the other hand, so far as she was concerned, no one should know that she went with his permission. The matter, therefore, was arranged that Eugenia should go, attended by Betty.

John Crofts having reached the London Inn in the afternoon, whereat he pretended he was to pass the night, discharged the postboy, and quickly taking a short stage on the western road, reached Brentford ere the shades of evening closed in. A short walk over Kew-bridge. by Richmond-park wall, brought him near the spot where dwelt the centre of his earthly hopes and cares. As the day grew dusky grey, and the long deep shadows of the stately trees threw gloom upon the sward of the park, he gently unlatched a side gate some few yards from the lodge, and stole along under the shade of a clump of laurels. Arrived at the end of the sheltering thicket, he was watching the glimmering light from the lodge window, when a light rustling was heard near him, and the next moment Eugenia clasped him by the hand; he drew her towards him, and folded her in a gentle embrace.

" This is too—too kind," said he, when his tongue resumed its office, for for a few seconds it refused to articulate; " this is too—too kind, my dearest Eugenia."

" Hush! hush! your mother is conversing with Betty, and if we must fly, the sooner we leave this fearful spot the better."

" I am ready; I have only to step into the town, where a conveyance for London will be immediately procurable."

" Nay, do not fear me, I can accompany you; risk not your own safety out of tenderness for me."

" Noble girl," said the lover, " I obey you."

They passed the outer gate, hastened a short mile to one of the principal inns, and while, by the advice of John Crofts, Eugenia strolled down the village and turned towards the bridge, her lover procured a post-chaise for London—a matter of no difficulty, as he was well known as a confidential servant of Sir Ebenezer.

As they passed near the toll-gate of the bridge, Crofts stopped the vehicle; Eugenia lightly entered, and away rattled the couple for London, as the safest spot for concealment, should pursuit be made.

The night of his arrival was indeed an eventful one for others in this story, as the reader has already seen. The murder of the post-boy had put the thief-takers on the alert; and in the course of the day Sir Ebenezer had arrived in town, and had an interview with the Secretary of State upon the subject of the murder, and the mysterious disappearance of Mr. Lynx, whose fate none doubted had been the same as that of the hapless youth. The result was a large reward offered on the part of the Crown for the detection of the murderers, and to this Sir Ebenezer added a promise of a like sum. The hopes of so rich a prize stimulated the zeal of the man-hunters of the police, and that day long were the consultations, and deep the potations, in the dark back-parlour of the Old Brown Bear, in Bow-street, as to the mode of tracing and effecting the capture of the villains.

"I'll tell you vhat it is," whispered Turner to his comrade, Pearce; "it's no use havin' a lot in it, else there'll be too many shares. This here job's Jerry Abershaw's work, and some of his pals. There's a young cove, too, as I've tvigged along of old Crocky Fuddlebrain, and he don't keep no secrets from me, though, to be sure, I pays him pretty tidy for vot hinformation I gets. Vell, this here younker's a*ther a by-blow * of old Sir Ebenezer's, and has got a sister as like him as two peas in a pod—but that's neyther here nor there. Vell, this lad bolts avay from home, and takes up vith Jerry and his gang, and now he's as an'inted young cracksman as ere a one in the long village. I sees him this very mornin', lookin' for all the vorld as if he'd bin on the tramp all night; he vas vell breeched, too, for he changed a yellow-man† to treat a moll‡ in Rats' Castle,§ vere he's been snoozin' all day. I've planted on him, though, and ven he leaves his Vestern hot-el this evenin', vich I make sure he'll do, ve'll trick him; for sartin 'tis ve shall light on Jerry, and 'tis 'twixt the lot on 'em; or if it ain't, vy, if needs be, ve'll *make it that vay,* and scrag the pair on 'em, vich vill be two more forties|| to add to the purse of two hundred canaries as the gover'ment and the old cove has already offered. But they'll show fight, Ben, for sartin; so ve must go prepared vith barking-irons and bracelets for more than two, if it should so happen."

Ben Pearce thought there was much feasibility in this, and while they were taking their fourth glass of stiff Jimakey, one of their watchers brought word that Walter had left the Rookery, and dodged by his, the watcher's, comrade, had betaken himself eastward. Buttoning up their coats, the pair of thief-takers hurried out, and taking with them two sturdy, resolute constables, wended their way on the track of the young thief. After stopping several times at liquor-shops, where he treated one or other of his flash acquaintance, Walter was leisurely walking down the narrow steep court at the end of Hatton-wall, which communicates with Saffron-hill, when he was seized from behind with a powerful grasp, and next moment his wrists were encircled with handcuffs.

"Take him avay," whispered Turner to one of his satellites, "and keep him safe till ve comes back. I say, Ben, it's clear enough now, he's bound for the old crib in Chick-lane; a desp'rate queer consarn that to storm, so ve'll just have half-a-dozen in all, afore ve tries to make the visit pleasant. Run to the Bear, and fetch Morris, Stevens, and Rose: they're about the gamest of the lot, and ve may vant 'em."

Mr. Pearce returned in half an hour with the reinforcement; young Walter, meantime, having been lodged in the watch-house near the old sessions-house, Clerkenwell. The officers advanced cautiously, yet, despite their utmost care, a cry of "The Philistines!" was heard by them as they reached the door of the Red Lion. The warning was, as we have seen, in time to allow the principal villians to escape; and Downy Dick, Joe Lovell, and a few who were carousing in the tap-room, were all that the myrmidons of the law succeeded in finding. Their fortune, as Mr. Turner termed it, was soon told. On Dick was found some of the money and a silver snuff-box, stolen from Sir Ebenezer's house; and on Joe Lovell some broken spoons, the produce of the same exploit, which Jerry and Houseman had given them as their share.

Those were not times in which any scrupulous tenderness for human life was fashionable, and, accordingly, Downy Dick made his worldly exit from the top of

---

* An illegitimate child.   + A guinea.   ‡ A loose woman.
§ A den in old St. Giles's rookery. || Blood-money.

Horsemonger-lane gaol, the offence being committed in the county of Surrey, and Joe Lovell, having been tried and convicted for a horse-stealing offence of some time gone by, died by "edge of penny cord," at Kennington Common, on the day following, it being the practice of our enlightened rulers in those days to furnish the public with recreation and edifying spectacles, by the erection of that great pulpit of public instruction, the gallows, in all sorts of places, on all sorts of pretexts, with what effect our criminal records fully show.

CHAPTER LVIII.

A CONSULTATION—VILLANY IN THE ASCENDANT—EUGENIA AND HER BETROTHED— THE WEDDING.

THE disappearance of the landlord of the Red Lion, of Jerry, Bill Houseman, and Rebekah Morse, left the thieftakers in full possession of the premises, which they by no means considered so desirable as the capture of Abershaw and Handsome Bill, for they felt assured if they could once get them under lock and key, the reward of blood money for the pair of them was as good as earned.

The articles found on Dick and his gipsy confederate, and which were stolen on the very night of the murder at Barnes, would have satisfied them as to being on the right scent, had it not received a confirmation, as it were, from the grave. Lawyer Lynx, though too weak to be removed, returned to consciousness before the night was over, and confirmed the suspicions of Dave Turner and his companions, by informing them that Abershaw and his gang were the parties who had robbed him, and confined him and the apothecary, although he had not witnessed any injury done to the boy who drove the chaise.

"I'll tell yer how it is 'xactly," said Turner, as he sat in consultation with Pearce, by the side of the lawyer's bed : " Jerry 's took hisself off with that 'ere troll of his'n, on the gipsy tramp, and catching of him 'ill be werry like lookin' for a needle in a bottle o' hay. Well, then, this must be the game, if so be as my conjectur' is right : we must tout the crib in South'ark and the Mint—for they won't kennel in that 'ere earth in Chick-lane for some time to come—and if so be we can eyther drop on to Patrico, as they calls him, or this here wench o' Jerry's, we may get a clue to him an' 'Ansome Bill ; as to this here lad " (Mr. Lynx half rose in the bed with ill-concealed anxiety), " why, I s'pose he'll be sent beyond seas, for his share in the robbery at Fitzroy Park, which I s'pose you've no doubt of his being concerned in ?"

The latter part of the sentence was addressed by way of query to the invalided lawyer, who, rejoiced at the opening prospect which this suggestion gave of getting rid of Walter, assented with all the energy his weak state would permit. Thus far, all things seemed *en train* for the successful issue of the schemes of Sir Ebenezer and the knavish Lawyer Lynx, on the principle that "the devil's children" have the good luck of their satanic parent.

When we last heard of John Crofts and Eugenia Lazenby, they were domiciled in London. Immediately on their arrival, Eugenia, with her quick and scrupulous sense of propriety, saw how improper it would be, and how derogatory to her character as a young, unmarried female, to reside under the same roof with her betrothed husband. They arranged accordingly. Eugenia was possessed of a few guineas, while John Crofts had supplied himself with fifty pounds, the accumulation of his savings. It was agreed, then, that Crofts should take a bed-room at a very quiet public-house in the vicinity of Tottenham-court-road, and that Eugenia should seek some respectable apartments in a private dwelling of moderate pretensions but honest respectability.

These they quickly procured in the house of a widow lady of limited means, at Somers-town. That suburban vicinity was then in a semi-rural state, and the lady with whom Eugenia was residing proved—so much in this world depends on what seems mere chance—the instrument, the unconscious instrument, of most important results to many of the personages of this history.

She was the relict of a captain of a West India vessel, from the port of Liverpool, who, after having the misfortune to lose his ship in one of the fearful tornadoes with which those tropical regions are frequently visited, obtained thereafter a situation as port surveyor and harbour master, at Fort Royal, in the island of Grenada.

With this worthy woman Eugenia was soon on the most familiar and friendly terms, and she esteemed herself indeed fortunate in thus obtaining so eligible a temporary home. The good lady, in order to add to the slender pension on which she subsisted, occupied herself in the making of many little articles of coloured grasses, leaves, feathers, &c., in the form of fly-brooms, fans, screens, &c., then much in vogue in the drawing-rooms and sitting-parlours of the wealthy.

In this light and feminine employment she readily offered to instruct Eugenia, whose natural good taste soon enabled her even to excel her kind mistress, in the elegance and contrasted colouring of the fancy articles she produced.

Crofts, too, was truly delighted, for although neither of them spoke directly on the subject, each had felt strongly that some means of subsistence, some method of earning an honest livelihood, must be hit upon before their slender capital should be exhausted. John Crofts, able, active, and young, feared not for himself; yet he knew that Eugenia's pride would not allow her to be dependent on him until she was his wife, and his deep, respectful love for her forbad him, under present circumstances, to talk even of wedding her to his poverty.

Three weeks rolled on, when one day Crofts, whose education had been a sound one, procured a moderately lucrative employment in the counting-house of a wholesale tradesman near West Smithfield. Their prospects were now altered, and within a month after this improvement in their circumstances, Eugenia Lazenby consented to become the wife of her devoted and manly lover, to redeem the promise made under far other circumstances, and, sinking all day-dreams of the past, find in the honest love of a true-hearted man a solace for the more splendid lot to which she had of late thought herself born. With this resolve, too, she determined to persevere in the humble employment to which she had devoted herself, and doubted not to find happiness in the lowly station in which it seemed to have pleased Providence to place her.

The day came; attired in spotless muslin, plain and pure as her hopes and intents, Eugenia, accompanied only by the kind old widow, a young female friend as bridesmaid, John Crofts and a brother clerk in the same establishment, who officiated as "papa," rode to the small old-fashioned church of St. Pancras. A license had been procured—albeit the expense dipped considerably into their slender finances—because they feared that the public calling of their names, for three successive Sundays, in a crowded church, might lead to some discovery by their persecutors.

After the ceremony, not the less solemn, decorous, and impressive from the absence of the accustomed bustle and display, a pleasant evening was spent at the excellent widow, Mrs. Melmoth's, where from this time forth the truly "happy couple" took up their united home; as for the old lady, her good heart rejoiced in the opportunity of making her fellow-creatures happy, and she never tired in her little attentions to promote their comfort, so true is it that all, even in the humblest stations, may bestow kindnesses, if their hearts beat with true benevolence.

CHAPTER LIX.

WALTER LAZENBY—AN ESCAPE—RATS' CASTLE—THE SURPRISE—THE ROOFS.

WE left young Walter Lazenby in the hands of the myrmidons of the law, by whom he was seized in the court near Hatton-wall which communicates with Saffron-hill, while on his way to the crib in Chick-lane, and by whom he was safely lodged in the watch-house near the old sessions-house at Clerkenwell. This was the first introduction of the unfortunate youth to a criminal prison; but his association with the most daring and hardened offenders against the laws, and his escape from the horrible den in which he had been immured by Sir Ebenezer, under the pretext of lunacy, caused him to look upon his present incarceration with other feelings than he would probably have experienced, had he not undergone this preparatory training, and taken his degree in the famous college of St. Giles.

Sitting down on the settle which ran round the dirty cell of the watch-house, he rapidly revolved in his mind the chances of escape. The only prisoners besides himself were two disorderly prostitutes, and two or three juvenile pickpockets, who were tossing for halfpence in one corner. Walter Lazenby, having decided upon the plan of operations which he intended to pursue, began dancing a horn-pipe, making all the noise he possibly could, and singing a low, flash ditty at the top of his voice.

"Kious, there, vill yer?" exclaimed the night-constable, in a hoarse, asthmatical voice, from the outer-room of the watchhouse. "Kim, jest stow that clatter, my young tulip. You'll vant that breath you're avasting of some fine mornin' at roll time."

"What's that to you, old cauliflower!" shouted Walter, through the keyhole. "Can't you mind your own business, and let a gentleman amuse himself as he likes?"

"Ah, you'll dance upon nothing, some day, and without music," responded the constable.

"You're a nice man, now, aint yer?" said young Lazenby, contemptuously. "If it wasn't for flash coves like us, what would become of such old hounds as you? S'pose there was no tobymen, no buzz-gloaks, no magsmen, what would become of all the beaks and traps, the charlies and the dubsmen? Why, you would have to doss in a sky-parlour, and live upon bacon rinds and 'tato peelings."

"You cantankarous young will'in!" exclaimed the watch-house keeper, in a passion. "Do you mean to say there'll ever be no magistrates?—no prisons?—no constables? I owes you vun, my young chaff-cutter, and now I'll sarve you out;" and he immediately unfastened the door, and rushed into the cell.

Walter Lazenby was standing close by the door, and dealt the old constable such a stinging blow on the left ear as he rushed in, like a bull at a gate-post, that he reeled against the damp wall of the dark and dirty cell. Recovering himself, he seized Walter by the collar as he was making off through the door; but at the same moment the young thieves in the corner advanced and attacked him in the rear.

"Here's a lark!" exclaimed Walter, striving to extricate himself from the grasp of the enraged constable. "That's it my kiddies! slog him—go into him—well done!"

The latter exclamation was occasioned by one of the boys having rushed between the constable's legs so adroitly as to throw him down, while Walter disengaged himself from his antagonist, and, giving him a kick in the ribs, sprung towards the outer door, leaving the constable fighting on the floor of the cell, with his juvenile assailants.

Having closed the door behind him, he turned into the first court he came to, in order to avoid observation, and walked rapidly away to Saffron-hill. Arrived in that salubrious and classical locality, he began to feel more at ease; and, pushing through knots and strings of Jew fences, Irish labourers, Italian music-grinders, orange girls, and prostitutes, he bent his way to Field-lane. Turning into a low boozing-ken in that narrow passage, he was not long in learning the surprise at the Red Lion, the dispersion of the Chick-lane gang, and the capture of Downy Dick and Joe Lovell. He immediately left the public-house; and as it was now dark, he hesitated not to ascend Holborn-hill, and again betake himself to Rats' Castle.

Here he met Sly Sally, and in the company of her who had been his mistress when he made his *debut* in a career of crime, with the fraternity of Chick-lane. Time flew on unheeded, until the hands of the smoke-begrimed Dutch clock had reached the "wee short hours ayont the twal." He was about to retire for the night, accompanied by the buxom Sally, when they were startled by a noise in the passage, and a cry of "the traps!"

"Steek the jigger!" exclaimed Walter; but it being too late for that operation to be performed, he extinguished the light, and rushed up a flight of dirty ricketty stairs which led to the dormitories. Two officers burst into the room as he disappeared, and, espying the door by which he had disappeared, were soon treading in his footsteps; but the long rooms and rambling corridors perplexed them, and rendered them uncertain of the direction taken by him whom they sought. Thus they lost much valuable time; but after much delay in searching through the upper rooms, they found an open window, and one of them observed that the sill was scratched as if by the nailed boots of a person getting through.

" He has gone this way,' remarked one of the officers; "for here are the marks of his feet."

" There he is!" cried his comrade; "I saw him dodging round that 'ere stack of chimnies."

" Where—where?" exclaimed the other, craning out of the window to catch a glimpse of the fugitive. "Oh, I see! Now run down to Davis and Hart, and tell 'em to look out in the street: we'll have him now." And while his coadjutor descended the stairs, he crept cautiously out of the window.

He slipped down the sloping roof into the leaden gutter, and began crawling over the tiles towards the stack of chimnies where he had caught a glimpse of the flying robber. Having accomplished this feat, with slow and cautious steps, and passed the chimnies, he came to the roofs of a court of houses which diverged from the street at that point; and turning to the right, he came to a skylight.

Finding it unfastened, he concluded that the fugitive had passed that way; and, creeping to the front of the roof, he called out to his associates to enter and search that house. Accordingly, Davis and another entered the house, while Hart kept watch in the court.

We will now follow the flying footsteps of Walter Lazenby, who had escaped by the window, as surmised by the officers, and crept over the roofs, in the hope of finding some avenue of escape from his pursuers. Dark clouds were flitting athwart the moon, throwing into alternate light and shade the chimnies and gables of Rats' Castle; and it was a momentary gleam of moonlight which had revealed his retreating form to the officers of justice. On reaching the skylight, he attempted to open it, but finding it fastened, he shattered a square of glass, and having turned the button which secured it inside, he opened it, and dropped lightly into the apartment, closing it behind him. The room in which he found himself was small and empty, but a light streamed through the chinks of a door which he must pass through to reach the stairs. A slight scream saluted his ears, but borrowing courage from despair, he opened the door, and entered the adjoining room.

Two young girls, whose only clothing was a ragged shift, were about to extinguish their rushlight, previous to laying down in their miserable flock-beds, when they were startled by the breaking of glass.

" Gracious ! what's that ?" exclaimed one.

" The cats," replied the other, yawning. But at that moment they heard some one drop into the adjoining room. They screamed simultaneously; and before they had recovered from their fright, Walter Lazenby opened the door, and walked in.

" Don't be alarmed," said he; " I am pursued for my life. Will you assist me to escape ?"

" What have you done, then ?" demanded one of the girls.

" Only a bit of moonlight on the high toby lay, over at Barnes," returned Walter, rapidly. " The traps are after me, and not having the key, I was obliged to enter this crib without knocking."

" Let's shove him between the bed and the mattress, Poll," suggested the girl who had spoken before. " He's not a very big'un," she continued, with an approving glance at the slight but symmetrical figure and dark handsome countenance of the youthful robber.

The bed and bedding were quickly lifted up by the two girls, while Walter deposited himself on the mattress, when they were again replaced. Poll then extinguished the rushlight, and footsteps being heard almost immediately ascending the first-floor staircase, they got into the bed, and pretended to be asleep. The door was bolted inside, and to the first summons of the officers they paid no attention; then, pretending to awaken, Poll desired them to wait until she had put on her petticoat, when she opened the door, and Davis and his companion entered the garret. They glanced sharply round the room, looked under the bed, and into the next room, and then took their departure, with a resolution to search every house in the court which had sky-lights in the garrets. Walter was then dragged out, almost smothered, from his concealment; and the two girls carried their kindness to such a degree, as amply consoled him for the more unpleasant portions of the night's adventures.

CHAPTER LX.

LAWYER LYNX—A MURDER—RETRIBUTION AND REMORSE—FLIGHT OF WALTER.

A MONTH rolled on, during which Walter Lazenby had heard nothing of Jerry Abershaw and his companions; and he himself had been obliged to skulk from the myrmidons of the law in the precincts of the Old Mint, in Southwark, the sanctuary in Chick-lane having been closed since the disappearance of Ben Hollins, on the memorable evening when Abershaw made the attempt on the life of Mr. Lynx. Downy Dick and Joe Lovell had suffered the last extremity of the law, as has been related in a previous chapter; for there were few offences at that time which were deemed expiable otherwise than by the bloody baptism of the scaffold and the rope, though the blood shed by the sword of the law yielded an abundant harvest of new crimes, like the serpent's teeth sown by Jason in the fields of Colchis—an apt illustration of the inefficacy of capital punishments to repress crime.

Walter Lazenby at length ventured to leave his hiding-place in the Mint, and in the dusk of the evening he directed his steps through the market-gardens, near the water-side. The night was dark and stormy, the wind blew in fitful gusts, and now and then a flash of lightning illumined the distant horizon. As he came near the Halfpenny Hatch, he distinguished the form of a man stealing along on the other side of the hedge which bounded the footpath: it was Ferdinand Lynx, who had recovered from the effects of the attack made upon him by Jerry Abershaw, at the den in Chick-lane, and was now on his way to the Mint, to ascertain the whereabouts of his execrable patron's nephew, and inveigle him, upon some pretence, into his power. But Walter Lazenby recognised him immediately, and sprang through the hedge. The lawyer, with the trepidation of conscious guilt, turned and fled, and Walter bounded after him with the agility of a young fawn. The lawyer led the chase towards the water-side, ever and anon casting on either side an anxious glance to ascertain if help were near, but not a human being was abroad; and in the wildness of his despair, he leaped into a boat, pushed off from the shore, and pulled into the stream. Walter soon found another boat, and stepping in, regardless of the ownership, he was soon in full pursuit of the flying lawyer.

The night was so dark that he could not see the chase, and the wind blew in such hollow gusts that he could not distinguish the dash of the oars; but a flash of lightning soon revealed the boat, tossed about on the rushing tide, Mr. Lynx in vain endeavouring to keep her head towards the opposite shore. Walter Lazenby drew a loaded pistol from his coat-pocket, and fired at the object of his hatred. The ball whistled so close to the lawyer's head, that he started, lost one of his oars, and the alarm so paralyzed his energy that the boat of his remorseless enemy bore rapidly down upon him.

"Help!—mercy!—spare me!" shouted Mr. Lynx, in an agony of fear; but the concluding words rattled in his throat as a bullet shattered his skull, and he tumbled into the river, a bleeding corpse! The boat drifted towards Westminster bridge, and Walter Lazenby, after rowing about to assure himself that his persecutor was indeed a corpse, pulled towards the Middlesex shore, and landed just below Millbank.

He had now taken the last step in the career of crime upon which the villany of his uncle had launched him; his foot was on the last round of that fatal ladder which conducts the unfortunate wretch who climbs it, to the gallows. He was now a murderer, and no remorse assailed his conscience for having taken the life of a fellow-creature: on the contrary, the excited state of his feelings, to which the fury of the elements lent its aid, prompted to fill the measure of his revenge, and incited him to fresh deeds of outrage and bloodshed. He had a glass of brandy at Knightsbridge, and walked on towards Hammersmith, crossed the river at Kew bridge, and pursued his way towards Richmond.

Sir Ebenezer Fitzroy was sitting in his library, awaiting the return of Mr. Lynx from his mission to Southwark, and listening in gloomy abstraction to the moaning of the wind among the old trees in the park, the pattering of the rain against the windows, and the rumbling of the distant thunder. Despite his repeated applications to the bottle on the table before him, he could not disengage his thoughts from the gloomy ideas which crowded upon his mind. He thought of the organized cruelty and oppression by which he had risen to opulence as a slaveholder, of the forged will by which he had robbed Walter and Eugenia of their inheritance, and of the chicanery by which he had maintained himself in his unrighteous position. He was roused from this gloomy reverie by the noise of what seemed to be some one scratching against the glass-door which opened on the lawn. He glanced in that direction, but saw nothing but the dim outlines of the dark trees swaying to and fro in the night wind. Again he heard the sound, and a superstitious awe began to steal over his mind; he shuddered involuntarily, and a cold sweat bedewed his pale forehead, as he distinctly heard the key turn in the lock. Then the door slowly opened; and, impelled by his fears, Sir Ebenezer rose from his chair, and extended his arm towards the bell-pull; but at that moment Walter Lazenby stepped into the library, and pointed a pistol at the head of his uncle, upon whom the sharp click of the lock sounded like a death-knell.

" If you touch that bell, I will blow out your brains on the instant !" exclaimed the injured youth, in a low but determined tone, which convinced Sir Ebenezer that his fate hung upon a thread.

" Would you murder me, Walter?—would you shoot your uncle, as if he were a mad dog?" stammered Sir Ebenezer Fitzroy.

" Have the ties of relationship been regarded by you !" replied Walter. "Have you not tried to hunt me to the gallows? Have you not robbed me of my birth-right, and imprisoned me as a lunatic? Villain, as you are, have you not done all this?"

Sir Ebenezer cowered before the repeated interrogatories of his injured nephew, and endeavoured in vain to falter out an excuse.

" Every dog has his day, Sir Ebenezer Fitzroy," continued Walter Lazenby ; "you have had yours, and now my turn has come." And he again raised the pistol.

Animated by despair, Sir Ebenezer sprang towards the bell-pull, and raised an alarm, just as young Lazenby discharged his weapon. The ball lodged in his shoulder, and with a cry of agony he dropped on the sofa. Walter heard footsteps approaching the scene of violence, and, with eyes inflamed with rage and revenge, he drew from his pocket a large clasp-knife, opened it, and sprang upon his intended victim.

" Mercy !—mercy !" shrieked Sir Ebenezer ; but the appeal was made in vain : the knife was plunged remorselessly into his heart, and the dark-red stream gushed with a gurgling sound over the rich carpet. Throwing down the knife, Walter Lazenby rushed from the apartment, just as several domestics entered by another door, and, bounding across the park, he leaped over the fence into the road.

At that moment the storm burst forth in all its fury; the thunder broke in appalling claps over the murderer's head, the forked lightning gleamed across his path, and the wind howled among the trees like a chorus of evil spirits. The serpents of remorse were gnawing at the heart of Walter Lazenby, and he rushed madly along the road which skirts Richmond Park, reckless of whither he was going, until he reached Putney. Fatigue then compelled him to slacken his pace, and on reaching Battersea, he turned from the road, and lying down in a cow-shed, endeavoured to forget the events of the last few hours in the oblivion of sleep.

CHAPTER LXI.

THE GIPSY ENCAMPMENT—A POACHING EXPEDITION—CAPTURE OF ABERSHAW—COMMITTAL TO HORSEMONGER-LANE GAOL.

As Abershaw and his campanions descended the dark culvert, on the walls of which, greenly damp and slimy, the bull's-eye lantern shed a flickering light, Rebekah Morse felt an involuntary sensation of alarm, lest she should lose her foot-ing, and be plunged into the black and turbid stream which rolled beneath; but she was light and agile, and moreover inured to scenes of difficulty and danger, and she reached the bottom in safety. At the bottom of the culvert, they found a narrow ledge of brickwork; and, with slow and cautious steps, the fugitives moved along it, so as to be out of sight of their pursuers, in case they should raise the trap, and peer into that dark and pestiferous vault. A legion of rats ran squeaking from their hiding-places, and plunged into the filthy stream with a sullen splash. Rebekah screamed, and the sound echoed strangely in the gloomy subterranean.

" Come, no screeching, 'Bekka," said Jerry Abershaw. "The creeturs is more frightened nor you have cause to be."

" What a stinking hole !" observed Handsome Bill, applying his finger and thumb to his olfactory organs. "I say, Ben, how far have we got to go in this fashion?"

" The tide will be running out in about an hour, and then we shall be able to wade down to the shore," replied Ben Hollins.

" And what then?" continued Bill.

" I perposes that we get over to the Surrey side, and look arter the Patrico," observed Jerry Abershaw.

This was agreed to; and when the tide had ebbed sufficiently to allow them to continue their subterranean journey, Black Ben leaped into the ditch, followed by Bill Houseman and Jerry, who assisted Rebekah down, and they began wading along the sewer. Ben Hollins led the way, and the others followed, Rebekah holding her clothes up to her knees, to avoid wetting and soiling them with the filthy water. After wading a little distance, they found a glimmering light struggling down a narrow shaft, and the rattling of wheels reached their ears, as if far overhead.

"We are now below Holborn-hill," said Ben Hollins; and the party continued their journey, passing underneath Shoe-lane, until they reached in safety the mouth of the sewer, near Blackfriars bridge. The moon was just struggling through a gathering mass of dark clouds, and her fitful light enabled them to pick their way through the mud until they found a boat, which they released from her moorings; and, getting in, Jerry and Bill Houseman took the oars, and pulled over to the Surrey side of the river.

They landed at Pedlar's Acre (now called the Belvidere-road), where they abandoned the boat, and walked briskly through the fields towards Kennington Common; and from thence, over the wide furze-covered commons of Clapham and Tooting, down to Phipps' Marsh. They had a half-pint of gin at the Swan, a small public-house by the roadside, and then pushed on over Mitcham Common, through Acbridge and Wallington, to the little manufacturing village of Carshalton. Passing through the Sutton turnpike, a spot well known to all frequenters of Epsom races, they trudged along the dusty road to the quiet rural village of Cheam, where they found the camp of the Patrico's tribe, pitched in a verdant nook, embosomed in old trees, the growth of a century, in whose lofty boughs the raven and the jay had their nests. They were warmly received by the old Patrico and his friends, to whom Jerry related the causes which had led to their flight from London; and then the little party sought repose, of which they stood greatly in need.

"What say you to a go in at the pheasants to-night, over yonder?" said the swarthy Tom Cooper, as the vagabond fraternity sat round a blazing fire, a few nights after the arrival among them of Jerry and his companions.

"With all my heart," responded Abershaw; and about midnight a party of six men, armed with guns, left the encampment, and proceeded towards the well-stocked preserves of Lord Elrington. The party consisted of Jerry, Black Ben, Bill Houseman, Tom Cooper, and two others of the gipsy tribe.

It was a fine moonlight night, and no sound was heard, save the murmuring of the wind among the trees, and the rustling of the dry leaves at their feet, as the poachers proceeded towards the preserves. A fine pheasant was soon found roosting in a fir-tree, and a well-aimed shot from Jerry's piece brought him to the ground. The report startled the birds from the trees, and as they flew affrighted from their roosts, the fowling-pieces of Handsome Bill and Tom Cooper scattered their feathers, and knocked over two more. In this manner they were rapidly filling their game-bags, when they found, by the rustling of the bushes, that another party was approaching them, and stood still to listen.

"The keepers, by George!" said one of the gipsies. "They are coming this way—let us nammus."

"What say you, Jerry?" said Ben Hollins; "shall we have a fight for it?"

"You may, if you fancy it," returned Jerry; "but I can't see the fun of being grabbed for a bird or two, and sent to quod, where we are safe to be bowled out and 'dentified."

"Then we'll give 'em leg-bail," said Handsome Bill; and throwing down the game, they started off towards the skirts of the preserve. The gamkeepers pursued them, and called to them to surrender; but they got away in safety, with the exception of Jerry Abershaw, who stumbled over a felled tree, and having hurt his leg, was captured and disarmed.

He was taken to the village round-house, and locked up for the night; and on the following morning he was ushered into the presence of a magistrate. The evidence of the keepers was deemed conclusive as to the trespass and poaching; and as the prisoner was not known to the keepers or constables, he was supposed to be connected with the gipsies. He was therefore committed to Guildford gaol for three months, and left the magistrate's room, laughing in his sleeve at the idea of the notorious Jerry Abershaw being in custody without being known. He was removed to Guildford in a light cart, and having undergone the full term of his imprisonment, was released by the turnkey; but instead of being set at liberty, as he expected, he was handcuffed, and taken before the magistrates.

Jerry turned pale when he entered the justice-room in the Town-hall; for there stood Ben Pearce, eager to have the renowned cracksman in his custody. It was no use to deny his identity, since there stood one there ready to swear to him, and Jerry preserved a dogged silence; he knew he had committed crimes enough to hang a dozen men, and therefore demanded not to know the crime of which he was then accused. But a few minutes sufficed to acquaint him that he was now charged with the murder of the postillion on Barnes Common; and the evidence of Mr. Lynx, and others, taken before the Richmond bench of magistrates, was read over to him. He had been recognised by the turnkey, and information of his capture having been sent to London, sufficient time had elapsed since his committal to enable Mr. Pearce to collect such an amount of circumstantial evidence as warranted his removal to Horsemonger-lane gaol.

Leaving him in safe custody in that prison, we will now take a perspective glance at other characters who have figured prominently in these pages. Ben Hollins, having ascertained that his neck was in no immediate danger, ventured to return to Chick-lane, where he continued for some time to keep the notorious tavern, the grim secrets of which were exposed to the public when it was pulled down a few years since, to make room for the continuation of Farringdon-street. Rebekah Morse, after the death of Jerry Abershaw, attached herself to Handsome Bill, who was hanged for a highway robbery a few years afterwards; but what ultimately became of the dark-eyed Rebekah, we have not been able to ascertain.

CHAPTER LXII.

THE DEN IN CHICK-LANE—THE SEARCH FOR THE PAPERS—WALTER'S INTERVIEW WITH EUGENIA.

WE left Walter Lazenby endeavouring to seek refuge in sleep from the horrors of his position; but his bleeding victims rose before his excited imagination, like the figures in some horrible phantasmagoria, forbidding sleep to visit the eyelids of the murderer and the outcast, and increasing tenfold the horrors of the night. Nature at length triumphed, and about daybreak the weary and miserable wretch sank into a profound sleep, induced by pure exhaustion, and when he awoke the sun was shining brightly. He arose, renovated in his bodily powers, and the energy and equanimity of his mind restored by his refreshing slumber; and, leaving the friendly shelter of the cow-shed, he crossed the ancient bridge of Battersea, and walked towards the crowded streets of our modern Babylon.

The subject which now occupied his mind was the recovery of the papers found by his associates on the person of the unfortunate Mr. Lynx, and which he had reason to believe had not been recovered by Ben Pearce, when that gentleman and his fellow-officers took a temporary possession of the old house in Chick-lane. These documents, he doubted not, would enable him to recover the property of which he had so long been unjustly deprived; and though he now saw that he had miserably mistaken the road to happiness, and that the crimes which he had committed or participated in would prevent him from maintaining his right to the property of his father, or from enjoying it even if he could recover it, yet he resolved to obtain possession of the documents alluded to, at any risk, and place them in the hands of his sister, Eugenia Crofts.

In pursuance of this resolution, he took a boat at Millbank, and was rowed across to the vicinity of Pedlar's Acre; from thence he walked through the fields towards Southwark, and waited the approach of night at a public-house in the Mint. About ten o'clock, he disguised himself in the garb of a sailor, and, crossing the river in a boat, he landed at Blackfriars, and proceeded by Shoe-lane to Holborn-hill; thence, turning off at Field-lane, he was in a few minutes standing in the shadow of the old Red Lion, in Chick-lane. The police-officers had abandoned their possession; and as Black Ben had not yet ventured to return, the tavern was unoccupied.

Walter entered the archway near Pickled-Egg-alley, leading to the back of the tavern, and having forced open one of the back windows, he entered, closed the shutters again, and, having lighted a dark-lantern, he commenced his search for the papers, which he had reason to believe had been left there by Ben Hollins, and had escaped the vigilance of Mr. Pearce and his subordinates. Having searched every part of the house in vain, he sat down in the bar, to resolve in his mind the probability of there being some secret repository which he had not yet visited. At length he bethought him that he had heard Downy Dick speak of the fire-place turning on a pivot, to form an entrance to a concealed passage; he immediately tried the grate in the bar, and after some delay, owing to a difficulty in finding the secret spring which acted on the hidden mechanism, the grate turned slowly round, and revealed the entrance of a dark passage.

A short distance up the passage lay a bundle of parchments and papers, tied up with red tape, where they had been thrown by Ben Hollins, before the evacuation of the tavern on the approach of the officers. Walter eagerly seized them, and hastily glanced over their contents; he secured them about his person, and quitted the house.

Return we now to Eugenia, her husband, and the worthy widow with whom they had been domiciled since their marriage.

The happy trio sat, on a summer's evening, in the pleasant little parlour which served them as a common sitting-room, the little window of which overlooked the extensive grazing fields of a dairy farm, which then occupied the meadows, now covered with streets and squares, lying between the southern end of Somers Town and the northern extremity of Camden Town. The day had been sultry, and the patient cows stood chewing the cud, or lazily flapping the teazing flies from their flanks; while others, knee-deep in a large sheet of water, formed against the declining light of the orb of day, as it sunk in the glowing west, a picture which Claude alone could tint.

As they sat at the window, admiring the quiet beauty of the rural scene, a young man advanced across the fields, and stopped under a tree at a short distance from the cottage of Mrs. Melmoth.

"My dear Eugenia," said the widow, for their intimacy was of the most friendly and familiar character, "who is that strange-looking young man under the tree, yonder? See! he is beckoning to some one."

"Oh, 'tis my unfortunate brother!" exclaimed Eugenia, turning pale. "He is beckoning to me—what had I better do?" and she glanced towards her husband.

"You believed him to be the victim of persecution," said John Crofts, "and I believe still that he has been unjustly deprived of property by the unfortunate Sir Ebenezer Fitzroy. Either he has escaped from the confinement in which the baronet placed him, or his death has occasioned his release, and he wishes to communicate with you, but will not come here on account of his dislike to me."

"I will go to him," said Eugenia, rising, "for I believe he has been the victim of a conspiracy;" and she crossed the fields to the spot where Walter Lazenby awaited her approach.

"Dear Walter," said she, "I am rejoiced to see that you are well, and have obtained your liberty again; but you look tired—will you not come in?"

"No, Eugenia," he replied, "for the officers of justice are searching everywhere after me, and may perhaps be even now on my path. My object in coming here was to see you once more, and to place in your hands these papers, which are useless to me, as my life is forfeited to the laws of the country; but when I am dead, they will secure to you the property of which we have been defrauded by our uncle?"

"He has been murdered, Walter!" exclaimed Eugenia, shuddering. "I trust his blood is not upon your hands?"

"Did he not hunt me, as if I had been a wild beast?" returned Walter, with forced calmness. "He goaded me to madness, and last night both he and Lynx paid the penalty of their misdeeds."

"But yours was not the hand that slew them?—you are not a murderer, dear Walter?" exclaimed Eugenia, clasping her hands, and looking earnestly at her guilty brother.

"I am a murderer, Eugenia; for I killed them both," replied Walter, with frightful calmness. "But they deserved their fate—their blood is on their own heads! Take these papers; they were stolen from Fitzroy Park, but not by me; they came accidentally into my possession, and they will be of service to you, though profitless to me."

Eugenia took the papers, with a heavy sigh; and Walter hurried from the spot, after tenderly pressing her hand, and proceeded to the metropolis, which was not then the overgrown Babel that it is now. Eugenia turned sorrowfully to the cottage, and, placing the papers in her husband's hands, fell on his shoulder and burst into tears. John Crofts allowed her grief to have quiet vent, and when she had become more calm, they read the papers and parchments; and smiles mingled with their tears as they thought of the bright prospect before them.

CHAPTER LXIII.

OLD LONDON BRIDGE—THE DEATH LEAP—CROCODILE FUDDLEBRAIN—CORONER'S INQUEST.

OLD London bridge was an unsightly structure, with houses on either side, overhanging the wide river, forming a continuation of Gracechurch-street, and serving to connect it with the High-street of Southwark. But these houses had been removed prior to the time of which we are writing, though the bridge was still far from being such a noble structure as that which at present spans what, in a commercial point of view at least, is the most important river in the world.

It was growing dusk, on the evening following the murder of Sir Ebenezer Fitzroy, when Walter Lazenby emerged from Cannon-street, and turned towards the bridge. His countenance was pale and haggard, his dark eyes gleamed with unnatural lustre, and every feature bore the impress of remorse and despair. The mark of Cain was on his brow; the air seemed filled with blood, and voices which no one else could hear called him "Murderer!"

He stood upon the middle arch of the old bridge, and the night wind bore the same cry to his ears, while shadowy figures flitted round him, and spectral hands beckoned him to the river. The cool air from the river, as it fanned his fevered brow, failed to chase away the spectres which appalled him; he pressed his hands over his face, but he could not shut them out; and, with the wildness of momentary insanity gleaming from his dark eyes, he mounted the parapet of the bridge: a cry of terror resounded near him, seeming to his distempered fancy the wailing of a ghost, and with an unearthly shout he threw up his arms, and leaped into the river!

The lights on the bridge and along the shore, which seemed to dance before his eyes as he fell from the giddy verge into the rushing stream, glittered like the eyes of a thousand demons: and the shadow cast by his descending figure on the water seemed to him like Satan hastening to seize his prey. He shrieked involuntarily, but the water rushed into his stomach and choked him; his brain became dizzy—a drumming noise seemed sounding in his ears—he tried to shriek again, but could not—his faculties forsook him, and the horrible sensation of suffocation was succeeded by utter unconsciousness.

The cry of alarm which had saluted his ears, as he leaped from the bridge, proceeded from Crocodile Fuddlebrain, who was now leaning over the bridge, watching for the re-appearance on the surface of the miserable young man whom he had been too late to save from the sin of suicide. For self-destruction is undoubtedly a great crime, however it may be glossed over by the fine rhetoric and false sentiment of Alexandre Dumas and Eugene Sue, and made to appear in their fictions as the result of a fine principle of honour. The morality of the act may be summed up in the consideration of a question which Sue, at least, will not answer in the affirmative: Should a man live for himself alone? Apart from all private and personal connections, there are duties which every man and woman owe to society in general, which it is incumbent upon them to fulfil. By the selfish and cowardly act of self-destruction, they deprive the community of their help, sever the bonds of fraternity which should unite mankind together, and rush out of life like a shrinking coward, seeking refuge in the grave from the evils which they have not the energy and moral courage to encounter.

> " What Cato did, and Addison approved,
>   Cannot be wrong,"

was the poor excuse by which the suicide Budgell sought to palliate his crime; but the example of the Roman stoic only proves that human nature is not perfect, even in its noblest specimens. Despair supplies the place of courage, in the last desperate act by which the suicide flies from evils often imaginary; as in the case of the soldier who, with delirium in his eyes, rushes madly into the thickest of the battle, not from excess of personal daring, but because he has not sufficient courage and firmness to remain in his rank, and receive the fire of the enemy.

Crocodile Fuddlebrain strained his watery eyes in vain—the neglected and misguided Walter came not again to the surface; but, borne through the arches of the old bridge by the rolling tide, which was now running out, the corpse of the suicide was carried down the river, and cast ashore in the sedgy marshes of the Essex coast. Here it was found by some fishermen from Barking, and carried to a public-house near the creek, where a coroner's inquest was held on the remains, and, in the absence of any evidence which could tend to throw light on the cause of death, a verdict of "Found dead" was returned.

Crocodile Fuddlebrain, however, had recognised the features of the guilty wretch, as the light of an oil-lamp fell on them when he leaped from the bridge, and waited on the Crofts, in the course of the following day, to acquaint them with the sad occurrence, and suggest what was best to be done in reference to the property of which the deceased and his sister had been deprived by the chicanery of Sir Ebenezer Fitzroy and Mr. Lynx, who had paid the penalty of their misdeeds in so awful a manner. The documents found by the wretched Walter, at the den in Chick-lane, contained every legal paper necessary to prove the legitimacy of the orphans, and their right to the property of which their uncle had so long deprived them; but considerable delay and difficulty occurred in establishing the identity of Walter Lazenby, and the proofs of his death. These quibbles were, however, removed at last, and John Crofts recovered the property in right of his wife. Thus was justice, though long delayed, done to the amiable Eugenia, and the memory of her mother cleared from the aspersions of calumny.

CHAPTER LXIV.

THE TRIAL OF JERRY ABERSHAW—THE SENTENCE—THE EXECUTION—THE GIBBET.

THE trial of our hero came on at the summer assizes for Surrey, which are held alternately at Guildford and Croydon; and, on a fine morning in August, Jerry Abershaw, and about thirty other prisoners, were taken to the latter town in the long black prison vans, and lodged in the gaol beneath the corn-warehouse at the south end of Butcher-row. On the following morning, he was escorted by constables to the Town-hall, and ushered into the presence of the judge.

Jerry tried to put the best face he could upon the matter; but, in spite of his endeavours to assume an air of nonchalance, he was pale and restless—his eyes wandered about the court, and now and then he clutched the front of the dock with nervous trepidation. But by degrees he recovered his self-possession, and as he listened to the evidence against him, the pride of successful villany inspired him with an air of boldness and cool impudence, and he cross-examined the witnesses with his usual effrontery.

But the evidence was too conclusive against him, and his character too well known, for him to have any hopes of acquittal, or of a commutation of punishment. Nerved by despair, therefore, his bearing to the last was bold and reckless; and when sentence of death was pronounced upon him, he loaded the judge with the most virulent abuse which the vocabulary of Chick-lane could supply him with. He was dragged from the dock, uttering the vilest imprecations, and taken back to the prison, from which he was removed to Horsemonger-lane gaol.

On the morning appointed for his execution, an immense crowd assembled in front of the gaol, just as the old Romans flocked to the Ampitheatre to see the battles of the gladiators, or the grandees of Spain to witness a bull-fight. Here some speculative itinerant vendor of cheap literature for the millions was reciting a copy of verses, supposed to have been sent the night before by the condemned housebreaker to his sweetheart; and there a knot of dirty ragged boys were tossing halfpence; here a pieman was inviting the bystanders to "toss or buy" his savoury comestibles, the contents of some looking like mutton, though they might have been puppy, and others representing veal, which might have been kitten; and there two Irish costermongers, having imbibed copious libations of "mountain dew," were stripping, to allow the fiery spirit to evaporate by blacking each other's eyes.

"The back o' my hand to you, you dirthy spalpeen!" said one.

"Bad luck to your sowl! is it Thady O'Brien you'd be afther insulting?" returned the other. "By Jasus! it's himself that'll have satisfaction for the same; and divil a mother's son in Tipperary can stand before an O'Brien."

"Dirty wather on your clane face!" exclaimed the offender, stepping back as the other advanced. "Can't you be afther putting off the scrimmage till the fun is over? Isn't it the bowld Abershaw we're come to see?"

The clock of St. George's church at this moment began striking eight, and the belligerents tacitly consented to a truce until the conclusion of "the fun." The criminal now appeared on the fatal platform, and looked around upon the vile throng with an air of cool audacity, which elicited shouts of approbation from that dense mass of human beings, the congregated villains and outcasts of the metropolis. The hangman, having completed his odious preparations, went below the scaffold, and in another moment the drop fell, and Jerry Abershaw swung from the fatal beam, convulsed and writhing in the agonies of strangulation!

"He died game, though, didn't he?" was the observation of an ill-looking ruffian near the scaffold, to another of the same genus.

"Out-and-out!—he was a reg'lar plucked 'un, warn't he?" returned the other; and the two fellows lounged into the nearest public-house, there to get drunk, and, perhaps, within a few hours to commit an offence of equal atrocity with those for which the wretched Abershaw had just suffered the last penalty of the law.

"Now then, who's for a meat-pie?" cried the pieman. "Here's your sort—mutton or veal—toss or buy, genelmen."

The two costermongers finished their fight beneath the shadow of the gallows, and the vendor of cheap literature stuck in his hat a rude representation of the execution, and began crying, in a lugubrious tone: "Here you have, just printed and published, for the small charge of one halfpenny, the full, true, and particular account of the life, trial, and awful execution of the notorious housebreaker and robber, Jeremiah Abershaw, who was tried and condemned at the last summer assizes, for a horrible, barbarous, and most atrocious murder, which he committed two years ago; also a copy of verses, which he sent to his sweetheart in the country, the night before his most awful execution; now printed and published for the small charge of one halfpenny."

The body of Abershaw was cut down after hanging the usual time, and taken into the prison, where the hangman and his assistants encased it in the irons in which it was intended to be suspended from a gibbet. It was then placed in the bottom of a cart, which the hangman drove away towards Vauxhall, accompanied by his assistants in the revolting office. The death-cart proceeded through Battersea, and drew up under a high gibbet which had been erected for the purpose on Putney heath. The iron-bound corpse of the robber and murderer was then lifted up, and suspended from the chain terminated by a hook, which swung from the arm of the gibbet by a ring in the semi-circular iron which passed over the head.

The cart was then driven away; but a number of persons had been attracted to the spot by that morbid love of the horrible, which prompts the untrained and uneducated—or badly educated—to seek out scenes of horror and wonder. One of these sight-seekers actually amputated one of the fingers of the corpse, and had a tobacco-stopper made of the bone; while others danced round the gibbet like cannibals, sung obscene songs, and passed the remainder of the day, and a considerable portion of the night, in drunken revelry.

Such are the deplorable effects of the Draco-like jurisprudence which punishes one crime by the commission of another, and confesses its incapacity to reform the criminal by putting him to death to hide its weakness. Since the period in which Abershaw lived, a considerable reform has taken place in our penal code, and the punishment of death is now only inflicted for the crime of murder. What has been the result? Offences against the person have proportionately diminished, as the exteriors of our prisons have been less and less darkened by the shadow of the gallows. Many a man who has been robbed has received his death-blow through recognising the robber, who has taken his life to prevent him from appearing against him for the robbery; thus the ferocity of our laws have defeated their avowed purpose, and actually caused blood to be shed, by awarding the extreme penalty of the law equally for stealing a yard of ribbon and for cutting a man's throat

If the aphorism be true which tells us that

> " Vice is a monster of such frightful mien,
> As, to be hated, needs but to be seen,"

then have we, in the preceding pages, done our part towards the amendment of the human race; for we have drawn aside the veil from the crimes and follies of a past age, and laid bare in all their glaring deformity some of the most prominent scenes of dissipation and depravity which then existed; we have drawn our characters from real life, and exhibited their vices and weaknesses in their proper colours, without holding them up for imitation. Many years have elapsed since the events here recorded took place: St. George's Fields are fields no longer, Rats' Castle has disappeared before the progress of our metropolitan improvements, and the terrible den in Chick-lane, which has supplied the materials in part of several modern romances, has been pulled down; and those who have not inspected its gloomy vaults and subterraneous passages have lost the opportunity for ever. Let us hope that the moral improvement of the denizens of those localities will be commensurate with the outward improvement of the localities themselves; if darkness and malaria have reared an Abershaw and a Lazenby, may improved condition produce improved characters, and the health and cleanliness of the body be the outward and visible sign of the purity and integrity of the soul.

THE END.

www.ingramcontent.com/pod-product-compliance
Lightning Source LLC
Chambersburg PA
CBHW08083825062 6
47161CB00009B/3113